Losing Mama

Losing Mama

Janet Mackey

Losing Mama

© Janet Mackey 2018

Published by
Lighthouse Christian Publishing
SAN 257-4330
5531 Dufferin Drive
Savage, Minnesota, 55378
United States of America

www.lighthousechristianpublishing.com

Chapter 1

Two miles down a rutted dirt road Miriam Cahill stopped at the end of a narrow lane and squared her shoulders before striding past the live oak tree and up the sagging wooden steps onto the porch of the little farmhouse where she'd lived since her birth twenty-four years before. It hadn't changed much in those years. Change would have cost money, and what precious little cash her father made from year to year had never gone to keeping the house in good repair. He never minded, in fact, never seemed to notice the crooked doors or cracked windowpanes. His pride didn't extend to the four walls and roof that protected his wife and four children from the rigors of daily life. Miriam glanced up to see that the house was dark. Not a lamp glowed anywhere. Strange, she thought. Where was he? She walked to the edge of the porch and looked down the driveway to see that the pick-up was gone as well. She shrugged, realizing that leaving would be easier without having to confront her father.

She walked into the house through a rusty screen door that had been ripped for as long as she could remember, and switched on the lamp at the end of the couch. She closed the wooden door behind her and knelt to light the space heater. The room was frigid with the cold. As the blue flames danced behind the grate, she glanced around. The curtains hung limply at the windows, the edges frayed and dusty. The sofa was threadbare along the arms, and the cushions sagged with the years of hard use. Simple planking comprised the floors, worn from time and the footsteps of weary feet. The house echoed with the silence, and in alarm Miriam looked up to see that Mama's clock was gone. The clock couldn't be gone! Pop and Grammy had given that clock to Mama as a wedding present. What happened to it? Miriam ran to her parent's bedroom to see that Mama's things were gone. The quilt had been removed from the bed, the photos were gone from the dresser, and her closet stood empty. Miriam stared in shock. Breathless, she leaned against the wall as she absorbed a truth that reviled her. The screen door banged shut, and she heard Daddy call out.

"Miriam, you here, girl?"

Miriam hurried down the hallway, stumbling into the front room where Daddy stood with his hands on his hips and a scowl darkening his face.

"How long have you been home? Is supper ready yet?"

"I just got here. Where are Mama's things?"

"I sold them. I asked you if supper was ready yet."

"You sold them? When? To whom?"

"I sold them to Mrs. Perkins. She paid me $16.00 for everything. Seems your Mama's things weren't useless after all."

"How could you?" Miriam wheezed, horrified at the idea. "How could you get rid of her things so carelessly? You knew Mary Elizabeth and I meant to sort out everything tonight."

"You and Mary Elizabeth wouldn't have sold anything to anybody. You'd have kept it for its sentimental value," he sneered, "and what good is anything if it won't bring a little money?"

Miriam couldn't believe what she was hearing. Daddy had sold Mama's things. Dear God, was he even human? She turned away from him, vaguely aware of the nausea rising up, determined to get away from this house and this man she couldn't bear to be near another minute.

"Where are you going, girl? Didn't you hear me ask if supper is ready?"

"I heard you. There's bread and cheese in the kitchen."

"Bread and cheese? You get in that kitchen and heat up something for supper!"

She walked to the front door with her coat and suitcase. Thank Heaven she'd thought to pack before the service. "I'm leaving. You'll have to be getting your meals by yourself from now on."

"Leaving? Have you gone crazy? Where are you going?"

"Did you think I'd stay after Mama died? I'm 24 years old. Most of my friends have already gotten married and had babies. I stayed while you sent Will to college. You laughed at me when I begged to go, too, and you kept right on laughing while I went to night school and got my degree so I could teach. I stayed when Mary Elizabeth and Toby eloped, and I watched you swallow your disapproval and welcome them back. I stayed to help Mama nurse Nan after she fell and couldn't live alone. I stayed because I knew how much it meant to Mama to have someone here to ease the hurt and unhappiness you brought to her every day of her life. I stayed for her. But there's no reason to stay any longer."

Miriam took a steadying breath as her father's face reddened. He spluttered. Her head high, she took a tighter grip of the handle of her valise and walked past his rigid, disbelieving figure, quietly closing the door behind her. At the bottom of the steps she heard the door flung open and her father storm across the porch.

"You go ahead and get out, then! But when you fall on your face, don't even think about coming back to this house. You've been disrespectful and ungrateful your whole life. You hear me, girl?"

"I don't expect anything from you. I stopped expecting anything from you a long time ago," she replied sadly, and with ever increasing urgency she walked down the lane and onto the road toward town.

Darkness was falling. The watery winter sun had already made its slow descent past the western horizon, and the skeletal black tree limbs stood starkly against a deep turquoise sky. Intermittent winds had settled into a lazy, ice-kissed breeze that idly fluttered coats and gave cheeks and noses a rosy tint. Everyone else had driven away from the barren rural cemetery long ago, eager to return to the warmth and normalcy of home and supper, where lamps burned brightly against the gloominess of the day, and the routine of chores pushed back thoughts of death and the heartbreaking tears of loss. In the stark loneliness of the empty landscape Miriam, unaware of the tears frozen on her cheeks, stopped before the simple pine box resting over an open grave and spoke softly to the mother she still couldn't believe she'd lost.

"Oh, Mama, I love you so." Miriam whispered almost in rhythm with the ebb and flow of the rustling leaves. "I miss you so much I ache all over. How can I ever sing again and not hurt for the sound of your voice? How can I ever cook over that old stove and not remember the thousands of talks we had while we worked together, and all the things you've taught me? I'm sorry for the dreams that died with you. I'm sorry your life wasn't happier. I tried to make things better." She gasped with the ache threatening to smother her. "Oh, Mama, I wasn't ready to lose you yet." The tears cascaded unchecked, and she hugged herself around her waist, almost as if to ward off the pain of such deep loss. "I hope you've found peace, Mama. I hope you've at last found that."

Aware of the encroaching darkness and the bone-chilling cold of the wind, Miriam took a deep breath as she tramped through the gravestones toward the cemetery gates. Miriam was no stranger to walking, but never before had she carried such a burden on her shoulders as she did this night. Exhausted and feeling old and used up, she trudged along and tried not to think about the dropping temperatures. She deliberately looked up from contemplating her shoes and tried to consider something other than her discomfort.

There was Mr. Adcock's farm with his ivy covered porch railings and green shutters. He and Miss Almira, his wife, had been good neighbors, willing to lend a hand if Mama needed them. They treated her like one of their own, and Miriam had grown to love them while still a little girl. She smiled as their lights shone in the darkness. She remembered the time Seth had been thrown from old Mollie when he was seven. He was out cold and bleeding from a gash across his head and Daddy nowhere to be found. Miriam and Mary Elizabeth had run for Miss Almira lickety-split. Seth had a pretty good headache for a few days, but Miss Almira had been right when she'd said he'd be fine. And, Miriam remembered, Seth was back on that stubborn horse's back within a week, despite Mama's protests. Miriam couldn't be too sure who was the more obstinate, Seth or the mare. He was certainly hard-headed.

The post office loomed in front of her, and Miriam realized she'd spent the entire walk to town daydreaming. Relieved to get out of this wretched cold, she stepped onto the sidewalk and strode around the corner and up the steps onto her sister's front porch. Toby swung the door wide as she reached for the bell.

"Miriam, what are you doing here? I was going to drive Mary Elizabeth out to the house after supper. Did you forget? Is something wrong?" Clearly concerned, her brother-in-law drew her into the house, a frown marring his usually cheerful features.

"Nothing more than has always been wrong," she responded, peeling off her coat, scarf, and gloves as she spoke. "I found out after I returned to the house that Daddy sold Mama's things."

"Sold them?" Toby interrupted. "Didn't he know you and Mary Elizabeth were going to sort through them yourselves?"

"Oh, yes, he knew. He knew that we wouldn't sell everything like he did. I figured I'd come on into town and save you and Mary Elizabeth the trip. Would have been for nothing anyway. And besides, I couldn't stay under that roof for one more moment. Can you put me up until I decide what to do? I think I'll try to get a job until I can apply for a teaching position for September. I'll never again depend on Daddy for one thing. He's a miserable, miserly, dried up old man, and I can't stand the thought of living with him for one more day," she ended on a sudden sob.

"Miriam, you come sit down on this couch right now.   You're frozen through," Mary Elizabeth commanded from the dining room doorway. "And what do you mean, Daddy sold Mama's things? Everything? How could he?"

"You know how he could, Lizzie. You grew up in that house the same as I did."

Mary Elizabeth sat down next to Miriam, stunned momentarily as she struggled to accept what she had been told. "The clock is gone? And the quilt? What about the watch pin?"

" He took it to Mrs. Perkins this afternoon."

"What a spiteful thing to do! He told me at the cemetery he'd see me tonight, and he said he'd help carry out the things I wanted to take with me."

"I'm never going back into that house as long as he's living in it, Lizzie. Can I stay here a few days? I can help out with T.J."

"You can stay as long as you like, Miriam," Toby said. "You're family; you don't even need to ask."

"Thanks, Toby. You know, Lizzie, when your husband was just a spindly-legged, skinny 12-year-old, throwing us into the creek and chasing us across the pasture, pelting us with cow pies, I never expected him to become such a fine, decent man. Seeing him now rather makes up for the torment we endured back then."

"I never actually hit you with any cow pies, did I?" Toby laughed. "That has to count for something."

"It counted for enough, I suppose, at least where Mary Elizabeth was concerned," Miriam replied, smiling. Looking from her petite, red-headed sister to the tall, dark-eyed man she had married, Miriam felt a huge jolt of love shake her to her toes. They were so good together. Toby with his patient, quiet ways and youthful face, and Mary Elizabeth with every good instinct a mother or wife might ever claim, had made a happy life together, and Miriam couldn't have cared for two people more.

Patting her husband on the shoulder as she rose from the couch, Mary Elizabeth turned to Miriam. "I've got pork chops that are going to burn if I don't get back to my dinner fixin's; come with me and help me, Mim."

Arm in arm, Miriam and Mary Elizabeth walked to the kitchen together. There was such comfort in routine chores, Miriam thought as she stirred the potatoes for dinner. She and Mary Elizabeth must have worked together to prepare a meal for the family hundreds of times. They had learned from a patient, loving teacher, and both were excellent cooks thanks to a caring mother who had taught them well. Miriam looked up at her sister, stirring at the stove and humming softly to herself in her sweet soprano. Her glossy red curls clung to her face from the steam of the pots, but her green eyes glowed as she glanced at Miriam and smiled.

"Do you remember the first time I made bread?" Miriam asked Mary Elizabeth.

"No one in the family will forget your first attempt at bread making. I think Mama wrote about it in the family scrapbook."

"Oh, she did not. You're exaggerating."

"She did too. I'd never seen a more pitiful pair of loaves of bread in my life. You must have kneaded that dough all day. We barely got a knife to slice through it, and then it was so tough no one could chew it. Even the pigs wouldn't have it."

"Who gave it to the pigs?"

"Will, of course. He didn't want you to know. You were only twelve, and he was afraid of hurting your feelings any more than we already had. You were so proud of that bread, but it was just inedible."

"My next attempt was certainly edible. Mama had an endless store of patience, helping me to feel better about my failure and encouraging me to try again. She knew the right thing to say."

"She was pretty good at knowing what not to say, too."

"Yes, she was. It just about broke her heart when Seth decided to quit high school and go to work, but she knew to try and talk him out of it was useless. He was so determined to help out around the house once he saw how much Mama was doing without because Daddy couldn't make the farm pay enough to keep us going."

"I'm not sure who was prouder of that first paycheck he brought home, either. Mama smiled all day that day. I think it could have been two dollars and she would have still behaved as if it was $200.00. She was so proud of Seth for taking that responsibility."

"She was proud of you, too. Eloping was a brave thing considering what Daddy might do, but you and

Toby knew your own minds, and Mama was about to bust her buttons at the way you spoke so confidently to him. She knew you needed to get out of the house, so she prayed for you both and trusted God to work out the details."

"I'll never know how she kept Daddy from trying to kill Toby. He was angrier than I'd ever seen him; I was scared to death at first. It took T.J. to bring him around even a little bit."

"Mama loved him so much. Her first grandchild."

"I'll tell him about his grandmother as soon as he is old enough to understand. I want him to know how much she loved him, and what a strong woman she was. We'll probably never know how much heartbreak she lived with in order to protect us. She got more of the back of Daddy's hand than I even want to think about."

Taking a deep breath, Miriam turned to her and smiled. "Let's not re-live those memories tonight, hmm? I want to laugh about every good thing that happened to us kids and be grateful we were brought up by such a remarkable woman. Let's not have Daddy spoil it for us, okay?"

"You're right. Call Toby to supper."

Chapter 2

The morning dawned bright and clear as Miriam turned over in bed, snuggling under the covers for one more lazy minute. She could hear Toby crooning to T.J. as he changed his soggy diaper and dressed him for the day. Coffee and bacon were bubbling and spitting in the kitchen, and the delicious aromas of both were more than Miriam could resist. She grabbed her worn flannel robe and let her nose guide her to Mary Elizabeth's cheery kitchen.

"Good morning, Lizzie."

"Morning, Mim. Did you sleep well?"

"I always sleep well." She smiled, biting into one of the buttery biscuits waiting to be dished up for breakfast. "Maybe that's my problem. I haven't made too much progress in looking for a job this last week. You're spoiling me with this good food and such a comfortable bed."

"Don't be silly. Mama has scarce been dead these two weeks, and I know for a fact that you're exhausted. You needed some rest, both body and spirit. When you're ready to look for a job, you'll find one." She looked up to see her husband of three years and her six-month-old son enter the kitchen.

"Hey, darlin'." Mary Elizabeth nuzzled T.J.'s neck as she walked past him to set platters of eggs and bacon on the table. "And how did the king sleep, sire?"

"Mother," Toby replied for T.J., "I've had a restful night's snooze and now I'm ready to eat! What have you got for a growing boy?"

"Your oatmeal awaits, your majesty," she said, chuckling. "Let's sit down; it's ready."

Miriam passed the first dish after Toby spoke his usual grace. "Here you go, brother-in-law. You haven't heard of any job openings in town, have you? I've got to earn my keep while I look for a teaching position for September."

"Braley's Insurance is looking for an assistant in the office," Toby mused as he sipped steaming hot coffee. "I heard Mike mention that he'd need a new waitress once Alice leaves to have the baby. Oh, and the library is looking for someone to work in the afternoons. Alice warned Mike that he might have to raise her salary or she'd take the baby and go to work for Martha Tate."

"The library. . . that sounds perfect. I'll walk down after breakfast and see if I can put in an application. Thanks, Toby."

"Here, T.J., honey. That tastes much better in your mouth than dribbling down your chin." His mama soothed him as she wiped up the mess. "I think the library sounds just perfect, Mim. You've loved books since you were a small girl. Surely applying is just a formality. Martha Tate has known us since we were the ones in diapers."

"Say a prayer for me. Might not hurt to keep your fingers crossed, too."

After breakfast Miriam hurried up to the post office and crossed the street to walk the four blocks to the Alberta Wilson Memorial Library. The brick two-story building stood on the corner across from the First Methodist Church, stately and dignified with its narrow windows and crisply painted white trim. Alberta Wilson had fought the town council for fifteen years to open a library, and Miriam heard that the mayor and councilmen had finally agreed in order to keep her out of the monthly civic meetings. She had been a force with which to be reckoned, but Miriam was glad for her foresight as she remembered the countless hours she had spent in the library, reading and doing homework. The serenity of the paneled rooms and Mrs. Tate's welcoming manner had been a refuge when home had been so miserable. To be able to work among the books she so loved would be an answer to prayer.

The door whispered on its hinges as Miriam pushed it open to walk inside. The smell brought back so many lovely memories. Mama took her to apply for her library card when she was just ten years old, and since the first one she'd worn out several. Books were such good friends, she thought to herself. Walking up to the desk, she smiled as Mrs. Tate looked up from her duties.

"Why, Miriam Cahill! How are you, dear? I'm so sorry about your mother. Christine was as fine a woman as I've ever known, and we were heartbroken to lose her. How is your family?" Hesitating, she added, "How is your father?"

"We're fine, Mrs. Tate. It's good to see you. I haven't been by in much too long, it seems. Will is still away at school, but his studies are going well. Daddy sees to it that his tuition is paid on time, and Will works part time to pay for his books and his room and board. He should be home in May. Seth is still in Ascension working at the feed store. He's the manager now, and doing well. He told me at the funeral that he's met a young woman; I believe he said her name was Polly. Seems my brother is thinking about settling down." Miriam smiled as she recalled Seth's enthusiastic description of his young lady at the house the day before Mama's funeral.

"Well, at 21 I'm sure a real home and little ones would be on his mind. You tell him to come by and see me the next time he's home. Are you here to check out some new books?"

"No, ma'am, I'm here to apply for your part time opening. I've moved out of the house and need to find a job for the spring. I'll be looking for a teaching job come September, but I'd love to work for you until the fall term."

"How marvelous, my dear," Mrs. Tate said as she smiled. "I'd be delighted to have you working for the library. It's afternoons from 1 until 6, and Saturdays from 9 to 1. With the new addition and the new books to catalog, I just can't keep up by myself. When can you start?"

"How about Monday?" Miriam asked.

"Monday it is, then." Pausing, she looked into Miriam's haunted brown eyes and plunged into what was probably none of her business. "Are you alright, Miriam? You said you've moved out of your home."

"I just thought it was time, Mrs. Tate. With Mama gone I'm not needed any longer, and I want to find my own place in the world, if you know what I mean. I'm eager to begin teaching so I can put my mother's hard work and hard-earned money to good use. She had an unshakable faith in my ability to be a good teacher, and I just can't let her down." A lone tear slipped down her face as she smiled at this kind-spirited woman who had been her friend since she was a child.

Mrs. Tate stepped from the desk to hug Miriam and pat her gently on the cheek. "Your mother was proud of you children every day of her life. You could never let her down or betray her memory in any way. Don't you worry about that." Taking a deep breath, Martha Tate patted Miriam's arm and smiled. "I'll see you on Monday."

Stepping out onto the busy Thursday morning town square, Miriam hadn't seen Martha Tate shake her head as she returned to her tasks, nor had she heard the quiet, "Couldn't live for another moment with that tyrant of a father is more like it."

Looking up into a sky filled with sunshine, she burrowed more deeply into her coat and walked back toward Mary Elizabeth's with a lighter step than she'd had in many a day. Taking a deep breath, she looked up to see Sheriff Brockland emerge from the post office and called a quick hello. In the distance she spotted The Lace Doily and decided impulsively, desperately hopeful, to make one more stop.

Jangling the bell above the door as she entered the second-hand shop, Miriam looked around at what many people considered treasures from a bygone time. Most of it looked to her like dusty cast-offs, but she wasn't interested in anything on the sales floor at that moment, anyway.

"Mrs. Perkins," she called. "Are you here?"

"Yes, dear, I'm in the far corner setting up a

display." Miriam looked toward the sound of the shop owner's voice and saw her hand waving between two low shelves. "What can I do for you?"

"Have you put out the pieces you bought from my daddy a couple of weeks ago? I believe there were four quilts, a clock, a watch pin, things like that. If you still have them, I'd like to speak to you about buying them back."

"I'm so sorry, Miriam. Those pieces sold just yesterday. I'm afraid they're not here any longer."

"You sold them? So quickly? I thought you appraised most of your things before you made them available for sale."

"Yes, normally I do, but someone came in looking for a large number of items, and he bought everything in the lot I purchased from Tom. I'm sorry, dear," she repeated as she stood to her feet, wiping wisps of graying brown hair from her cheeks and slapping at the dust on her skirt with a soft cloth.

"It's okay, Mrs. Perkins. You couldn't have known that I wanted them back. Thank you, anyway."

"I was mighty sorry to hear about your sweet mama. She was a lady through and through, Miriam. Her passing has left a hole in many a life, I know."

"Thank you for saying so. We do miss her terribly. Goodbye, now."

More upset than she'd believed possible, Miriam trudged back to the house. The idea had come so quickly, but she'd been sure she could have made payment arrangements to get Mama's things back. Anger anew boiled up within her, and her breath gusted out in tiny clouds as she silently cursed her father once again for his unfeeling greed.

The warmth of the indoors seeped into her bones and relaxed her rigid posture as Miriam walked back into the house, hanging her coat in the hall closet and walking down the hallway in search of Mary Elizabeth. She was in the kitchen, just as Miriam had surmised, cutting ham sandwiches in half and pouring glasses of milk for their lunch.

"We'd better eat up while we can. T.J. will be up from his nap soon, and he's in a frightful mood waiting for that new tooth to erupt. It may take both of us to keep him happy this afternoon."

"Poor little guy. We could rub his gums with whiskey, if you had any," Miriam replied.

"Miriam Cahill, shame on you for even suggesting such a thing! You know I don't have any liquor in this house, nor would I ever -" she ceased her spluttering as she looked up to see Miriam holding her sides and trying not to laugh out loud.

"Oh, Lizzie, if you could see your face!"

"Well, I couldn't believe you'd think I would even consider giving whiskey to that sweet baby," she finished on a chagrined note. "You got me; go ahead and laugh if you must."

Miriam burst out with the giggles she'd been holding in, and soon she and Mary Elizabeth were both guffawing and trying not to make too much noise.

"Mama always did say you had a bit of the devil in you, Mim."

"I just kept everyone from thinking too much. It was difficult enough living with Daddy's angry outbursts and erratic moods as it was; no need in dwelling on what couldn't be changed and letting it depress us."

"No one could be depressed for long around you

and Mama. Y'all were quite the pair."

Smiling, Miriam spoke. "I got the part-time job at the library. Mrs. Tate seemed happy to have me. I start on Monday. Could you help me make a new dress over the weekend?"

"You know I will. Congratulations, Mim. You'll love working at the library, and keeping busy will help you begin to heal."

"I stopped by Mrs. Perkins's shop on the way home. I had this idea that I could pay her a little bit of my salary each week and buy Mama's things back."

"Oh, Mim, what a good idea! I never thought of asking her to do something like that. What did she say?"

"She told me she sold everything yesterday."

"Already? How did she sort through everything so fast?"

"She didn't. Someone came in and bought two lots without even sorting through them. He got the things Daddy sold."

Bursting into tears, Mary Elizabeth pulled out a chair and sat heavily at the kitchen table. "I was hoping to save the clock for T.J. Surely Daddy wouldn't have objected to his first grandchild having something from his family. Did he resent Pop and Grammy so much?"

"He never gave them a moment's thought. This was about the money, and you know it. What I can't understand is why he sold the pictures. Why would anyone want our family photos? The frames were cheap; no one could find any value in those, surely."

"I don't have one picture of Mama to keep for T.J.," Mary Elizabeth sobbed as Mim sat beside her and felt a few hot tears slide down her own cheeks. "How did Mama live with Tom Cahill for so many years? We could have lived with Pop and Grammy. Mama could have gotten work somewhere. Why did she stay?"

"I guess we'll never know for sure. Maybe there was some bit of hope that he'd change. She used to talk about the first year they were married and the way he used to tease her and make her laugh. Something changed him, and Mama must have hoped she could love him long enough to get back the man she married. I have to admire her courage, but I think if it had been me I'd have bundled up my children and run as far away as I could get."

"I talked to her about Daddy and his anger several times, but she refused to speak ill of him to me or answer any of my questions. When I saw how upset she got at my probing, I decided to stop asking."

"Did she -" Miriam began, only to be interrupted by the loud wailing of her infant nephew. "Gracious, you were right, Lizzie. That's one unhappy young man."

"Will you get him for me, Mim?" Mary Elizabeth asked as she rose from the table, wiping her eyes on her apron. "I'll warm his bottle and see if we can't find some way to take his mind off his misery."

Miriam walked into T.J.'s bedroom and picked up the red-faced, kicking little bundle, patting his back as she settled him on her shoulder. "Hey, mister, what's this? There's no need to carry on so. Your mama will make your gums feel better in a jiffy, and then maybe we can play with your truck. Would you like to play with Auntie Miriam for a bit? Your Grammy used to wish she could play with you more, but the illness had already made her weak by the time you came along. Oh, but she was so proud of you, T.J. She used to hold you and tell you about your uncles and how they used to tease your mama and me. They threw us in the creek once, and we were dressed up for the revival meeting, too. Oh, my, your Grammy was so put out! Will apologized to her and gave her the grass snake he had in his pocket. She made him put the snake back where he'd found it, of course, but Will couldn't understand why she got so upset. After all, it was just a snake. I'm sure you'll bring home your share of snakes. Just be sure you let your Daddy show you the harmless ones first, okay?" She blew raspberries on his tummy and listened to him giggle as she walked into the kitchen with him. "Here we are, Mommy. He and I have just had an interesting talk about snakes."

"Snakes? What are you up to? Thank goodness he can't understand a word you're saying." She shook her head as she put the bottle in his reaching hands. "Snakes. As soon as we're done with our lunch, Aunt Mim, we'll pick out some fabric from my sewing room for your new dress."

"Thanks, Lizzie. Why don't I do these dishes, hmm?"

Toby walked in later that evening to find his son asleep on the couch, snuggled in the blanket his mother had knitted for him, and his wife and sister-in-law cutting out pieces for a dress.

"Domestic bliss is a wonderful thing," he called out from the front door.

"Toby." Mary Elizabeth looked up in surprise. "You're home early, honey. Is this a good happenstance?"

Reaching to envelop her in a hug, Toby smiled in that secret way he had and replied, "The best of happenstances. I've got something to show both of you.

It's out in the truck."

"Well, go get it. We could use a nice surprise about now."

Walking back in a few minutes later, Toby gently set the box he was carrying in the overstuffed armchair and began, "I made a visit today to an old friend of ours and made a couple of inquiries. Took me away from work for about two hours, but I figured it would be worth it when you see what I've brought home." He reached into the box and pulled out a quilt. Still puzzled, Mary Elizabeth took the coverlet into her arms and looked up at her husband's smiling face.

"I don't understand, Toby," she said, only to be interrupted by Miriam's soft cry.

"It's the quilt Mama made for Seth, Mary Elizabeth. Look! Everything Daddy sold is here. Toby, how did you do this? I went by the secondhand shop this morning and asked about Mama's things, and they were gone."

"I know; Mrs. Perkins told me. I knew how much this meant to you two, so I was determined to get it back. I had to track down the man who bought these things, but he was most understanding when I explained what had happened. He let me buy everything for what he paid Mrs. Perkins."

"Oh, it is all here!" Mary Elizabeth exclaimed. "Mim, here's the clock, and the pictures! Oh, Toby," she cried, flinging herself into his arms. "I think I love you more in this moment than I ever have before. Thank you, honey."

"Aw," he grinned. "Twern't nothin'."

"Thank you, Toby," Miriam added. "You know, I think I love you, too." She smiled and sorted through the items in the box until she'd lovingly removed and stroked each piece. "Mary Elizabeth, why don't we put the clock on the mantel right now?"

"I think that's a good idea, Mim," Lizzie answered, wiping the tears that were once again coursing down her cheeks.

Watching Mary Elizabeth with a smile on her face, Miriam reached for the stack of pictures her mother had protected so carefully over the years. The shining faces of her brothers stared back at her from the snapshot on top. When she reached for the next photo, her fingers found instead a small envelope tucked between the images.

"Lizzie," she said quietly, "it's addressed to you, and it's in Mama's handwriting."

Chapter 3

Mary Elizabeth accepted the envelope with hands that were beginning to shake. Breathing deeply, she sat on the couch and gently pried the flap up and withdrew the pages within. As she opened the letter, several bills fluttered to the floor. "Oh, my. Miriam, look." She bent over and retrieved five fairly crisp ten-dollar bills. "How did Mama ever manage to get $50 dollars?"

Miriam joined her sister on the sofa and urged Mary Elizabeth to read the words written in their mother's familiar and much-loved hand.

Dear Mary Elizabeth,

I know there won't be too many days left for me on this earth, and I wanted to be sure this got done for you to find after I'm gone. Oh, my child, how I have loved you and your brothers and sister. You children were the spots of shining light in a life that became quite dark and desperate almost before I could realize it was growing so. Please don't feel sorry for me, though; I have loved your daddy and have sorrowed for the bitter man he became. I don't make excuses for him; he carried his anger like a gauntlet and used it to make himself miserable and lonely.

That was his choice. I hope I was able to stand between you children and his self-pity enough to make a difference in your lives. I'm so proud of my children, of Will for working so hard at college, and of Seth for becoming such a good provider and hard worker. They will both make wonderful husbands and fathers some day. I'm proud of you, Mary Elizabeth, for grabbing onto your dream and making a happy life for yourself with Toby. He's a fine man, and I know I can trust him with you and T.J. after I'm gone. And I'm proud of my Miriam, for the love she was willing to share with us, even to the point of sacrificing her own dreams. That's why the money is in this letter; it's hers. I want her to use it to make a new beginning for herself somewhere away from Cedar Springs. She owes nothing to her father now, but I'm afraid some false sense of family obligation will cause her to stay in that house and take care of Tom. Don't let her do it, Lizzie. Promise me that you will give her this money and help her to find her own happiness. I don't worry about you and the boys, but Tom might try to hold on to her. I couldn't bear knowing she gave up even one more day. I will miss you, my dears, but I know our separation is only temporary. Tell T.J. every day that his grandmother loved him.
I love you all,
Mama

    As the words faded and the room grew quiet, Miriam turned to Mary Elizabeth and clutched her in a sobbing embrace. What must Mama have denied herself in order to save so much money? The sound of Toby's sniffles drew their attention to his tearful face, and Mary Elizabeth stood to take him into her arms.

"Whew," Toby remarked. "Christine was a remarkable woman. What a gift she has given to you."

"I can't keep this money," Miriam said as she looked down at the bills in her hand. "This should be divided among the four of us."

"Oh, no, it shouldn't." Mary Elizabeth declared. "Mama was right. I'm proud of you for getting out of that wretched house, but you have given up too much already to assume responsibility for more than you should have. Besides, I'm not about to be the one to break a promise to Mama. This money is yours, and you will use it to make a new start once you find a teaching position. That's settled."

Miriam hugged her younger sister once again, then clasped the money to her chest and smiled a tiny, sorrow-laden smile. "If you're sure I'm doing the right thing, then okay. I'll do as she asked. I want her to be proud of me."

"Oh! Why won't this thing stay level?" Miriam complained as she tried for the third time to anchor the shelf in the library's newest addition. "My thumb is blistered and there's a roll of skin peeled from my little finger and you still won't stay where you belong." Swiping the hair plastered to her face, she addressed the source of her frustration. "Okay, here we go again, you stupid shelf, and this time we do it my way."

The front door to the library whispered open and with it the sounds of a busy Saturday morning filtered in from the street beyond. Farmers were in town for supplies and to check cotton and wheat prices, their wives eagerly looking forward to visiting seldom seen neighbors and the added pleasure of eating lunch at one of the local cafés.

"I'll be with you in a moment," Miriam spoke to the newcomer.

"Take your time," a familiar voice replied.

With an un-librarian like squeal, Miriam lunged to her feet and dashed across the room into the waiting arms of her youngest brother.

"Will! What are you doing home?" she asked as she squeezed him breathless.

"It is May, big sister." He laughed as he set her on her feet.

"Yes, I know, but. . ." she began.

"I made arrangements to take my exams early," he interrupted. "I wanted to see if I could make some kind of difference in the farm if I got home two weeks early. Dad isn't exactly ambitious these days about getting the crops in the ground. It may be too late already, but I'm going to try to increase the number of acres we plant this year," he explained. "Besides," he added with a new twinkle in his eye, "I missed my sisters and their good home cooking. I need some pampering."

"Well, you'll have to be pampered at Mary Elizabeth's, because I'm living with her and Toby until I find a teaching job."

"I know, sis. I've already been to Mary Elizabeth's. Daddy wouldn't even allow me to speak your name when I got to the farm this morning. I had to get the story from Lizzie."

"Will, I just couldn't -"

"Stop." Will gently covered her mouth with two fingers. "I think you did the right thing. You don't need to explain anything to me, and you certainly don't need to justify any of your behavior. I know why you got out, and I'm proud of you for having the courage to walk away. I'm angry with Dad. He was harder on you than the rest of us, acting like you owed him something and never measuring up to his expectations. I'm glad you're working here and making plans for your new life, and I'll do anything I can to help. And," he added as he flung his arm across her shoulders and walked her back to the shelves where she had been working, "there's no time like the present. Let me at this stubborn old shelf."

Miriam locked up the library promptly at one o'clock and smiled to Will as they began the short trip back to Lizzie's. Comfortably arm in arm, Miriam marveled at this broad-shouldered, handsome young man who was her youngest brother. He was easily four inches taller than Daddy's 5 feet, ten inches, well-muscled and tanned, with wavy hair the color of honey and snapping brown eyes. Good looking to the point of being 'pretty,' he had an easy-going manner and patient gait that someone might mistake for laziness, but Miriam knew better. Will was an excellent student with dreams of his own about a farm that would someday rival any in the state, equipped with the latest implements. He wanted to try new hybrid seed and many of the newest techniques he was learning at college. His brain was quick to absorb the chemistry behind the ideas, and he excitedly awaited the day when he could buy his first few acres and till up the first rows of his crops. Cheerful and upbeat most of the time, it was only in his most private moments that he pondered the shame of the farm on which he grew up, the softly spoken words he had sometimes overheard about "lazy Tom Cahill" and the "pretty little farm he was letting go to ruin." Will had vowed long ago to have the best farm in the world and never give anyone else the opportunity to speak ill of his land and abilities. He loved the animals, as well. As a child he'd named every barn kitten and fluffy new chick born on the farm and now looked forward to rising each morning to the comforting cackle of the chickens, the lowing of the milk cows, and the imperious crowing of the rooster as he summoned the farmyard to wakefulness.

A strident voice cut through Will and Miriam's comfortable stroll, and Will turned to see Marcus Thompkins sprint across the street and skid to a stop in front of his sister.

"Hello, Miriam," he spoke to her. "It's nice to see you again." Then, grabbing Will in a bear hug, he slapped him on the back and laughed aloud at the sight of his old high school chum.

"How are you, man? How is school? Aren't you in your second year? We've missed you around here, son. What are your plans for the summer? Say, why don't I meet you at the post office tonight about 7:30? Erwin and Carl and I are going out to Ronnie's; come along and see everyone again. And you can meet my cousin, Sonny. He's just back from seminary and visiting the family for several weeks this summer. He's something of a quiet guy, but you'll like him just the same. Don't be late!" Slapping Will on the arm one last time, Marcus dashed off with a wave and a shout to someone coming out of Callahan's General Merchandise.

"My!" Miriam chuckled. "He certainly has mellowed, hasn't he?"

"He's a good old boy, sis. Just a little enthusiastic at times," Will said, laughing. "It will be good to see those boys again, though. I don't do much but study at school."

"You tease," Mim responded. "Now walk me home; I'm starving and I'm sure I can smell Lizzie's roast chicken and lima beans from here."

"Race you!" Will taunted and ran off.

"You got a head start, little brother," Miriam called as she raced to catch up. "No fair, no fair!" Their laughter mingled and faded as they made their breathless way up the street to Toby and Lizzie's front porch.

The door opened before them and Miriam stared into the smiling face of her youngest brother, Seth. She flung her arms around him, knocking him backwards and almost toppling them onto the living room rug.

"Easy, Mim. You'll wreck the priceless antiques!" Seth kissed both her cheeks and then reached around her to shake Will's hand.

"I'm so happy to see you, Seth, but what are you doing here?" Miriam asked, wiping the tears from her face. "I thought you worked on Saturdays at the feed store."

"I do, Mim, but if the manager can't manage a day off for himself once in a while, what kind of a manager is he anyway?" His laughing eyes and wide grin reminded Miriam of just how much she'd missed Seth and his irrepressible good humor. His hair still dangled over one eye in a cowlick that refused to be tamed, and Miriam was glad to see the 'boy' hadn't completely left him. Time enough to grow up yet, she thought to herself.

"Will wrote me that he'd be home this weekend from school, so I decided to make it a family affair for the entire family. We haven't been together since the funeral, and I know we need time to talk about some things. I have some news to share; I'll bet the rest of you do, too." He smiled a mysterious smile and turned to put his arm around Mary Elizabeth, who had just walked into the room. "Mama would have been pleased to see us like this, don't you think?"

"Yes, she would have. Nothing meant more to her than her children. I'm so happy you're here."

Toby walked up behind Mary Elizabeth and laid his hands lightly on her shoulders. "Say, is anyone else hungry, or is it just me?"

"Everyone wash up," Mary Elizabeth requested. "I'll dish it up in a jiffy." Wiping a stray tear, she thought to herself that she'd been doing entirely too much of that lately. She rinsed her hands and dried them on her apron before putting lunch on the table. A contented group of young people talked and laughed around a table laden with roast chicken, mashed potatoes, gravy, lima beans, carrots, and rolls. Miriam had made a chocolate cake for dessert.

Seth leaned back and patted his middle, sighing deeply. "No one cooks like that for me in Ascension. I make do with the boarding house meals, but Mrs. Stewart's gravy is lumpy and her soups are runny and bland."

"I'm so sorry to hear that," Toby replied, looking up and down Seth's tall, angular frame. "You do look like you're wasting away."

"Oh, poor Seth, subjected to such poisonous fare," Will taunted. "At least you don't have to eat dorm food. After a while, everything tastes the same. Well, except for the chocolate pudding. I think they add cough syrup to it. It's horrible, and no one eats it. Why do they keep making it? They must throw it out by the gallon."

Everyone chuckled at his lament. "I'm sorry you fellas can't have Mary Elizabeth's cooking all the time, but that's a pleasure reserved for her husband alone, and don't think I'm not grateful." Toby smiled. "I know what I've got in the little woman."

"Little woman?" Mary Elizabeth piped up. "You watch it, mister, or you'll be doing these dishes yourself!" She swatted his arm with a dish towel as she rose to clear the table.

Wait, Lizzie, please," Seth interrupted. "I want to talk to you a minute. Sit back down, okay?"

"This isn't bad news, is it, Seth?" Mim asked. "I'm not sure I can handle anything else right now."

"It's not bad news, Mim." He smiled and took a deep breath. "I'm getting married."

Everyone cried out in joy and rushed to embrace him, congratulating him and asking for the details.

"Polly wants to be married the first Saturday in August, so we're planning a simple wedding at the Methodist church in Ascension. Miriam, she told me to ask you and Mary Elizabeth to sing a hymn during the ceremony, and Toby, we'd like you to be an usher. Will," he asked, turning to his brother, "will you be my best man?"

Gripping his arm, Will grinned and replied, "I'll be the best one you've ever seen."

"I hope y'all will understand what I'm about to say; I sure wouldn't hurt any of you for anything." Taking a deep breath, Seth announced, "I'm going to invite Pop to the wedding."

"I don't object, Seth," Miriam answered, "but do you think he'll come?"

"No, he won't," Will spoke up. "He's worse than he was before Mama died. I couldn't get him to speak a word about Miriam moving out. He has a perpetual frown on his face now, and he growls more than he speaks. If I weren't so determined to do something about the farm I'd be gone tomorrow. Once this morning I was sure he was about to hit me. You can ask him, but you're wasting your time, I promise you."

"How did he get this way?" Toby asked this clan into which he'd married. "I've always known him to be sullen, and I certainly never knew he was abusive to any of you until Mary Elizabeth and I began going together, but she has told me how happy he and your mama were that first year or two. What changed him?"

"I know a little of it," Miriam said. "Mama told me that she had gone out once or twice with Uncle Jim before she dated Daddy. She said that they had a good time, but she was never serious about Uncle Jim. They were just good friends. He was funny and easy to talk to. By the time she turned 18 and got to know Daddy, she knew Uncle Jim wasn't for her. It took her a long time to convince Daddy that she was interested in him, though. Grandpa had spent his lifetime telling Daddy how worthless he was next to his brother. Uncle Jim was going to be something in this world, and Daddy would never be anything but a dirt farmer. He wanted his father's approval so much, but mostly what he got was ridiculed and beaten. Grandpa was a strong advocate of 'Spare the rod and spoil the child,' but that only applied to Daddy and his sisters. Uncle Jim was Grandpa's favorite, so he was never whipped. When Daddy and Mama got married, he was so crazy in love with her he could forget she had gone with Uncle Jim. I'm sure even Grandpa's cruelties weren't as important any longer."

"I remember now." Mary Elizabeth took up the story. "Mama told me that Daddy came in for lunch one day the second year they were married. Uncle Jim had come to see him, and while he waited for Daddy he and Mama were visiting in the kitchen. Daddy came in and found them laughing together and assumed the worst. He threw Uncle Jim out of the house and swore he'd kill him if he ever came back. Mama begged him to see the truth, but he was so jealous he wouldn't listen. Mama told me that was the first time he ever hit her."

"Miriam, do you know what I just realized?" Seth said. "Everyone looked at him as surprise registered on his face. "You were born two and a half years after they were married. Mama must have already been pregnant with you at that time, but she didn't know it yet. If Daddy assumed that she and Uncle Jim had been together, he must have thought that you were. . ."

"Dear God!" Mary Elizabeth breathed in astonishment. "Has he believed all these years that you were Uncle Jim's child?"

"Oh, he couldn't have believed that of Mama!" Miriam objected. "She used to tell me of the fun they had that first year. She took lunch out to him in the fields and they'd have picnics together. Once she took lunch to him in the barn and one thing led to another and. . ." Seth and Will looked at one another and smiled. "He used to bring wildflowers to her when he came in for dinner. They loved to listen to the radio together, especially The Grand Ole Opry on Saturday nights. Mama said that sometimes they'd dance together."

"Jealousy is a powerful emotion, honey," Toby argued. "It can eat away at a person, and Tom must have been jealous of Jim long before Christine entered the picture. Their history together only made it worse. What a shame, to let your own insecurities ruin the love you have for a woman who clearly loves you, and to turn that love into bitterness and self-pity."

Tearfully Miriam responded, "I've spent my entire life trying uselessly to win the approval of a father who doesn't even believe he is my father.   What an unspeakable irony."

Mary Elizabeth reached across the table and took her hand. "You've suffered the most because of Daddy's ugly imaginings, but you surely don't blame yourself for any of this, do you?"

"I used to. I used to cry myself to sleep at night wondering what I could do to have him love me. I tried my best every day to make him notice me, show me some kind of affection, but I can't even remember a time when he hugged me. I thought it was because there was something wrong with me. This is priceless," she sobbed. "At least I know now it was nothing I did, and nothing I tried to do could have made a difference to him. Can you imagine? I was so pathetic, following after him like some lost puppy, and all these years he's despised me."

"You were never pathetic, Mim," Will insisted. "He was the pathetic one. He's driven everyone away who's ever cared anything about him, and he did it to himself. Mama must have loved him more than I can even imagine to stay with him knowing what she did."

"She did love him, but we don't often hear of women who leave their husbands and file for divorce. Most women stick it out no matter how badly they're treated because most don't have anywhere else to go and no way to support themselves without their husbands. What was Mama going to do if she did pack us up and leave Daddy?" Mary Elizabeth countered. "I'm sure she felt trapped at times, but she hoped that someday she could convince him of his mistaken ideas and win him over again. She never gave up hope for that."

"I used to get so angry with her for putting up with Daddy's meanness to us. I used to wish she would surprise him one day in the barn with the shovel and knock him senseless," Seth commented, his jaw flexing in anger. "I dreamed of how I'd sneak up on him sometime and beat him with my baseball bat. I could see it, and later on I'd be scared to death that I could even think about doing such a thing."

"You were an angry, confused little boy, Seth," Miriam told him. "We used to wish he'd go away and leave us alone at the least. It was only natural to feel that way; we lived with a tyrant."

"Was your growing up as sad as this sounds?" Toby asked.

"Actually, no," Miriam explained. "Mama loved to sing and tell us stories. She made the chores fun for us kids. Each of us was given two rows in the garden to tend, and we made it a contest to see who could grow the best vegetables each summer. Laundry was an assembly line kind of thing, and we used to make up songs as we each did our part."

"I remember swimming in the creek every summer," Seth added. "We swung from one of the tree branches growing out over the water to see who could get closest to the middle of the current. We played in the mud and skipped rocks, brought home lizards and snakes, just like normal children."

"We were normal children, you idiot!" Mary Elizabeth chuckled. "What I loved best were the evenings after supper when we'd watch the fireflies out in the meadow," she remarked, a distant look in her eyes. "The barn cats would rub up against our legs and meow for us to pet them. Looking up into the sky at the full moon drifting across the clouds was one of my favorite joys.”

“Those times were special because of Mama,” Miriam said. “She taught us about nature and helped us to make up games. Playing with her made everything fun. Daddy worked out on the farm all day, so we seldom saw him, remember? After supper he’d read the newspaper in his easy chair. He never got involved in our play. It was easy to be grateful that he didn’t come around. When he did, one of us usually got backhanded for something he didn’t think we should be doing.”

“If he was so busy on the farm,” Seth interjected, “then why was it such a pitiful money maker? We never had any money for anything. Mama had to make do with so little. Other farms were profitable, even smaller ones. I don’t understand it.”

“He worked all the time,” Will said, “but he was no farmer. He overplanted his fields until the soil was useless. He planted some crops way too late, and he never kept up his equipment. That’s why he could never make a living at it. I think he resented the fact that Uncle Jim had chosen not to be a farmer and was making a handsome living working at the mercantile for Mr. Callahan. Maybe he just didn’t have the heart to work at it after what he believed about Mama and Uncle Jim.”

“He was also just plain lazy,” Mary Elizabeth added. “He never did one thing to make any repairs around the house. Some didn’t require anything more than a little time and effort and some supplies from the barn. That never seemed to matter; he just didn’t care if the house fell apart around us.”

“I could almost feel sorry for him if I didn’t know

what those years of abuse did to Mama," Miriam said.

"I loved your Mama almost like she was my own," Toby began in a thoughtful voice. "She welcomed me with a big hug and a plateful of food every time I came to play. Her gingerbread was the best I'd ever had. She fussed at me just like she did all of you, and when there were chores to do she expected me to pitch in as well. She made me feel like I was a part of your family, and I couldn't wait to finish my work at home so I could get to your place. Of course, once Mary Elizabeth set her cap for me, how could I resist two such comely ladies?"

The comfortable silence was interrupted by T.J.'s sudden squeal. Everyone started and then laughed. "Well, I guess the king has decided he's been ignored long enough!" his mother laughed. "Come, your highness. It's time to find a clean diaper and a nappy time friend. Excuse us, please." She snuggled her son close as they made their way to his bedroom. Toby and the others could hear her lovingly murmuring to him in the way only mothers knew how to do. Will stood up from the table and walked to the door.

"I should get out to the house. I want to make plans for an early start in the morning before I meet Marcus later tonight. Tell Lizzie I said 'Thanks' for lunch."

"Anytime, Will. Hey, aren't you going to church with us in the morning?" Toby asked.

"I guess I should, I suppose," Will remarked. "Can I come back here for lunch?"

"You know you can, you clown." Toby laughed. He thumped Will on the back as he walked out the door. Helping Mim clear the table, he remarked, "That kid brother of yours is a pip. I certainly married into an interesting family."

"We're one of a kind," she agreed, grinning at him. She looked up as Seth walked into the room. "Are you washing or drying?"

"What?" he sputtered. "But I'm a guest. Surely you can't think -"

"Let him take a nap, Mim, like he'd planned," Mary Elizabeth spoke from the living room. "T.J. is asleep, and you know I don't want any of these men in my kitchen. I'll wash." Giggling, the sisters disappeared into the back of the house.

Chapter 4

Three weeks later Mary Elizabeth found herself walking up the driveway to the farm in search of Will. She needed to ask a favor, and since it was such a lovely morning she decided to bring T.J. so they could both enjoy the soft breeze and the glory of the daffodils. Mim had offered to watch the baby, but Mary Elizabeth had another idea in mind. It was difficult to concentrate on the beauty around her with so much else to think about. She supposed this was a fool's errand, but she could be stubborn, too, and it was about time Tom Cahill saw his grandson. She called out to him as she took T.J. from his stroller and walked up the front steps. The third one sagged even more than she remembered, and the yard bristled with weeds of every description. Had there ever been a time when grass could find a toehold in this jungle? If so, she couldn't remember it. The screen door whined as she reached the porch, and she looked into the face of a father she hardly recognized. His hair had grown shaggy and was even grayer than she remembered from the funeral. He'd not shaved in several days, and the gray stubble on his chin made him look even older than his 48 years. His clothes were unkempt and wrinkled, and the shirt so dingy with stains and dirt it was anyone's guess what the original color had been. Shocked, Mary Elizabeth cleared her throat twice before she could speak.

"Daddy, I brought T.J. for a visit. Toby and I thought you might come by the house, but you haven't. Is anything wrong?"

"You haven't seen me because I'll not be under the same roof as your sister."

"You can't still be angry with Miriam for wanting a life of her own."

"She had a life, here, with me. Her mama would have expected her to stay on and take care of me, but she couldn't get out of here fast enough after the funeral. If she doesn't care about what happens to me, then I don't care if I ever see her again."

Furious with his selfishness and self-pity, Mary Elizabeth stood up to her full 5' 4" and unleashed the years of anger she'd been holding back.

"How could she care if you lived or died after the way you've treated her? You ignored her completely unless you were hitting her or yelling at her for doing something you didn't like. I've never heard you speak a kind word to her. Mama said you refused to hold her when she was a baby. She's been more of a servant in your household than she ever was a daughter. If you'd treated me that way, I'd have gotten out at the first opportunity myself. The only reason I'm here this morning is to give you a chance to see your grandson, if that matters to you. I'm beginning to think nothing matters to you except all the years of feeling like you've been wronged by the people who loved you most. I'd be inclined to feel a little sorry for you if you weren't such a miserable excuse for a husband and father. Look at you, unshaved, filthy, and letting this house fall down around you. You have no pride at all, do you?" Taking a steadying breath, she added, "This was a mistake; I shouldn't have come out here this morning. Why don't we just agree to leave one another alone from now on?" Turning to go, she gasped when she felt his hand grab her wrist in a crushing grip.

"You dare to come out to my house and speak to me that way? Who do you think you are, girl?" he roared. "I'll live as I want, and do as I want, and you'll say nothing about it. This is my house, daughter. Your mama thought she could do as she pleased, but I showed her she was wrong. As long as I kept a roof over her head, she had no say about anything." He shook her so violently she was afraid T.J. would fall.

"Let go of me, Daddy. You might hurt T.J."

"Did you think the sight of that baby would make me feel any more obliging to you? You took in your sister, gave her a home, made her a part of your life even after you knew she'd betrayed me. You're no better than she is." He pulled his hand up to strike her when a shout from the barn halted him. Mary Elizabeth turned to see Will running up to the house, shouting at their father to let her go.

"Leave her alone, Pop," Will commanded. "You're hurting her, and scaring T.J., too. Let her go."

"Don't tell me what to do, boy," Tom began, but Will walked up to him and gently took T.J. from Mary Elizabeth's arms. Soothing him absently, he turned again to his father and spoke with quiet authority.

"I said to let her go, and I meant it. I'm not the frightened little boy I used to be, and you're not going to hit her, or me, ever again. I can hold my own with you now, and if you insist on taking this any further, I won't be the one bruised in the morning."

Tom's face flushed a deep red as he stared into his youngest son's face. His breath came in great gasps. "Get her out of my sight," he spat, flinging Mary Elizabeth's arm away so forcibly that she stumbled. "You can get out, too," he pointed at Will and ground out.

"I'll be staying, and you can't do anything about that, either. I'm working this farm, which is more than you've done in the last few months. You're eating because I'm making meals every day, and there's money in your pocket again because I take more pride in this land than you ever did. You won't be throwing me out anytime soon, and you know that's God's truth. Why don't you go back in the house?"

Seething, Tom stalked back inside and slammed the door against the sight of the two young adults he had fathered. He sank into the overstuffed chair that had been in this living room for over twenty years, unmindful of the dirt and sags. What had become of him, that his kids could treat him so? It was humiliating, that's what it was, but for the life of him he couldn't seem to work up the energy to do anything about it.

Will handed his nephew back to Mary Elizabeth and hugged her to his side. "Don't think about it, Lizzie. You need to put him out of your life and get on with taking care of Toby and T.J. Something in him died when Mama died, and I don't think even this young 'un is going to penetrate the wall of misery he's built around himself. Now go on home."

"Oh, Will, how do you stand it?" she cried softly. "How do you live in this house with him? I'd go mad if I had to put up with his tirades."

"He never speaks to me. He sits in that old chair most of the time, eats what I fix for him, and ignores me. I keep busy with the chores during the day, and then work in the barn until bedtime most nights. I think I've made some real progress. I never thought I'd be washing bedclothes and towels, but you do what you have to. Besides, it's only temporary. I'll go back to school in September, and then he'll be alone in this place again. I'm sure that's how he prefers it."

"I thought I'd try to reach him for T.J.'s sake. Guess I was wrong to come out here."

"You weren't wrong. You love your son and want him to have a grandfather. It's not your fault that this is the grandfather he's got. It's going to be Dad's loss ultimately if he continues to turn his back on us. Nothing can be done; I've given up trying myself. Go on home, sis."

"Can you come for supper? Toby and I want to talk to you about something."

"Sure thing. I'll get washed up here and be on your front porch about 6 o'clock. What's for supper?"

"Pork chops, fried potatoes, corn on the cob, squash, and peach pie."

"Maybe I'll be there at 5:30." He grinned.

Hugging him for one long moment, she smiled her thanks as she walked down the front steps and secured T.J. in his stroller. He watched her make her way to the road, waving as she turned at the corner. "God bless her, she tried," he thought aloud as he returned to the barn.

"Honey," Toby sighed as he tossed his napkin on the table next to his plate, "if you keep feeding me like this I won't be able to get through the door. That was sure good." Leaning over, he kissed her on the cheek and sat on the couch. "I think I'll let my stomach settle before I try to move. Anybody's guess as to whether I could make it across the street after making such a pig of myself."

"You don't need to worry about getting fat, Toby. You burn it off at work every day. If I didn't feed you so well, you'd waste away for sure!" she replied, laughing as she got T.J. out of his high chair.

"I sure hope you're right, or you'll be letting my pants out soon."

Following her husband into the living room, Mary Elizabeth settled her contented son on her lap and turned to Will, who had stretched out in a comfortable chair, his impossibly long legs reaching for the overstuffed ottoman.

"Will," she said, "do you remember Anna Davis? She sings in the choir at church."

"Sure, I do. She's the one with the pretty alto voice and curly brown hair. You're not trying to set up a blind date or anything, are you, Lizzie?" He smiled as he asked, but his eyes held a glint of steel.

"Oh, of course not. You've still got two more years to go at school. I know you're not ready to get married yet. Besides, she's two years older than you, so I know you wouldn't be interested. I have another idea in mind."

"Well, speak up. I'll agree to almost anything that isn't a date."

"I want you to consider singing a duet at church with her before you go back to school in the fall." Seeing the thundercloud descend on his brow, she spoke at a faster pace. "I know you didn't like to sing at church when we were younger, but I figured you'd grown out of that by now. You sing like an angel, so it can't be -"

Slapping his feet onto the floor in front of his chair, he interrupted, "You're right, I don't like to sing at church, even now. I'm not an angel, I'm a college student and poor farmer's son, and I won't be doing any singing at church with Anna or anyone else."

"But, Will, why not? What do you have against singing?" she asked plaintively.

"Lizzie, I don't owe you an explanation, but I'll give you one anyway, and then I don't want this brought up again, okay? You've begged me to sing off and on for years, and the answer is always going to be the same. I used to sing around the farm; I know you remember." He paused at her nod. "But what you don't know is that I got laughed at for my singing once. Dad heard me in the barn. I didn't know he was standing there until I'd sung the whole song and heard him applauding. I thought at first that he liked what I'd done. Then he told me he didn't know he had three girls in the family. When I asked him what he meant, he said I sang higher that either you or Miriam. Told me I made a mighty fine little girl and he'd have to see about Mama making me a dress. I hated him for making fun of me like that. I was only 10, and I loved to sing, but I haven't sung another note where anyone else could hear me since and I'm not about to start now. So forget it!" He lunged up and headed for the door. "Supper was good; thanks." With that pronouncement he stormed outside and slammed the door in his wake.

"Whew!" Toby muttered. "You sure touched a raw nerve, honey."

"I had no idea," Mary Elizabeth murmured. "How could Daddy have treated Will that way, so cruelly . . . and his own son. I thought he loved Will. He's paid for his college tuition. Am I being deliberately blind to his good points, or does he just not have any?"

"You've been hurt, Lizzie; you all have. It must be especially difficult for you because of T.J. I can't imagine doing something so hateful to my son, but then I don't understand your father. You can't help but be angry, and you see your childhood through the miseries he caused."

"I wish I'd never said a word to Will. I don't like the idea that I'm the reason he had to dredge up that awful memory."

"Lizzie, don't be ridiculous. You couldn't know; Will himself said that. He'll be okay; Will isn't the kind to brood or hold a grudge."

Before she could respond, the door opened and Miriam walked in from her dinner engagement with Mrs. Tate. "What's wrong with Will?" she asked as she hung up her scarf and purse. "He stormed past me out on the road and didn't even look back as I called to him."

"It's my fault," Mary Elizabeth sighed. "Pour yourself a cup of coffee while I get T.J.'s bottle for Toby and I'll tell you about it."

Toby hoisted T.J. into his arms and bounced him up and down on the way to the bathroom. "Come on, old man. It's time for you and me to have us a bath and a long talk about your mama and your granddaddy and one or two more grown up things. What do you say? Ready for a heart-to-heart with your Daddy?" T.J. giggled as Toby jostled and tickled him. Miriam turned to see Lizzie watching after them with tears flowing freely down her cheeks.

"Lizzie, what is it?" Miriam asked with a frown on her face. "What's wrong?"

"Nothing's wrong, Mim." Mary Elizabeth smiled through her tears. "I was just counting my blessings because I have such a patient husband who loves his boy without reservation. I know I'm lucky."

Miriam hugged her briefly and smiled, then she stepped back to remark, "I know this has to have been brought on by something Daddy did or said. And I'll just bet that's why Will is walking around in an angry fog, right?" At Mary Elizabeth's nod, Miriam turned her toward the kitchen and responded, "Let me fix T.J.'s bottle while you tell me what happened." Mary Elizabeth sat wearily in a chair while Miriam began her preparations at the sink. "The whole thing is my fault, Mim -" she began.

Summer heat settled over Cedar Springs as the days wore on. Soon it was July, and Miriam marveled anew at how much she had come to love working at the library and making preparations for the day she would be on her own, teaching school and living the life she used to dream about as a girl when she hid in the barn and lost herself in the pages of her library books. She had taken a portion of the money Mama had saved for her to buy fabric so that she and Mary Elizabeth could fashion a wardrobe. Lizzie was such an accomplished seamstress that Miriam usually allowed her sister to design the dresses and contented herself with installing zippers, buttons, and hems. They were beautiful, and Miriam was going to be so proud to wear them when she began teaching full time in September. She hadn't begun her search for a new job yet, but she knew this idyll must soon come to a close or there would be no jobs left for her. Still, it felt like a little bit of paradise had come to visit her to be living in Toby and Mary Elizabeth's home, enjoying a job she loved and no longer having to worry about what Daddy might say or whether or not he'd take a swing at her. The peace that had settled in her soul was almost overwhelming. Lizzie's home was warm, loving, and filled with laughter. Miriam wanted the same for herself someday. Many years had passed since she'd dreamed about a future, but she was dreaming with a vengeance once again, and it felt good.

Some Sunday afternoons, while Mary Elizabeth and her 'boys' took a much-needed nap, Miriam would wander around town, or walk down some country lane or another, and then the memories would come. She remembered times when they were children, playing in the barn, swimming in the creek, feeding the animals. She thought about the games they played, like Flying Dutchman, Piggie Wants a Signal, and Red Rover. Mama had played with them sometimes; oh, how she'd loved those times. Often her memories were washed with tears. Miriam had loved her mother completely, and missing her was an ache that lived with her no matter what else she might be feeling. Accepting that her grief had to run its course, Miriam wept when the emotions overwhelmed her, laughed when the remembrances were happy, and rejoiced that she'd had such a woman to raise and love her. She knew she'd been richly, sacrificially loved, as had each of Christine Cahill's children, and she knew at what cost that love had come. Flashbacks to her father's tyranny often followed those thoughts, and she accepted them as a part of what made her the young woman she had become. Growing up had not been easy, but thank God those times were behind her forever and she could concentrate on making her own happiness from now on.

Once in a while the walks had been nothing more than an opportunity to enjoy the light breezes that blew or to exult in the summer wildflowers and the shade provided by the towering oaks and pecans, sycamores and cedars, and countless other trees that filled the surrounding farmlands with such beauty year round. Her musings might drift to Seth's upcoming wedding next month. Lizzie and she were working on dresses for the ceremony, and through letters that had flown between them and Polly they had settled on pale blue with lace collars. Polly had requested that they sing, "Blest Be the Tie that Binds," one of Miriam's favorites. She could almost burst with her happiness for Seth and his bride; she looked forward to knowing this new sister and couldn't wait for August 16th to arrive. Miriam dared to hope, in her innermost spirit, that she might find that kind of love someday. She shied away from most young men because of her fear that she'd repeat her mother's mistake, but her fear couldn't quash that flickering spark that promised faithfulness and love and commitment. She even prayed for that unknown young man whom she hoped would someday be her husband. It might seem foolish to others, but she knew God looked into her deepest being and understood what she hoped for her future. Goosebumps rose on her arms as she considered what the next few years might bring, if she could find the courage to actually begin dating. Crossing her fingers, she giggled at her own silliness as she continued on her meandering way.

On this particular Sunday afternoon, just two weeks before Seth's wedding, Miriam was wandering happily on the lane that led to the river. She loved the sound of the water bubbling up from the spring, trickling over the rocks and gently roaring as it picked up speed around the last bend. The live oaks grew over the water in a tranquil green canopy, and the grass was lush and thick from its proximity to the water. Without conscious thought she found her feet leading her to one of her favorite spots, a canopied glade profuse with wild violets and alive with birdsong. She was glancing up into the trees looking for what birds she could see when there was an abrupt explosion of noise in the underbrush to her left. She turned in time to see a horse and rider bound from the woods and leap across the road just inches from her nose. Crying out in astonishment, she stumbled backward and lost her footing, falling into a thicket of brambles and twisting her right leg awkwardly beneath her. The rider came dashing back onto the road, calling out as he approached her, "I'm sorry, miss; I'm so sorry! Solomon got spooked and I couldn't slow him down in time. Are you hurt? Let me help you up." She took his hand as he pulled her to her feet. Gingerly she put her weight down and found her leg wasn't seriously hurt, just tender in a spot or two. Brushing her skirt free of debris, she looked up to respond, "I'm fine, really. You surprised me, and I stumbled. Thank you for coming back to check on me."

"I was afraid I'd maimed you for life, at least. I'm glad you're ok. I'll try to keep a tighter hold on Solomon from now on." Smiling, he aked, "I've never seen you around town before, have I? Are you visiting someone in Cedar Springs?"

"Oh, no, I live here. I've lived here all my life. I

was just thinking I'd never seen you around town. Do you live here?" She was thinking that if she'd ever seen this gorgeous man before she surely would have remembered. He was tall and broad-shouldered, his legs long and deliciously clad in faded dungarees. His hair was so blond it could almost be called silver, and his eyes were aquamarine blue. He smiled, and those eyes sparked like firecrackers on the fourth of July. Oh, yes, she thought, she'd have remembered him for sure.

"No, I'm spending some time with my aunt and uncle this summer before I continue my summer internship. I'll return to school in the fall."

"If you don't mind my saying so, you look a bit old for college."

"Why, ma'am, I'm a spry young boy of 25! Actually, I'm a third year seminary student. My name is Sonny Williamson."

I'm Miriam Cahill, and it's very nice to be run over by you, Sonny Williamson." She smiled as she worked to stop fidgeting and hold her hands still at her sides. He was just so handsome! And being this close to him made her nervous. "Who are your aunt and uncle?" she asked.

"Thaddeus and Margaret Thompkins."

"Oh, you're Marcus's cousin. He mentioned to Will that you were visiting."

"Will? Will Cahill is your brother?" At her nod, he said, "I remember meeting him a few weeks ago at one of Marcus's 'quiet affairs.'"

"Marcus is known for his enthusiasm," Miriam responded as she chuckled with him. "I remember one time when Will and Marcus must have been about nine. They'd managed to catch a mockingbird at recess. The poor thing must have been trapped in some underbrush or something. Those two took that bird into the classroom and turned it loose. It was bedlam! The teacher was yelling to get it back outside, the kids were laughing and jumping off their desks trying to catch it, and that terrified little mockingbird was dive bombing all over the room, desperate to find a window so it could escape. And in the midst of the chaos, there sat Will and Marcus, grinning like fools at one another. It didn't take Miss Elliot long to decide who was to blame."

"I've heard about the Great Mockingbird Caper," Sonny replied. "Uncle Thaddaeus applied some serious persuasion to Marcus's backside. He told me he had to eat dinner that night standing up."

"Will had to clean out the horse stalls for a week. He declared there was no worse punishment devised by man."

An impatient whinny startled them both, and Solomon ambled out of the trees to nudge Sonny's shoulder. Laughing, Sonny retrieved the reins and turned to Miriam.

"You're sure you're okay? I could take you to a doctor or something -"

"No, no, I'm just fine," she insisted, "but thank you just the same."

"Then I'll be on my way. Aunt Margaret will be expecting me for supper. It was very nice meeting you, Miriam."

She admired the easy way Sonny swung into the saddle and turned Solomon on the road headed west and away from her. Saluting from his perch, Sonny smiled as horse and rider trotted away.

Drawing a deep breath, Miriam thought aloud,

"Yes, sir, if I could work up the courage to date, I wouldn't mind starting with him." Humming softly, she resumed her walk to the river.

Chapter 5

The Methodist church in Ascension looked like most every other church Miriam had ever seen. Its white steeple clearly visible as it rose over the eastern end of Main Street, it boasted a large set of steps leading up to double doors painted a smooth cream. The shutters were dark green and rather simple, but they lent the exterior of the church a certain elegance. The pews were polished pine with dark green cushions, and the chancel area and aisle were carpeted with worn runners in shades of brown, yellow, and red, like the leaves that might flutter to the ground in a late autumn wind. Miriam marveled at the beautiful flowers that festooned the sanctuary; daisies and daffodils and marigolds were everywhere. There was a wooden arch at the end of the aisle, and it was woven with greenery and clusters of violets and roses. She was enchanted. Here in this peaceful chapel she could hear the whisper of the breeze in the trees on the lawn and the quiet noises of preparation going on in the pastor's office and Sunday School rooms down the hall. She expected Mary Elizabeth and the organist to find her here any minute so that they might rehearse their duet, but she wanted a few moments alone before the wedding began.

"Mama," she whispered. "It's Seth's wedding day. You'd be so proud of him today, Mama. He's got a good, steady job, and he's found a fine girl to marry. Her name is Polly. You'd like her, Mama. She has a pretty, heart-shaped face and blond curls that fall almost to her waist, and eyes that look on Seth with open adoration. They love each other so much. Did you and Daddy look at one another that way in the beginning? Were you ever as happy with him as Polly is with Seth? I hope so, Mama. Oh, how I hope so. I'm going to be sure Polly's uncle takes a picture of the four of us together today. You would have liked a picture like that."

Hearing the pastor's door swing open, Miriam wiped at a stray tear and turned to introduce herself to the balding man with the kind eyes walking toward her.

"Hello," he began. "I'm Reverend Mitchell," he said as he reached for the hand she had extended to him.

"It's so nice to meet you, Reverend." Miriam smiled in greeting. He had the gentlest brown eyes she'd ever seen, and his short, stocky build couldn't detract from the friendliness mirrored in his open face. That sincere countenance saved him from being considered stuffy, she concluded to herself. "I'm Seth's sister, Miriam."

"I'm delighted to meet you, Miriam. This is quite a day for Seth and Polly. I've known her since she was a little girl running around with her blond curls in a long ponytail, threatening her older brother with every kind of mischief. She's grown up quite well, don't you think?"

"Yes, I do. She's a lovely person. We've already grown to love her. Mary Elizabeth and I couldn't be happier to have a new sister in the family."

"I've become very fond of your brother since he's begun worshipping with us. He's a fine young man and will make Polly a grand husband. It's my honor to marry them today."

"We're very happy for them. They make a sweet couple."

"Yes, they. . . what in the world?" he declared as he heard a great crashing noise coming from the vestibule. "What is this about?" he asked her as he hurried toward the noise.

Following quickly behind him, Miriam gasped in horror. A man in filthy overalls and boots so worn they were separating at the soles had fallen on the floor just inside one of the front doors. He was bleeding from a gash in his arm and couldn't seem to regain his footing, in spite of the swaying and stumbling he was doing. Reverend Mitchell rushed to help him to his feet, only to have the man brush him aside violently.

"Leave me alone!" he roared. "I can get up just fine."

Miriam's hand flew to her mouth as she recognized the man's voice. It couldn't be, she thought miserably. It just couldn't be; he couldn't be here doing this on the most important day of Seth's life. Staggering to his feet, Tom Cahill looked up to find himself staring into the horrified eyes of his eldest daughter.

"Daddy!" she whispered. "What are you doing here?"

"I come to see my boy get married, you stupid girl. Why else would I be here?"

Reverend Mitchell attempted to intervene, alarmed by the way this man was glaring at his daughter, but Tom would brook no interference.

"You just mind your own business, preacher," he threatened. "This is none of your concern, y'hear?"

"Reverend," Miriam spoke quietly as she stared at her father. "could you please go find my brother?"

"Do you think it's wise to involve Seth on his wedding day?" the minister said.

"Not Seth, Reverend, Will. He should be in the Sunday School room with Seth. Just tell him I'd like to see him; Seth doesn't need to know about Daddy."

"Will you be all right, my dear, while I'm gone?" He hesitated as he turned to leave.

"Of course I'll be." She spared him a glance and smiled. "Just please hurry."

The minister's footsteps echoed in the corridor as Miriam turned her attention to her father once again.

"Why doesn't he need to know about me? Didn't you hear what I said? I told you I come to see Seth get married. He invited me, didn't he? Must've wanted me. Go tell him I'm here."

"He invited you, yes, but he didn't expect you to show up here in your filthy work clothes. What's the matter with you?"

Tom looked down at his clothes as if seeing them for the first time. "I reckon I'm not exactly fancied up and readied for church, but this is nothing more than honest dirt. Shouldn't embarrass no one, least of all you," he spat. "Who are you to criticize how I look, anyway? Now go get Seth," he commanded as he grabbed her arm and steering her down the same corridor into which the minister had just vanished.

"Will is coming; I'll wait for him."

"Go do what I said!" he yelled. "Who are you to

back talk your Daddy?"

She opened her mouth to speak just as she heard Will's voice from behind. "Miriam, what's going on?" Staring beyond her to the tattered old man whom he recognized as his father, he demanded fiercely, "Dad! What are you doing here? Why are you dressed like that?"

His father sneered at Will as he had just done to his firstborn and growled, "I come to see Seth get married! How many times are you going to make me repeat myself? Now show me where he is," he insisted as he shoved past Will.

"No, Dad, you can't!" Will began, as Miriam added, "Daddy, you mustn't. This would embarrass Seth horribly."

"Dad," Will interrupted, "how did you get here anyway?"

"I drove my truck. How else do you think I got here? Now are you going to take me to Seth or not?"

"No, I'm not," Will replied calmly. "You're going to get back in your truck and drive straight home. I've got two dollars in my pocket," he spoke as he turned Tom back around to the door, "and I want you to buy yourself a sandwich and then head on back."

Tom yanked his arm from Will's grasp and shoved him viciously toward the wall. "Git yore hands off me, boy! Who do you think you are, ordering me around like this? I'm here to see Seth!" he yelled.

Miriam hurried to Will's side, asking in despair, "What do we do now?"

A door closed quietly behind them, and Will and Miriam turned to see Reverend Mitchell walking toward them with two sheriff's deputies. She breathed freely for the first time since she had heard her father's voice. "Thank Heaven," she whispered.

"Ma'am," the tallest of the two deputies approached her. "Is there any trouble here? Reverend Mitchell called us about a disturbance."

Hesitating slightly, Miriam found herself unsure of just what to say. Before she could speak, however, her father pushed her aside and strode up to the officer until they were almost nose to nose. "There's no trouble here unless she causes it."

"Miss?" he questioned Miriam again.

"This is my father," she explained. "He has come to my brother's wedding, but I'm quite sure my brother wouldn't like to see him like this."

"You shut up!" Tom screamed at his daughter. "No one asked you to interfere!"

"Sir." The second deputy stepped forward. Miriam noticed that the name tag on his uniform said Tucker. "You need to calm down. We're just trying to understand why the Reverend felt it was necessary to bring us down here."

Fed up and thoroughly exasperated, Will spoke up. "Officer, this man is my father as well. We are Will and Miriam Cahill. He has already shoved me into a wall, and he's pushed my sister several times. We don't want him here."

"Why you rotten -" Tom cried as he reached for Will. "I'll take you outside and show you how to talk to your daddy!"

Before he could grab Will, the officers took a firm hold of each arm and stopped his progress. "Let me go," he snarled. "This is none of your business, and you need to keep away from me and how I deal with my children."

"Calm down, sir," the deputy requested. "We're going outside for a little talk, okay?"

Struggling mightily, Tom tried repeatedly to wrest his arms from the officers' grip, but he was unable to free himself. Miriam watched helplessly as he was handcuffed and manhandled into the back of the police car, yelling and kicking out at the men who held him fast. Will's arms around her trembling shoulders were a great comfort, and she turned her face into his shirt as the police car pulled away. What began as a trickle of tears built up within her until Miriam wept in great sobs that shook her to the very depth of her soul. Will hugged her tightly and let her cry it out, then offered her the handkerchief he'd placed in his back pocket earlier that morning.

"I'm sorry, Will. I just couldn't seem to control myself. I'm so lonely for Mama today anyway, and then to have Daddy show up and cause this trouble was more than I could face."

"I didn't mind, Mim. I am worried a little about you, though. Do you think you can get through the wedding?"

"Of course, I can. I wouldn't disappoint Seth and Polly for anything. In fact, can we keep this to ourselves until after the wedding? There's no use in upsetting everyone if we don't have to."

"I can keep quiet about it, but your nose is as red as the light on a Christmas tree. You'd better go to the ladies' room. Are you beyond repair?"

"Gracious, I hope not. If Lizzie comes up here, keep her busy. I'll be right back!" She sprinted to the restroom after grabbing her handbag from the back row of the sanctuary. Gazing at her reflection in the mirror above the bathroom sink, Miriam realized Will had been right. Her nose glowed so fiercely it looked like a neon sign outside a saloon. She retrieved her powder and set to work.

Emerging a few moments later, she spotted Mary Elizabeth in the narthex speaking to a gentleman she'd not seen before. Hearing her footsteps, they both turned in her direction, and Miriam's stomach did a little flip-flop.

"Miriam!" Sonny Williamson declared delightedly. "What a great surprise to see you again." He clasped her hand in both of his as he smiled into her flustered face.

"Sonny!" Miriam managed with a tremulous smile. "What are you doing here?"

"Mim!" reproved Mary Elizabeth. "Where are your manners?"

"I'm sorry, Lizzie, Sonny. You took me by surprise. Are you -?"

"This is the summer internship I mentioned to you. I'm spending eight weeks here in Ascension before I return to seminary. Working with a pastor-mentor gives me an opportunity to consider what kind of ministry I would like to pursue after I graduate. Besides, I'd met Reverend Mitchell last year when he taught a class I attended, and the chance to learn from him again was too good to pass up. I admire him a great deal."

"I'm happy to meet you, Reverend Williamson," Mary Elizabeth responded. "If you'll excuse us, Mim and I need to practice our duet for the ceremony. Mim?"

Looking down, Miriam realized that her hand was still clasped warmly in his. Blushing to the roots of her hair, she pulled away and murmured, "Please excuse me," before turning toward the doors.

Smiling, Sonny followed them into the chapel. "You can't escape me that easily, Miss Cahill. I'm the pianist." He grinned into her stunned face. "I'm ready to rehearse when you are."

"You're the pianist?" she blurted out.

"Mim! What is the matter with you today?" Mary Elizabeth whispered in her left ear as she plowed into her sister from behind. "Why are you just standing there? Come on!" Grabbing Miriam's arm, Mary Elizabeth dragged her sister toward the front of the sanctuary. Stumbling twice, Miriam regained her equilibrium just as they reached the steps leading into the chancel.

"I'm sorry, Lizzie. He just took me by surprise," she spoke in a hushed voice. Smoothing back her hair and brushing the front of her dress, Miriam looked up and smiled as Sonny took his place at the piano.

"We'll talk about this later, big sister," Mary Elizabeth declared as she cleared her throat and opened up her hymnbook. Smiling at Sonny, Lizzie spoke for both she and Miriam. "Ready, Reverend Williamson. Could you play the last line of the hymn as an introduction for us? We thought we'd sing the first two verses."

Sonny smiled and played the music to one of his favorite hymns. At once he was captivated by the perfect blending of Mary Elizabeth's pure soprano and Miriam's smoky alto.

"Blest be the tie that binds our hearts in Christian love.
The fellowship of kindred minds is like to that above."

The girls began verse two as an acapella offering,

for Sonny had stopped playing and was openly staring at the two of them. Their voices trailing off, Miriam turned to him and asked, "Is something wrong?"

"Hmm?" He spoke as if from far away. Clearing his throat, Sonny replied, "No, no, of course not. I'm sorry, ladies, but I was so taken by your beautiful harmonies that I simply forgot to play. Forgive me. Shall we take it from the top once again?"

This time the song flowed perfectly as Mary Elizabeth and Miriam poured forth the words in perfect accompaniment to Sonny's instrumental offering.

"Ladies, that was lovely." Reverend Mitchell spoke from the back of the sanctuary. "I know Seth and Polly are going to love it."

Miriam smiled at the minister, then turned to glance at Sonny. She found him staring unashamedly at her face, grinning as if he knew a great secret. The twinkle in those startlingly blue eyes was impossible to resist.

The wedding had been everything the young couple could have hoped for and more. Miriam recalled their laughing faces as they exchanged their vows, and then the light shining in their eyes throughout the reception as they were hugged by everyone at least twice, Polly's mother bursting into tears at roughly seven minute intervals. T.J. had charmed everyone, but by the time Seth and Polly had fled the hail of rice two hours later he was exhausted and wailing so that everyone within a mile of the church must surely have known it. The Cahills were more than tired and quite ready to wend their way home.

There had been an uncomfortable moment in the

parking lot when Will announced that he needed a lift to the police station. After explaining about what had happened with their father, Toby had given him $10.00 and had said, "Go bail him out and take him home. I'll see to it that the girls get home. Be careful, Will. He's going to be in a vicious mood."

Tom had in fact refused to go with Will in the beginning. He was furious with his youngest son and blamed Will for getting arrested in the first place. When the officers saw how abusive Tom was becoming, they took him before the Justice of the Peace. A few harsh words of his own and a threat to spend ten days in jail had Tom agreeing to let Will pay the fine and take him home. He muttered and sulked all the way to Cedar Springs, but thankfully there were no more incidents.

Drinking tea on this early Saturday morning a week later, Miriam smiled as she thought about what had taken place. What a day! Lizzie had been driven to tears several times this past week as they discussed the contumacious old man their father had become. At least Will would be leaving for college this Friday. She and Lizzie worried about him spending his time out at the farm with Daddy so unpredictable and hateful since Mama had died.

She couldn't wait for Mr. Brindle to bring the mail. She had mailed off several applications for teaching positions back in July, and here it was four weeks later and not a peep from anyone. Determined to make her own way for the first time in her life, Miriam had crossed her fingers and sent off applications to Birtwhistle, Elm Grove, Martinsville, Heber Springs, Crosswinds, and Hodges. Surely someone needed an elementary school teacher!

Toby and Mary Elizabeth were still asleep. Miriam had awakened at 6:30 when T.J. fussed. She gave him his bottle and rocked him back to sleep so his mama and daddy could get some extra rest. His round baby face and chubby legs never failed to make her smile. Tobias Jamison Woods was already a heartbreaker. His deep brown eyes were just as warm as his daddy's, and when he smiled and those dimples peeked out from his delightfully pinchable cheeks, you were sunk. No one could gaze upon his sweet innocence and not fall completely in love. Too eager for news about a job to be able to go back to sleep, she'd brewed herself some tea and was peacefully sipping, thinking about the turn her life might soon take.

She hoped she could find a boarding house that would allow her to paint and make some personal changes to her room. She had dreamed of how she'd decorate a place of her own since she'd been a little girl. There would be lace curtains at the windows and braided rugs scattered on the floor. She would cover her bed with the quilt Mama had made and remember each loving stitch every time she looked at the soft blues and greens that made up the coverlet. The kitchen she'd paint a pale yellow, or maybe a light blue. Someday she hoped to have dishes with sunflowers on the border, and a bright sunflower painting over the table. The linens she would stitch with a lace border, and she'd find bright blue and green plates to hang on the walls.

More than making her first home into a comfy place that suited her, though, she longed for a space of her own, a place in which to create new and imaginative ways to teach her students, a place to dream about the future for her family, to sit in the evenings and write letters to Will and Seth and Lizzie, to share everything about her job and her friends and the new life she'd make for herself. Miriam wanted more than anything to put away the frightened little girl she'd been, waiting for Daddy's next ugly word or the next bruise on Mama's cheek or upper arm. She wanted to be free to cook when she wanted, tidy up as she pleased, go to all the movies she could afford, and not worry about doing what was expected or her duty. She looked forward to that sense of freedom, knowing somehow it would feel even better than the independence she'd already tasted living with Toby and Lizzie and working at the library.

Would her children like her? Would they want to learn what she could teach? Would there be one who might share her love of books and look forward to their weekly trips to the school library? Would they bring gifts for her at Christmas and hug her on their way out the door in the afternoons? With a contented sigh, she arose from the table to put breakfast on the stove. She'd heard Toby's boots thump against the floor and knew the family was beginning to stir. Her dreams would have to wait for another time, but they were never out of her mind.

The sound of Mr. Brindle's footsteps on the front porch an hour later startled Miriam from her place on the sofa. She'd settled down with her latest novel from the library to await the mail and had almost dozed off. Hurrying to the door, she flung it open just as the erstwhile mailman was about to place the envelopes in the slot.

"My gracious, Miriam! I'm not as young as I used to be. My heart can't take such surprises. What are you so eager to find, anyway, that it's worth knocking a few years off my life?"

"I'm sorry, Mr. Brindle. I didn't mean to startle you. I'm looking for a reply to my job applications, and it's been weeks! Is there anything today?"

He smiled a lazy grin and handed over the stack of letters. "Never know, missy; never know." Whistling softly, he turned and strolled back to the sidewalk.

"Thank you, Mr. Brindle!" she called as she began looking through the handful of letters. Next to last was one with a Martinsville ISD return address typed in the upper left hand corner. Ripping into it, Miriam read hastily as she walked back into the house.

"Miriam, aren't you going to close the door?" Mary Elizabeth asked as she walked in from the kitchen. Miriam looked up at her sister with tears pooling in her eyes and replied, "It came, Lizzie; listen. . .

Dear Miss Cahill,

We received your application and were most impressed with your college records. If you should still be interested in a position, we have an opening in the fourth grade for the upcoming school year. Your beginning salary would be $3,600.00. Should this meet with your approval, we will expect you on August 26 to sign your contract and attend orientation. There are two boardinghouses in Martinsville, as well as several fine families who house our teachers. The fees are nominal. I'm sure you will have no trouble finding suitable lodging.

We look forward to meeting you. If you have any further questions, we can address them at that time.
Yours sincerely,

Jonathan Butler

Superintendent of schools

Mary Elizabeth found her own eyes swimming with tears as she grabbed Miriam in a fierce embrace. "Oh, Mim, I'm so happy for you. You're officially a school teacher. Toby," she called to the back of the house. "Toby, come quick!"

Chapter 6

Miriam stepped off the bus on the Martinsville town square and looked around with eager eyes. She wanted to absorb every detail of her new home. She retrieved her suitcases from the driver and thanked him as he smiled and responded with a "Not at all, miss." Miriam could imagine him walking up the steps of the wood framed home he'd shared with his wife of 35 years and petting the mutt his son had named Poochie over ten years ago as he made his tired way inside. Smoothing her hair and shaking out the hem of her dress, she hefted her bags and walked down the block and into the quaint little post office building. Post offices must smell the same everywhere, she mused, like dust and lavender toilet water. Strange, she smiled to herself. The gentleman in the window looked like Pop, she realized. He had an almost completely bald pate, with just a rim of gray dusting his elephantine ears. The heavy rimmed glasses he wore could do nothing to disguise his smiling hazel eyes, and the pipe in his teeth was lightly puffing out a rich aroma that contained just a hint of cherry. He even smelled like her beloved grandfather.

"Good morning," she said.

"Good morning, young lady," he replied as he looked up. "What may I do for you this morning?" he asked with a grin.

"I'm looking for the superintendent's office. Could you give me directions?"

"I can do that, Miss. . .?"

"Oh, I'm Miriam Cahill. I'm the new fourth grade teacher at the elementary school."

"Well, isn't that nice," he replied. "I'm Amos Guthrie, Martinsville postmaster for, oh, nigh unto 47 years. Welcome to town. Do you have a place to bed down yet?"

"No, sir. Could you recommend something?"

"I sure can! My sister-in-law runs a boarding house just a few blocks from the school. She takes in teachers every year. A mite nosy, but cooks just like your mama. You'll like her place just fine. Name's Myrtle Henson, by the way. And you get to Jonathan's office by walking two blocks thataway," he pointed, "and turning the corner onto Sycamore. Can't miss it."

Smiling her thanks, she reached for her bags when Mr. Guthrie called out, "Hey, there, young woman. You don't need to be a'totin' those suitcases all over town. You just leave them with me and I'll see that they get to Myrtle's this evenin' when I close up shop."

"Oh, thank you." Miriam breathed a deep sigh of relief. Her arms felt like limp spaghetti already, and she hadn't even walked a full block. "I'll appreciate that so much."

She heard him whistling as she stepped out onto the square once again. Hugging herself briefly, she started toward Sycamore at a steady clip. She was so excited to be in Martinsville beginning this new life for herself. The few weeks she'd had to prepare had been a whirlwind of sewing dresses and packing what she believed she'd need. Lizzie helped her buy a new hat and pair of shoes; she'd felt so extravagant outfitting herself to be a schoolteacher for the first time. Determined to make the most of this adventure, Miriam smiled and spoke to everyone she passed along the way. The chubby matron in the flower patterned dress, the young mother with a blond-headed toddler in her arms, the clerk sweeping the sidewalk with his long sideburns and white apron all smiled and answered back politely as they went about their day. The courthouse was a two-story white brick building with black shutters and imposing staircases leading into huge double doors. She saw a five and dime, an ice cream shop and a café' that said, "Lucille's" on the front window. Across from the courthouse were a beauty shop, a hardware store, and a dress shop. There were large ceramic urns of flowers along the sidewalk, the zinnias filling up the pots with their lush colors. Miriam was pleased with everything she saw.

She spotted the trim, brick building which housed the district offices for Martinsville schools. The cream colored brick was saved from being dull by the deep green of the stately magnolia on the front lawn and the line of rose bushes blooming along the west wall. Stepping across the paving stones, she entered the front door and introduced herself to the secretary at the front desk.

"I'm Miriam Cahill, the new fourth grade teacher. I wondered if Mr. Butler had a moment to see me."

"I'll tell him you've arrived, Miss Cahill. Please take a seat," the severe looking woman told her as she rose from her chair. Miriam started at the sound of her voice; she sounded like her throat had been lined with gravel. Her graying black hair was pulled back in a bun so tight Miriam wondered how she managed to see. She was short and somewhat round, like a small snowman, and the black dress belted at her almost invisible waist did little to soften her frowning features. The black glasses that hung on a neck chain finished the look perfectly, Miriam thought. Usually not so cold-blooded, she couldn't help but think that this woman greatly resembled a bat.

Clearing her throat, the woman indicated for Miriam to follow her into an office at the end of a long, terribly dark hallway. Well, Miriam considered, the surroundings were perfect for her assessment of the secretary. This place was a cave.

Jonathan Butler, the district superintendent, rose to greet Miriam with a warm smile. "Welcome, Miss Cahill. Please sit down. Can I offer you a glass of water, some coffee?"

"No, thank you. I'm fine, and I'm eager to see my school and my classroom."

"Of course you are. If we could get your signature on your contract and a few other bits of office flotsam, we'll be on our way."

He reviewed the terms of her contract and pointed to the line where she signed her commitment to those stipulations. Shivering slightly, she told him, "I can't quite believe I'm actually doing this after I've dreamed of it for so long. I'm so excited to be teaching school, Mr. Butler, and I'm very appreciative of this opportunity."

"We're glad you're here, Miss Cahill. You are going to find Taylor Elementary a special place in which to work. The principal is an excellent leader and mentor; you can go to him with any problem and find his door open. We have some of the finest educators in the state working for us here in Martinsville. You will find the teachers at Taylor helpful and friendly from the outset." Placing the next form in front of her, he explained briefly and indicated where she was to sign and date the document. Two forms later he rose from his place behind his desk and responded, "If you would come with me, we'll walk to your new school and let you have a look around."

"Thank you, Mr. Butler. I never expected such personal treatment. I'm sure you must be busy."

"That's true, but I believe in having as hands-on an approach as possible. You will see me wandering the hallways and perhaps even sitting in on your class from time to time. Don't be nervous in the least; it's just my way." Pointing to the school campus about four blocks ahead, he told her, "There's Taylor. What do you think?"

"Why, it's gorgeous! I never expected such a large campus with so much playground equipment in the yard. You have tire swings in the trees!"

"Martinsville has been very fortunate to have parents who are willing to donate their time as well as their resources. We had some bake sales and a few other fundraisers in order to buy the extra playground equipment, and the fathers donated the tires and ropes and hung the swings. You may be in for a few more surprises once we get inside the building."

She was indeed surprised, and delighted, to see each classroom door painted a bright color; there were reds, blues, greens, yellows, and purples, and curtains at the windows. What a marvelous idea! Plants decorated the teachers' desks and windowsills in the classrooms, and there were paintings and posters on the walls. Each classroom had a corner dedicated to reading, with braided rugs and pillows on the floor. The more she observed, the more she marveled! Never had she imagined such a school. These few homey touches removed the utilitarian quality of most schools she had seen, and attended herself, and made her feel comfortable. She imagined the same could be said of the children.

Anticipating her question, the superintendent explained, "We have a very creative, forward-thinking principal, William McAnaly. This was his brainchild, and I must admit it's been most successful. Would you like to meet him now?"

"I certainly would," she responded eagerly. "I'm more excited about teaching here now than I was before."

Laughing, he led her down the corridor to a large set of glass doors. The office was filled with planters and photographs, and the chairs were deep and upholstered in the most beautiful blue plaid fabric she'd ever seen. They looked like they belonged in someone's parlor rather than in a school office. Miriam couldn't wait to write all of this to Lizzie. She wouldn't believe any of it!

A statuesque woman of about 50 walked into the office from a back hallway and approached Miriam and the superintendent. She was easily 5 feet, 10 inches tall, and her blonde hair was pulled back in an elegant French braid. She wore a tailored suit of deep green with a cream colored, ruffled blouse underneath. The cameo at the neckline was stunning. Smiling, she took off her glasses and addressed her boss.

"Hello, Mr. Butler. Is this Miss Cahill you have with you?"

"Yes, Mrs. Abernathy, it is. Miriam, I'd like you to meet Margaret Abernathy. She is Mr. McAnaly's secretary and a top-notch office manager. You'll enjoy getting to know her."

"How do you do, Mrs. Abernathy?"

Shaking her hand, the older woman replied, "Miss Cahill, we're happy to have you at Taylor. Anything I can do to help you along the way, you just let me know. And, please, call me Margaret."

"Then I'm Miriam, and thank you."

"Margaret, do you have my copy of the -" began a gentleman who had entered from his office at the back of the waiting area. Looking up, he broke off what he had begun to say. "I'm sorry. Hello, Jonathan. I hope this is Miss Cahill you have with you."

"Miriam Cahill, meet William McAnaly. I was just introducing her to Margaret."

"Miriam," he said as he offered his hand. Miriam found herself face to face with a man in his late 50's with thick gray hair and serene blue eyes. The lines that crinkled around his eyes made him seem friendly and approachable. His upper lip was covered by a bushy gray mustache, but she could still see the dimples in both cheeks as he smiled. "It's so very nice to meet you. Welcome to Taylor. I'm afraid you've caught me on a very busy morning. Would you mind if we talked as we take you to your classroom?"

"Thank you, Mr. McAnaly. I'm eager to see my

room."

Feeling a little breathless, Miriam allowed herself to be swept along an outside hallway to a bright green door. The number above read "27." Opening the door wide, the principal gestured for her to precede him into the room. She walked into a bright, sunny space outfitted with two huge blackboards covering adjacent walls. The third wall contained a row of shelves about three feet up, and then there was a narrow counter above which hung a coat rack and a bulletin board. The last wall was banked by four large windows. Twenty child-sized desks were lined up in five rows across the center of the room. In one of the far corners was her own library space with several large pillows and a rocking chair. Miriam was enchanted.

"Feel free to make this space your own, Miriam. We love to see plants growing and science experiments going on, as well as the children's artwork and academic successes posted everywhere you have the room. The workroom is next to the front office, just down the hall from where you came in. I'm sorry to be so abrupt, but I must meet a deadline with some paperwork. I would encourage you to look around today, visit some of the other rooms to see how our teachers have begun to prepare for the new year. Introduce yourself to anyone working in her room. Visit the library; Mrs. Pollard is there today and will be happy to answer any questions you may have. Jonathan, if you both will excuse me?" With that, he turned and hurried back from whence they had come. Miriam looked up as they left and wondered briefly about the pencil sticking out of Mr. McAnaly's back pocket. She chuckled when she heard him mutter, "Now what have I done with that pencil?"

"Miriam, you must excuse me as well. I've got to

get back to my own beginning-of-the-year preparations. If you need anything, come see me. Do you have your schedule for the new teacher orientation?"

At her nod, he said, "Excellent. I'll leave you to carry on."

Pleased to have a moment to collect herself, Miriam looked at the form she'd been given. She had the rest of this week to make her room ready for her students. School began promptly at 8:30 on Monday morning. She walked over to her desk and sat down in the upright chair. She'd make a cushion for this seat as soon as possible. Something with bright, primary colors would be nice, and she'd do the same for the rocking chair. Unable to resist, she moved to the chalkboard and wrote her name with a new piece of chalk she'd found in the tray. Stepping back, she read, 'Miss Cahill.' She thought a moment and then added Monday's date and 'Welcome to 4th Grade.' Hugging herself, she spun in a circle.

"Oh, Mama, I wish you could see me today! I'm standing in my classroom. Beginning on Monday morning I'll officially be a school teacher. I'm not sure I believe it yet. I'm so excited, but I'm scared to death. I wish you were here to give me some advice about what I've chosen to do with my life. You'd like Mr. Butler and Mr. McAnaly, I think. They seem like very professional men with some good ideas about teaching children. I know I'm going to love my fourth graders. And I'm going to be the best teacher anyone has ever seen. I'm going to make you so proud of me, Mama."

Overcome with emotion, Miriam found herself hugging her arms even tighter around her middle as she sobbed. She felt like she'd miss her mother forever, that the ache would never go away. It had only been seven months since her precious Mama had died, and so much had changed in that short time. Talking to her mother seemed silly sometimes, but it brought her such comfort that she continued to do it while keeping it to herself, like a marvelous secret that only she knew. Walking back around the desk, she sat in the chair once again and let the tears flow, knowing that it was impossible to hold the grief back once it overtook her. After several moments she was able to dry her face with a handkerchief and decided to take Mr. McAnaly's advice about looking around.

Walking down the hallway from her classroom, she found most rooms empty. Peering in the narrow windows that flanked each door, she found the rooms laid out just like hers, with a few preparations obvious in one or two of them. She could almost hear the children whispering and the tablets rustling as she looked from room to room. Would Monday never get here?

The room at the end was open, and she heard singing as she approached. Stepping across the threshold, she found a woman of about 30 standing up on a chair, stapling paper to the corner of her bulletin board. Leaning too much of her weight on the stapler, she lost her balance and teetered on the chair, grabbing for the edge of the board and desperately trying to find some purchase.

"Here, let me help," Miriam commented as she rushed forward. Holding the chair steady, Miriam grabbed her hand and righted the woman just before she would have toppled.

"Whoops! Thanks for saving me, sweetie. Say, I haven't seen you around before. New teacher?" she asked as she stepped down from her perch.

"Yes," Miriam responded as she introduced herself. "I'm in room 27."

"Well, it's a pleasure to meet you, Miriam Cahill. I'm Annie Buchanan, and I can see that we're going to get along just fine. I've been here at Taylor for five years, and I don't think I could work anywhere else. This is the best staff in the world, and there's no finer principal that Bill McAnaly. Have you met him yet?"

"Yes, just a few minutes ago. He seems like a very good principal. In fact, everyone has been so friendly I'm feeling a bit overwhelmed." Her lips trembled a bit as she smiled.

"We don't mean to scare you; we're just happy to have you. Sit right down here and tell me about yourself. You're new to Martinsville?"

Determined not to let this first experience of being on her own intimidate her, Miriam told Annie about growing up in Cedar Springs with Lizzie, Will, and Seth, and about striking out on her own after her mother had passed away this past winter. She told Annie about T.J. and Seth's new bride and that she hoped she was going to be a good teacher. Looking into Annie's clear, gray eyes and open, somewhat square face, Miriam knew she'd found an ally. Annie Buchanan was short and rather stubby; Miriam judged her to be about 5 feet, 2 inches tall and slightly rounded, but she had an ear-to-ear smile and the loveliest river of dark red hair Miriam had ever seen. It curled past her waist. In spite of her diminutive size, Miriam guessed correctly that Annie Buchanan was a force with which to be reckoned. She had a booming laugh and a confident demeanor that appealed to Miriam instantly, perhaps because she saw herself as so timid and uncertain. She hoped she and Annie could be friends.

"What about you, Annie? Are you from Martinsville?"

"Born and raised out in Lubbock. My daddy is a rancher. I'm here in Martinsville because my mama's sister lives here, and she wrote to me about the schools needing a 3rd grade teacher a few years back. Took me a while to get used to so many trees. I felt pretty hemmed in that first year. But I met Buck a few weeks after I started teaching here, and we've been married for the past four years. He's with the forest service. My Daniel is with Aunt Sarah; she keeps him for me while I'm working. He's three years old and just full of the devil. Buck says he gets it from me; I'm sure he's right." She laughed. "My mama used to tell Daddy that I'd outgrow it, but I never did. Glad of it, too. I may surprise you from time to time, but you'll never call me dull." She laughed her outrageous laugh and threw her arm around Miriam's waist.

"Come on, sweetie. I'll give you the Annie Buchanan new teacher tour."

Miriam and Annie walked out to the playground and Miriam took a few turns on one of the tire swings. She felt the carefree happiness she'd known as a little girl running around the farm with Lizzie, and before she knew it she was laughing out loud just like Annie. They talked about the children, the other teachers, and Annie's view on just about everything in the world. She delighted Miriam. Before too long Miriam was telling Annie about her mother.

"She was an extraordinary mother. She met us at the door after school each day with snacks and icy cold milk. She made up games for us to play, and sometimes she'd play, too. She quizzed us for our tests and read stories to us and took us to church every Sunday. I miss her. She was so sick that last few months that all I could do was sit by her bedside. She and I talked about our favorite parts of my growing up, and she told me about her own family, things I'd never heard before. Her grandmother had been a Cherokee medicine woman; her name was Minerva. I guess that makes me part Cherokee, too," she wound up, smiling at Annie.

"I guess most of us are part Indian of some kind. I'm Kiowa. Daddy used to tell us stories about our great great grandfather. I've seen some of the beadwork the Kiowa do. It's beautiful." Pausing for a moment, Annie said, "Listening to you talk about your Mama makes me wish I was closer to mine. Don't get me wrong; she took real good care of us. My brother and I had a great time riding with Daddy as he checked fences or herded the cows from one pasture to another. We used to like taking hay out to them in the winter best of all. The ground would be crusted over with ice and snow, and the sky was such a brittle blue our eyes would ache with the shine. The air was so cold it hurt to breathe. But Mama was so busy being proper and teaching us how to be ladies and gentlemen that she never could unbend enough to just be our mama and have a little fun. We're more like polite strangers than mother and daughter. That may be partly because she just never could tame me." Snickering, she added, "Gave it the old college try, though, but I wasn't cut out for frills and tea parties and garden clubs. Can you see me pouring tea in some parlor with Queen Anne chairs and lace doilies? What a hoot!"

Annie and Miriam discovered a mutual love for books and sassafras tea and a shared dislike of sewing clothes and ironing sheets. They laughed all the way back to Annie's classroom where they parted company for the afternoon. Miriam promised to find her on Thursday when she returned to make her room ready for the new year. On impulse, she hugged Annie and thanked her for making her feel so much at home. Annie smiled that ear-to-ear grin and told her she'd bring the sandwiches for lunch on Thursday.

Miriam smiled as she strolled back to the post office. She realized she was starving! In her zeal to find out about her new job she'd forgotten about eating lunch. Walking into Lucille's, the diner on the corner, she was charmed by the ceramic frogs she saw everywhere. There were frogs on the curtains and the napkins at the tables, and a long shelf above the door hosted an army of the fat little green amphibians. A waitress waved her to a table and arrived in a moment with a pad and pencil. Miriam ordered soup and a sandwich and settled back in the comfy booth to enjoy the decorations and consider her morning. What a morning it had been, too!

The whirlwind had begun at six this morning when she'd arisen to finish the last of her packing and get ready to catch the 7 o'clock bus. The ride had been an adventure in itself; she'd loved seeing the endless green of the pastures dotted with Herefords and Black Angus, placidly chewing their cud or enjoying an early morning drink. The farms along the way had been idyllic, the sunshine casting shadows over the barns and ripening fields of milo. She had seen several tractors heading out and one farm wife hanging her sheets out on the line to dry in the late summer breeze. This part of Texas was beautiful, whether it was early spring and the landscape looked like an ocean of bluebonnets or high summer with black-eyed susans, roses, and zinnias blooming everywhere. Whether pine or cedar, pecan or sycamore, the trees boasted a dozen different shades of green as they bloomed and then turned to fire in October and November, the leaves turning blood red, deep mustard yellow, and every orange shade one could imagine. Miriam loved it; she was home. And today she was beginning a new life in a new part of that home.

Ready for the next step in a day full of surprises, she found her way to the boarding house that Amos Guthrie had recommended. Unsure of what to expect, she was nevertheless stunned as she rounded the corner and saw the stately home perched magnificently in the middle of the next block. Three stories high, it was painted a beautiful shade of pale yellow with white shutters and trim. There was a big pecan tree in the front yard, and a mammoth oak filled up the rest of the yard from the side of the house to the street. She had never seen such a gorgeous old tree. The house was framed with azaleas, and there was a rainbow of color in the flowerbeds lining the walkway. She walked up the six wide front steps to a huge wraparound porch where waited a swing and two gliders made homey with fat throw pillows and hanging baskets overflowing with ivy, geraniums, and ferns. She knocked on the door and waited while she heard shuffling beyond the yellow curtains that framed the windows.

An older woman who looked to be about 65 opened the door and smiled warmly. "You must be Miriam. Come right in, my dear."

Nonplussed, Miriam stammered. "But how, when?"

Myrtle Henson's white hair was elegantly coiffed in a style that reminded Miriam of a fluff of cotton candy. Her lean frame was resplendent in a teal blue and green print dress, belted at the waist and adorned with a scarf tied at the neckline and a single strand of pearls. Smiling, she replied, "Amos couldn't wait to tell me about you. He hurried over here on his lunch break and brought your suitcases. He told me then you'd be coming. I hope you don't mind."

"No ma'am, I don't mind. I'm just surprised, I guess."

"Let me show you the apartment. I aired it out this afternoon, and if it suits you we can talk about house rules and rent."

"I'd like that. Thank you, Mrs. Henson."

Myrtle Henson led Miriam up the staircase to the last door on the right. She opened it into a tidy living room. Furnished with a wooden rocking chair and plush sofa in a lovely shade of cream, Miriam looked around and was pleased with the space. There was room for a dining table and two chairs in the corner that led into the compact kitchen. The countertops were white tile, and the cabinets were painted the same pale blue as the walls. Walking back across the room, Mrs. Henson opened a door into the bedroom. It was quite large, with a full-size four poster bed covered in a white bedspread and pale green throw pillows. The windows fluttered with white lace curtains – Miriam almost squealed in delight at the sight of her beloved lace curtains – and the room was painted a pale green to match the accessories. A marble-topped dressing table rested between the two largest windows, and a matching dresser complete with an oval mirror stood opposite the bed. There were two overstuffed chairs in the sitting area beyond the bed, with a stately secretary and overstuffed ottoman. It was light and sunny and everything Miriam could have wanted.

"If you want to make any changes, please feel free to do so. While you live here this will be your home, and I want you to do what you would like to make it personal to your tastes. If you wouldn't mind, I'd like some say about any major changes, but I would be happy to consider anything you thought you might like to do. The bathroom is through that door, and there is a closet as well. I have only one other boarder on this floor at the moment. She is a secretary at the courthouse and is just about your age. If you like what you see, how would you feel about $40.00 a month?"

"I love it, and I'll take it. There are a few boxes of things arriving on the bus tomorrow. If you don't mind, I'll unpack and get comfortable. It's been an exhausting day. Can you tell me where the market is? I'll need to stock the kitchen tomorrow."

Chapter 7

Humming to herself, Miriam opened the boxes that had been delivered that next morning by bus from Cedar Springs. She gently folded the quilt Mama had made her and smoothed it across the foot of her bed. It blended nicely with the colors already in the room. She unpacked a few basic dishes, some bathroom items, and her few photographs. Already the apartment was beginning to feel like home, and Miriam couldn't have been more pleased. She had collapsed in bed the night before and was asleep almost before her mind could form a complete thought. She was determined to get a letter off to Lizzie tomorrow, though, so she made sure the note paper and her pens were laid aside so that she could find them easily tonight after supper. She considered everything she wanted to share with her sister as she absently hung her dresses in the closet. The letter was growing longer the more she thought about it, but she didn't want to leave anyone or anything out. Lizzie and

Toby would want to hear it all.

Her thoughts were interrupted by the sound of her front door opening. Strange, she had been told that she would have privacy here at Mrs. Henson's. Who would just enter her room without knocking? Walking cautiously to the bedroom door, she peered into her living room to see a young woman holding the picture of the four of them at Seth's wedding. She cleared her throat and the woman spun around to face her. She was, quite simply, stunningly beautiful. Her black hair hung down her back in thick, springy curls and her black eyes dominated her delicate face. She was short and curvy, her tiny feet strapped into high-heeled sandals and her skirt swishing with its full pleats as she moved. She looked like a pixie.

"Hi. I'm Gladys Betts. Mrs. Henson told me she'd rented this apartment to you, so I thought I'd drop by and introduce myself. You've done some nice things to this room already."

"Did you knock? I'm sorry if I didn't hear you," Miriam remarked.

"No, sorry, I didn't. Seemed like a waste of time; you were going to let me in anyway, right?" She smiled disarmingly at Miriam.

"I guess so," Miriam agreed. "Still, it would have been nice if you had waited until I could invite you in. Next time, knock, please?"

"Sure, if you're going to be stuffy, I guess I can knock." Turning to the picture in her hand, she pointed at Seth and smiled. "Who's the looker? Boyfriend, or have I got a chance at him?"

"He's my brother, and that was taken at his wedding," Miriam responded as she took the photo from

Gladys' hands. Replacing the photo, Miriam turned to Gladys and asked, "Would you like to sit down?"

"I'd rather help you unpack, if you like. Too restless to sit for very long, you know? I have to sit in that dinky office in the courthouse all day, but I hate it. How about I start on this box over here?"

"Well," Miriam hesitated, "I guess I could use a little help. Those things go in my dresser drawers in the bedroom. I'll handle them myself in a bit. You could put my towels in the bathroom shelf."

"Afraid I'll see your 'unmentionables?' What a stupid word. Even dumber idea. We wear the same thing, don't we? Sears and Roebuck advertise it in the catalogs, and everybody's seen those. Just false modesty, if you ask me. I'm not ashamed of what I wear or how I behave. Life's too short to worry about what everyone else thinks."

"I'm a very private person, Gladys, that's all."

"No chance of being private in my house. I've got six brothers and two sisters. Us girls shared one room, and we all used the same bathroom. I'd a never gotten my turn if I'd waited until it was empty," she declared.

"You mean your brothers and sisters walked in on you while you were in the bathroom?"

"Every day. Just the way it was. You get used to it, you know."

"I could never grow accustomed to such a thing," Miriam asserted as she unloaded boxes.

"Owen and Clyde, my two oldest brothers, were the worst about it. They were forever trying to figure out a way to separate us girls from our clothes. My sister, Katie, and I paid them back one Halloween, though. We knew they were going out that night after supper, and it was already dead of winter that year.   I'm from Oklahoma. Anyway, we'd been iced in for two weeks. Katie and I had gotten Edgar, our cousin, to help us move the outhouse back about four feet.   Then we covered up the hole with leaves and underbrush. It was so pitch black and icy cold that we knew they wouldn't notice anything. Sure enough, they walked right over the hole and sank into that nasty mess up to their necks. You never heard such hollering in your life! Had to strip naked and wash off in the horse trough. There was a mighty wind blowing out of the north that night, and them naked as jaybirds and turning blue. Had to burn their clothes. Mama wouldn't touch 'em to try to get 'em clean. Katie and I were grown before we admitted what we'd done. I was sure Clyde was going to beat me to a pulp even then." She shook with was going to beat me to a pulp even then." She shook with laughter until the tears glistened on her cheeks.

Despite her horror, Miriam couldn't help but join in with a few chuckles of her own. It was the most outrageous story she'd ever heard, and Gladys was the most outrageous person she'd ever met. It occurred to her that this world was full of a vast rainbow of people who were nothing like her and her family. The idea of getting to know them frightened her a bit, but she was excited about the prospects as well. With the additions of Annie and Gladys in her life she knew she had made a colorful beginning.

Miriam was up at six on Thursday, too eager to decorate her room to sleep. The box she had filled with her classroom preparations was sitting by the front door, ready to go. She ate a banana and slice of toast for breakfast and dawdled over the paper, but it was no use.

She fidgeted for 45 minutes before finally deciding the building would be open by the time she arrived, and then she hefted the box and headed out the door.

She hummed as she hung the simple curtains she had fashioned yesterday. They were bright and sunny, with butterflies and ladybugs dancing along a crisp white background trimmed with red and black rickrack. She thought they were wonderful. There had been enough fabric left to sew up two pillow shams, and she had covered two inexpensive pillows she'd found on the bargain table with them. She covered her reading corner with several additional pillows and decorated her desk with a globe, an aging snapshot of her mother, and a funny-looking ceramic cow she'd been given by her grandmother when she was ten. She covered the bulletin board with bright yellow paper and then centered a poster she had lettered with the classroom rules. Comic strips from the Sunday newspaper framed her efforts, quite nicely she thought.

The next half-hour was spent writing the assessment test she had drafted onto the chalkboard. Mr. McAnaly had told her she could check out her teacher's editions today, but she wanted an idea of her students' skill levels before she began her actual lessons. Hoping to begin the process of getting to know her students, she had prepared three simple activities she was sure would give her some insight into their personalities as well as their academic abilities. So engrossed was she in her tasks that the voice at the door nearly stopped her heart.

"Hey, sweets, how are you this morning?" Annie boomed. "Say, I like the curtains. Did you do those yourself? I'm proud of you, Miriam. You said you weren't much of a seamstress."

"I don't like fashioning clothing, but stitching a straight seam isn't difficult. I enjoyed doing something that brought me one step closer to Monday. I can't wait for classes to begin!"

"Your room looks more than ready. I'm impressed."

"I hoped to remember some of the basics I learned at teacher's college, but it's been two years ago since I got my certificate."

Interrupting with a boisterous guffaw, Annie replied, "You'll find out soon enough that most of what you were told in college works best in theory alone. These are living, breathing, squirming, active ten year olds, and you have to be two steps ahead of them at all times. They will lie to you, ask permission to do something they know is against the rules, and insist that just this once they really do know better than you do and you can trust them. You will repeat yourself until you feel like you're blathering, and at least two of them will insist you've never said a word! Keeping them engaged and productively occupied is like herding cats. Tell me how much practical advice you used from teacher's college at the end of Monday, okay? C'mon, let's go eat lunch. I've been smelling those tuna fish sandwiches all morning, and I'm starving."

"How can I eat after you just told me all that? I'm not prepared for Monday if that's the case. What am I going to do?"

Putting her arm around Miriam's shoulders, Annie smiled and said, "Go with your instincts, sweets, and you'll be just fine. 90% of this job is love and patience, and I've got a feeling you have all you need of both of those."

Somewhat mollified, Miriam allowed Annie to lead her to the classroom. She wasn't so sure she was ready for Monday.

Sitting at her kitchen counter later that evening, she reviewed everything that she had done for the first day of school yet again, uncertain now of what to do or how to proceed. Annie had shaken her up. Staring into space for the tenth time in the last 15 minutes, she found herself speaking to her mom as if she were in the room listening.

"Mama, I don't know what to think. I was so sure I could be a good teacher, and now I'm so scared to even go into the classroom on Monday I think I'm going to hyperventilate. What should I do? Maybe we wasted the money you spent on teacher's college. Is it so important that I be a teacher? I could get my job back at the library in Cedar Springs. Mrs. Tate was happy with my work. I loved being among the books every day, and I was good at my job. This is just too risky; there's too much at stake!

"I don't know anything about herding cats. We've never even had a cat in the house!" Aware of what she'd just considered, she smiled. Before too long, she was howling with laughter and wiping tears as they ran down her cheeks. It felt good to laugh like that, even if it had been at her own expense. Sometimes she was a complete idiot. "I guess I'll give it a try, Mama. Wish me luck."

Moving to the secretary to write a letter to Seth and Polly, she was startled for the second time that day by someone intruding on her without any warning. Gladys threw open the door to Miriam's apartment and strode in with a disarming smile on her face.

"Hey, Miriam. I heard the laughter and was sure

I'd missed the party. So here I am."

"There's no party, Gladys, and you promised me the last time that you would knock first before just barging in."

"Oh, for Heaven's sake, you are a prude. I didn't catch you naked or anything, so why are you making such a fuss?"

"I don't think this is making a fuss. I'm simply asking you to have enough respect for my wishes to knock before you come in. This is my home, Gladys, and neither you nor anyone else can come and go as you please, okay?"

"As you wish, Your Highness," Gladys responded with a sweeping bow. "Jeez, you are such a piece of work."

"If you're through ridiculing me, would you please go home? I've got some work to do."

"What kind of work? Is there something I can do to help?"

"I'm writing a letter to my brother," Miriam replied with exasperation. "Goodnight, Gladys."

"Are you going to sit in this apartment and brood about your new job all weekend?"

"No, I'm not going to . . . how did you know I was brooding?"

"Saw it on your face, hon . . . Want to go to the movies with me Saturday afternoon? Get your mind off things for a while."

"That's very nice of you, Gladys. I think I would like to go to the movies."

"Good. I'll see you at 1:30, and I promise I'll knock." With a breezy "Toodles, hon!" she was out of the apartment and gone as quickly as she'd come.

"Whew!" Miriam thought to herself. "She wears me out." Shaking her head in wonder, she returned to the secretary to resume her letter. At least her news to Seth and Polly wouldn't be dull.

Monday had dawned bright and sunny, and Miriam stood at the entrance to her classroom as nervous as she'd ever been in her life. Annie had come by for a quick hug and pat on the back earlier in the morning. The physical contact, as slight as it had been, had made Miriam stumble forward and almost fall. She had to get control of these butterflies before she made herself sick.

"This is ridiculous, Miriam," she thought to herself as she rubbed the gooseflesh on her arms. "You are a grown woman and more than capable of doing this job." She wasn't sure she believed the pep talk.

Startling visibly as the bell rang, Miss Cahill smiled in her attempt to look professional in the navy blue dress Lizzie had made for her. It had a white Battenburg lace collar and thin fabric belt that cinched her waist. Her flat black shoes had been comfortable when she'd bought them, but now her feet ached abominably. Stress did strange things to the body. Looking up, she saw a woman approach her with a young girl in tow. They walked up to her and smiled.

"Miss Cahill?"

"Yes, I'm Miss Cahill," Miriam spoke as she held out her hand.

The woman took Miriam's hand and shook it firmly. Miriam could feel the roughness of her palm and the calluses that lined her fingers. These were the hands of a hard-working housewife. Remembering her own mother's hands, Miriam relaxed somewhat.

"I'm Sally Woodson, and this is my daughter, Emily. She is in your class."

Smiling at the sweet little girl standing by her mother, Miriam took her hand and spoke more confidently than she felt. "Emily, I'm happy to meet you. Welcome to 4th grade. Please find your desk; each one has a card with a name printed on it." Turning to Mrs. Woodson, she remarked, "I'm happy to meet you, Mrs. Woodson. I know Emily and I are going to have a very good year together."

"My Emily tries hard, Miss Cahill, but she doesn't catch on to things as quickly as the other kids. Her daddy and I work with her at home as much as we can. We don't want her to get behind."

"I'll take good care of Emily, Mrs. Woodson. If there's ever anything you need to tell me, or if you ever want to check on her progress, then please feel free to send a note or come visit our classroom. I want my students to succeed."

"Thank you," she responded and waved to Emily as she turned to go. Miriam spared a moment to watch Emily as she sat in her desk. She was slightly built, with long brown hair braided over each shoulder. Dark framed glasses dwarfed her petite features. Her back ramrod straight, she looked as if she'd bolt right out the window at the first opportunity. Miriam's heart melted right on the spot.

"Miss Cahill?" the next mother interrupted Miriam's thoughts. "I'm Lucy Dixon, and this is Sylvester. Say 'Hello,' son."

The next 20 minutes were a blur of parents and

children. Miriam directed each child to find his or her seat, and before she knew it 18 faces were staring her with expressions that registered eagerness, resignation, hesitation, caution, uncertainty, and misery. Miriam closed the door and moved to her desk. Starting to sit in her seat, she changed her mind and on impulse moved to the front of the desk and hoisted herself onto its top. One or two faces registered surprise, but no one spoke.

"Good morning. I'm Miss Cahill, and I'm happy to have you in my classroom. I'm sure you know that I'm new to Taylor, so I'm going to need a great deal of help from you to make sure I do everything properly. Will you agree to be my classroom helpers?" She paused to see most of the little heads nod, while a few exchanged questioning glances with one another. One little boy, Thomas, she thought she remembered, shrugged his shoulders. Smiling to herself, she began again. "As I call each name on this roll sheet, I need you to stand up and tell me one thing about yourself you'd like me to know. Can you do that? We'll start with Susan Aldrich." An elfin blonde in the front row stood up and spoke with a shy smile. "I'm Susan, and we have a new baby in our house. Adam was born two months ago."

"Congratulations, Susan. I'm sure you're the best baby-sitter in the world. What's your favorite thing to do for Adam?"

"I like to give him his bottle. He's a real good eater, and Mama says he burps louder than Daddy."

The children giggled for a moment, as did Miriam.

"Thank you, Susan. I'll look forward to meeting Adam someday soon."

Susan sat back down as Miriam called out the next name. "Lucas Ashfield, where are you?"

A tall, stocky boy with strawberry blonde hair stood up in the third row toward the back. "I'm Lucas," he spoke in a loud voice, "and my Daddy says I'm the best farm hand he's ever had. He lets me feed and groom the horses every night before supper."

"I'm sure you are a very responsible hand, Lucas. Which horse is your favorite?"

"Randy. He's the biggest we got – 18 hands, and won't let anyone ride him but me and Daddy," he answered with the pride evident in his voice. "He's black with a white blaze. Daddy bought him the year I was born."

"Do you like to ride, Lucas?"

"Yes'm. I spent all summer on Randy. Sure was hard to come back to school." Realizing how his comment might have sounded, Lucas turned a bright pink and muttered, "'Scuse me, Miss Cahill. I didn't mean no disrespect."

"I know you didn't, Lucas. I found it difficult to end my summer, too," she confided with a grin. 'Please sit down."

"Our next student to share will be . . . Beth Blackman," Miriam said as she looked up. No student rose at her request. "Beth? Stand up, please."

A lovely girl dressed in what had to have been an old work dress of her mother's tried to sink out of sight into her desk, but Miriam picked her out easily. She had an olive complexion and deep hazel eyes that were framed by the thickest, darkest lashes Miriam had ever seen. Her shoulder length hair was a rich, chocolate brown, and the sides were held back by two bobby pins. Her shoes were scuffed and worn, and the socks on her feet were frayed at the ends. "Beth, can you stand up?"

The little girl ducked her head, refusing to look at anyone, but Miriam saw her head shake clearly enough. Stumped for a moment, Miriam wondered how to handle the situation. She wouldn't embarrass the child for anything, but she wanted to begin right away to help her gain some confidence. An idea sprang to her mind.

"Which of you would like to introduce Beth to me? Can one of you tell me about your friend?"

Emily's hand flew up and she spoke, "I can tell you about Beth, Miss Cahill."

"Thank you, Emily. Why don't you do that for us?"

Standing to her feet, Emily walked over to Beth's desk to stand beside her. "Beth is 10 years old, and she has five brothers and sisters older than her. Her daddy died last year, and we sew doll clothes together, and Beth is the best singer I ever heard."

"Thank you, Emily. You did a fine job. It's very nice to meet you, Beth. I have two brothers and a sister, myself. Do your brothers ever pick on you?"

The dark head nodded. Miriam took that as an encouraging sign and decided to move on to the next student. Thirty-five minutes later, Miriam had found out a little something about each of her charges. It was a good beginning. Clipping the attendance slip to the classroom door, Miriam asked each student to take out a pencil.

"We're going to start with an arithmetic lesson -" Day one had begun.

Standing on the edge of the playground, Miriam watched the children swing or play catch or Red Rover or whatever game struck their fancy. She had learned quite a bit about the group already. Beth Blackman wasn't the only shy child in her class. Herbert Mitchell and Simon Newsom were unwilling to speak out very much. Estelle Chapman was a rather plain looking girl, but she had a sharp mind and intelligent eyes that spoke of a wisdom beyond her years. Miriam felt an immediate kinship with this little sprite. Ruthie Mayhew was somewhat spoiled; she tossed her hair and spoke with elaborate gestures while smoothing the ruffles on her obviously very expensive dress and pinafore. Bobbie Oliver looked as if she could hold her own with any boy in the class. Right now she was leading the way in a spirited game of dodge ball.

Calling to them, Miriam had them line up and walk quietly back into the classroom. Settling them into their desks, she pulled out a book and told them she would like to read a story to them for a few minutes. Speaking in a clear, expressive voice, Miriam shared Tom Sawyer with them. She quickly realized that they were enthralled. Smiling and adjusting herself on top of the desk – she'd discovered that this was her favorite teaching perch – she read until she was almost hoarse. Coming to the end of the chapter and closing the book, a chorus of protests greeted her.

"Read a little more, Miss Cahill . . . That's too good a spot to stop . . . Just one more page?"

"We haven't done our Geography and Science lessons yet. I'll read more tomorrow. I'm so happy you like good stories. On Friday we'll go to the library and each of you may check out books of your own."

Going to the low shelf, she removed a box lid filled with small cups of growing plants. She had seeds, leaves, and bean pods ready to discuss with her class how plants grow. They were eager to share what they already knew, and several told of how they helped plant corn or cotton with their daddies or tomatoes and cucumbers with their mamas in their kitchen gardens. Miriam listened eagerly to each one as he or she clamored to share, and she guided them into additional knowledge with terms and concepts as they needed them. Looking up at these glowing faces, Miriam had something of an epiphany. She knew beyond the shadow of a doubt that she'd found her place in the world, and she thanked God for it. Many people stumbled through their lives, doing what had to be done to keep food on the table and a roof over their heads, but those were just jobs, nothing more. Miriam recognized this as the calling it was, and in doing so had to blink back the tears that pooled in her eyes. She was in love with these children and the opportunity she'd been given to be their teacher.

Dismissing them at the end of the day, she erased the board and make preparations for the following day's lessons. Humming as she worked, she found herself sharing her day with her mother.

"Mama, I've finished my first day as a teacher. It was glorious! I love my children, and I love teaching them. I'm so grateful that you sent me to teacher's college. I love you so much for never giving up on my dream. Oh, Mama, I wish you could be here to meet my kids and sit in on my classes. I've found my place. I've found where I belong."

After the last lesson had been readied Miriam straightened up her books and made sure she left the room tidy before turning out the lights and closing the door. She had stayed until almost five, so she was surprised to see Annie's door still open. Walking down to room 31, she realized that her new friend was engrossed with writing arithmetic problems on the chalkboard. Quietly stepping into the classroom, Miriam said, "Annie?"

Dropping the chalk and spinning around to stare at Miriam, Annie clutched her chest and grabbed the chalk rail for support.

"Miriam! You nearly scared me to death! What are you doing tiptoeing around like that? You should let a body know you're here."

Trying not to laugh out loud at Annie's consternation, Miriam walked forward to hug her and apologized. "I'm sorry, Annie. I didn't mean to scare you. I just came to see how you and your students enjoyed your day."

"We had a fine day. I like every one of the little stinkers. One or two are going to be real ring-tailed tooters, but I 'spect we'll get along well enough once they realize who's robbin' the train. Takes a couple of weeks to iron out the kinks, but we manage. What about you? Are you still thinking about tucking your tail between your legs and runnin' back home?"

"Oh, no, I love it. The children and I had such a good day today."

"Who do you have in your class?"

"Let's see . . . Susan Aldrich, Lucas Ashfield, Ruthie Mayhew, Bobbie Oliver, Emily Woodson, Beth Blackman, Estelle Chapman, Sylvester Dixon, Herbert something." She smiled apologetically. "I don't have their names down quite yet."

"Herbert Mitchell, and you're doing fine. Watch out for Ruthie Mayhew. She's been spoiled by her councilman daddy and thinks she's better than the others. She can be mouthy if you let her get the better of you.

Beth and Susan and Emily are gems. They will be your best helpers; you can trust them with anything. Beth is going to need a tender hand for a while. She feels like the world has fallen in on her since her daddy died earlier this year. She was quiet before, but she's so shy now she barely holds her head up. Breaks my heart to think of her mama struggling so. The church has helped out as best we can, but it's going to take some time for the world to right itself for that poor family. Is Peter Pritchard in your class?"

"Yes, I remember him now that you mention it. He seemed to be sizing me up most of the day."

"That's very perceptive of you, sweets. I knew you'd handle this job just fine. He was sizing you up, and before too long he's going to see just what you're made of. Don't you let him get the better of you. If you feel you have to call his mama, she'll come to school and sit with him and make him behave, but you'll never have control of him again if you ask her to do that. You just hold the line with him, and he'll settle down soon enough. Are you done for today?"

"Yes, I was just going to drop by the market and pick up something for a celebratory dinner."

"Plans have changed. Buck is making his famous fried chicken and dumplin's for supper tonight. It's become a first day of school tradition around our house, and there's enough to feed Cox's army. You're coming home with me."

"Annie, I don't want to intrude on your family time. I'll just go home and . . ."

"You'll do no such thing, and don't make such a fuss. If I didn't want you, I wouldn't have said anything. Besides, I'm dying to show off my Daniel. He's just too sweet for words."

Finding it impossible to resist Annie's natural ebullience, and grateful to have this most unique woman as her friend, Miriam allowed herself to be nudged out the door. Arm in arm, they made their way to Annie's house.

Chapter 8

"Buck, honey, I've brought company for supper," Annie called as they walked into the front door of a tidy little shotgun house nestled in the prettiest yard Miriam had seen in a long time. The flowerbeds were thick with chrysanthemums and hydrangeas, and a huge magnolia tree dwarfed the left side of the porch. There were pecan trees in the back yard and a long row of blooming irises bordering the garden off to the side. The porch boasted swings at either end, and the screen door opened with a welcoming squeak. Miriam loved it. Just as she was getting a first impression of chintz curtains and cushioned rocking chairs flanking a low sofa, a spinning tornado known as Daniel Buchanan launched himself into his mother's arms from his hiding place behind the hallway door.

"Hi, Mama. Who'd you bring home to supper?"

"Hey, Danny boy. This is my new friend, Miriam. You may call her Miss Cahill. She teaches at Taylor with me. What have you been doing today?"

"Aunt Sarah and I picked t'maters today. And she let me water her garden. I got all muddied up and had to be washed off with the hose. She said there weren't no other way to get a dirty boy clean. Sure was fun! Maybe she'll let me water the garden tomorra, too. Daddy picked me up and we're makin' fried chick'n for supper. I dragged it through the flour 'fore he put it in the pan. And I didn't even spill, much."

"You've had a grand day, haven't you? Can you say hello to Miss Cahill?"

Looking around his mother's shoulder, he looked into Miriam's face with the most solemn eyes she'd ever seen. They were hazel and almost hidden by an unruly mop of red curls. His fair complexion was dotted with freckles, and his square little chin boasted a dimple. When he smiled his entire face lit up in a grin reminiscent of his mother. "Hi," he spoke quietly.

"Hi, Daniel. It's nice to meet you."

"Danny boy, why don't you take Miss Cahill to meet your daddy?"

"Sure, he's in here." Wriggling down from Annie's arms, he grabbed Miriam's hand and almost dragged her into the kitchen. "Daddy, add another chick'n leg to the pan. Mama brought comp'ny home for supper."

A stocky man about Miriam's height looked up from the stove where he was keeping an eye on several pots and a huge cast iron skillet stuffed with frying chicken. The room smelled so good that Miriam could feel the saliva pool in her mouth. Buck Buchanan was about 35, and neither the frilly apron he was wearing nor the flour that was dusted halfway up his muscled arms or smeared across his bearded face did anything to minimize her impression that he was the toughest guy she'd ever come across. He had arms like a longshoreman, and his face was crisscrossed with lines made from too many hours in the sun. Annie's husband sported a crewcut the same honey blonde color as his beard, and he looked up from what she assumed was chaos to smile and welcome her to their home.

"It may look like a mess," Annie spoke from the doorway, "but he's the best hand in the kitchen I've ever seen. Buck works for the fire department. That explains the muscles and the fact that he's as good a cook as I am. Honey, can I help?"

"I've got it, Annie. Fifteen minutes and we'll be pulling up to the table. Pour yourself and Miriam a glass of tea and go put your feet up. I know it's been a long day."

"You got yourself a deal, sugar. Thanks," she added as she gave him a peck on the cheek and reached up behind him for two glasses.

Dinner was a relaxed, happy affair, and Miriam felt as at home as she did at Lizzie's table. These were remarkable people. Annie and Buck both treated Miriam like one of the family, and Daniel was indeed too sweet for words. He reminded her of T.J., and she found herself drawn to them in a way she had not expected. Could she have found something this rich and good so quickly after embarking on her own? She would go cautiously, for that was her way, but she felt very fortunate to have this family include her in their circle. A small part of her grieved for what her life might have been like had her own father been more loving and less pugilistic, but she blessed Heaven for her mother and the rest of her family, and she determined even more to find this kind of happiness in her own life someday.

That first day set the tone for the weeks to come. Miriam loved preparing the daily lessons and teaching them to her students. She grew to love her kids even more as time went on, even the crafty ones like Peter Pritchard and the prissy ones like Ruthie Mayhew. It was her job to encourage the very best from them, and often they responded in a way that delighted her and encouraged her in her efforts. Beth and Estelle had quickly become her favorites, even though she knew choosing favorites was unwise. Beth had slowly begun to warm up to her, and just yesterday she had looked Miriam in the eye and smiled. That smile lit up Beth's whole face, and Miriam's spirit glowed all the way home that afternoon. Estelle was of more than average intelligence, and Miriam soon found that her wisdom had come at a price. Her parents were dirt poor and struggled just to feed their six children on a consistent basis. Estelle often came to school with dark circles under her eyes, and Miriam knew that as the eldest, this eleven year old child shouldered the burden of caring for her younger siblings while her parents toiled to make the farm pay. Her father had taken a part-time job, so Estelle and her mother worked the fields sometimes to take care of the crops. As much as the children loved to read, Estelle burned with a hunger to read and learn everything she could. Miriam had begun to loan Estelle books to read after she'd completed her lessons, and she devoured them as she sat in Miriam's rocking chair in the corner. This was why she had become a teacher, and she found immeasurable joy in caring for these children.

There had been one or two rocky moments along the way these first six weeks, and Miriam knew she still had much to learn. The first problem came when she spoke to Jack Michaels about his failing arithmetic grade. He mumbled something she couldn't understand and promised to try harder. The grades did not improve over the next several days, so she paid a visit to Jack's home to see if he might need some extra help. Mrs. Michaels was very polite, but she couldn't understand why Jack was doing so badly. His homework was correct when she checked it, and he loved arithmetic last year. Miriam suggested he stay after school for tutoring. As Mrs. Michaels was about to agree, Jack burst into the room and yelled.

"It's her fault! It's her fault, Mama. I told her that I couldn't see the board from the back of the room, but she wouldn't listen. I do know how to do the problems, but from where I sit I just can't see them," he wailed and ran out the front door into the yard.

Visibly shaken, Miriam realized that Jack had indeed told her that he couldn't see the board, and she had not taken the time to listen. Mortified that she had caused him such distress, Miriam apologized to Mrs. Michaels and assured her that she would move Jack to the front of the room. She stuck her foot in it, though, when she asked if Mrs. Michaels had ever considered getting Jack glasses.

"His father and I can't get him something we can't pay for, Miss Cahill."

Before she could do any other damage to this nice family, Miriam had fled. She had wept on the way back to Mrs. Henson's and then brooded about it for days. She couldn't believe she'd been so insensitive to the needs of this little boy. She cursed herself for being an idiot and felt awkward around her students for the next week. It had taken days for Jack to even look at her again, and Miriam was grateful. She didn't know how to handle the situation and was just too humiliated to ask Annie for help in straightening it out. Finally, one Thursday afternoon, Annie inadvertently put her out of her misery. Stopping in at Miriam's door, Annie interrupted her as she was writing the arithmetic lesson on the board for the next morning.

"You been avoiding me, sweets? I haven't put you off for any reason, have I?"

"Gracious, no, Annie. I haven't been avoiding you," she responded.

Unaware that her face was a perfect mirror for her churning emotions, Miriam smiled gamely and went back to her task.

"Then why do you look like thunder? What's wrong, Miriam?"

Sitting down at Miriam's desk, Annie crossed her arms and looked as if she was preparing for a siege. Desperate to find some absolution, Miriam heaved a deep sigh and spilled out the entire story.

"Oh, Miriam, I know how upset you are, but you're making way too much of this. Did you think you were never going to make any mistakes at this job?"

"Well, no, of course not, but you didn't see how upset he was."

"No, but I've seen dozens of others, and they all get over it. By the end of the week you will be Jack's favorite teacher again, and this will be forgotten. Don't be so hard on yourself, sweets. It goes with the territory."

"Are you sure, Annie?"

"Take it from an old pro at making mistakes, okay? C'mon, dry those tears. I'll walk you to the corner."

This and several other incidents had put some serious dents in Miriam's growing confidence, but Annie had been solid reassurance and Miriam believed she was doing better. She loved teaching, but dear Heaven, this job was tough.

The briskness in the air awoke Miriam from her musings as she made her way to school that early November morning. There had been frost on the ground for the past two days, but somehow she had missed that autumn had arrived. The children had so loved dressing up for Halloween and making suet for the birds. At her encouragement they had brought Indian corn and hay shocks with which to decorate the classroom, and their artwork adorned the entire bulletin board. With a start she remembered that she needed to purchase her bus ticket back to Cedar Springs for Thanksgiving. How had three months sped by so quickly?

Miriam had been delighted with everyone she had met in Martinsville. Mr. Guthrie had quickly become her favorite person in the world. He called her 'Missy,' and treated her like a princess every time she mailed a letter or bought stamps. His usual greeting began with, "Boy, if I were 40 years younger . . ." Miriam adored him. She had become acquainted with Hazel at the grocery store and Curtis at the filling station. She walked down there on Saturday mornings sometimes for a soda and some bubble gum. He was a delightful old gentleman, and his stories about his grandson, Billy, entertained her for hours. The office staff and librarians at Taylor had gone out of their way to make her feel welcome, and had pointed her in the right direction about something more than once. She couldn't be happier about teaching among such dear people.

In spite of their rocky beginning, Miriam and Gladys had settled into a comfortable routine of sorts.

Once or twice a week Gladys would eat supper with Miriam, bringing over tuna sandwiches or apples or some such to contribute to their Dutch treat. Miriam had found that she did like Gladys, but her forthright manner and lack of social graces did take some getting used to. They had gone to the Saturday matinee a few times, and Miriam enjoyed the company. She certainly never knew what was going to proceed from Glady's mouth. She was unashamedly outrageous.

Miriam's real joy had come from her friendship with Annie. She treated Miriam like a beloved sister, and many Sunday afternoons had been spent on Annie's front porch talking together and sipping iced tea. A great deal about her father had been shared during those quiet times, and the burden Miriam had been carrying for her entire life had been lifted somewhat by allowing Annie to share it. She had told her about Lizzie and Toby, and T.J., as well as Seth and Will. Typically much more reticent about family affairs, Miriam felt no embarrassment at sharing so many private details with Annie. Never had she known such a good listener.

This lovely Sunday afternoon found the two friends talking about Annie's marriage to Buck. At first Annie had been unwilling to consider a firefighter for a mate. The risks he took exacted their own toll on her, and she wondered if she could bear up under that kind of stress. She had walked away from their growing relationship twice, but Buck had been gently persistent, and eventually he had won her over. Miriam got lost in the wonder of Annie's descriptions of their lives together.

"He's my best friend. I can tell him anything and know he will accept and understand. He's my greatest cheerleader. I think I could tell him I'd like to run for president of the United States and he'd simply ask what he could do to help. Huh, can you see me as president? What a laugh that would be! I'd tell some foreign minister just how I felt and set foreign relations back 100 years! Buck knew I was mouthy, o'course, before he popped the question, and it didn't seem to matter to him one whit." She sipped the icy goodness in her glass and stared at Miriam. "Now, I'm changing the course of the river's flow for a minute here. Call me nosy if you want, but I just gotta ask. Why isn't there a Mr. Cahill?"

Pausing to reflect for a moment, Miriam explained. Annie noticed that she had a far-off look on her face, so she simply rocked and waited. "You know what my childhood was like, at least some of it. I wasn't free to consider a beau while Mama was alive. She needed me. And since she died, there hasn't been time."

"Pooh!" Annie interjected heatedly.

"Pooh?" Miriam asked, chuckling. "Where did you get that one?"

"Never you mind. Get back to the story."

"I did meet someone this past summer, but all I've done is meet him. I don't even know him."

"Well, who is he? How did you meet him?"

"He tried to run me down with his horse."

"He what? Why haven't I heard this one before now? You keep way yonder too much to yourself, sweets."

Miriam smiled and told her about meeting Sonny, and then again about seeing him at Seth's wedding. Annie's eyes glistened with interest as she took it in.

"I think he's the finest looking man I've ever seen, and I believe he's a good man, as well. There's something in his eyes that draws me," Miriam added.

"But I'm really daydreaming now," she concluded wistfully. "I doubt he even remembers my name."

"I don't know about that, sweets. You'll just have to wait and see what happens, won't you?"

Miriam walked down the tree-lined street later that afternoon in a swirl of autumn leaves. The black outline of the bare limbs had a stark beauty that appealed to her, and she drew in a deep breath of utter contentment. In no hurry, in spite of the nip in the air, she mused about how much her life had changed in just the short span of a year. She had lost Mama, moved out, worked at the library, left Cedar Springs to teach school, and was making her own way for the first time in her 24 years. She would soon be 25; December 3 was quickly approaching. It felt so satisfying to know she was making her own way financially as well. There was no question that she'd never be rich on a teacher's salary, but she had a homey place of her own and there was money left over for her savings each month after she paid her few bills. She thought she might treat herself to a new dress for her birthday. She'd never bought a dress from a boutique before. Thinking over what style she might like, she nearly stepped on the envelope laying just inside her front door as she returned home after a busy Monday in the classroom. She saw that it was from Mary Elizabeth, but it was fatter than usual. Shedding her coat and scarf, she picked up the letter and settled herself in the overstuffed armchair that had quickly become her favorite and tore open the envelope. Wrapped around another envelope addressed to her was a short note from Lizzie.

"Dear Mim,

This came in the mail yesterday. I guess he didn't

know that you'd begun teaching in Martinsville. Hope you're happy with what he has to say! We're looking forward to having you home again for Thanksgiving.
Love,
Lizzie"

Turning the enclosed envelope over, she realized with a gasp that it was from Sonny. Her hands shook slightly as she withdrew the letter and read.

"Dear Miriam,

I hope you won't mind that I'm writing you, but you've been very much on my mind ever since we met up at Seth and Polly's wedding. I am going to be in Cedar Springs over the Thanksgiving break and would like to see you. With your permission, may I come by Saturday afternoon?
Your friend,

Sonny Williamson"

Grinning as she re-read the letter, Miriam felt a funny little flutter in her stomach. Springing up from the chair, she sat at the secretary and composed what she hoped was a casual response to his request.

Dear Sonny,

I am no longer living in Cedar Springs. I have taken a teaching job in Martinsville and am living there now. I will, however, be visiting with Toby and Mary Elizabeth over Thanksgiving weekend, so please do come by on Saturday afternoon. I will look forward to seeing you again. We'll expect you about two o'clock.

Sincerely,

Miriam Cahill

Grabbing her coat and scarf, she sprinted all the way to the mailbox on the corner. With her fingers crossed, she sent up a silent prayer and dropped it in the box. Things were looking up!

Chapter 9

The bus rumbled up to the square in Cedar Springs and shook slightly as the airbrakes hissed its arrival. Alighting with a huge smile on her face, Miriam met the answering smiles of Toby and T.J. Laughing, she wrapped her arms around them both and gave them a huge hug.

"I'm so glad to be home," she said. "Oh, I've missed you so much."

"A'nie Mim, we has waited and waited," T.J. told her as he stretched out his arms for her to hold him. Snuggling into the lining of her coat, he looked up with his huge brown eyes and patted her cheek. "I love you, A'nie Mim."

Big tears pooled in her eyes as she hugged him yet again and told him she loved him, too.

"Excuse me, miss?" the driver interrupted. "I have your suitcase."

"Oh, thank you. Toby, could you get my bag for me? I'm afraid it's quite heavy."

"Never knew a female in my life who didn't think she needed to pack her entire closet for just a few days. Don't guess you'd be any exception." Toby's tongue-in-cheek pronouncement had her laughing in response.

"Never you mind, mister. You be nice to me or I won't give you your present."

"The company of the prettiest sister-in-law in the world and presents too? Be still my heart," he joked as he retrieved the suitcase.

"You never stop, do you?"

"Not as long as there's breath in my body," he declared, his right hand solemnly placed over his heart. "Put that boy down. He's as heavy as a fat cat fallen into the cream jar, and he can walk quite well on how own. We've been practicing, haven't we, old man?"

'T.J. walks, A'nie Mim."

"I can see that! When did you sneak off and grow up?"

The short walk to the house was accomplished with great laughter and easy banter. Mary Elizabeth met them in a flurry of hugs and flying aprons.

"I've missed you so much I thought some days I couldn't stand it! Oh, I'm so glad you're home. Get that coat off and come on back into the kitchen. I've got stew on the stove and cornbread in the oven and lunch is almost ready. I want to hear everything."

'I've been writing you every week since I got to Martinsville. I'm not sure what else there is to say," Miriam answered as she followed Lizzie to the back of the house.

"It's not the same. I want to know about Gladys and Annie and your students and the girl at the beauty shop and Mrs. Henson and everyone else, and you're not to leave out anything, you hear?"

"Yes ma'am. Could I sit down and catch my breath first?"

"I'm sorry, Mim. I don't mean to overwhelm you.

I'm so proud of you for how hard you've worked to be a good teacher and make your own way, but I got spoiled this past summer having you around every day. I've been downright lonesome for you. Dish up the stew into those bowls, and I'll pour the tea. We can eat."

"Ah, man-trappin' stew," Toby exulted as he straddled a kitchen chair.

"Toby, you know I don't like that expression," Mary Elizabeth scolded with a frown on her face.

"It's nothing to get upset about, honey."

"That grin isn't going to get you out of this, Toby. That expression makes it sound like I tricked you into marrying me or something equally as distasteful. Please don't call my chicken stew that terrible name."

"Lizzie, you know very well. . ."

"Do either of you want to hear my news or not?" Miriam interrupted in mild exasperation.

"You're right, Mim. I'm sorry. Toby and I will talk about this later."

Toby ducked his head and took a quick sip of his iced tea. The look on Mary Elizabeth's face did not bode well for his afternoon. One of these days he was going to learn when he was about to go too far.

The meal began with a slight frost in the air, but Miriam ignored it as she caught them up on her life of the past three months. They laughed at Gladys' nosy, bossy ways, and Toby loved the story of her brothers in the outhouse hole. Miriam told them some personal thing about each of her students, and it was clear to anyone listening how much she loved them and what teaching meant to her. Before they knew it, Lizzie had brought out deep bowls of egg custard and a steaming pot of coffee.

"Lizzie, I have certainly missed your good

cooking. I can keep myself from starving, but what you do with food is an art. That was delicious."

"Mama taught you well, too. You just haven't had a chance to develop any great skills heating up soup for yourself every night. Your time will come."

Looking over at a very sleepy little boy, Miriam asked if she might put him down for his nap.

"I've missed taking care of this little guy more than you can imagine. Toby, if you'll warm his bottle, I'll take him to his room."

"Hot dog, honey." He grinned like an idiot. "If Mim is going to put T.J. down, you and I can fool around in the kitchen," he said, leering at his wife.

Blushing to the very roots of her hair, Mary Elizabeth shook her head as she cleared the table. "You're incorrigible. What am I going to do with you?"

Moving up to put his arm around her shoulder, he murmured in her ear, "I have an idea or two if you'd like to talk about it."

"Oh, you!" She chuckled as she loaded his arms down with plates. "You're washing, dear. Follow me."

Sighing deeply, Toby laughingly complained, "So much for fooling around."

It had been the grandest Thanksgiving celebration Miriam had ever imagined. Will had arrived on Wednesday evening just in time for supper. Toby had accused him of doing it on purpose. Mary Elizabeth had made pumpkin and mince pies before Miriam had arrived on the Tuesday afternoon bus, but the two sisters had prepared cornbread for the dressing, a cherry pie, an apple pie, and a German chocolate cake. Neither were worried too much about leftovers, either. With Seth and Polly's early arrival on Thursday morning, the day had begun on a festive note and had remained so throughout dinner and a lovely afternoon of sipping coffee and enjoying one another's company.

The girls had outdone themselves. Dinner had included heaping bowls of chicken and dumplings, dressing the way Mama had made it, green beans, black eyed peas, fruit salad, Waldorf salad, and biscuits. Everyone had eaten themselves silly. T.J.'s feet hadn't touched the floor all day. He had been the center of attention, reaching out for one set of willing arms or another, talking and giggling until he was utterly exhausted and terribly fussy. Miriam had put him down for a nap after lunch, then she and Lizzie and Polly had cleared the table and washed dishes.

"Polly," Miriam spoke as she took yet another dish from the drainer to dry. "How are you and Seth getting along? Still happy you married that brother of ours?"

"Delirious. But one of you could have told me he doesn't know why closets were invented." They burst out laughing as she smiled. "His shoes and socks fall wherever he is when he takes them off. I think he believes that we bought chairs so he'd have a place to drop his shirts and pants without ever needing to find the hamper! Heaven forbid I'd actually like to sit in a chair. There's never an empty one," she finished on an exasperated laugh. "Other than that one little fault, I'd say married life is just about perfect." Grinning cheekily, she added, "He makes me tingle every time he comes near me. I'm so crazy about him I grin like a fool all the time. Is this how love feels?"

"Yes, it does," Mary Elizabeth responded. "And

thank God that it does. I'm so happy being married to Toby that sometimes I still can't believe it's true. He is such a good man, and I've never seen anyone so much in love with his son the way Toby is with T.J. He makes me tingle, too. What a delightful way to put it, Polly."

"Gee," Miriam sighed. "I wish I knew what you two were talking about."

"Oh, stop." Mary Elizabeth popped her arm with a dish towel. "You know very well what I'm talking about. Just because you're not married yet doesn't mean no boy has ever made you feel tingly inside. Who was that skinny boy in your 7th grade class? Norbert something. You mooned over him that entire first term. Mama had to repeat herself so many times I was convinced you were losing your hearing."

"Ah, yes, Norbert. I wonder what ever happened to him?" Miriam grinned.

"Polly, he was the homeliest thing you've ever seen," Mary Elizabeth hastened to tell her sister-in-law. "All elbows and knees, and as clumsy a kid . . . he couldn't walk across the floor without tripping over his own feet. And what feet they were! You could have put out grass fires with those feet."

"Lizzie, is that nice?" Miriam scolded with a grin on her face.

"I know, Mim. Speaking of him like this is mean, but you know it's the truth. I felt sorry for him, but it's God's truth just the same."

"Yes, I'm afraid you're right. Polly, his ears were huge, and they looked like someone had glued them to the sides of his face. His hair was straw colored and stuck up like someone had cut it with pruning shears. I was so much in love with him I was positively goofy. That's not the tingly feeling I'm talking about, though, and you both know it. I want what you two have found. I want to glow with love for someone the way you both do for your husbands. I want to be intimate with someone, and I'm not just talking about going to bed with him." She paused. "Although, I won't mind that aspect of being married," she added as she blushed a becoming pink.

Laughing with her embarrassment, Polly added, "I know what you mean. Seth and I know one another's dreams, our secrets, our private thoughts and wishes. Sharing my life with him, as well as my bed, has made us a part of one another. I can't imagine having that close a relationship with anyone else in the world. It's very special. So tell me, Mim, is there anyone about whom you've had those thoughts?"

Her blush deepening to a bright red, Miriam grabbed up a plate and dried furiously.

"Mim?" Mary Elizabeth coaxed. "What have you not told me?"

"There's nothing to tell yet."

"Oh sure. That's why you could light up a dark street with your face."

"Who is he, Mim?" Polly asked as she turned from the sink. "Look, we've washed the dishes. I think we could all sit at the kitchen table with some coffee, don't you, Lizzie?"

"Good idea," Mary Elizabeth agreed. "I'll get the cups. Mim, you've got some talking to do."

"You both are making too much of this."

"If there were nothing to it, you'd tell us," Mary Elizabeth objected.

"Fine, I'll tell you why I blushed, but you're going to be disappointed," Miriam said. She sipped her coffee.

"You let us be the judge of who's disappointed," Polly asserted.

"Do you both remember Sonny Williamson, the pianist at the wedding?"

"Yes, vaguely," Polly answered.

"I remember him," Mary Elizabeth said slowly. "You were tongue-tied around him, right?"

Miriam frowned at the description. "Well, I wouldn't call it tongue-tied exactly."

"Be that as it may," Mary Elizabeth interrupted, "what about him?"

"Didn't I tell you that I had met him earlier?"

"You said you'd seen him in town."

"Well, I didn't exactly meet him in town. There was a little more to it than that."

"What? What more to it?"

"What are you trying to tell us, Mim?" Polly asked.

Reluctantly Miriam told the two women about her encounter with Sonny in the woods last summer. Gasping at her account of how he'd come flying right in front of her on Solomon, they both smiled as they saw the look on her face as she told the rest of the story. "And," she finished, "that letter you forwarded to me two weeks ago was a request from him to stop by on Saturday. I wrote him back and told him it would be fine with me if he wanted to come over," she concluded on a whisper.

Her face splitting in a maddening grin, Mary Elizabeth teased, "Fine with you? You're so excited you can hardly sit still, aren't you? Tell the truth now."

"You look like I did the first time Seth noticed me," Polly said, smiling as well.

"Yes, I'm excited. I think he's just about the most

handsome man I've ever met. He has a kind, quiet way about him that appeals to me, and his eyes could make me lose my good sense. Truthfully, I'm scared to death. I've never dated in my life. I don't know how to handle myself, or what to say. I still can't believe he's asked to see me. He couldn't possibly be interested. I'm practically a spinster, for Heaven's sake."

"That's enough of that kind of talk, Mim," Mary Elizabeth frowned as she scolded. "It's not your fault that you never dated. Chalk that up to Daddy, along with about a thousand other things he did to ensure that you had no life of your own. I can understand that you're nervous, too, but that's no excuse for being so self-deprecating. You are a beautiful young woman with a great deal to offer someone." At Miriam's snort of disbelief, she turned to her new sister-in-law. "Help me out here, Polly. Maybe she'll believe you."

"Miriam, when Seth first introduced me to his sisters, I was scared to death. I didn't grow up around girls much; it's just my brother and me. The girls I had known in school could be spiteful and ugly if they thought I had crossed their boundary in some way. But you and Mary Elizabeth opened your arms to me and welcomed me as if I was your long lost sister. You especially were kind to me, and I've never forgotten how hard you worked to make me feel at home. You are an excellent teacher; I've read the letters you've sent to Seth, so don't try to contradict me. It's true that you're reserved, especially around strangers, but I've never met anyone with a greater gift for compassion and giving. Your hair is your crowning glory, and your loving spirit shines in what I think is a very pretty face. Don't be so down on yourself. I believe this man is interested or he would never have contacted you in the first place. Don't you agree, Lizzie?"

"I do. So come Saturday you're going to put on your best dress and we'll wash and set your hair, and then we'll just see what happens when he gets here, okay?"

Wiping the tears from her face, Miriam smiled. "I'm sure I don't deserve those lovely words, Polly, but it felt good to hear them. Thank you."

"You do deserve them, Mim. Why can't you believe them yourself?"

"Oh, that's a conversation for another time. Shouldn't we offer some of this coffee to the fellas? It's gotten awfully quiet in there," Miriam hastened to add.

"It's quiet because they're asleep," Mary Elizabeth told them. "I'd like to explore Polly's question, Mim. Think you're up to it?"

Shuddering, Miriam looked from one loving face to another and shrugged. "I guess so, Lizzie. Polly, what do you want to know?"

"Seth has talked about how you grew up. I know what your father did to him, and how he treated your mother. Does how you feel about yourself now have something to do with what happened then?"

"It has everything to do with it." Miriam's smile was edged with sadness. "Daddy resented me just as much as he did Mama. We've recently come to believe that he thinks I'm not his child."

"What do you mean?"

Miriam explained about Uncle Jim and her mother as the tears flowed in earnest. Polly held her hand as she listened quietly to Miriam's heartbreaking words.

"I wanted so much to please him. I tried all my life to do what he asked, what he demanded actually. I endured his slaps and hateful words and tried to lose myself in the books I checked out from the library every week. It was easy to believe that there was something wrong with me that kept him from loving me. Nothing I did ever made any kind of difference in the way he treated me. I guess being the oldest I felt the greatest responsibility for Mama and the others. It was a burden I accepted almost without conscious thought. When Seth or Will got into trouble, I wanted to make it all right again. If Lizzie was the one who made him angry, I'd put myself between the two of them. I guess I thought I could keep them from getting hurt if I put myself in the middle. Mama seemed to depend on me so much that I came to believe that part of the reason I was put on this earth was to ease some of her unhappiness. When she got sick, I stepped in to take care of her. Lizzie was married, and she had a right to her own life. I was glad for her that she'd gotten out. Seth was gone, and Will was away at college. They each had managed to find their own way in spite of Daddy's iron fist bearing down on us. It wasn't until I began living on my own and teaching at Martinsville that I realized just how much of my own dreams I'd set aside. I don't think I ever knew what freedom felt like until then. I've been living in chains for most of my life. Somehow it seems that I should be happy for that and not hope for more. This is so much more than I ever thought I'd have. Maybe I don't deserve to have that special someone in my life," she concluded, a hitch in her voice. Giving in to the hurt she'd bottled up for most of her life, she put her head down on the table and sobbed.

At the same time that Miriam was bearing her soul to Polly and Mary Elizabeth, her father was crawling around in his attic searching for his birth certificate and muttering to himself. The dust lay thickly on everything that had been stuffed into this airless hole over the years, but he didn't let that deter him. Determined to collect the disability to which he felt entitled, Tom furiously swept boxes aside as he looked for the strong box he was certain Christine had put up here ages ago.

"Useless gov'ment rules and regulations. All I want is what's coming to me, and they insist that I prove I'm who everybody knows I am. Just foolishness, that's what it is. If they think I'll give up though, they can think again. I'll find that piece of paper if it's the last thing I do."

Reaching past a huge box filled with old clothes, Tom crawled into a far corner and stretched up for a handhold by which to hoist himself up. The beam proved to be too smooth for a good grip and he fell, slamming his right knee onto an ornately carved wooden box he hadn't seen. The pain shot up his leg in an agonizing ribbon of fire. Rubbing his bruised and dented kneecap, he scooted over to take a closer look and realized he had found what he was looking for. It was Christine's strong box.

Flipping the latch, he found it crowded with papers, photographs and letters. Curling into the tight space between several boxes, an old bicycle, and the tarnished remains of an ancient mirror, Tom placed the box on his lap and searched. He couldn't imagine why anyone would want to keep so much useless junk, but it was just like a woman, he figured. Nothing but a nuisance to have to look at every piece in order to find the one thing he'd come for, but there it was. Casting the photos aside carelessly, he discovered a group of letters. He was just about to discard them when he recognized his brother's handwriting on the one on top. The bile rose in his throat when he saw that it was addressed to his wife.

"I knew it," he thought as his eyes glazed over. "I knew it all along. She was stepping out on me, and with my own brother. I should have killed them both. All along I knew, and now I've got the proof."

He started to rip the letter in half, but something malicious in him made him stop.

"Nossir. I'm going to read this for myself and see the words written in black and white. Then I'm going to wave this under Will's nose when he comes home and make him show his brother and sisters. Then maybe they'll give me the respect I deserve. I'll show them just what kind of a mother she was."

Stuffing the envelope in his shirt pocket, he resumed his search for the errant birth certificate.

Able to compose herself at last, Miriam sat up and wiped her eyes only to find that Polly and Lizzie were weeping as well. She hugged them both as they shed fresh tears, and then Mary Elizabeth got up to find handkerchiefs for everyone.

"I'm sorry, Polly, Lizzie. I didn't mean to wallow in this. I thought I'd put my hurt and anger away a long time ago," Miriam apologized.

"Oh, Miriam, I'm the one who should apologize," Polly spoke gently. "I didn't mean to upset you so much."

"She needed to get it out, Polly," Mary Elizabeth said. "No one can hold in that kind of emotion and be healthy. It's like a fester; she needed to lance it. Maybe she can feel better about herself now that some if it has been shared.

"Miriam," Lizzie turned to her beloved sister, "you must surely know that it was not your role in life to make Mama and us children happy. No one can take on the burden of someone else's happiness. You have been given a job in this life, and I believe you fulfilled some of it just by being a loving daughter and sister. You have been given a passion for teaching, and that fulfills some of your purpose, too. But I believe with all my heart that God made you to be a wife and mother, as well."

"That's right," Polly asserted.

"You have such a loving, giving nature. And you wouldn't want to be married and have children of your own if you weren't meant to do so. Just look at the way you love and care for T.J. Your instincts are strong. Give yourself and the good Lord a little credit. I'm thrilled that Sonny Williamson is going to come calling on you day after tomorrow. Let's make it worth his while, shall we?"

Smiling through the last of her weeping, Miriam squared her shoulders and said, "Okay, I'll trust you and Polly about this. Will you help me style my hair?"

"That's more like it." Mary Elizabeth smiled. "We'll dazzle him. You just wait and see."

"Mama?" A small voice called from the doorway, startling the trio.   "I'm hungry-"

Saturday morning was frosty, with a bright sun glowing in a cloudless sky. Miriam had walked to the market with Mary Elizabeth early, and the ice in the wind had exhilarated her as much as it brought out the roses in her cheeks and reddened her nose. She had never been more nervous in her life as she was about meeting Sonny this afternoon, but the thought that he might be interested in her had her nerve ends jumping like grease in a hot skillet. She was impatient, convinced that two o'clock would never come, and just as terrified that it would.

She and Mary Elizabeth had pressed her favorite dress, a black polka dot with long sleeves and slight vee to the neck. The collar was white, fashioned like the lapel of a man's jacket. Belted at the waist, the full skirt fell to just below her knees. She knew it flattered her skin and the deep color of her hair. After shampooing it that morning, Mary Elizabeth had set it in rollers to dry. It rained over her shoulders in a shining fall of curls, and Miriam knew it had never looked better.

She was just dabbing a bit of cologne behind her ears when she heard the knock at the front door. Her pulse rate crescendoed, but she forced herself to relax as she reached for her coat and scarf. Toby was shaking hands with Sonny as she stepped into the living room. Riveted to him, she couldn't believe how good-looking he was. The black leather coat he wore over a navy turtleneck sweater and dark slacks hugged his solid frame and accentuated every muscle. She thought ministers were supposed to be flabby and round, but this one certainly wasn't. He looked strong and capable of doing any kind of manual labor asked of him. His hair shone like a halo of silver against the dark of his clothing, and his blue eyes sparked even more than she had remembered. Her heart fluttered just as it had the last time she'd seen him.

Hearing her footsteps, he turned and smiled warmly. "Miriam," he spoke, walking forward to take her hand. "I'm glad to see you again. You look lovely."

"Thank you," she replied, a little breathless.

"I hope Toby and Mary Elizabeth won't mind if we don't stay to visit, but I'll have to be leaving for Ascension this evening, so we don't have much time to spend together this afternoon. Might we go?"

"Of course. We'll be back in a little while, Toby."

"Good to see you again, Sonny. Come back when you can stay longer. Mary Elizabeth hasn't had a chance to impress you with one of her suppers yet; can't let you miss that," Toby told him.

Turning to have Sonny help her with her coat, Miriam looked up into Toby's grinning face and saw his covert little wink. The look she shot him said clearly, "Don't start!" Winking again, he walked around the two of them to open the door.

"Toby, Mary Elizabeth, good to see you. Give Will my best when he gets back," Sonny said. Addressing Toby as they stepped onto the porch, he grinned, "and I'll bring her back safe and sound."

Helping Miriam into the front seat of the sedan parked at the street, Sonny trotted around to the driver's door and climbed behind the wheel. He started the engine and pulled away from the curb, heading toward the town square.

"I thought about taking you to the movies, but then we wouldn't have much opportunity to talk. Would you mind if we had coffee at Lazenby's instead?"

"That would be fine," Miriam responded. "I'm happy to go wherever you have in mind."

"At least we'll be snug and warm in the café. It's been bitterly cold the past two days. I guess Old Man Winter will be here before we know it." He navigated the brick streets smoothly as he spoke.

'I love the winter. I wish it snowed more often. The bite in the air and the frost on the ground is exhilarating. That's my favorite time to take walks and be outside."

"I love every season. There's something fresh and new about each time of year as it comes in its turn. The wildflowers in the spring, especially the bluebonnets, lift my spirits and remind me of playing in them when I was a boy, and the autumn colors and smells make me think of hayrides and harvest moons. Summer nights are fun because of the breezes and the fireflies that dance over the pastures. Isn't it incredible that there's so much glory in nature? I guess I learned to appreciate it twice – once as a farm boy growing up in the country, seeing my father work to live in harmony with nature, and then in seminary learning to love the God who fashioned it all to work together in harmony in the first place."

"What a lovely way to express it. You have quite a way with words, Sonny."

"Why, thank you, ma'am. Is it working? Am I impressing you yet?"

Frowning with uncertainty, she saw his eyebrows jumping up and down as a huge smile engulfed his face, and she knew he was teasing.

"My, yes, I'm very impressed, sir. What other parlor tricks do you have up your sleeve?"

Pleased to see that she enjoyed his quirky sense of humor, Sonny chuckled and turned into the café's parking lot.

"You never know, my dear Miss Cahill. You just never know."

He opened her door and offered his arm to escort

her into the café. They found a booth not far from the jukebox and settled in with two steaming cups of coffee. Miriam relaxed as Sonny asked her questions about her students and her apartment and living in Martinsville. He was an attentive listener, drawing her out and making her feel comfortable. She marveled at him as they shared things about their families and careers and hopes for the future. His family stories delighted her.

"My dad has been a wheat farmer for over 30 years. He loves the land, and our farm has been in his family for over 100 years. The house sits on five acres and is surrounded by huge oaks and cottonwoods and sycamores. Mother has a large kitchen garden, and she cans over 400 jars of fruits and vegetables every summer. Her pear preserves won first place at the county fair when I was in high school. My favorite place in all the world is the swing that hangs at the far end of the porch. Seems I've spent my entire childhood in that swing, throwing baseballs up against the house, and hearing Mother fuss at me to stop, watching the rain blow by in great sheets, hearing the owls call out in the barn. I love that swing. I've even slept in it a few times when the house was too hot and I couldn't stand my bed a minute longer."

"I envy you having such a loving family and a home that's withstood the test of time." The wistful quality in Miriam's voice gave Sonny pause. "Do you have any brothers or sisters?"

"I have four younger siblings. Esther is 18 and fresh out of high school. She wants to marry Chad Boyd, but Dad and Mother are insisting she take some college classes first. She's in secretarial school, but she's adamantly against going back in January. The skirmishes have been legendary." He laughed as he remembered his mother's latest description of their onging battle. "My two brothers, Caleb and Gideon, are 16 and 13, and they are both first rate farm hands. The light of our lives is Rebekah. She's 10, and she'd be spoiled rotten by now if it weren't for Mother's wisdom when it comes to raising children. She's got a wicked fast ball, and her knees look like road maps they're so scarred with scrapes and cuts. She couldn't care less about dresses or ribbons or anything that would give anyone the impression she's a girl."

"She'll care when it's time. It's clear you dote on her, but I can see the love you have for your other brothers and sister, too. They sound like a great family, Sonny."

"They are. I've been very blessed to have my family love and support me as they do." Pausing to sip his coffee, he looked up and asked, "What about your family, Miriam? You haven't told me much about your own upbringing."

Sipping her coffee as she gathered her thoughts, she composed a tidy little answer of half-truths, and then looked in Sonny's sincere eyes as she opened her mouth to speak. In a flash that polite response flew from her mind and she found herself blinking back tears.

"Miriam," he said, reaching for her hand. "I'm sorry if I've intruded where I don't belong."

"I find myself wanting to tell you about my family. Are you sure you're up to it? It's not a very nice story."

"I'll listen to whatever you want to say, Miriam, but it's not necessary to tell me anything if you'd rather not. I'd never want to do anything to embarrass you," he said, hoping to reassure her.

Smiling as she blinked back the emotion threatening to spill over, Miriam told him about growing up on the little farm that Tom Cahill seemed inept at managing. Before she realized what she was doing, most of the uglier events from her childhood had come pouring out. Sonny listened intently as he held her hand, lightly grazing his thumb back and forth across the pulse point in her wrist. Nothing she had experienced in a long time had felt as soothing as that gentle caress. He interrupted her with a question once or twice, but for most of the next hour, he merely took in what she seemed determined to say. With a deep, cleansing breath, she looked at him more directly than she had since she'd begun her narrative, and said, "So much for a pleasant, uneventful afternoon. You might wish now you hadn't asked."

"On the contrary. I'm honored that you felt like you could share such a difficult story with me. You have a depth of courage that astounds me, Miriam. It's one thing to talk about standing up to adversity when it's merely an abstract thought in a very happy life; it's something altogether different to live with such abuse and emerge healthy and whole. I admire you for that, and I'm sure you learned to have that kind of courage from your mother. She must have been a remarkable woman. I wish I could have known her."

"I wish you could have, too. She was the heart of our household."

"I'm going to make it a priority to pray for your father. I believe that God can reach even the most hardened heart, so I'm going to ask Him to minister to your father. Wouldn't it be incredible if your relationship with him could be restored?"

"I'd like to build a new relationship with him,

Sonny. I'll feel better knowing you're talking to the Lord about Daddy. I'm afraid my anger has gotten in the way of my praying for him."

Smiling at her, he responded, "I'll pray about that, too. Now, as much as I'd like to stay right here with you for the rest of the evening, it's time I was making my way to Ascension. I'd better get you back to Toby's. Before we go, though, may I ask you a favor?"

"Of course."

"May I write to you once I return to seminary?"

"You'd like to write to me?"

"Yes, I would. You've been very much on my mind since we 'ran into' one another last summer, and I'd like to get to know you better. May I have that privilege, Miriam?"

"Yes. I'd enjoy your letters, and I promise to write back as often as I can."

"I'll look forward to them. I have a feeling we're going to be good friends, Miriam. Thank you for spending this afternoon with me." He grinned. Leaning toward her as he drew her scarf around her neck, he kissed her lightly on the cheek. Surprising her once again, he settled her hand in the crook of his arm and walked her to his car.

Standing on Mary Elizabeth's front porch ten minutes later, Miriam waved to Sonny as he drove off. Smoothing her fingers along the cheek he had kissed, she hugged herself and laughed. Giddy with the joy coursing along her veins, she danced in a circle along the wooden slats of the covered porch. Life was good, she thought to herself, and getting better all the time. Humming, she made her way into the house.

School had only been back in session for a week when Miriam's first letter from Sonny arrived in the mail. She dropped her purse twice before she could get her front door opened and actually step into her apartment. Dropping everything in the floor, she ripped the envelope in half and yanked out the letter.

Dear Miriam,

I've only been back in classes for three days, but it feels like a month since we spent last Saturday together. I hope you have not regretted what you shared of your life with me. I was honored that you felt you could trust me to that extent. Be assured that I have firmly placed you and your father at the foot of God's throne and am trusting that in His time all will be well.

I am taking three classes this term, and then I'll need only two more semesters to complete my degree. The idea that I have only one year to go is thrilling; the classes I must successfully complete in that year are less so. Please don't misunderstand; I love knowing that what I am learning will someday be put to good use in whatever ministry I undertake, but my professors hold us to very high standards. I have little free time to call my own. I've already been assigned a research paper in my Acts of the Apostles/Pauline Epistles class, and my assignment for Church History includes an intensive look at the life and theology of John Calvin. He was a brilliant man who lived during the Protestant Reformation, and I have found his commentaries to be fascinating. I am taking a Pastoral Care class. The work can seem endless!

I share my complaints with a fellow student who

has become one of my best friends here in seminary. His name is Mike Nelson, and his father owns the feed store in a little town north of Houston called Humble. Mike and I are just two good old country boys who have a good time swapping stories and making fun of the food in the mess hall. I never saw so much gray, tasteless slop in my life! Thank Heaven our mothers take pity on us and mail us care packages from time to time. I can smell Mother's oatmeal cookies from miles away, and Mike's mother makes gingerbread that is so good it can make you weep. We'd starve if it weren't for the two of them.

I have one particular professor whom I greatly admire. His name is Dr. McLaurin, and he teaches New Testament Greek. He is unassuming in stature, with a leonine mane of white hair and an endearing Mississippi accent. His genteel nature hides a sharp wit and brilliant mind, and his classes are certainly challenging. Mike and I hope we can make the same kind of difference in our ministries someday that he has already made in ours.

Esther has lost another front line attack. Mother wrote me that she is once again firmly entrenched in school for another semester, grumbling nastily but attending classes just the same. Chad told her he'd wait for her until the moon disappeared from the night sky, but poor Esther fancies herself a grown woman and is sure that waiting for marriage until she's a withered, used up old woman of 20 is a fate worse than death.

Rebekah qualified for the all-district spelling bee this week at school. She wanders the house now with her nose in the list of words, spelling everything the family utters and declaring to the world that the trophy is hers. What a girl! I told Mother that her passions would stand her in good stead someday, and that those tantrums she had as a toddler were going to pay off eventually. I'm still not sure she believes me!

Take care, Miriam. I eagerly await your return address in my mailbox. I can't wait to hear about Gladys and your students. Tell Mr. Guthrie at the post office I am eternally in his debt.
Affectionately,

Sonny

Miriam read the letter four times before she gathered her belongings from the floor and changed into her robe. The more she got to know Sonny, the more she liked what she knew. He was intelligent, caring, and obviously crazy about his work and his family. And then there were those eyes, she sighed. One day at a time, she thought to herself, as she sat down at the secretary to compose her reply.

The letters flew back and forth for the next three weeks, and in Sonny's last short note he asked once again to see her over the Christmas holidays. He had a month between semesters and had planned on spending a few days with his uncle and aunt in Cedar Springs. Miriam would have been delighted to hear his mother's comments on his sudden interest in Uncle Thaddeus and Aunt Margaret. She had asked him if there was anything, or anyone, else, drawing him to Cedar Springs, to which he had merely smiled. The truth was he felt drawn more and more to Miriam, and hoped she might be the woman God meant to share in his life and calling. Her hair shone like a fiery sunset, and gleamed like silk as it cascaded down her back, and her peaches and cream complexion made his fingers itch to stroke her face. Just looking at her alone was enough to make him drool, but when you added her intelligence and gentle, compassionate spirit, he feared he was already in over his head. He quite frankly thought she was wonderful. Therefore, any opportunity to spend time with her was not to be frittered away frivolously.

Esther had given him some wise advice about a Christmas gift, and the scarf he had chosen was one he hoped she liked. He thought the mint green and soft peach hues were a perfect compliment to her coloring, and the fabric flowed like water through his fingers. In order to make it a little less personal, he had added a volume of poems written by his favorite British authors. The collection included the works of Wordsworth, Shelley, Keats, Coleridge, and Lord Byron. Sonny knew he was a romantic at heart, but he loved the images in them, and he hoped she enjoyed reading them as well.

Miriam was overjoyed to be seeing him again in a few days, and she had shopped for hours before she found the perfect gift. She knew he loved to read, so she bought him a copy of *The Pilgrim's Progress* and a novel, *Jude the Obscure*, by Thomas Hardy. Hardy wrote so exquisitely that she wept each time she read any of his works. Sonny was picking her up the Wednesday after Christmas for a drive into the country and then dinner at his aunt and uncle's.

Chapter 10

In the pre-dawn darkness of her bedroom, Miriam slept, dreaming of blue eyed stallions named Solomon and a warrior with silver hair. T.J. had been up later than usual the night before, shaking packages under the Christmas tree and trying to play with the balls hanging from the branches of the pine tree in the front window of Toby and Mary Elizabeth's living room. He didn't understand what Christmas was about, but the excitement in the air was enough for him to be fussy and unwilling to go to sleep. There were strange goings-on all around him, and to sleep might mean he'd miss it. The mattress bounced slightly as someone skulked into Miriam's quiet room and straddled her in the middle of the bed. The intruder dug her fingers into Miriam's ribs and shouted, "Santa Claus has been here!" Just a hair shy of screaming, the mists cleared from Miriam's mind and she realized that Mary Elizabeth had pinned her to the bed and was tickling her furiously.

"Lizzie," she gasped, slapping at her sister's relentless hands, "are you out of your mind? What are you doing?"

"It's Christmas, Mim. Come on, get up. I can't stand it another minute. We're going to have a few quiet moments to open our grown-up presents, and then Toby is going to wake up T.J." Crawling off the bed, she said, "I've got coffee brewing on the stove and biscuits ready to go into the oven. You'd better hurry or you're going to miss out." Laughing, Mary Elizabeth sailed out of the room.

"Crazy," Miriam muttered as she stumbled up from the bed and grappled with her robe. "Why do we have to do this now? It's not even daylight out yet. What time is it anyway?" She peered through sleep-fogged slits at the alarm clock on her dresser. "It's not even six o'clock! She is crazy," she grumbled. Shuffling into the hallway, she looked up to see that Toby was sitting by the tree, but he wasn't in any better shape than she was. "Does she do this every year, Toby?"

"Every year since I married her, yes ma'am," he slurred, the enormous yawn threatening to swallow his face.

"Don't be mad at me, you two," Mary Elizabeth begged from the doorway. She walked into the room carrying a tray laden with steaming cups of coffee. "We never got to do this when we were kids growing up. Don't you remember, Mim? We had to wait until Daddy left the house before we could even open our presents. I used to dream about celebrating Christmas with as much noise and fun as I could imagine. You wouldn't take that away from me just for a little more sleep, would you?"

Reaching gratefully for his coffee, Toby tugged Mary Elizabeth onto the floor next to him and hugged her.

"Honey, you get as rowdy as you want, but I reserve the right to take a long nap this afternoon, okay?"

Smacking his lips exuberantly, she dove under the tree to retrieve the gifts she had so carefully wrapped over the previous two weeks. Miriam had never seen anyone get as excited about Christmas as her younger sister. Toby had told her that Lizzie insisted she go along to chop down the tree; only a perfect one would do. The one standing in front of the window now was only about six feet tall, with one huge gap in the limbs and several other limbs crooked and overlapping. Lizzie insisted that it was beautiful. She had labored over the ornaments she had fashioned, decorating the balls with glitter and yarn and draping popcorn strings across every inch of the tree. Huge lights were intertwined with the glittery tinsel she'd bought at the five and dime, and a foil star pointed gracefully upward from the topmost peak. Gazing at it as she knew Lizzie did, Miriam saw not the flaws and inexpensive decorations, but the magic that was a part of all Christmases. Her tears clouded her vision as she wished fervently that she could be sharing this with her mother.

Handing a box to both Mim and Toby, Mary Elizabeth insisted that they open these gifts first. Toby reciprocated with a box of his own for his wife. Miriam found a lovely hand knitted sweater of soft blue, with a cowl neck and ring of tiny pink and lavender embroidered flowers gracing the bodice. It was exquisite, and she knew that it must have taken Lizzie untold hours to stitch it. She hugged it to herself, her eyes swimming with tears at the love she knew had gone into the making of so precious a garment.

Toby was holding up a flannel jacket, and he knew as well that his wife had sewn this for him. Every stitch was tiny and perfectly spaced, and the lining was of a smooth, cream-colored satin. He watched Mary Elizabeth open the gift he had given her, smiling as she drew out the wooden carving of T.J. standing before her, his arms reaching up for his mother to hold him, his face alight with pleasure and hers glowing with love. She launched herself into his arms, hugging him fiercely and thanking him over and over for the exquisite statuette. Miriam was floored by the craftsmanship. Clearly anyone could recognize his wife and son's features in the faces carved in the wood, and their emotions were boldly declared.

"Miriam," Toby spoke, holding out a box for her. "I made this one for you." He smiled. She opened the simply wrapped package to find another statuette . It was of her and Mama, standing side by side, one of Christine's arms around Miriam's waist, and the other one pointing into the distance.

"Oh, my," Miriam exclaimed. She looked up to see both Toby and her sister smiling at her with tears streaking their faces. Clearing his throat, Toby added, "It's called 'Dream.'"

"Do you like it, Mim?" Mary Elizabeth asked softly.

"Like it?" Miriam answered. "I think it's the best gift I've ever received, along with my gorgeous sweater. Thank you both. This has been a very special Christmas already, and somehow it feels like Mama is sharing it with us."

"I think so, too," said Toby softly.

"Oh, now it's my turn," Miriam exclaimed. Reaching toward the back of the tree, she withdrew two flat boxes wrapped in bright red paper and adorned with silver stars. Toby tore into his first, finding a Canon 35 mm camera. He couldn't believe his eyes. She had included four rolls of film and a carrying case.

"Miriam, I'm overwhelmed. How did you know

that I've wanted one for years? I never thought I could afford one. Thank you, honey," he replied, hugging her.

"Mim, it's gorgeous," Mary Elizabeth interrupted as she pulled her gift from its box. Holding it up against her frame, she smoothed the material and hugged it. Toby watched her face light up as she jumped up to try it on. Miriam had splurged for Mary Elizabeth, too, and had found a full-length coat made of the softest suede she had ever seen in a rich chocolate brown, with a fake white fur collar.

"I love it, Mim. It's the prettiest coat I've ever had." Looking over at her husband, she teased, "Now you won't have to look for yours every time I borrow it to go outside and then forget where I've put it."

Toby laughed as he gathered up the scattered remains. "Miriam, I'm in your debt. You have no idea how many times I've sprinted to the mailbox in my shirtsleeves because Lizzie couldn't remember where she'd dropped my jacket."

"I'm glad you both like them. I want you to know how much I've come to count on the two of you for your support and encouragement this past year. Moving out on my own has been better than I could have imagined, but I've never been as scared in my life. Knowing I had a place to run to made it easier."

Hugging her tightly, Mary Elizabeth murmured, "Mama would be proud. Merry Christmas, Mim. Now, let's go wake up a certain young man!"

After the gifts had been opened and miles of paper and ribbon gathered for the trash, after the huge turkey dinner had been devoured, after everyone had napped and eaten turkey sandwiches for supper, Miriam sat in the quiet of the rocker on the front porch and considered what had transpired for her in the past year. Last Christmas Mama had been ill, and Miriam had fought desperately to care for her, to do something that would reverse the effects of the tuberculosis and give her even one more moment with her mother. She had fought against the bitterness and hurt that threatened to engulf her each time she reached out to her father. He had been so cold, so callous about losing his wife; Miriam hadn't been able to stand the sight of him. She couldn't understand why he wouldn't even come into Christine's sick room to visit with her, and his stoicism in the face of her death baffled Miriam. She had made the break from the life she had come to despise, and now she was Miss Cahill and had so many new people in her life to love. Marveling at the way just a few months had changed her life, she thought once again of her mother and of how much Christine had dreamed for her eldest child.

"Merry Christmas, Mama. I've had such a nice day with Mary Elizabeth and her family, but I would have traded it all for just another few minutes to spend with you. I know you're happier now, and the joy you're experiencing couldn't compare to anything you knew here on earth, but I still miss you dreadfully and have so much I'd like to share with you.

"Will is coming into town tomorrow. He spent Christmas with his friend, Jarrod, and his family. He hasn't said anything, but I suspect Jarrod must have a sister or something, because Will's letters have been full of how much time he's spending with his friend. Seth and Polly will be here tomorrow, too. We'll have a lovely family dinner together and share the gifts we've been thinking up for each other. I'm happy to have drawn Seth's name. I've found a Bible to give him for

Christmas. Every husband and father, when he becomes a father, should have a family Bible from which to read and in which to keep the family's history. I hope he likes it.

"It saddens me when I think of how Daddy so disdained the family Bible your folks gave you when you married. He is still such a bitter, dried up shell of a man, Mama. I hope he can find his way out of the misery he's created for himself, but I can't be his happiness for him. I can love him, and I'm trying to do that in spite of how cruelly he's treated us. I know that holding onto my anger and hurt only diminishes me, and I don't want to live my life regretting what can't be changed.

"I have a new friend, Mama. His name is Sonny. We write letters to one another while he's attending seminary, and he's coming over in a couple of days to see me. I dream of what my life might be like to have him care for me. Do I dare to hope for such a miracle in my life? I know you wanted such happiness for me. I am happy, Mama, and I have you to thank for bringing me to this place in my life. I love you so much, Mama. Merry Christmas."

Wrapping her shawl more firmly around her shoulders, Miriam softly hummed one of the hymns she knew her mother had loved.

"When peace like a river attendeth my way,
When sorrows like sea billows roll,
Whatever my lot, thou hast taught me to say,
'It is well, it is well, with my soul.'"

Miriam arose around seven the next morning to help Mary Elizabeth make preparations for the rest of the family. After a breakfast feast of waffles, link sausages, and canned peaches from the pantry, Toby took T.J. out for a run. Truthfully, though, Toby was going to do the running while T.J. rode in his Radio Flyer and had the time of his life. It was one of his favorite games to play with his dad.

Miriam began slicing potatoes for the scalloped potato casserole Mary Elizabeth had planned, and the lady of the house cut up the two chickens she planned to fry a bit later on. The cake was stirred up and in the oven, and the two loaves of bread that had been set to rise would go into the oven when the cake came out. Mary Elizabeth hummed as she worked; she was never happier than when she was in her kitchen, making her home a true place of peace for Toby and T.J. She had a surprise to share with everyone once they'd had dinner and exchanged gifts, and she was about to burst with the news. Toby didn't even know that she'd gone to the doctor two weeks ago and confirmed her suspicions. He had told her the baby would come sometime in August. In her heart of hearts she hoped for a girl, one with Miriam's luxurious hair and her mother's sweet disposition. She had already picked out a name, too – Rachel Christine. She could see her already, this precious new life that grew inside her.

Her thoughts were interrupted by a burst of noise from the living room. Will and Seth must have arrived. Wiping her hands on a dish towel, she brushed back an errant lock of hair and scurried into the front room with Miriam at her heels. There was a mad rush of hugs and kisses and flying coats and scarves, then everyone gathered around the kitchen table to drink coffee and share news while Polly joined in the effort to get dinner on the table.

Will grabbed T.J. as he settled himself in a chair, tickling him and nuzzling his neck with his cold nose.

Squealing with delight, T.J. patted Will's cheek and begged, "More, Unca Will, do more." Grinning, Will was happy to comply.

"Hey, T.J.," Seth said, "come over here a minute. I've got a secret to tell you."

Clamoring into Seth's lap, T.J. put his ear close to his uncle's face. He loved secrets. Speaking loudly enough that his stage whisper could be heard by everyone, he told his nephew, "How would you like to have a cousin to play with soon?" Drawing back, T.J. registered his confusion with the look he gave Seth, but no one else was confused. In a moment the kitchen was in happy chaos as Polly confirmed Seth's announcement. Yes, she was expecting a baby. They had just found out a few days ago, and the baby was due in September. After everyone had hugged Polly and Seth and settled down again, Mary Elizabeth smiled and looked at Toby.

"Well, I was going to wait until later to share my news, but I don't think I can. T.J. isn't only going to have a cousin come September. He's going to have a baby sister or brother as well."

The stunned look on Toby's face was priceless, but the tears in his eyes bore witness to the joy that flooded his soul at the news. Grabbing Mary Elizabeth in a bone-crushing hug, he spun her around the room and laughed aloud as he kissed her over and over. "Really, Lizzie? Are you sure? Are you okay? Have you seen the doctor?"

"Honey, put me down before my cake falls. I'm fine, and yes, I've seen the doctor. I went Tuesday a week ago. I hope you don't mind that I waited until today to tell everyone at once. He says I'm due in August."

"I don't. Let's knock on the neighbors' doors and

tell everyone! Another baby," he responded. "Whew."

Lunch was a happy affair with lively discussions about maternity clothes, baby clothes and baby names and all the questions Polly had wanted to ask Lizzie ever since she had found out that she herself was pregnant. Miriam couldn't imagine a happier time in which to have such news. She loved Mary Elizabeth's idea of a girl's name, and she secretly hoped for a niece as well.

The family spent the day playing dominoes and cards until Polly and Mary Elizabeth couldn't hold their eyes open another minute. There were more hugs and kisses as everyone bid the others good night, and Toby promised everyone he and his brothers-in-law would make breakfast the next morning.

"Uh, are you sure?" Will asked dubiously. "I've managed to learn a few things in the kitchen or I would have starved at the farm this past summer, but things like biscuits are beyond me."

"I can't even do that much," Seth added.

"I've got it under control, gentlemen," Toby assured them. "Trust me," he added as he winked.

The next morning the girls were astounded to see the table laden with a platter of scrambled eggs, enough bacon to have come from an entire side of pork, hash brown potatoes, and cinnamon toast.

"Toby," Mary Elizabeth marveled as she sat down in the chair her husband held for her. "How did you manage this feast?"

"Simple, my dear. I've been watching you for over three years." As she stared, he added, "and I called my mother this morning and got the instructions."

"I knew it," she declared. "Still, this is impressive, and we girls are grateful to you for putting this together for us. This was another Christmas gift, wasn't it?"

"You bet." Polly smiled as she sipped her coffee. "Seth, does this mean I can expect breakfast in bed from time to time?"

"Ah, honey, we'd better talk about that another time, okay?"

There were chuckles all around as everyone enjoyed the meal, and then it was time for Miriam's brothers to head home. She shed a few happy tears as she watched Will climb into the truck for Toby to drive him to the bus stop on the square, and she waved until he and Seth and Polly were out of sight, too. Oh, how she loved her family.

"Lizzie," she called as she returned to the kitchen a few minutes later, "is there time to wash my hair before Sonny gets here this afternoon?"

She walked into the room to find her sister crumpled on the floor, unconscious. "Lizzie, honey, oh no. Lizzie, wake up! Sweetie, can you hear me?" she demanded as she massaged Lizzie's arms and looked frantically for some answer to why Mary Elizabeth was passed out cold. Grabbing the telephone, she dialed zero and waited an endless ten seconds for Delia Edwards to answer.

"Operator," she began.

"Mrs. Edwards, this is Miriam Cahill -"

"Oh, hello dear. How are you? I believe Mary Elizabeth did tell me you were coming for Christmas. How are you enjoying -"

"Mrs. Edwards, forgive me for interrupting, but I need you to call Dr. Meyer for me. Lizzie is unconscious, and I can't wake her up. Can you ask him to come right away?"

"Oh, mercy! Yes, honey, he'll be along as soon as I can patch through a call."

Hanging up, Miriam ran back into the kitchen to find that Mary Elizabeth was struggling to sit up, rubbing the back of her head as she looked around, dazed.

"Miriam? What happened?"

"I don't know. I walked back into the kitchen to find you had passed out on the floor. I called Dr. Meyer, and he'll be here shortly. Lie still."

"I don't want to cause anyone any trouble. I was just dizzy for a moment. Help me up."

Reluctant to do so, Miriam was about to argue when Toby walked into the house.

"Toby?" Miriam called, "Come on back here, please."

"I got Will to . . . Lizzie, honey, what's wrong?" he asked as he fell to the floor beside her.

"I don't know, Toby. I just got a little dizzy, and I guess I passed out. Help me up."

"Maybe you should stay put. Miriam, call the doctor."

"He's already on his way."

"Toby," Mary Elizabeth spoke with some exasperation. "Dr. Meyer can't examine me if I'm on the floor. Help me up."

Gently bringing her to her feet, he eased her into a chair and turned to get her some water when he heard the doorbell chime.

'I'll go," Miriam replied.

A few moments later a well-dressed man in his mid 50's walked into the kitchen. His somber eyes registered his concern as he approached Mary Elizabeth.

"Well, my dear, I didn't expect to see you quite so soon. What happened?"

"I felt a little dizzy, Dr. Meyer. I suppose I passed out, but I'm feeling better now. Is this necessary?"

"Why don't we have a look-see since I'm already here, hmm?" Turning to Toby, he asked that they help her to the couch in the living room. Toby went to check on a napping T.J., and Miriam returned to the kitchen to finish the cleaning up that Lizzie had been doing when she fell ill. She had been working about ten minutes when Dr. Meyer called for them to return to the room.

"She's fine. She's just pregnant, and I suspect she overdid it for Christmas and all the company you had. There is the possibility that she's a little anemic. I took some blood for testing, but I want her to start on these iron supplements today. If she rests this afternoon, I'm sure by tonight she'll be back to her old self. Mary Elizabeth, you're going to have to take it easy, my dear. That's an order. Toby, you'll see to it?"

"Certainly, Dr. Meyer. Thanks for coming so quickly."

"Not at all, not at all. I'll be by in a few days with those blood results and to check in. Good day."

"Can I get up now?" Mary Elizabeth asked as she swung her legs to the floor.

"Just a minute, there, ma'am," Toby cut her off. He grabbed an afghan from the back of the sofa and covered her with it. "You are to rest until I say you can get up. No more scares like that. My heart can't take it."

'I'm sorry, honey, but this is unnecessary. I'm pregnant, not recovering from a near-death experience."

"Toby's right, Lizzie. There's nothing that needs to be done until lunchtime. You can certainly spend an hour on the sofa without the house falling into disrepair. I'll take care of T.J. when he wakes up, so you and Toby enjoy your time together. You get precious little time alone as it is."

Seeing she was outnumbered, Mary Elizabeth relented. Toby sat down at the foot of the sofa and drew her legs into his lap. Miriam left them quietly talking.

"Is she okay?" Sonny asked, glancing at Miriam as he drove down the quiet country road.

"Dr. Meyer says she'll be fine. I'm sure the holidays and the work she did preparing meals and decorating for Christmas just exhausted her. Toby will be the world's best watchdog now that he knows she overdid it. In fact," she added, chuckling, "if I know Toby he's going to hover and worry until he drives her just a little bit crazy. Men are such ninnies when their wives get pregnant."

"Pregnancy is terrifying to men. We know nothing about it, and it's all so mysterious and secretive. It's no wonder we act like our wives are going to break. We're helpless, and that's a very uncomfortable feeling. I'm sure I'll behave even more ridiculously than Toby and drive my wife batty as well."

"It's a perfectly natural happening, you know. Women have been having babies for centuries."

"It's one of God's greatest miracles. I find it fascinating that a man and a woman can create a new and unique human being, with the best parts of both of them. There is so much that could go wrong, and yet most babies are born perfect and healthy. What a gift. And while I can acknowledge the wonder of being pregnant and giving birth, it is still incomprehensible to me how a woman endures. It's true that women have been having babies for centuries, but they've been laughing at their men and their ineptness for centuries, as well, so I'll happily join the ranks of the ninnies and know my wife and all the females on both sides of the family will laugh at me when it's my turn."

"I'm happy you can be so broad minded about it, Sonny."

Laughing with her, he changed the subject. "How have you been, Miriam? I've missed you this past month."

"I've been busy with my children, mostly. The four weeks between Thanksgiving and Christmas might as well be one long holiday. They are so excited they can't concentrate on anything, so lessons are more tedious, the days drag by endlessly, and the kids are so fractious they're almost impossible to control. And I loved every minute of it."

"You've found your calling, haven't you?"

"Yes, and it feels good. You've found your calling, too, Sonny. I know you're going to be a great minister when you graduate and are sent to your first church."

"I hope so. I know I'm going to give it my best."

"What do you like most about ministry?"

"Oh, without a doubt I love the pastoral care aspect of ministry. I like knowing I can bring comfort to someone in need, or make someone in the hospital feel better. My greatest joy is bringing God to someone who needs a special touch. Does that sound pompous?"

" Everyone wants to feel as if they are making a difference in some way. One of the things I love most about teaching is helping one of my students comprehend a new fact or idea that he's never considered before. It opens up an entirely new world to him. What better way to make a difference than to minister in Jesus' name to someone who needs Him? That can make an eternal difference."

"Exactly. I'm glad you understand. After pastoral care what I love most is to teach. I hope I'll have many opportunities to share God's word with the people in my church.   There are so many miraculous events and fascinating people in the Bible. Do you know the story of David and Bathsheba?"

"Yes, of course. David is one of my favorite people from the Bible, so I've read as much as I could about him. One of the stories I love most is the one about finding Jonathan's crippled son and bringing him to live in his home. There was no one more human than David. He actually planned Uriah's murder just so that he could have his wife. When I think of David and his flaws, and then read about how God used him to do such great things, such loving and compassionate things, like taking in Mephisbosheth, I'm just awed.

"I'm particularly fond of Gomer. She was just about the last woman our modern society would consider worthy of God's attention, and just look at how often Hosea goes after her. I'm comforted knowing that God pursues me that lovingly even though I'm unworthy as well."

"I've found the story of Elijah and the prophets of Baal to be exciting and inspiring. Did you know that when he taunted the prophets he was actually asking them if their god was using the restroom? That tickles me."

"I never knew that about the story. You must

have an advantage because you've studied in the original languages."

"The translating is tough sledding some of the time, but the payoff is well worth the effort and time. I think those little details make the stories more human, more alive. That's what I want to teach to others. So many people believe the Bible to be some ancient, dusty, irrelevant volume of lovely stories. Why, there's more violence and cruelty, adventure and romance, and love and revenge in the Bible than anything we could hear on the news or read in the paper. The men and women of the Bible give us stirring looks into every human emotion and behavior possible, and from them we have much we can learn about ourselves and how we're to love God and treat one another. Studying the Bible is one of the most exciting ways I spend my time."

Miriam looked at Sonny as he turned to watch the road winding out before him and realized that there was so much she liked about this man. He was clearly passionate about his life's work, and she admired that tremendously. She understood where that passion came from; she had that same fire for teaching. He was unutterably genuine, so easy to be with. She hadn't spent a great deal of time with him yet, but she knew her feelings were growing stronger each time she read one of his letters or talked with him. She had no past experience by which to judge, but if this wasn't love, then she was very much in like! The thought made her chuckle before she could stop herself.

"What's funny?" Sonny asked as he looked over at her.

"Oh, nothing really. I was just th-thinking," she stammered. Yikes! What am I doing? I can't tell him how I feel; what can I tell him? Miriam, she thought to herself, you've put your foot into it this time.

"Can you tell me?" he asked with an expectant look on his face.

"I was just looking at your profile and thinking how much I like you," she blurted before she could stop herself. "I mean, I was . . .um. . . oh, help."

She could feel her face flaming; it must be as red as a cooked beet. She was mortified at what she'd just admitted. Her eyes filled with tears as she realized he was pulling the car over to the side of the road. Oh, Miriam, she thought, you've blown it now.   He's going to turn this car around and take you right home and that's the last you'll see of Mr. Perfect Minister.

Stopping the car under the shade of a towering cottonwood tree, Sonny killed the motor and turned to his companion, who was studiously attempting to blend in with the passenger door window.

"Miriam, can you look at me?" he asked. She just sat there, terrified to move and have him see the tears on her cheeks.

"Miriam, please. I'd rather not speak to the back of your head, but I will if I must."

Miriam's sighed, which sounded more like a pitiful little hitch to her, and turned slowly to look at Sonny's face. Bracing for the worst, she was astonished to find him scooting across the seat and wrapping her in a gentle hug.

"Oh, Miriam, please don't cry. I know you're embarrassed by what you just said, but you don't need to be. I'm delighted to know that you like me. It makes it much easier for a coward like me to admit just how fond I've become of you."

"You mean," she struggled to say, "you're not going to take me home?"

"Heavens, no! I'm going to take you to Uncle Thaddeus' just like we'd planned. But first I want to say something. Will you listen to me?"

She merely nodded.

"Good. Ever since Solomon and I almost ran you over last summer, I've been thinking about what a nice person you seemed to be. Some girls would have peeled a layer off my hide off for knocking them down the way I did you, but you weren't angry in the least. Nothing you said could have been remotely considered rude. I just marveled at that. And then I saw you again in Ascension and heard you sing. I knew only the purest of hearts could sing as you did and express your feelings as clearly as they shone in your face. You are a lovely woman, Miriam, and I find my feelings for you growing quite strong. So you see, I'm very happy to know that those feelings are reciprocated. I'd like very much to continue this friendship and trust God for where it leads. Can we agree to do that?"

"Oh, Sonny," she exclaimed as she threw her arms around him, "I'd like that, too. I'm so glad you don't think I'm too brazen or outspoken."

"I could hardly think that. You are the soul of propriety," he teased, "so I hope you won't be too outraged if I do this."

Before she could anticipate his next move, he had reached up to stroke her cheek and place the softest of kisses against her mouth. She was stunned. His kiss rocked her to the soles of her feet. Pulling back to smile once again, he hugged her fiercely and then moved to his side of the car once again.

"If we don't hurry, Aunt Margaret's lunch is going to be cold and she'll have something to say. Are you okay?"

Once again Miriam could only nod, but Sonny didn't seem to mind. He nodded in response and pulled back onto the road. They traversed the rest of the trip silently, which was fine with Miriam. She was still in shock, but it was the nicest feeling in the world at the same time. Sonny had kissed her! He hadn't minded that she'd been so forward. She hugged the feeling to her like a beloved quilt as she glanced his way from time to time. He was quite a guy.

"There it is," Sonny declared a scant ten minutes later. "Looks like Marcus is on the porch waiting for us. Can you take it?"

"I like Marcus. He likes to live his life out loud, to quote a friend of mine, and that's fine with me. I am a little nervous about being here with your family. What if they don't approve?"

"I approve, and that's enough for them. Besides, how could they not love you? Relax," he encouraged. Jumping out of the car, he hurried to open the door for her. Taking her hand, he entwined their fingers together. Miriam stopped and stared at their joined hands for a moment, and noticing her hesitation, Sonny turned to her and asked, "Is this okay with you?"

Miriam smiled her response. "It's very much okay with me."

Tightening his hold, Sonny grinned, and his incredible blue eyes dazzled her with their glow. Hand-in-hand they made their way up to the house.

Later that evening at Mary Elizabeth's she relived her afternoon with Sonny's aunt and uncle as she and

Lizzie sat drinking coffee. Toby had gone to bed soon after putting T.J. down for the night, and the sisters were taking advantage of these solitary moments together.

"What do you think of his aunt and uncle?"

"I like them very much. They were gracious and welcoming, and I lost my timidity very quickly. His Aunt Margaret is every inch the southern lady, but she was such a generous hostess I didn't feel like a bug on the end of a pin at all. Her living room was very formal, with muted mint green carpet and the most gorgeous silk wallpaper you've ever seen. It was done in stripes the color of the carpet, with the cream stripes in between laced with pale dusky pink roses. Her furniture is very elegant, and at first I hesitated to even sit down. Then Marcus threw himself across the sofa and propped his feet up on the glass topped coffee table."

Laughing quietly, Mary Elizabeth remarked, "Well, so much for formality."

"You're right. After then I didn't feel as awkward. We had a lovely dinner. She had baked two huge chickens, and they were so tender and good. There was a sweet potato casserole, turnip greens, and pecan pie for dessert. I drank enough tea to swim home, I think," she concluded, chuckling.

"It was more than that, though, Lizzie. We never had much chance to have people over or be invited to someone else's home when we were growing up. How could Mama have explained Daddy to anyone? Besides, there wasn't much extra money to be cooking supper for guests. But since I've been on my own I've gone out with Gladys, had supper countless times with Buck and Annie, and now I've been a guest in the Thompkins' home. It finally feels like I have a place in the world, that I'm accepted and welcomed outside of my own family. I like that feeling. I especially like being accepted by the people Sonny cares about," she added quietly.

"You like him, don't you, Mim?" Mary Elizabeth asked gently as she covered Miriam's hand with her own.

"Oh, yes, Lizzie, I do. He's such a good man, compassionate and giving, friendly and open and accepting of who I am. I've told him so much about our growing up, things no one else outside the family could possibly know, and he seems to understand. His letters have given me an insight into his life that I'll bet it took you the entire first year of your marriage to learn about Toby. Sonny is smart, and funny, and he loves his family, especially his sisters. I hope he'll invite me to meet them someday. He's the best part of my life, Lizzie. When I think about what might be, the feeling warms me all over."

"You sound like I did when I first fell in love with Toby."

"It's too soon to know if I love him, but I'm willing to wait and see." Miriam's grin reminded Mary Elizabeth of an imp bent on a little harmless mischief. She wouldn't tell Mary Elizabeth about the drive home from his Uncle Thaddeus's. Thoughts of that time with him made her blush to her toes. Too, the details of her friendship with Sonny belonged to just she and Sonny. She had waited so long for someone to single her out in this way, and the joy of his arm around her shoulders and the sweet little kisses she had shared with him as he dropped her off was hers to savor alone.

The next five months were going to be long ones, she knew. There were no more extended holidays until the close of school for the year in May, so she would have to content herself with the letters they would exchange and the memories of her time with him this holiday. Sighing deeply, she rinsed her coffee cup and bid her sister a quiet goodnight.

Chapter 11

Curled up in her favorite chair, Miriam was reading yet again from the volume of poetry Sonny had given her at Christmas. She loved the words of Wordsworth best, but all the authors swept her away with their lovely verses and fanciful notions. Keats' "Ode on a Grecian Urn" was one she particularly fancied, caught up in the idea of one perfect moment frozen in time, to be relived again and again as the mood beckoned. She supposed it was rather like having a photograph now, a special one that reminded its owner of happy times and much-loved people.

She had received a letter not long ago with photographs of Mary Elizabeth and T.J. and was delighted to see that Toby was enjoying her Christmas gift so much. The quality of the snapshots attested to his growing skill as well. Mary Elizabeth's letters were full of updates on her pregnancy, her growing girth, and the soft blankets and nightgowns she was making for their latest addition to the family. Miriam was compiling a library of some of her favorite children's books for T.J. and the new little one to share. She had found a leather-bound volume of poetry that included Longfellow, Lowell, Emily Dickinson, Walt Whitman, and Eugene Field. How she thrilled at the words herself as she read, and her students loved the poems. "The Midnight Ride of Paul Revere" and "Wynkyn, Blynkyn, and Nod" were their favorites. She prayed that both of Mary Elizabeth's children came to love books as she did.

Seth and Polly had written her several times, discussing their ongoing debate about baby names. Polly wanted to name a boy after her father, but her dad's name was Stanley, a name Seth had never much liked. Seth liked Bradley, and Polly had refused to even consider it. She'd been bullied by a Bradley as a young girl in school. The names for a girl were even more hotly contested. Seth liked Ruthie, Martha, and Erma Jean. Polly considered them detestable. Her choices of Millie and Betsy he considered too cutesy, so the war waged on. Miriam could tell from the easy bantering in the letters that they were both deliriously happy with this new baby and making plans almost too quickly to carry them out. She contented herself with the waiting by sewing diapers and nightgowns. She would never be the seamstress that Lizzie was, but she could sew a nice straight seam, and a new baby deserved her best effort. She was making quilts for both new babies, and fashioning those was such fun she didn't consider that a chore. She couldn't wait for Lizzie and Polly to see them.

She and Sonny had written back and forth about several books they loved and recommended to one another. Sharing her love of books with Sonny was just one of the things that made her smile these days. His colorful stories about his family made her laugh, and his encouraging words about her teaching seemed to provide a boost just when she needed it. One letter had been dedicated to stories about his grandfather, a hellfire and brimstone preacher in the pulpit and a quiet, humorous fisherman out of it.

Sonny's reminiscences about time with his grandfather made Miriam ache for the affection they so clearly shared one with another. He wrote about what he was learning in his classes. Miriam marveled at his insights and the intelligence with which he had been gifted. She could feel the smoothness of the tabletops and smell the muskiness of the volumes of books in the library, so vivid were his descriptions of his time there, studying and writing. She thrilled to read that he loved the library as much as she. She shared his reverence for books, and learning about his life made her days sweet and full of hope for what they were becoming to one another. He had sent her a sweet Valentine's card in February with a silly rhyme he'd composed to her. She couldn't have been more enchanted. When he'd read in her letter that she'd spent two weeks in January battling a cold, he'd mailed her a funny get well card and a can of chicken soup. In March he'd sent a card with flowers on it to wish her a happy spring. April had found an Easter card that had brought tears to her eyes. She found herself reading them over and over, along with his letters, as much as she did the poems. Lizzie had grilled her for details about her relationship with Sonny in the last several letters, but Miriam kept most of her thoughts to herself. Sonny was too special, their growing friendship with one another a warm place in her heart she held too precious to discuss, even with someone as close as her own sister.

She poured her heart out in her letters to him. She

shared her dreams for the future, the anxieties that stemmed from her father's abuses, and the loss of her mother that still consumed her from time to time. Sonny seemed to understand, and his responses comforted her as no other words from anyone else had done. His latest letter had included an invitation to spend a weekend in June with his family. She was eager to accept, but scared to death at the prospect of meeting his family. There was to be a family reunion that Sunday afternoon, so she would find herself in the midst of the entire Williamson clan. The prospect was terrifying.

A knock at the door interrupted her wanderings. Knowing it was Gladys, she merely snuggled more deeply into the chair and called for her to come in.

"I haven't heard a sound from this apartment in days," Gladys griped the moment her foot was across the threshold. You haven't snuck off and become a nun or something, have you?"

"Don't be ridiculous, Gladys. Sit down," Miriam told her.

"Well, I just figured something must have happened. Those gals take vows of silence, don't they?"

"That's monks, Gladys. What are you doing up so late?"

"Late? It's just 9:30. Don't tell me you're ready for bed?"

"See this robe? See these slippers? Yes, ma'am. I'm just finishing some reading, and I'm going to bed. My alarm goes off at 6 o'clock so I can get ready to go to work. You remember work, don't you, Gladys?"

"You are the original stick-in-the-mud," her friend complained.

"You bet; now if you'll find your way back from

whence you came, I'm going to sleep. Good night, Gladys."

"Wait just a minute, Miss High and Mighty. I've got a proposition for you." Gladys smiled, but her eyes smoldered as she stared at Miriam. The calculated quality of the look made Miriam feel like a prize animal on an auction block. The feeling unnerved her.

"I'm sure it can wait." Miriam replied in an attempt to distract her.

"It'll only take a minute, so listen." She dropped onto the couch and grabbed a pillow to hug as she spoke.

"I have a friend, the sweetest guy in the world, and he's going to be in town Saturday night a few weeks from now. Why don't you go out with him?'

"I don't think so, Gladys. I'm not big on blind dates. Besides, my children and I have planned some very busy days these last two weeks of school, and I would prefer to focus my time and attention on them."

"It's not such a big favor I'm asking. Charlie is one of my oldest friends. I've known him since we were kids. He's got a couple of days off, and he's coming to see me. I already had plans for Saturday night, so I thought you could keep him company. Please?"

"Gladys, I'm not interested in meeting anyone. I've been writing letters to someone who is away in school. He's the only man I want to get to know right now. You can change your plans for that night."

"No, I can't. This isn't an arranged marriage, Miriam. It's dinner. Surely you can unbend enough to entertain my friend for a couple of hours. I'll tell him it's all arranged, hmm?"

Jumping up from the sofa, Gladys hurried to the door before Miriam could blink.

"You're a peach, toots. I'll tell Charlie to pick you up at 6:30. School will be out for the year and you can kick up your heels to celebrate the summer, okay? Thanks."

"But Gladys, I didn't say . . ." Miriam called, but it was too late. The Phantom was gone.

"What has she gotten me into now?" Miriam huffed, exasperated. "That girl wears my patience thin. I think I may find a new boarding house when I come back in September. I love Mrs. Henson, and this apartment is comfortable, but I think I could live without Miss Betts as a neighbor." The idea appealed to her the more she considered it. Making preparations for bed, she thought about what kind of place she might find.

The last two weeks had indeed been hectic. The children had finished their final examinations with scores that pleased Miriam enormously. They had worked very hard, and she continually praised the learning and growing they had done. Beth Blackman seemed much happier these days. She opened up more in class, and she, Susan, and Estelle had become fast friends. The last day the children had showered Miriam with gifts and hugs and promises to visit when school commenced again in September.

Buck had barbecued what Miriam was certain was an entire side of beef, and she had celebrated the closing of the school year with the Buchanans in style. There had been baked potatoes, roasted corn on the cob, squash, beans, and homemade bread. Daniel and Annie churned strawberry ice cream to go with Miriam's chocolate cake. The table groaned with each new platter or bowl it welcomed. Annie had invited Mr. McAnaly and his wife, along with several other teachers and their spouses, and everyone joined in with the raucous fun.

They had divided into teams and gone on a scavenger hunt, looking for silly things like leftover potato salad from someone's refrigerator, a man's left cowboy boot, an unused bar of Dial soap, and a dill pickle. Miriam was nervous at first about walking up to a stranger's door and explaining such shenanigans, but everyone seemed to enjoy the fun, and the members of the winning team were each given a card of buttons from the local five and dime. Annie organized a three-legged race, a potato sack race, and a sing along. Miriam had never had such a rollicking good time. She thanked the Creator yet again for this job and these wonderful, caring people with whom she worked. Her first year as Miss Cahill had been a roller coaster ride fraught with danger and excitement, perilous dips and frightening turns, but love for her kids and the satisfaction of her calling kept her on track, and she knew she would bask in this joy for the entire summer.

Since time marched on in spite of her dread of her impending blind date, Miriam soon found herself contemplating her Saturday night with Charlie Carpenter. If there had been any way to cancel without seeming ungracious, she would have done so in a heartbeat. She had tried talking Gladys out of it on two other occasions, but Gladys brushed her off as if her opinions were of no consequence. Charlie would be a fun time for her, and she couldn't back out now anyway; the plans had been made. Resolving to make the best of it, she put on her game face and set about getting ready. After all, it was only one evening. What harm could come to her?

Miriam inspected her image in the full length mirror before her. The sage green dress she'd chosen was flattering to her figure without risking her modesty. The scoop neck and mother-of-pearl buttons suited her easy-going sense of style, and she added teardrop earrings and bone colored pumps to the ensemble. A knock on the door interrupted her final perusal. Hurrying to the living room, she swung it open to find Gladys on her threshold.

"My, my, don't you look prim!" Gladys remarked as she circled Miriam like a vulture searching for scraps. "You'll never interest him dressed like someone's schoolmarm."

"I don't look like a schoolmarm," Miriam protested. "This is one of my nicest dresses. What's wrong with it?"

"Charlie likes to let his hair down. How are you going to burn up the dance floor in that?" She waved her arm in Miriam's general direction like a queen dismissing her errant handmaiden.

"Maybe this wasn't such a good idea, Gladys. I know Charlie is supposed to be a great guy, but I don't want to go out with anyone else. I've told you about Sonny . . . " she began.

"Well, Sonny isn't here. I told you before, this isn't a marriage. Besides, he is a great guy," Gladys interrupted, "the best, and you should be grateful I set up this date!"

"I'm not grateful and you know it. You bullied me into this. That fact notwithstanding, I am who I am, and I'm comfortable in this dress. If Charlie thinks I'm stuffy and a bore I imagine the evening will end very early. I'm only doing this as a favor to you anyway."

"Yes, so you've said, a hundred times." Gladys

opened her mouth to continue, but the rat-a-tat-tat on the door stopped what Miriam knew was about to become a tirade. Grateful for the interruption, she sidestepped her friend and opened the door. Her smile faltered as she stared up into eyes the green of a crystal clear lagoon. His smile and raven black hair rendered her momentarily speechless. Charlie Carpenter was gorgeous.

"Miriam?" he asked. "How are you? I'm Charlie Carpenter."

She reached out to shake his offered hand, quickly regaining her equilibrium. It was foolish to behave this way, she scolded herself, even if his gray slacks and cotton shirt hugged his wide, well-muscled frame so well. This wasn't a date, and he wasn't Sonny. Still, she wished she had more experience when it came to casual dating. She wished she didn't feel quite so gawky and naive.

He stepped into the foyer and spotted Gladys. "Hey, Gladys. How are you, honey?" He casually embraced her and dropped a kiss on her cheek.

"Keeping busy, sweetie, keeping busy. I was just telling Miriam to have a good time tonight. You be sure she enjoys her evening, y' hear?" With a wink and a kiss idly blown in his direction, Gladys sauntered out the door.

"I'm ready, Charlie," Miriam spoke quietly as she returned from her bedroom with her purse and shawl. He held the door as she moved gracefully down the porch steps toward his black pick-up. He opened the passenger door and helped her step up into the cab of his Ford. The interior was spotless. There were no boots or rope in the floorboard, no gun rack in the rear window, no clutter or dust on the dash. It was cleaner than her apartment, Miriam ruefully admitted to herself.

"Your truck is certainly well-kept, Charlie. Did you clean it especially for this evening?"

"I keep my truck this clean all the time. One of my quirks, I guess." He smiled as he fired up the engine. "I hope you're hungry, Miriam. Murphy's is a plain little diner, but their food is popular for miles around."

"I've been looking forward to dinner at Murphy's all week. I've only eaten there one other time, but the meatloaf was better than any I've ever had."

In the 15 minute drive out to Murphy's, Charlie and Miriam settled into an easy camaraderie. He told her about growing up on his grandparents' farm after his mom and dad died when he was six. He loved the farm, he said, but his real love was horses. He had hired on at a cattle ranch in nearby Crosswinds the previous fall, and he believed he'd found what he was meant to do with his life. He talked about going to school with Gladys and what a good friend she'd been, especially in grade school. He'd been desperately lonely for his folks, clumsy and shy, and an easy target for every bully in town. "Gladys was fierce in her defense of me, even if she is two years younger. It still makes me laugh to remember how loyal she was. She's a great gal."

"I met Gladys when I moved into Mrs. Henson's boarding house. She helped me unpack and showed me around town. We haven't missed a Saturday afternoon movie in months. I've been lucky to have such a good friend," Miriam remarked, trying to believe it and not focus on her current irritation with the bossy Gladys Betts.

The truck rocked slightly as Charlie turned into Murphy's parking lot. Miriam enjoyed the feel of his hand at her elbow as they walked into the diner. Everything about this man pleased her, and she relaxed as her concerns about this evening disappeared in the face of such sincerity and open friendliness.

Dinner was a comfortable affair. The pork chops were served family style, and Miriam had seconds of the fried okra, sautéed squash, and black eyed peas.

"Gracious, I'm stuffed." She sighed, settling back into the green vinyl of the booth.

"Tastes like my grandmother's been cooking back there," Charlie remarked, grinning. "Ready for some cherry pie?"

"Oh, no. I couldn't eat another bite. But I'll sip my coffee and let my food settle if you'd like some dessert."

"Not this time, I guess. I'll pay the check, and we'll go."

As the two young people strolled out into the balmy evening, Charlie asked Miriam if she'd like to go for a drive before he took her home.

"If you like," she answered. Truthfully, she would have rather gone home, but she didn't want to appear rude to Gladys' friend.

He helped her onto the bench seat once again and pulled onto the highway. He wandered around the town square, pointing out the lighted dome of the courthouse and the stately pecan trees that graced its lawn. They drove past the high school with its stone wall and ancient oak trees. The night sky was filled with stars and a thumbnail moon glowing pale and misty in the deepening night. Miriam shivered a bit at the sight of the lunar 'smile' of a crescent moon; somehow those smiles seemed a bit malevolent to her. "Childish notions," she thought to herself. Charlie turned the corner at Grant but did not bear right as Miriam expected him to do.

"Charlie, you didn't turn onto Miller. This is the way out to the feed lot. I should be getting back."

"I just thought we'd find a quiet place to get to know one another better. Aren't we having a nice time becoming friends? Relax, Miriam. You're in good hands."

Miriam followed his advice with a few steadying breaths. Charlie had been a perfect gentleman all evening, so she felt somewhat silly at her nervousness now.

The Ford shuddered over a cattle guard as Charlie turned off Route 17 and into an abandoned pasture. He inched into the grass at the side of the rutted dirt road. The engine stilled, and the startling silence slowly gave way to familiar and comforting night sounds: the chorus of the crickets, the distant lowing of a cow, and the whisper of a summer breeze gently stirring the trees.

"Isn't this nice?" Charlie spoke softly. "I love to come out here from time to time with special friends, like you, Miriam. Lower your window so we can take advantage of this breeze. Tell me about your job."

"Well, I teach elementary school; you knew that. I taught fourth graders this past year, but I'm to be moved to third grade when school begins in September."

"What made you decide to become a teacher?"

"Circumstances, mostly. I helped take care of my brothers and sister, and then night school was all my mother could afford when I told her I wanted to go to college. My choices were limited, so becoming a teacher just seemed the natural decision."

"Do you like teaching school?"

"I love it. My children are sweet, and hungry to

learn. I use every opportunity I can to teach them about the world around them. When it rains I talk about the water cycle. When it's time to plant the crops, we talk about seeds and how they grow. We use harvest time to compute profits and costs so they can practice their addition and subtraction, and so on. I try to add a bit of whimsy whenever I can. I read them stories about dragons and knights and other fanciful notions," she explained animatedly. "I can't imagine doing anything else."

"I admire you, Miriam. It must be deeply satisfying to see your students succeed like that."

"It's very satisfying, but I'm sure your work is satisfying, too. If you're doing something you love, it must bring you great pleasure."

"I love to be outside every day, even if the saddle can make you bone weary and the cows try to go everywhere but where you're trying to herd them."

"You talk like you've seen my students! Following directions is a skill with which they constantly struggle."

"My grandfather wasn't too happy about my wanting to be a cowboy. He wanted to send my father to Baylor, but Dad and Mother eloped before Granddad had the chance to see his son get a college degree. So when I graduated, there was no question that I would attend Baylor."

"Did you like college?"

"I suppose. I enjoyed the learning, but I wanted more than anything else to be outdoors. I have my undergraduate degree, and I know Granddad hoped I'd go on to law school, but that kind of life wasn't for me. I'm much happier on a horse."

Charlie's smile died away to be replaced with a gaze so intense that Miriam found herself reluctant to look at him. He reached over to cover her hand with his own, and she pulled away.

"Charlie, this has been very nice, but I'm not comfortable being out here with you. It's so lonely. Please take me home."

"Miriam, honey, relax," he cajoled as he scooted across the seat to put his arm around her shoulders. "I like you. I want this to be a good time for both of us."

Miriam pushed herself away from his arm. "If you aren't going to take me home, then I'll walk back to town," she declared, reaching for the door handle. Charlie simply reached around her and closed the door.

"Come on now, don't be this way. Let's have a good time," he persuaded, reaching for the buttons on her dress. "You know," he mused, reaching up to stroke her hair back from her forehead, "you have the most gorgeous hair, so soft and silky. I like it very much." She slapped his hand repeatedly, but Charlie was relentless, his smile never wavering. Miriam hit him, demanding that he leave her alone.

"Charlie, stop. No! I don't want this. Let me go."

She managed to fumble behind her and slip the door handle up. As Charlie paused to unbutton his own shirt Miriam turned quickly and plunged out the door, stumbling as she ran toward the highway in her frantic attempt to get away.

"Miriam, come back here," Charlie called. "What are you doing? Honey, I'm not going to hurt you. Come back now, before you get into trouble."

Sobbing, Miriam ran faster. She could hear

Charlie's thudding footsteps growing closer, but the road was rutted and there was virtually no light coming from anywhere to illuminate her escape. Just as she reached the shallow ditch around the cattle guard, Charlie lunged and grabbed her arm. They both stumbled, falling together into the weeds. She fought, trying to pull away, begging him to let her go. Relentlessly he hauled her to her feet and dragged her back to the truck, and in spite of her kicks and screams she was powerless to break free from his grasp.

"I don't understand why you're making such a fuss, honey. This is unnecessary, you know."

"Charlie, please," she whispered, "don't do this, please. I just want to go home."

"Honey, honey," he crooned, "haven't we had a nice time together? I just want to show you what a special girl you are. Won't you let me do that?" As he spoke, he smoothed her hair back from her forehead, caressing her as gently as one might a small child. The entire thing seemed unreal, somehow. This soft-spoken, charming cowboy surely wasn't intent in his aim to force her into intimacy, yet Miriam could make no mistake that he was calmly undressing her. Gathering her wits once more, Miriam fought with every ounce of energy she could muster, hitting and slapping Charlie, kicking his legs and wishing desperately for something with which to hit him hard enough to knock him out. Damn him and his spotless truck! Charlie merely grasped her hands and held them above her head, raising his voice above her struggles to capture her attention.

"Miriam, stop." He kissed her cheek. "I'm going to take care of you," he soothed. His hand stroked her cheek as he kissed her chin, her eyes, her hair. "Calm down; you're wasting your time, anyway."

Finally realizing that there was nothing else she could do, Miriam squeezed her eyes tightly shut and softly wept as Charlie reached under her skirt. She heard her Daddy's voice in the images that flooded her mind, calling her as she ran toward the barn and away from the sight of her mother's bruised face and bleeding lips as she sat in the bedroom floor, sobbing from the angry beating she had once again endured.

'I'm going to find you, girl. Come on out now and make this easier on both of us.' Miriam strove to quiet her harsh gasping, knowing if he found her she'd find her own face bruised come morning. Sometimes he'd give up and go back to the house, and Miriam hated herself for hiding and leaving her mother to his tirades. They never knew what might set him off; sometimes he'd yell because dinner was cold, or maybe Will was crying too loudly from his crib. No one breathed easily until he'd slammed into the truck and roared off toward town, but then Mama could calm their sobs and make everything all right again.

" Charlie, stop," she begged once again. "Stop!" she screamed. Breaking his hold on her hands, she once again pushed at his chest with all her strength, but his weight as he moved on top of her was too great. She gasped for air as she whimpered. He lightly slapped her face and told her once again to hush. She turned as far away from him as she could and sobbed, helpless to stop him from brutalizing her. Again her thoughts drifted from what was being done to her. . .

'Miriam, you get in here and help your Mama with these children! I'm sick and tired of you running to your room when there's work to be done.'

'But, Daddy, I was just going to get my book to read after supper.'

'How many times have I told you to stop wasting your time with those useless stories?' he barked. 'They won't feed you or put clothes on you or get your chores done. You live in the real world, child, and you owe your time and energy to your family. I'll not have you daydreaming over some book!' Miriam watched helplessly as her father snatched the book from her hands and flung it viciously into the stove. 'You have time to see to your work now.'

Crying out in pain, just as she'd done that night when her father had burned her book, Miriam moaned and shrank away from Charlie, but he was relentless, mindless now of who was beneath him or of the damage he was inflicting. Miriam retreated from the horror of this reality once again. . .

Reeling from the sting of the repeated slaps, she staggered back against the kitchen counter and stared at the rage on her father's face, terrified as she watched him come at her again. From the door she heard the steel in her mother's voice as she told her father to stop hitting her. 'Stop it, Tom, or I'll get the shotgun and make you stop. You aren't going to take your anger at me out on her, or the other children, ever again, do you understand?' Stunned to hear her mother's ultimatum, Miriam watched him spin around and glare at her, his chest heaving. 'You dare to talk to me like that, woman? I am still your husband, and you will do as I say in my own house.'

'Miriam,' her mother addressed her calmly, never breaking eye contact with her father. 'Go on to your room, love. I'll take care of this now.'

Horrified of what might happen if she left, Miriam

nevertheless heeded her mother's gentle command and fled to her room. She leaped onto her bed and prayed as she'd never prayed before, asking God to keep her mama safe. She never knew what Mama said to Daddy, but that was the last time he ever raised his hand to any of them again.

The ugly memories assaulted her endlessly, scraping along her skin until she was raw with anger, sorrow, and an emotional pain just as acute as that Charlie was inflicting on her now. After he was done, he moved away to get dressed again, admonishing Miriam to button up. She had pushed herself into the door as far away from him as she could get in the confines of the pick-up, lost in her humiliation.

"Miriam, sugar, button up. I can't take you home looking like that." He smiled, but Miriam had withdrawn so far into her misery that she was unaware of Charlie's presence in the truck.

"Oh, for goodness' sake," he mumbled, and reached across the seat to restore her clothing himself. Humming, he drove her home. At the door to the apartment he placed a gentle kiss on her forehead, whispered a soft "Good night," and guided her through the door. The last sound of which she was even vaguely aware was Charlie's whistling as he trotted down the steps and climbed into the Ford to drive away.

Chapter 12

Stumbling in the dark of her apartment, Miriam faltered. Her legs were numb, wooden, and reluctant to obey her commands. Sitting on the edge of the bed, she smoothed her skirt, plucking at the buttons Charlie had done up crooked. She finger combed her tangles with hands that trembled, then lay back on the pillow, curling into as small a ball as she could manage, hugging herself in an iron grip and trying not to cry. She lay like that for several hours, watching the moon travel across the sky as the night waned, occasionally moaning and swallowing back the screams she knew weren't far away. The sky had just begun to lighten with the dawn when she finally surrendered to an exhausted sleep.

"Miriam? Are you awake?" Jerking awake at the sound of Gladys' voice, Miriam bolted from the pillow. "Miriam? Let me in; I want to hear about last night." The steady knock-knock-knock repeated itself three times before Gladys gave up and walked away. Miriam waited until she heard the footsteps fade, then limped into the bathroom in a manner reminiscent of Quasimodo attempting to navigate a waltz. She stared dully at her reflection for several moments, acknowledging the matted hair, streaked make-up, and scraped elbows before she looked down at her dress. The skirt was torn and filthy, her legs scratched and bloody. She winced at one particularly painful spot below her left knee; a pebble had been driven into her flesh, causing her shin to swell visibly. All at once she couldn't move fast enough. Frantically she shed her dress and the rest of her clothing, shoving everything, even her shoes, into the trash can. She gasped and heaved as the sobs overtook her. She turned the taps in the bathtub, running the water as hot as she dared. Just as she stepped into the tub she begin to retch. Vomiting into the toilet, she threw up over and over until her stomach was empty and she could taste the bile on the back of her tongue. Swallowing convulsively, she got into the tub and drew the shower curtain, releasing the spray to pour over her forcefully, relentlessly. The water flayed her skin as she held a washcloth to her mouth and screamed and screamed and screamed. She scrubbed herself twice, doing everything she could think of to wash off the humiliation and pain inflicted on her last night, then stood under the spray until it ran cold. She wrapped her hair in a towel and her battered body in her blue chenille bathrobe, collapsing into the overstuffed chair by her bed. Exhausted and afraid, she was unsure of what to do next. As had become her habit, Miriam began once again to speak to her mother.

"I need you today, Mama. Oh, Mama, I tried to get away. I fought back just like you used to with Daddy, but it didn't do me any good either. He seemed so nice, so friendly. I thought I could trust him, because he's Gladys' friend. Did she know what he had planned?" A new pain sliced through Miriam's heart as she fought back the idea that Gladys could have known about Charlie's intentions. Even Gladys couldn't have done this to her. Dear God, no, don't let Gladys have known. "Mama, it hurts. He hurt me. Help me."

Miriam sat unmoving for over an hour, crying softly and doing her best not to think of anything. The headache that had begun in the shower now pounded so hard she could feel her stomach begin to roil. She managed to walk into the kitchen long enough to swallow two aspirin with a glass of water, then she lay down in her darkened bedroom, begging God to let her drift off to sleep once again. "Don't think," she told herself in what was becoming a mantra. "Don't think, just don't think." The headache dulled somewhat, and Miriam felt the abyss of sleep overtake her. "Thank you, Lord," she sighed as she drifted off.

"Miriam?" The call came from far away as she turned over and tried to burrow further into her pillow.

"Go away, Gladys. I can't handle you right now." Instinctively Miriam knew it was her neighbor, back to hear the juicy tidbits from her Saturday night experience with Charlie. She groaned at the irony of that thought; juicy tidbits it would be, all right, if she cared enough to open the door.

"I know you're home, and I'm starting to get worried. If you don't open the door I'll just get Mrs. Henson to let me in. She's worried about you, too. Come on, Miriam, open the door," Gladys demanded as she relentlessly knocked. Knowing her headache would return with the insistent pounding, Miriam stood with reluctance and walked to the door.

"I'm fine, Gladys, but I'm tired and I don't want to talk to you right now. Can you be satisfied with that?"

"No! I want to hear about your date. Give!"

"We went to dinner at Murphy's, he took me for a drive, and then he brought me home. Now go away." She moved to close the door, but Gladys stuck out her sandaled foot with the hot pink painted toenails and blocked the way. Strolling into the apartment, she collapsed into Miriam's brocade covered chair and propped her feet on the coffee table.

"Charlie Carpenter takes you out for an evening of fun and entertainment, and all you can tell me is that you went to dinner and came home? Something is wrong with this picture. Didn't he like you? Were you rude to him or something? He's gorgeous, Miriam; I can't believe you could do anything to scare him away. Do you know what an opportunity this was for you?"

Miriam walked over to Gladys and slapped her hard across her left cheek. Gladys fell back, stunned at the idea that her friend could hit her at all, let alone with such force. "Get out."

"What do you mean? Mir. . ."

"Get out! Now! I don't want to hear another word about opportunity."

Gladys grabbed Miriam by the shoulders and shook her. "You tell me what is going on. Why did you slap me?"

"He raped me, Gladys! We had a lovely dinner, and I thought he was just exactly the nice guy you'd told me about. Then we went for a drive, and he forced me to have sex with him. I fought him off as long as I could, but he was stronger. I begged him to stop, but he wouldn't. Your good friend had a wonderful time, yes, ma'am. But I lost my virginity in the process. Is that a good enough story for you? Now get out." Crying softly once again, Miriam walked to the door and held it open for Gladys to leave. Instead of leaving as Miriam desperately hoped, Gladys shut the door and turned to face her friend once again.

"Well, I might have known you'd do this," she sneered. "What is the matter with you, Miriam? Surely you knew a guy like Charlie would expect the evening to end like that. Why did you put up a fuss? If you'd just gone along with him like you should have, you wouldn't be so upset now. It'll be a cold day in Brazil before I try to give you another chance to loosen up a little."

Miriam stared at Gladys in horror. It was true. She had known Charlie would expect to be intimate with her, and she had said nothing. Did Gladys not know her at all? How could she think Miriam wanted casual sex, like it was some sort of recreation to work off a big meal? Sickened in the face of such cold-blooded arrogance, Miriam grabbed Gladys' arm and, catching her off balance, opened the door and shoved her out, Gladys spluttering and protesting with every uneven step. Slamming the door in her face, Miriam ran back into her bedroom, sobbing. She threw herself down on her bed, but a moment later she sat up and stalked back into her bathroom. Staring at her reflection in the mirror, she snatched open the vanity drawer and grabbed a pair of scissors. With jerky, haphazard swipes she cut off her hair in great handfuls, relentlessly hacking until there was nothing left but spiky ends sticking out all over her head. "There," she thought to herself. "No man will ever admire my hair again."

She discarded her robe for slacks and a shapeless old shirt. Squaring her shoulders, she strode into the kitchen to heat up some soup and make plans. She may have been in circumstances beyond her control last night, but she would never be out of control of her life again. Rummaging in her catch-all drawer in the kitchen, she found a tablet and pencil. Dishing up the canned soup, she sipped and began writing a list.

Chapter 13

The bell hanging from the front door of the beauty shop made a cheerful jingling sound as Miriam walked in early Monday morning. She loved the smells that greeted her - the permanent solution, the shampoos and hair spray. There was something fun and exciting about the aromas of a beauty shop; to Miriam they meant new possibilities, new looks, new chances for someone to change her life in some way. That was very much on her mind this morning as she had arisen early to put her new plan into action. The first step was to do something with the hair she had so recklessly butchered the day before. A scarf covered up the damage as she'd walked into town, but she couldn't wear a scarf forever.

"I'll be right with you," a voice sang from the back room.

"It's only me, Tina," Miriam called back.

"Hey, Miriam, what are you doing here so early in the morning? Did we have an appointment that I forgot about?"

Looking at Tina McMillan made Miriam smile. She had curly black hair that hugged her plain, round face and tiny black framed glasses that sat on her nose by way of a beaded necklace attached to the ear tips. The glasses rode low, making her look much older than her 35 years.

Tina said they gave her dignity. What struck Miriam was Tina's insatiable love of life. Her dark brown eyes glowed with friendliness and a joie d'vive that was impossible to resist, and her rambuctiousness was just the balm Miriam's battered spirit needed this morning.

"We don't have an appointment, Tina, but I need your help. I'm afraid I had a fit yesterday and cut my hair. Can you style it into something for me, do you think?"

"You cut your hair? Whyever would you do such a thing, sweetie? Take off that scarf and let me have a look."

Miriam slowly removed her cover-up and jumped when Tina gasped aloud.

"It's terrible, I know. Can you fix it?"

"Of course I can fix it. You just come right over to this shampoo bowl and let me get started. We'll have you ship-shape in no time." Tina had seen the tears pool in Miriam's eyes as she walked across the room and wisely chose not to ask Miriam for any more details. That was another reason Miriam liked Tina so much. She knew when to keep quiet.

"We'll use this new gardenia scented shampoo I bought just last week. I couldn't resist it once I got a whiff. You'll love it, too." Tina adjusted the temperature of the water and hummed as she worked the lather into Miriam's scalp. "Have I told you about my Sam's latest idea," she began, chattering on about nothing in particular in order to help Miriam to relax a bit. "He thinks we should raise poodles. Have you ever heard the like? I don't much cotton to the idea. What would we do with a house full of prissy little dogs like poodles? In this part of the world we've got a better chance of making money raising hunting dogs. At least I could be sure we'd sell a few of those. But who would buy one of those yapping little fur balls? And then what would we do with them, stuck and no way to make any of our investment back? I told Sam he'd been out in the sun too long."

Scrubbing gently as she prattled, Tina spared a glance at Miriam's face and didn't like what she saw. Her complexion was pale, and the dark circles under her eyes made her look bruised. Her hands trembled in spite of the tight clench in which she held them. Concerned, Tina debated whether or not to ask what was at the heart of Miriam's hatchet job on her hair. It looked like she'd been at it with a pair of gardening shears.

"Did I tell you about Sam's mother?" Tina asked as she wrapped Miriam's shorn locks in a towel and moved her to a chair. "She's decided that Sam and I need to be eating better. That's mother-in-law talk for 'You don't know how to cook, hon.' She's bringing food over every two or three days, telling me it's just to help out because I'm so busy at the shop. Busy. Huh! I'm no busier than I've been the past 16 years I've been doing this, and Sam hasn't died of malnutrition yet. I told him to tell her to mind her own business, but he says he'll hurt her feelings if he tells her that. He hasn't worried that she's hurt my feelings about a thousand times in all these years we've been married. Treats me like I'm an imbecile or something - not cooking properly, working too much, not taking the kids to the Methodist church with her. I've been a member of the Blessed Souls Pentecostal Church since I was a girl, and if it's good enough for me it's good enough for my kids. Now -" she breathed deeply. "Let's see what we can do about this new hair style you've given yourself."

Removing the towel from Miriam's head, Tina picked up a comb and began smoothing through what was left of Miriam's silken locks. Once she'd sectioned it off with clips, Tina saw that she could style it into a cap of wavy curls that hugged her ears and brushed the collar of her blouse. If she were careful, she mused, she could just pull it off with what hair Miriam had left her to work with. Soothed by Tina's gentle fingers on her scalp, Miriam sighed deeply and worked to empty her mind of any thought. After a moment, she closed her eyes and gave herself over to Tina's ministrations.

Forty-five minutes later, Tina gave Miriam's hair one final pat and stepped back.

"Ok, doll, open your eyes and tell me what you think."

"Oh, I like it, Tina," Miriam told her as she turned one way and then another to look in the mirror. "It's fine," she replied, and then to her utter humiliation found herself weeping as she stared at her reflection.

"Miriam, sweetie, what's wrong?" Tina demanded as she grabbed her in a big hug. "What is it? What's got you so upset that you'd hack off your hair in the first place? Can't you tell me?"

Miriam clung to Tina for one desperate moment, then pulled away as she groped for her wallet. "How. . .how. . .how much?"

"I'm not worried about the money. Miriam, what's wrong?"

"Thanks, Tina. I've got to go." Miriam smiled at her friend through her tears, then turned and ran out into the street as Tina called after her. The pleas went unheeded. By the time Tina reached the sidewalk, Miriam was gone.

She hurried back to her apartment with her head down and her face averted from everyone who passed her. She couldn't face anyone else this morning. The world still functioned as it had before Charlie had raped her, but for her nothing was the same. Why was everyone so cheerful, so industrious? Didn't they know that the world had ended two days ago? Couldn't anyone else see it? The sky was blue with a light sprinkling of high, fluffy clouds, but Miriam felt as if she were caught up in a tornado, viciously spinning out of control around her. Racing up the stairs to her apartment, she closed the door behind her and collapsed into a chair, her heart beating furiously. She was clammy, drenched in sweat, and her face felt pale and bloodless. Sitting bonelessly in the chair, she found that while her heart had slowed to its normal pace, she was exhausted. There was no energy in her body, not one drop. Pulling her throw pillow from the small of her back, she hugged it to her chest and calmed herself. Her thoughts flew like debris in the wind, swirling in circles, hurtling past her, threatening to strike her and knock her to the ground. It took every bit of control she could muster in order to still the chaos, but she managed it. Before too long she felt her eyelids grow heavy, and giving in to the exhaustion, she slept.

Rousing from the awkwardness of sleeping doubled over in an easy chair, Miriam moved slowly and stretched her numbed limbs to work out the kinks. Walking into the kitchen, she was astonished to find the back yard filled with shadows. It was dusk; she had slept for most of the day. Funny, she still felt as exhausted as before. Emotionally, if not physically, she was no better off than she had been. Why had she believed she might be? "Damn him," she swore violently, and then was thoroughly ashamed of herself for uttering the thought. She had no appetite, but knew she must eat. There was a can of soup and some crackers in the pantry; they would do for now. As she warmed the soup, she thought of what she would face in the days to come. Groceries had to be bought, bills had to be paid, and she had to come up with some kind of letter to send to Lizzie. Why had she written her about her date with Charlie in the first place? Freezing in horror, Miriam realized that Lizzie would expect her to come home for several weeks this summer. Panic gripped her much as it had when Charlie's bulk had overwhelmed her in the cab of the truck two nights ago. She couldn't go home. Lizzie would take one look at her and know what had happened. What would Toby think of her, of what she had allowed to happen to herself? Try as she might, she couldn't place all of the blame on Charlie, or even Gladys. She knew she must have done something, said something, to make Charlie believe she would be willing to have sex with him. How could Toby ever respect her again once he knew that? He might try to keep her away from T.J. The idea of that had her knees buckling. Groaning in agony, she collapsed to the floor as the sobs engulfed her yet again. She huddled there until she smelled the soup beginning to burn, and grabbing the countertop for support, she pulled herself to her feet and wiped her eyes. Removing the pot from the burner, she poured it into the bowl she had waiting and carried it to the table. She stared into its depths for more than fifteen minutes before she could rouse herself enough to pick up the spoon and eat.

Remembering a conversation she had had with Annie a few weeks ago, Miriam knew how she could avoid a trip to Cedar Springs. She would find a summer job. School had only been out a week; there were several things she knew she might do. Determination gripped her again. Reaching for her list, she added, 'Find a job' to the other things printed on the tablet.

Knowing how difficult writing to Lizzie and Sonny was going to be, she decided to get that particular chore out of the way today. Reaching to smooth back her long mane of hair that no longer existed, she fumbled twice before she could remember what she'd done. She walked into the bathroom, hesitating slightly before looking at herself in the mirror. It wasn't too bad. She might grow to like it short, given time. Returning to the living room, she sat down to compose her letter to Sonny first.

Dear Sonny,

I have been considering your sweet invitation to meet your family this summer, but I'm afraid I won't be able to come. I've found it necessary to take a job here in Martinsville for the summer. Maybe we can get together in August before the term begins again for both of us. Please convey my regrets to your family. I'm sorry this didn't work out.
Affectionately,

Miriam

She read it through twice and decided it would do nicely. When she could muster up the courage she'd write a newsy letter to him, but cheerful banter wasn't possible right now. Come to think of it, she wasn't sure she'd be capable of cheerful words ever again. The letter to Lizzie was a bit trickier. She composed and discarded several before she decided that what she'd written would suffice. She addressed and stamped both envelopes and then walked them to the mailbox, deciding to send them as soon as possible before she changed her mind. Thinking ahead to her list of chores, she bought a paper from the newsstand and made her way back to her apartment. She was surprised at how winded she was. Her legs were trembling and her heart was pumping furiously. On the verge of panic, she sat on the sofa and put her head between her knees, panting and whispering the words of the 23rd Psalm. "The Lord is my shepherd, I shall not want . . ." After a few moments she felt herself calming and sat up once again.

"That's the way, Miriam. You can do this," she told herself. Opening the paper, she found the classifieds and scanned them for job opportunities. She saw ads for secretaries, cashiers at the market and the soda shop, and a Tupperware saleslady. Rejecting them all, she knew she'd feel better with a job away from the public, at least until she'd regained her equilibrium. Spotting what she hoped was the answer to her search, she circled a listing for a bookkeeper at Robinson Motors on the edge of town. Hiding away in an office balancing numbers suited her perfectly. She'd apply in person tomorrow morning.

Restless and edgy, she prowled the apartment for a few moments and then snatched the paper up once again. She had to get out of this boarding house. Getting away from Gladys was paramount. How could anyone deliberately do such a horrible thing? She had arranged that date with Charlie thinking that Miriam needed to 'loosen up.' Shuddering with the revulsion and anger once again, Miriam fought the sudden urge to walk over to Gladys' apartment and slap her face again just as

Daddy had once done to her. She wanted to hurt her, hurt Charlie, release her swirling emotions in a violent manner until she was physically spent and her mind emptied of rational thought. Maybe then she'd be able to settle down once again. She sat on the sofa and scanned the classifieds, this time for a more suitable apartment. There were two listings in her price range. She circled both of them, deciding to check both of them out tomorrow as well. Flipping on her radio, she scanned the dial until she found some quiet music. Sitting back to rest her head on the back of the plump cushions, she let the music seep into her battered body and slept.

Chapter 14

The next morning Miriam found herself more ready to seek out a job than she would have imagined yesterday. The thought of getting control of her life drove her in a way she had not expected. Up before dawn, she had taken her time getting dressed, experimenting with her new haircut and finding it a style she liked. Certainly the shorn locks took less time to dry and curl. She chose a navy blue shirtdress, belted at the waist. It was plain and, she hoped, businesslike. After a simple breakfast of cereal and juice, she walked across town to the car lot. The sky was a clear blue, with only a sprinkling of puffy, white clouds. The sun bore down, but a light breeze made the day bearable. Shoring up her confidence, she opened the double glass door to the showroom and walked in with her head up. A salesman descended on her in an instant.

"Good morning, miss; may I help you?"

"Yes, I'm here to apply for the bookkeeper's job," Miriam spoke softly but clearly.

"If you'll come with me, I can show you to Mr. Robinson's office. He's holding interviews this morning."

"Thank you," she answered, walking down the utilitarian hallway. Everything in this showroom was gray – the linoleum on the floor, the walls, even the frames on the doors and windows. She supposed that was to allow the brightly colored cars and trucks to stand out. While she understood the concept, she found it dreary.

"Here you go, miss." The older gentleman smiled. "Have a seat. Mr. Robinson's secretary will be with you shortly."

"Thank you for your help," she responded, almost smiling at the salesman. Somehow she couldn't quite manage a real grin, but he seemed satisfied and walked away.

Miriam barely had time to catch her breath when the door to the large office opened up and a woman of about 25 stepped out. She had hair the color of milk chocolate and deep violet eyes. Miriam had never seen such eyes. They were large and rimmed with thick, black lashes. Her nose was straight, her lips full and shapely in a lovely, delicate face. The dimples in her cheeks gave her a youthful quality, but she was dressed in a professional manner and seemed to know her business.

"May I help you?" she asked Miriam.

"I'm here about the bookkeeper's job," Miriam responded.

"If you would fill out this application, I'll let Dad . . . uh, Mr. Robinson, know you're here," she said with a smile.

Miriam completed the basic form and returned it to the secretary.

"Oh, thanks," she said as she accepted the clipboard. "You're only the third person to apply in over two weeks, and we're desperate to find someone. The other two couldn't add two and two, but you look like someone who could handle our system. If we don't find someone soon, he may make me do it, and I'm dreadful with anything mathematical. I can't even balance our checkbook! My husband gave up on me last year and realized he'd have to manage our budget himself."

"I taught Math to fourth graders last year; I feel certain I can manage your bookkeeping system," Miriam assured her.

"Great! I'll tell him you're ready to see him. By the way, I'm Melissa. It's nice to meet you."

"It's nice to meet you, too, Melissa."

Melissa disappeared into her father's office with the application, and after a few minutes the door opened and she asked Miriam to step inside. Mr. Robinson was a tall man, well over six feet, with graying blond hair and the same dimples and smile he'd passed on to his daughter. Miriam felt comfortable.

"Miss Cahill, I'm impressed with your application. But tell me, why are you giving up teaching to become a bookkeeper?"

'Oh, I'm not giving up teaching. I will return to my classroom in September, but I would like to find something with which to occupy my time this summer. It seemed a waste to sit in my apartment for three months. I could use the income a summer job would bring."

"Well, I had hoped to find someone to fill the position permanently, but I'm sure Melissa told you we are quite desperate to find someone now. Our quarterly statements are going to be late in another three weeks, and there's simply no one who has the time to add the bookkeeping duties to his regular job. Could you start tomorrow?"

"Yes, I could. I'm hoping to find an apartment closer to you than the one where I currently live. Could you make any recommendations?"

"Why, yes, I can. I know of a garage apartment for rent quite near here, and I know the woman who would be your landlady. I think you would find it most suitable." Writing down the address, he rose to escort Miriam to the door. "We'll expect you tomorrow morning at 8 o'clock. By the way, how far is the walk for you now?"

"Almost three miles," Miriam admitted.

"Why, that's much too far. Melissa, come here a minute, please."

Quicker than a flash Miriam found herself with a ride to and from work until she could move into a closer apartment. The idea of riding with Melissa appealed to her, and she blessed Heaven for watching out for her once again.

Leaving Robinson Motors, she paused to look at the address Mr. Robinson had given her. To her surprise, it was the same as one of the ads from the paper. His directions were easy to follow, and in just ten minutes she had found the simple frame house. A sign read "Room for Rent" beside a freshly painted dark green door, and the shutters and trim were a soothing camel brown. The porch was compact, but there were two chairs flanking the door, and ivy grew up and across the corner posts. Happy red geraniums waved in the breeze from a huge terra cotta pot. Miriam liked the neat, trim appearance of the house. She knocked on the door. An elderly voice called out to wait just a moment, then the door was opened by a tiny, white-haired lady in a black dress and black house slippers.

"May I help you, young woman?" she asked.

"I'm Miriam Cahill, and I'm here about the apartment for rent. Mr. Robinson said to tell you that he sent me over."

"Ronnie Robinson? How nice. Come in, dear, come in. I'm Mrs. Barnes, and I'm happy to know you."

Miriam entered the living room and was surprised to find it almost overwhelmed by an upright piano. There was an elegant sofa upholstered in a light floral print across from a stone fireplace, and two rocking chairs completed the grouping. The mantle and the bookshelf in the corner were filled with framed photographs of children. She was delighted.

"Sit down, child. Tell me, how do you know Ronnie?"

"He's my new boss. I'm the new bookkeeper at Robinson Motors, starting tomorrow. I live at Myrtle Henson's boarding house, but it's too far to walk from there every day. He recommended I look at your apartment."

"It's out back, above the garage. I can't climb those stairs any longer, but I'd be happy to have you look around and see if it suits you. It's not as big as Myrtle's, but it does have a kitchen. I'm certain it would meet your needs. I'm asking $25.00 a month."

"May I go take a look now?"

"Certainly. I'll get the key and show you the way."

Miriam walked through the dining room with her into her kitchen at the back of the house. There was a utilitarian looking table in the alcove and a freezer against the wall opposite the back door. Every available niche had a plant in it. They were hanging over the freezer, the table, and the sink. A plant stand in the corner held three lovely blooming plants, and the table boasted a huge curling ivy in a basket. Miriam looked beyond the kitchen into a bedroom, although it looked more like a greenhouse. There were pots of violets, cactus, aloe vera, mother-in-law tongue, and a host she couldn't identify. Looking through the screen door, she saw the garage at the back of the lot. This wasn't a wide parcel of land, but it extended almost across to the next block.

"Here you are, Miss Cahill. Please take your time."

Accepting the key, Miriam climbed the staircase to the apartment, not sure she liked the idea of being so high up. She supposed she could get used to it. Opening the door, she found herself in one large room. There was a dresser and bed in the corner of the room opposite the door, and room for her table and chairs at this end. The kitchen was separated by a waist-high dividing wall, the kitchen side filled with shelves. Two doors opened off the room, one the entryway into a decent sized closet and the other into a tiny bathroom. She would need to buy a chair and coffee table, along with a lamp and a few other necessities, but she liked this plain little space and the privacy it would afford her. Getting away from Gladys was so important to her that this apartment became perfect for her on the spot. Opening what she assumed was the pantry, she was startled to find another door beyond the wall of shelves. To her delight, it opened onto a wide staircase leading down into the garage. Miriam found these stairs to be much sturdier than those outside. She intended to ask Mrs. Barnes if she might use them.

Stepping into the kitchen, she found her new landlady setting out icy bottles of Coca Cola and a saucer of sliced banana bread. This was the first of many such occasions.

"Come sit down, my dear, and tell me what you

think," the elderly woman invited. Miriam found herself grateful for the woman's hospitality and gladly accepted the drink.

"I like it very much, and I'll take it."

"Splendid. When would you like to move in?

"This Saturday? Would that suit you?"

"Yes, I think so. That would give me time to ask Melissa to air it out for you. I'll wash up the linens."

"Oh, please don't go to any trouble on my account. I can do that myself if you could let me have the key."

"Nonsense, child. I'll make sure everything is ready for you." Seeing Miriam open her mouth to argue, she smiled and replied, "and I'll hear no more about it."

"Yes, ma'am," Miriam said. She sipped her cola and asked Mrs. Barnes about the pictures she'd seen in the front room.

"Those are my grandchildren and my students. I used to teach school a long time ago. I taught piano for years. That old upright belonged to my mother, and I can't bear to part with it. There's not room for it in this tiny house, but I manage. I still play from time to time, too. It soothes me in a way nothing else can."

"I wanted to take lessons when I was a girl, but there was never the extra money. I do love to listen to piano music."

"I'll teach you."

"Oh, I couldn't ask that of you," Miriam protested.

"You didn't ask; I offered. And it's settled. We'll begin next week after you get moved in, yes?"

"Yes, ma'am; thank you. I'm looking forward to learning how to play."

"I'll enjoy giving lessons again. It's been such a

long time since I advertised my services. So you see, my dear, you'll be doing me a favor."

"Oh, Mrs. Barnes," Miriam said, "would you mind if I used the staircase inside the garage to come and go? I'm a little unsure of myself on the outside stairs."

"I forgot to mention that those stairs are there. Surely you may use them. There is a door on the side of the garage that is never locked, and a light switch just to the right. Make yourself at home."

Miriam lingered over the banana bread, enjoying this woman and the simple beauty of this little kitchen. She felt peace steal into her soul, and knew it was because of Mrs. Barnes. Reluctantly she rose to carry her dishes to the sink, then bid Mrs. Barnes farewell.

Mrs. Barnes walked with her to the door and patted her arm as she sent her on her way. "I know we're going to get along quite well, Miss Cahill."

"I'm sure we will, and please, call me Miriam."

"Very well, then, you must call me Isabel. And by the way, Ronnie Robinson is my son-in-law. He married my Caroline. You couldn't be working for a nicer fella. See you Saturday."

Miriam walked with a lighter step back to her apartment. She had just four days to get packed up and moved out of Myrtle's boardinghouse. Hating to give her landlady the news, she decided to get it over with rather than dread it for days. She found Mrs. Henson on the front porch, rocking and fanning herself with a towel.

"Hello, Mrs. Henson," she said as she ascended the steps.

"Hello, Miriam, dear. How are you enjoying your summer?"

"It's been strange not having to get up at 6 o'clock

every morning, but I'm afraid I'm going to soon grow to love it. Mrs. Henson, may I speak to you about something?"

"Certainly. Sit down, please. My, hasn't it turned hot?"

"Yes, it has. Mrs. Henson, I can't live here with Gladys Betts as my neighbor any longer."

Myrtle responded with a nod of her head. "I'm afraid I understand only too well. She takes some getting used to. Still, I had hoped you and she might get along well enough that you could teach her how to be more of a lady." Shaking her head, she said, "Well, I'll be sorry to lose you, Miriam. Is there anything in particular you'd like to tell me?"

"No, ma'am. I just find her rude and manipulative. She never respects my privacy, and she tries to manage my life. Before you rent the apartment again, you might put a lock on the front door. Gladys walks in whenever she wishes."

"Oh, dear, I am sorry to hear this. When are you thinking of moving out?"

"This Saturday. I'm paid up through May, and I'll give you the rent for the first two weeks of June before I leave. I'm sorry it didn't work out. I love that apartment, and you've been a very nice landlady. I simply have to get away from Gladys."

"I understand, Miriam. Come, I have some boxes in the storage shed out back. I'll help you get packed up if you like."

Miriam and Myrtle worked the rest of the afternoon on boxing up her few belongings. She was going to miss this place, particularly her favorite overstuffed chair. When most of her things had been packed, she stepped back and wiped the sweat from her brow.

"You were right, Mrs. Henson. It is hot today. I think that's all I can pack for the moment. The last of my things I'll load up Friday night. One of the girls at the car company will come get me Saturday morning, and I'll settle up with you then. I do appreciate your help. Can I fix us some lemonade?"

"Oh, no, dear. Thank you, but I've got work in the kitchen waiting for me."

"Mrs. Henson, would you please not mention this to Gladys? I'd rather avoid her questions if I could."

"Not a word, I promise." Patting Miriam's hand, the elderly woman made her way downstairs.

Miriam was ready when Melissa pulled up to the curb and honked the next morning. The car was a glistening maroon four-door sedan, with a roomy interior and every extra Miriam imagined one could find on a car. The chrome alone nearly blinded her.

"This is beautiful, Melissa. You must enjoy driving it," Miriam commented as she slid into the front seat.

"I do. Helps that your dad owns the dealership. He leases it to me at a reduced rate. Stephen and I could never afford anything this grand on what we make."

What does your husband do?"

"He works for the light company. He's a lineman. Says he'll never be happy working in an office cooped up when he can be outside in the fresh air and sunshine. I think there's too much sunshine around these parts come June, July, and August, but he loves it."

"I appreciate you picking me up like this. Oh, it

will only be through Friday, though. I'm moving this Saturday."

"I know," Melissa responded with a grin.

"How do you know?" Miriam asked, confused.

"Isabel told me when I stopped by yesterday afternoon."

"Isabel . . . you mean Mrs. Barnes? But, I don't .. . ohhhh," Miriam finally caught on. "She's your grandmother!"

"Yep! And delighted you're moving into her apartment. She told me about you yesterday and wants me to help her get the place ship-shape."

"You don't have to do that, Melissa," Miriam argued.

"Oh, yes I do. Isabel asked me to, and I'm not about to be disrespectful by refusing. But I did have an idea. It won't take me anytime to dust and sweep out the place Friday afternoon, and if you want to help, Isabel will fix us both supper."

"I'd like that very much. It's a deal." The girls grinned at one another and had a nice time getting acquainted on the short drive to the car lot.

Miriam had needed no time to understand the bookkeeping system Robinson Motors employed, and by lunchtime she was well on her way to making the job her own. She paused a moment over her tuna fish sandwich to think about getting away from Gladys and her horrible memories and what it was going to take to put the rape behind her. Concentrating on this job would give her plenty to think about so that she couldn't dwell on what had happened. The piano lessons would be another distraction for which she was very appreciative. You can do this, Miriam, she thought to herself for the hundredth time.

Saturday morning found Miriam up and ready to go before seven o'clock. She had made arrangements for Melissa to be there by 7:30, hoping Gladys would still be in bed and miss the entire thing. When she heard the door open without a knock, she knew it was not to be.

"Hey, Mir," Gladys called out. "How about . . .say, what's this?" She indicated the packing boxes with a wave of her hand.

"If you couldn't figure it out for yourself, I'm moving," Miriam responded with just a hint of ice in her voice.

"I knew you might still be miffed at me about Charlie, so I've laid low for the past week. Aren't you over that yet? You don't have to get in a huff and move out."

"Miffed? Is that what you expected? I was humiliated and brutalized, and then I find out you had a hand in setting up the whole thing, and you thought I'd be miffed? You stupid cow. Get out."

"You can't talk to me like that, missy," Gladys snarled, her eyes narrowing to slits.

"I'll talk to you any way I please," Miriam shot back, picking up a pair of scissors from the countertop. Advancing on Gladys, she repeated, "Get out, now, and if I were you I'd make myself scarce for the next hour or so. You don't want to be anywhere near me right now, lady."

Seeing the fire in Miriam's eyes, Gladys turned and bolted for the door. "Good riddance, then Miss High and Mighty. I tried my best, but if you're going to be a prude and a grouch, I'll be happy to leave you alone." The door slammed as Miriam lunged for it.

She leaned her head on the smooth wood. The scissors clattered to the floor as the sobs began from the very pit of her stomach and overtook her. Crying out, she stumbled into the kitchen and grabbed the first thing she could find – the glass she'd used for her orange juice. She hurled it against the wall and heard it shatter. Reaching into the cabinets, she grabbed every glass, every bowl, every plate she could find and threw them against the wall. The shards flew everywhere, catching the sunlight from the kitchen window and showering down in a rainbow of light.

"That's for you, Gladys, and you, Charlie. I hate you both for what you did to me!" she cried out, sobbing and gasping as her shoulders heaved and her eyes blurred over and over with the torrent of tears. She stood there for quite a while, and then realized with a start that Melissa would be there any minute. Running to the bathroom, she splashed cold water on her face and re-applied powder to try and cover the ravages. It didn't help much, but any little bit she could do to restore her equilibrium would make her feel better.

Walking back into the kitchen, she regretted what she had done for Mrs. Henson's sake alone, so she took a loose sheet of paper from the supply in the secretary and composed a short note.

Dear Mrs. Henson,

I am sorry for the mess I made in the kitchen. I have enclosed $20.00 to replace the broken items. If there is any justice in the world, you'll make Gladys clean it up. Sincerely,

Miriam

She stood the note up against the vase of flowers on the coffee table and gathered up her things as she heard Melissa's knock at the door.

"Well, Mama, I'm making yet another start in my life. I hope I can put what Charlie did to me behind me for good. I know I can't live like this any longer, haunted and afraid and feeling like my life is over. Wish me luck."

Chapter 15

Miriam found, much to her surprise, that she liked the bookkeeping job. She was indeed in a tiny office away from most of the people employed by Mr. Robinson, and the work was time consuming without being too complicated. The routine comforted, and Melissa was an easy-going companion. They ate lunch together most days, and Miriam was content to let Melissa do all the talking. She had an endless store of anecdotes about her family and her husband, all of which amused Miriam and kept her mind from wandering to what she was desperately trying to forget.

Isabel Barnes was a Godsend. She had been true to her promise to teach Miriam the piano, and the exercises were such fun that Miriam practiced every night in Isabel's tiny living room. The little house was warm and peaceful, and Isabel had a caring teaching style that soothed the hurting places in Miriam's spirit. Unable to see the sadness that she bore so clearly on her own face, Isabel recognized it nonetheless and determined to reach out to this young woman. She hoped that one day soon Miriam might share the reason for her sadness and be able to overcome it. She had become fond of Miriam very quickly and soon realized that the loneliness that often plagued her was a thing of the past. Perhaps these two souls had needed one another, and God had seen fit to bring them together. Whatever the reason for Miriam's presence in Isabel's life, they were happy with one another, and their days were full once again.

Isabel couldn't hear the cries and moans that filled Miriam's nights as she re-lived the rape in her dreams over and over, but she noticed the light that Miriam left burning all night in the apartment. She woke up gasping and drenched in sweat, the darkness disorienting and terrifying. Having that little measure of comfort was the only way she could even hope to sleep.

Before Miriam could blink three weeks had gone by. The dark circles were worse than ever, and she grew more exhausted as the nightmares worsened. Her hair grew limp and dull, and the bruising around her eyes returned with a vengeance. Her step was plodding, her responses listless, and concentrating was a Herculean effort. One evening, in spite of her valiant efforts not to do so, she nodded off while playing the simple piece Isabel had given her. Concerned with her fatigue, and the deep shadows around her eyes, Isabel decided to finally speak up.

"Miriam, dear, wake up." Shaking her gently, she repeated her request. "Miriam, dear, wake up."

Jerking her head up, Miriam felt herself blushing in embarrassment at what she'd done.

"Oh, Isabel, I'm sorry. I guess I didn't sleep well last night."

"Miriam, you haven't slept well any night you've been here. I've seen the light you leave burning, and I've seen the sadness on your face. Can't you tell me what plagues you? I'd like to help."

Feeling the tears begin to drop onto her cheeks, Miriam turned her face away and helpless to regain control of her emotions. "I'm fine, Isabel, just tired," she insisted.

"Hogwash, child. Whatever has you upset is eating you alive. Look at you – you're skin and bones. I'm sure you're not eating properly. You drag yourself to work every day and drag yourself home. Why, you walk as if each step is of such colossal effort that it may be your last. You must find a way to get over whatever is tormenting you."

Turning Miriam around to face her, Isabel counseled gently, "I love you, child. Your coming here has been a great blessing to me. You have taken away my loneliness and given this old piano new life. Let me help you, please. What's wrong?"

Collapsing in Isabel's arms, Miriam clutched at her blouse and sobbed and sobbed. Isabel stroked her hair and murmured comforting words to her as she let her cry it out. Gradually Miriam regained her composure, and the story unfolded. At first the words were jumbled and broken, interwoven with tears and labored breathing, but the more Isabel sat quietly and listened, the easier it was for Miriam to recall what had been done to her. "So you see," she finished, "I had to make a new beginning, away from Gladys. I've got to put this behind me, but I don't seem to be doing such a good job of it so far."

"My precious child, no one can just put something that horrible behind them. You've been holding this bottled inside you for weeks, hurting and hating. Emotions this strong must be dealt with openly, or they'll fester and consume you."

"I never thought of it that way, but I do feel like I'm being eaten alive from the inside out. I haven't had the courage to tell anyone else what happened. I kept hoping that if I ignored it, I could just forget it ever happened. I can't bear to let my family know about it. What if they blame me for what Charlie did to me? I couldn't survive that," she whispered, her eyes sunken and afraid.

"I think you need to talk about it. That young man who did this to you is the only one who bears any blame, Miriam. You told me your neighbor made these arrangements with just such an outcome in mind. And I don't believe for one moment that you gave that despicable young man any ideas. He knew what he'd planned to do long before he ever picked you up for dinner."

"Do you think my family will understand, Isabel?" Miriam questioned.

"Tell me about your family," she invited.

Miriam told her about Lizzie and her brothers, about their parents and losing her mother eighteen months ago. She shared a bit about what it was like growing up and how Tom had treated them.

"My dear, I can hear the love in your voice when you speak of your mama and those other children. From what you've said, they love you just as much. You've endured more than God ever intended a child to bear. I think you're doing them a disservice by not sharing this with them. Haven't they helped you with your grief from the death of your mother?"

"Yes; I couldn't have moved out on my own or made a new life for myself without their support. They mean everything to me."

"Then trust them with this. They'll help you to heal from this loss as well," Isabel assured her.

Holding her arms open, Isabel smiled and said, "Come here. I find I have need of another hug."

Miriam laid her head on Isabel's shoulder and listened to her speak quiet words of reassurance for the rest of the evening.

The following Saturday Miriam awoke with more energy than she'd had in over a month. She had slept better since she'd shared her agony with Isabel, and they had talked several times about Charlie and what had happened. Miriam was able to speak freely about him and the hatred she felt simmering in her for what he'd done to her. She spoke about Gladys' betrayal and how foolish she felt about trusting a stranger as she had. Each time she and Isabel talked the wise grandmother reassured Miriam a little bit more, and the band around her chest that had been choking her for weeks loosened. It was a beginning.

This morning she was going to buy a few items for her apartment. She wanted a new chair, an end table and lamp, and a bookshelf for her keepsakes. Her paychecks from Taylor would continue throughout the summer, and with the salary from Robinson's she had the extra she needed to fix up the little room a bit.

Wandering the square, she found some lovely dishes in an antique shop and some ready-made curtains in a yellow stripe that was dotted with tiny, bright red cherries. They cheered her, and she decided they would look perfect in her kitchen window.

She debated over three chairs that were in her budget before deciding to take the tufted one in burgundy. The lamp and end table were easy to choose, and the furniture store promised to deliver them Wednesday afternoon. Pleased with what she had found, and feeling more like herself, she treated herself to lunch at Lucille's. The roast beef was almost as good as Lizzie's, and the lemon pie was more tart than sweet, just as she preferred. The walk back to the apartment was pleasant, and she was able to get indoors before the summer heat to which all Texans were accustomed overtook her. She decided she even felt like reading a book, something on which she had not been able to focus since Charlie had dropped her off at her front door.

Monday afternoon she found two letters in the mail, neither of which she was ready to open. Picking them up, she walked to Isabel's kitchen door and called to her friend, asking if she could come in.

"Miriam, dear? Come in this house. I was just watering my plants. Sit right down at that table and I'll slice us some banana bread. Would you like a Coke float?" Spotting the letters in Miriam's hand, she set down the watering can and walked to the girl hesitating in the doorway.

"I worried about you when I saw those letters. Would you like to sit down here and read them with me?"

"Could I?" Miriam walked to the table on legs that quivered and opened the one from Lizzie first.

"Here goes," she said with a tremor in her voice.

"'Dear Mim,

We got your letter that you weren't coming home for the summer, and we wondered if there might be something wrong, but Toby said I should trust you and wait for more news. Honey, it's been weeks and we haven't heard a word. I'm worried sick about you! Why

haven't you written? What is going on, Miriam? If you don't write me back with some kind of explanation by the end of next week, I'm going to be on the next bus to Martinsville, and there's nothing Toby or Dr. Meyer will be able to say to stop me.
I love you always,
Lizzie'

"I was afraid of this," Miriam said. "She shouldn't be riding the bus anywhere right now. She's going to have that baby in just a couple of months. What should I do?"

"Why don't you read the other letter first?"

"It's from Sonny. I'm even more afraid to read it. I haven't written him in weeks, either, since I told him I couldn't meet his family in June like he'd asked."

"Don't imagine the worst. See what he has to say," Isabel urged, patting Miriam's hand.

"Dear Miriam,
I was sorry to receive word that you couldn't go with me to meet my family, but I'm more concerned that I haven't heard from you since then. Is everything okay? Have you been ill? I've been in prayer for you all these weeks. My spirit has been troubled for you. Can't you let me know that you're all right? I'm anxiously awaiting some kind of word.
Affectionately,

Sonny"

"And who is Sonny?" Isabel asked with a knowing smile on her wizened face.

Miriam told her about meeting Sonny and the corresponding they had done since Christmas.

"This proves my point, child. They are worried sick and deserve some word from you. I want you to consider going to see your family this upcoming weekend. You could ride the bus to Cedar Springs on Friday evening. Ronnie would let you go early if you asked. I think you need to share this with your family." At the look of stark fear on Miriam's face, she amended her advice. "At least tell Lizzie. See what kind of reaction you receive from her, yes?"

"Oh, Isabel, I don't know . . ."

"How did you feel after you told me, hmm? You said yourself you felt better. Remember what I told you? You can't let this fester and eat away at you. The more light you open this up to, the faster the wound can heal. Go see Lizzie. You've got to tell her something. I'm quite sure you wouldn't feel comfortable sharing this in a letter, and if you choose to write a letter, what are you going to say? You know your sister better than I do; would she be appeased with anything less than the truth?"

"No, no, she wouldn't. Okay, Isabel, I'll think about buying a bus ticket." She smiled as tears pooled in her eyes. "I love you, Isabel. I don't know what I'd have done if I hadn't found you waiting for me here."

Gathering her close, Isabel said, "I love you too, child. You were an answer to my prayers, as well. Now, how about that coke float?"

Miriam had decided by Wednesday that she had to go home. Lizzie deserved the truth, and facing her would only get more difficult the longer she waited. On

Thursday she bought her bus ticket, and on Friday afternoon she packed for the weekend. Walking to the bus station, she almost changed her mind, but Isabel's words propelled her into the seat waiting for her in the rumbling conveyance. She had the entire trip to think of how she would tell Lizzie, but the words wouldn't come together. Walking from the bus stop to the house was an endless agony. She felt like a condemned prisoner being led to the hangman' noose. By the time she had reached Lizzie's front porch, her hands were like ice. Setting her suitcase down with a thump, she knocked on the door.

Mary Elizabeth's astonished face greeted her as the door swung open. "Mim!" Her sister grabbed her in a fierce embrace, made all the more impressive by the inches she had added to her middle since Miriam had last hugged her in December.

"My, you are pregnant, aren't you, little sister?" Miriam smiled.

"Never mind that. Come in this house. Why didn't you let us know you were coming? Why haven't you written? Don't you know I've been worried sick? Sit down and let me fix you some iced tea. Are you all right? Have you been ill? What have you done to your hair?"

"She might answer one of those questions you're hurling at her if you'd let her breathe, honey," Toby gently scolded from the doorway. "Miriam," he said as he moved to embrace her, "you've had my household in a dither for weeks." Looking at her face, he saw the sadness, and the fear, and smiled. "You're home now, and we'll deal with it, won't we? Why don't you go on into the kitchen and spend some time with Lizzie. I'll sit with T.J. for a spell. By the way," he added as he grinned, "I like your hair."

The tears spilled over as she saw the compassion in his face. "Thanks, Toby," she whispered.

"Go on with you," he teased as he reached up to wipe away the errant tear that was making its way down her cheek.

She walked into the kitchen to find Mary Elizabeth bustling to pour ice and tea into three glasses.

"Lizzie, Toby is with T.J. He doesn't want any tea right now. Could you just sit down for a minute? I've something I need to tell you, and your rushing around is making me nervous."

Turning to smile at Miriam, the words she was about to utter died the instant she saw the expression on her sister's face. Sitting down with a thump, she asked, "What is wrong? Why are you crying? What have you not told me, Mim? I need to know."

"Yes, I know you do. I should have told you this weeks ago, but I thought that I could ignore it and it would go away."

"Thought what would go away?"

"You're going to need to let me say this in my own way, Lizzie, or I'll never say it at all. Could you just hold my hand and let me do that?"

"Of course. I'll try to behave."

"I moved out of Mrs. Henson's boarding house in June. I'm living with a dear lady named Isabel Barnes now. She convinced me that I needed to come home and speak to you about what happened." Steadying herself, she began her story. "Two weeks before school was out Gladys came over. She had a favor she wanted to ask of me . . . ." By the end of the tale, the tears were pouring freely down Mary Elizabeth's face.

"Oh, Mim, why didn't you tell us? Why did you

try to hide what that monster did to you?"

"I was afraid, Lizzie. I convinced myself that I must have done something to lead Charlie on. I thought somehow it was partly my fault, and I was afraid you and Toby might blame me in some way."

"Oh, no, Mim, none of this was your fault. Don't ever think such a thing. Oh, honey, I'm so sorry you've had to go through this by yourself. I'm so sorry," she repeated as she moved her chair next to Miram's. Reaching out, she hugged Miriam tightly as they both sobbed.

Half an hour later the much calmer twosome were sipping iced tea and catching up with one another's lives.

"So you like living with Mrs. Barnes?" Mary Elizabeth asked Miriam.

"Very much. She's been such a support to me these last few weeks. There's not much of her. She's no taller than my shoulder, and I'll bet on her best day she wouldn't tip the scales at more than 90 pounds, but there's a core of steel in her. She doesn't mince any words, ever, but there's such wisdom and concern in what she says that you can forgive her bluntness. She's teaching me to play the piano."

"No kidding." Lizzie smiled to her sister. "I've always wanted to learn to play. Sitting at a piano softly performing the music of Mozart of Chopin has been one of my dreams. Well, maybe someday." Shaking off her idle musings, she asked, "Are you any good?"

"I'm fair. I've not learned enough to know if I have any innate talent for it. Playing the exercises is fun, and I've been practicing every night. It is a comfort to me, and it kept my mind off Charlie and that night. At least I thought it did."

"Your landlady was right; you can't keep this bottled up inside of you. I'm proud of you for breaking all those glasses and dishes at Mrs. Henson's."

"You're what? Have you lost your mind?"

"No, I haven't.   You needed some kind of emotional outlet, and I think breaking all that glass was healthy. You didn't hurt yourself, or Gladys, although she deserved it, and you didn't do anything illegal. The way you described your feelings, it seems to me it could have been much worse."

Snorting with laughter, Miriam responded, "I guess you're right. I hope Mrs. Henson made Gladys clean up every sliver of it, too."

"You know, Mim, I could almost feel sorry for Gladys," Mary Elizabeth said.

"How could you feel sorry for Gladys?" Miriam asked, astonished.

"Anyone who views casual sex the way she does can't possibly be virtuous still. She's given herself to someone, maybe several someones, and she still doesn't seem happy with herself. You said so in one of your letters. I think she's looking for something that her life is missing, some happiness, some fulfillment. If she's doing that by seeking out relationships with men, she's going to wind up miserable. No one finds true contentment that way."

"She hates her job, and there's a restlessness in her I noticed from the beginning. You're right about that. I'm going to have to put some time and distance between us before I can feel sorry for her, though. I'm still too angry about her role in what happened that night."

"I can understand that. I'm glad you're away from her. I'd like to have a few minutes with her myself." The two sat quietly for a few moments, sipping their drinks, before Mary Elizabeth asked, "Do you like being a bookkeeper?"

"It's fine as long as I know it's temporary. I'm in a room by myself with no one to bother me, particularly any men, and the monotony appeals to me right now. I'm going to try to look forward to going back to school in September, although I'm not ready to think about it now."

"Have you thought about quitting your job in Martinsville and coming home?"

"Sure, I've thought about it. I've wanted to run in a hundred different directions in the past five weeks, but I'm not going to quit my job. That would mean that Charlie has more hold over my life than I'm willing to give him. I've gotten away from Gladys, so I'm reasonably certain that I'll never run into Charlie again. I don't want to leave Annie and Mr. McAnaly and the professional way the school is administered. I'd like to think I've got enough of Mama's courage to face down my demons and come out a winner."

"I have faith in you, kiddo," Mary Elizabeth asserted as she squeezed Miriam's hand. "I've got something to ask you, speaking of courage."

"What's on your mind?"

"I'd like your permission to tell Toby what has happened to you. And I think you should tell Will and Seth."

Miriam said, "I understand why you'd like to tell Toby. He knows something has been wrong. But why do Will and Seth have to know?"

"Do you think they don't know that something has been wrong? Seth's last letter wanted to know if I knew why you hadn't written or come back to Cedar Springs this summer. Will has hounded me ever since he got back from school. They both know something has happened to you, and they're worried, too. Mim, haven't we been there for one another when times with Daddy were particularly difficult? Haven't we supported one another and helped each other sort out problems and face unhappiness together?"

"Yes, we have. Oh, I know you're right. It was just so hard admitting it to you. How am I going to tell Will and Seth?"

"I'll be holding your hand the entire time. You can do this, Mim. Mrs. Barnes was right. You can't hold all this inside you. It needs the light of day. You'd become bitter and unhappy and let this assume too large a place in your life if you never told anyone. You said yourself you don't want Charlie to hold sway over your life. Well, you break those bonds a little bit more each time you let someone else know what you've endured. Toby and Seth and Will need to be able to help you through this, too. They love you."

"I love all of you, too, Lizzie. I've known I had your love and support. Okay," she said, squaring her shoulders, "I guess there's no time like the present. Let's go tell Toby.

Miriam didn't stumble over the words quite as much when she told her story to Toby. Maybe Lizzie and Isabel were right. The power of the rape was lessened the more she shared her story. She hoped that was the case. Her insides were like jelly once again as she wrapped it up, but she had held tightly to Lizzie's hand during the telling, and Toby sat quietly listening without interrupting. She saw his jaw clench several times as she shared just how relentlessly Charlie had pursued her each time she'd run away and how brutal the attack had been. When she was done, he sat for a few moments in utter stillness. The ticking of the clock sounded like hammer blows in the quietness of the room. He rose from his chair and walked to Miriam. Reaching for her hand, he helped her stand to her feet and then he wrapped her up in his arms and hugged her tightly while his breathing became labored and he struggled with his anger. Miriam could feel how tense he was, but his arms were gentle as he held her. Finally, he pulled back, and she could see the sheen of tears in his eyes.

"Miriam, you know I've loved you ever since we were kids playing together. When Lizzie and I married, it didn't seem strange to count you as another of my sisters. I've felt like that for as long as I've known you."

"I know, Toby. I've loved you as I've loved Will and Seth. You're my big brother," she replied.

"Well, as your brother, I'd like to ask your permission to find this sorry excuse for a human and thoroughly kick his sorry backside," he said through clenched teeth.

Lizzie gasped. "Toby, honey, you aren't serious!"

"I'm very serious, Mary Elizabeth. He's done to Miriam what no man has a right to do, ever. He deserves to pay for it, and I'd like to be the one to deliver the bill."

Miriam smiled sadly. "Oh, Toby, I appreciate your outrage. I've wanted to kick his backside a few times myself. But I don't want you to do that. It won't change what he's already done to me, and I don't want our responses to be out of hatred. We're better than that, aren't we?"

"I'm not so sure I'm better than that," Toby argued. "I want to loosen a few of his teeth; I can't help that I feel that way. But for your sake I'll sleep on it tonight and see if I can't feel a little less murderous in the morning." Taking her shoulders in a firm grasp, he looked intently into her face and asked, "Are you okay, honey? Has sharing this with us been too much for you?"

"No, of course not. I was foolish not to have come running back here in the first place."

"No, you weren't. You dealt with it in the only way that made sense to you at the time. I'm proud of you for taking back your life when many women would have done something more self-destructive. I'm very glad the only thing you went after was your hair," he chuckled, ruffling the short curls. "But in the future, if you find you need us, could you please take pity on your poor brother-in-law and just come running at the start? Lizzie hasn't been herself since you wrote that you weren't coming home. I'm sure junior there is going to be born with a twitch."

"He is not, you idiot," Lizzie insisted. "Do you think the two of you could stop hugging one another long enough to help me off this couch? My center of gravity has shifted recently."

"Hold on, sweetie, I've got you," Toby said as he held out his hands to give her a boost. "I think we're ready for bed. Emotional exhaustion is worse than working hard all day. Miriam, I'm glad you're home. We're here for you, okay?"

"Okay, Toby, and thank you again."

"Oh, hey, he just kicked." Mary Elizabeth grinned at them. "Mim, give me your hand. Can you feel that?"

"Can I feel it? I'm surprised you're not turning somersaults in response to those kicks. That's incredible. And by the way, that's a girl in there. She's got a lot of her grandmother Christine in her."

Another ten minutes of hugs and reassurances and the three of them were happy to make their way to their bedrooms. Miriam was exhausted after sharing what she'd held locked inside for so long. She knew it had been hard for Toby and Lizzie to hear it, but she was glad, nevertheless, to be home. She could actually believe that she was going to survive. Up until recently, she'd not been so sure.

Toby drove out to the farm the next morning after he dropped T.J. off at his mother's house and told Will that Miriam had come home. He invited him to come over for lunch and promised that she was okay. Will assured him that he'd be there; the anxiety that had dogged him about Miriam was a nagging little itch at the base of his neck that he couldn't dispel. He'd tried everything he could think of to reassure himself, but he knew the only way he'd be satisfied would be to see his sister for himself.

The knock at the door at 12:15 was so abrupt that Miriam jumped, even though she had been expecting Will for the last half hour. He opened his mouth to speak when he looked up and saw her hair.

"Miriam, what did you do to your hair? Why did you cut it off?"

"I'm happy to see you, too, little brother," she replied with a tremulous smile.

Folding her in a tight embrace, he asked his own set of questions at rapid-fire pace, not giving her any more opportunity to respond than Mary Elizabeth had done.

"Must run in the family," Toby mused out loud as he walked up behind the two of them. "You're letting the heat in, you two," he scolded lightly.

"Oh, sorry," Will said as he released Miriam and closed the front door. "Where have you been for the past six weeks? Dealing with Dad has been bad enough without worrying about you, too," he fussed as he put his arm around her again. Now that she was here, he couldn't seem to let go of her. He'd imagined every kind of nightmare for too many days.

"Come sit on the couch, and I'll tell you where I've been. Toby, would you and Lizzie sit with us? I'll take some of that moral support you promised," Miriam said.

"Will, do you remember my neighbor, Gladys Betts? I told you about her when we were here at Christmas."

"Sure I remember her. You said she had taken some getting used to," he answered.

"Yes, that's right. Turns out I couldn't get used to her after all," Miriam responded.

"I don't understand. What does your neighbor have to do with why you didn't come home?" he asked, beginning to feel impatient and trying not to let it show.

"I'm sorry, Will. I'll get to the point," Miriam said. Slowly the story unfolded as it had for Lizzie and Toby the night before. Will sat silently throughout, but his face registered more stunned disbelief than the anger Toby had shown. When she finished, she said, "That's why I cut my hair. Charlie made such a point of admiring it that looking at it the next morning made me sick to my stomach. So I got a pair of scissors and hacked it off. If the girl at the beauty shop hadn't been so good with her scissors, my hair wouldn't even be presentable. I did a job on it."

"Thank God," Will murmured out as Miriam finished her story.

"I beg your pardon?" Miriam asked.

"What did you say?" Toby questioned.

"Will, how could you?" Lizzie said, horrified.

"No, no, you don't understand. I was sure that Miriam was about to tell me that she had cancer or something and was dying. I'm so grateful that it's not that, I guess I said what I did without thinking. I'm sorry, Mim." Running his hand through his hair, Will jumped up and paced the room. "How could your friend do this to you? Huh, some friend she turned out to be. And just what kind of a jerk is this guy? Do you know how I can find him? Toby, get the truck. We'll go find this creep who thinks he can treat women, my sister, that way, and explain the facts of life to him."

"No, Will, going after Charlie Carpenter isn't the answer," Miriam insisted.

"It's my answer, Mim. I want to kill this guy!"

"Toby felt the same way. I guess it's a pretty natural reaction," Lizzie added.

"Come on, Will," Toby interrupted. "Let's take a walk while Lizzie gets dinner on the table."

At first Toby thought Will was going to refuse, but he finally nodded and followed Toby out the door.

Chapter 16

"Whew! "I don't ever want those two to get mad at me," Miriam exclaimed, shaken. "I never saw either of them so worked up before."

"Nothing like this has ever happened to someone they loved before, Mim. Seth is going to respond the same way, and I have a feeling their reactions combined will be nothing compared to Sonny's."

"Sonny," Miriam groaned. "How am I going to tell Sonny?"

"The same way you told us," Lizzie answered as they walked to the kitchen.

"Lizzie, how can I tell this to Sonny? If our friendship is going where I think it's going, and I sure hope it is, won't he feel like I'm damaged goods or something when he finds out that Charlie had me first?"

"Don't be ridiculous! You were raped. That has nothing to do with a loving sexual relationship between a husband and wife. You aren't damaged goods, Mim. I know you might feel that way, but that's only because you've never had a physical relationship with anyone. That violent attack you endured was more about power and control. You said yourself you didn't want to be out of control of your life, right?"

"Well, yes," Miriam responded.

"Has your being raped made you want to go to bed with every man you see?"

"No!" Miriam said, horrified at the thought.

"You're right, it hasn't. That's because rape has nothing to do with sex. Get it?"

Mary Elizabeth saw for herself the realization dawn on her sister's face. "Yes, I get it. I just hope Sonny gets it," Miriam said softly.

"Trust me, Mim. If he cares about you at all, he'll get it. He's going to want to kill Charlie, too. You need to prepare yourself for his anger."

The front door opened and Miriam heard Will and Toby talking as they entered the kitchen. Will stepped around the table and engulfed Miriam in a bone-numbing hug.

"I love you, Mim. I love you so much. I'm sorry I got so angry at what happened to you that I forgot to tell you that."

"It's all right, Will. I understand how you felt, believe me. I've thought about slowly killing Charlie Carpenter a dozen different ways."

"I'd like to be the one to tell Seth, if you don't mind. I'll drive up to Ascension next Saturday and have supper with he and Polly and tell them both. You don't need to go through the story again."

"I'd appreciate that, little brother. It's not an easy story to tell."

Will reached for Miriam's hand. "I think you should get away for a few days. A change of scenery might help you to put this into perspective."

"How is going away going to help me with this?"

"I think you should take a trip. Go to San Antonio or Corpus Christi or somewhere you've never been before. You could clear your head. You'd be away from Martinsville and your memories. Just for a couple of days. I think it would do you good."

"Will may be right," Toby added. "You've been running this around in your head for weeks now, and that's understandable. God knows I couldn't have handled myself as well as you have. But you might like a change of scenery for a couple of days. Why don't you think about it?"

"I believe you need to get away for a few days. You've never been to the beach. Why not go down to Corpus Christi for the weekend? The ocean has a way of helping you to put things into perspective."

"Let's sit down, everyone. I've got dinner ready to dish up," Lizzie said.

"You know," Toby said thoughtfully. "This is the first time I can remember when Will didn't ask what we were having ahead of time."

Everyone laughed as the bowls were passed around.

"These aren't usual circumstances, Toby," Will said with a pink glow on his face. "Knock it off, will ya? I forgot to tell y'all before now," he added, "but something strange happened with Dad right after I got home in May."

"Stranger than usual? How could you tell?" Miriam asked with a wry note to her voice.

"This was about a letter I found on the kitchen table," Will said. "I'd gotten in late on a Thursday night after my last tests, so I went right to bed. Next morning I went into the kitchen to make some breakfast – y'all should have seen how he lives. There were dirty dishes everywhere and the trash bin had overflowed onto the floor. The faucet was dripping, and from the looks of things had been doing so for a long time. Empty bean cans were lined up on the cabinet, and there was stale bread piled up on the table. I started to clean up some, and I found a letter leaning against the salt shaker. Just as I picked it up, Dad roared from behind me to give him back his property. He snatched it from my hands and stalked off muttering about 'giving me what for if I ever bothered his proof again.' What do you suppose he meant by that?"

"With your father," Toby said, "it could mean anything."

"Did you see to whom it was addressed?" Mary Elizabeth asked.

"I didn't have a chance to see anything. He moved faster than I'd ever seen him. He went out to the truck and drove off a few minutes later. I wish I knew what he did with it. I'd sure like to see it for myself."

"That is strange," Miriam commented. "Will, are you sure you're happy spending your summers out at the house? Seems to me you could be working somewhere closer to the school and making money while you're at it."

"Yes, I'm sure. I know my efforts won't mean much until I can work the place full time, but I am doing some things to make it better in the short term. It feels good to help that sad old farm. I think Mama would be pleased, too. I've dreamed for years, ever since I was a kid, of restoring what Dad took from that place. If I ever feel like I'm wasting my time, I'll quit."

Will looked at Miriam to ask a question and found

her sitting with a distant look on her face, tears winding in little rivers down her cheeks. Reaching over, he took her hand and asked quietly, "What is it, Mim?"

"Hmm?" she asked from that far off place to which she'd drifted. "Oh, nothing I guess." She sniffed as she once again focused on Will's face. "I just love you all so much, and I'm so sorry to have to bring such terrible news home to you, and I . . . oh, I miss Mama." The tears began anew as Will squeezed her hand and Mary Elizabeth laid her head on her shoulder.

"We're not sorry, not one bit," Lizzie reassured her. "This is where you should come every time you need something. That's what family is for," she declared. "I know what you mean, though; I miss Mama, too. She would have been so excited about this baby, and some of the time I think I can't bear knowing that these two precious children are going to grow up without knowing their grandmother."

"You'll tell them, honey, and they'll know her through you and Miriam and their uncles. We'll make sure of it," Toby told her in an attempt to comfort his wife.

"Come on, Mim." Mary Elizabeth wiped her face and stood, more ponderously than normal. "I've got a coconut cake that's been waiting all morning for one of us to dive in. Anyone save room for dessert?" she teased.

With Mary Elizabeth's encouragement, Miriam penned a letter to Sonny that evening. She tried three different times before she composed one that satisfied her. Walking with Lizzie to the post office, she slipped it in the outgoing slot before she changed her mind and snatched it back. Isabel had been right; Sonny deserved to know. She had avoided him for far too long, but the deed was done. Now all she could do was wait, and hope.

She didn't have to wait long. The following Friday afternoon she and Isabel were just sitting down to her piano lesson when they heard the front door rattle with a bold knock. Isabel asked her to answer it, and when she swung the door open she stood face to face with a frowning Sonny.

"Miriam," he breathed, and then she was in his arms. He held her in a firm embrace while he stroked her hair over and over. She was flabbergasted at his response, and at the same time she had never been so glad to see anyone in her life. He drew back to frame her face with his hands, and said, "I got your letter, and I had to come see you for myself. Are you okay, really and truly okay?"

"Yes, yes, I'm fine," she assured him. "I'm so happy to see you, Sonny, but you didn't need to drive all this way. It must have taken you all afternoon! Come in, and meet my friend and landlady."

Keeping her hand firmly in his, he allowed himself to be led into the living room to meet Isabel. Recognizing their need to spend some time together, she excused herself and went into her bedroom.

"Sit down on the sofa, Sonny. Can I get you something to drink?"

"Ah, sure. Anything will be fine."

Smiling, she told him, "Isabel keeps a steady supply of Coca Cola on hand. I'll get us a couple of those."

Returning momentarily with the icy bottles, she handed him his and sat beside him on the sofa.

"I knew something was wrong when you hadn't written," he told her, "but I never imagined you'd suffered through anything this horrible. I had to read the letter several times before I could take it in. I couldn't imagine how anyone could be so evil. God has dealt with me all week because of my anger. I wanted to find Charlie Carpenter and give him a little Old Testament justice."

"Old Testament justice?" she questioned.

"Yes, an eye for an eye!" he replied vehemently.

She smiled, and the response gave Sonny the opportunity to expel a long breath and soothe the tense atmosphere a bit.

"Lizzie said your anger would be fierce. I guess she was right," Miriam admitted.

"Fierce doesn't even come close. I wanted to hurt him, and that stupid Gladys Betts as well. I'm so glad you're away from her. I think you were wise to find another place to live. And," he added, looking up, "I like your short hair. I'm sorry you felt the need to cut it off, but I certainly understand why you did it. It's very becoming."

"Thank you. I was so hurt and angry and tied up in knots that first few days after he raped me, I thought I was losing my mind," she admitted.

"How are you managing now?" he asked.

"I'm better. I'm more tired at the end of each day. I think it's from having to work so hard not to think about it. It's a constant presence, like a rock in my shoe I can't reach to throw away. Does that sound silly?"

"No, but maybe you need to think about it. Maybe we can pray that God will show you how you can turn such a wretched experience into good in your life."

"How can God turn this into anything good?" she asked angrily.

"Don't try to force the thoughts from your mind.

Ask God to take away their sting. Don't you think He is hurting for you, too? You're His child, Miriam. I know your Mother would have sorrowed for you had she lived to know of what you were forced to endure. God loves you just as much as your mother did, and more. He's grieving for His wounded child, too. Let Him comfort you and help you find peace about this. If you don't deal with it, Charlie wins."

She sat quietly for a few moments, looking into his face intently. "I think I understand what you're trying to say. Can I think about it for a few days?"

"Why, sure. I'm sorry if I sound like a preacher, honey. I came just to be with you, to reassure myself that you were okay. And to tell you one more thing: this doesn't change how I feel about you one bit, except to care about you even more. You're very special to me, so I don't intend to let Charlie win, either."

"Thank you for coming."

"You're welcome." He smiled. Reaching up, he cradled her cheek with his hand and gently pressed his lips to hers. "Now then, I'm starving," he said as he stood to his feet. "Think you'd like to walk downtown with me and let me buy us some supper? I've got to find a motel for the night, and then tomorrow I thought we'd take a little drive. You could show me around Martinsville. How does that sound?"

"Sounds good. Come on, we'll tell Isabel our plans."

Charlie held the door to Lucille's and Miriam entered the café. The aromas from the kitchen tempted both of them. Leading her to a corner booth, Sonny slid in beside her and looked around.

"I love the frogs! This place is great. Is the food good?"

"The food is very good. I can recommend the sandwiches and the roast beef. I haven't tried anything else."

A smiling waitress brought glasses of water and menus, then looked up to see Miriam smiling at her.

"Hello, Miriam. I didn't even look up to see it was you. How you been, sugar?"

"I've been fine, Linda. And you?"

"Can't complain, sugar, can't complain. My Ernie got fired a couple of weeks ago, and now all he does is lay on my couch and dirty up my coffee table. Can't get him to fix anything around the house, either. Had to cut the grass myself this last Sunday afternoon. He's not so old he couldn't help out around the house a little. Look at me; 48 and still on my feet 10 hours a day. Man's a disgrace, I tell you, a disgrace." Looking at Sonny, she asked, "You new around here? Haven't seen you in here before. You make sure you treat this little lady good, you hear? We watch out for Miriam, you know."

"Linda, this is my friend, Sonny. He's in his last year of seminary."

"Seminary, huh? Well, I guess I can trust you then. Welcome to Martinsville, preacher. What do you folks think you'd like to eat?"

"How about the chicken and rice?" Miriam suggested.

"Sounds good, with green beans and carrots?" Sonny added.

"I like that," Miriam confirmed. "Thanks, Linda," she remarked as Sonny handed the convivial waitress the menus.

"You two want some iced tea? Best in town right here," Linda offered.

"We'd love some iced tea," Sonny said. "Thanks for looking out for us, Linda." He smiled.

Sonny watched avidly as Linda sashayed to the kitchen to place their order. She wore a sleeveless cotton blouse in bright kelly green and a pair of capri slacks in a garish purple and pink print with a background the same hue as the shirt. Her high-heeled slings were purple with a pink bow across the top, and they clicked on the linoleum floor as she walked. He looked askance at Miriam, a question in his eyes.

"I know she's a bit much, but her heart is pure, and she does look after me. She was absolutely sincere about that. I love her, so you can stop teasing. You're almost as bad as Toby," Miriam laughingly scolded.

"That's bad?" Sonny asked with a grin.

"Tell me about seminary, instead. You have just one semester to go, isn't that right?"

'Yes, I'll graduate mid-year in December. I had planned to continue as intern in Ascension until I can be assigned a church in June, but I'm not sure those plans are going to hold up. I've got some decisions to make soon."

"You sound very mysterious, Sonny," Miriam remarked.

"All in good time, my dear," he responded, patting her hand. "I did very well on my finals this past spring, and I'm taking two classes this last semester. The workload should be lighter, at least theoretically. Most professors have their own ideas, though. How do you like being a bookkeeper?"

"It's been a lovely job for this summer. I like Mr. Robinson and Melissa, his daughter, and the work is less than challenging. Still, my office is quiet and away from anyone who might ask questions I've not wanted to answer, and the extra money has been very nice. Mr. Robinson told me last week he'll try to hire someone soon enough that I can train them before I have to return to school in September. He's been more than accommodating, and I'm grateful to him."

"He sounds like an understanding employer. I'm glad you found this job when you needed it."

"Here you go, children," Linda announced as she placed iced tea and steaming plates of food on the table. "Anything else you need, just whistle," she added as she sauntered away.

Shaking his head ruefully, Sonny remarked, "She's quite something."

"Yes, she is, in the best sense of the word," Miriam assured him. Picking up her fork, she contemplated the huge portions of food in front of her. She quickly put the fork back down and reached for his hand. "I forgot that we should hold hands to say grace. Usually I just think the prayer by myself."

Sonny took her hand and spoke a short prayer for both of them, then he picked up his fork. Taking a bite of the chicken casserole, he closed his eyes and looked toward Heaven with utter contentment shining in his face.

"My, oh, my, this is good. Better than my mom's, but don't you dare tell her I said such a thing," he said.

"Your secret is safe with me," Miriam promised.

"No wonder you like to come here," Sonny remarked between forkfuls.

"Butch is a great chef," Miriam told him.

"Butch? What does he look like?"

"Like you'd imagine he'd look, but he's a very nice man and a whiz in the kitchen." Miriam chuckled as she explained. "I'd like to take lessons from him someday."

"This little town is quite a place, Miriam," Sonny told her.

They spent the rest of dinner in companionable conversation, Sonny telling her about Esther and Chad's wedding plans. She still had a year of secretarial school to go, but she was planning the wedding in the hopes their parents will relent and let them marry a year early. Miriam filled him in on Mary Elizabeth's and Polly's pregnancies, their name debates, and her plans to be there when the babies were born. He was a most remarkable man, Miriam thought as she listened to his description of an incident in one of his classes. Another man might have turned away from her after hearing about the rape, and she had given him an opportunity in the letter she'd written to distance himself from her. Instead, he'd swooped down on her like some hawk diving for an unsuspecting mouse in a winter meadow, holding her and reassuring her and behaving as if she were just the same. His behavior made her feel like she was the same, somehow, when she knew in her darkest moments that what Charlie had done to her would be a scar on her soul for the rest of her life. I could live with this man forever, she thought to herself. Miriam thought about what she'd just admitted to herself. Sitting up abruptly, she swallowed the chicken she'd been eating and gulped down more than a third of her iced tea.

"Miriam, are you okay?"

"I'm fine, Sonny, just swallowed wrong." She picked up her fork once again and resumed the meal. Do

I really think that? Could I be happy living with him forever? The warmth began in her chest and spread throughout her whole being until her fingers tingled and she felt a silly grin begin to spread across her face. She covered it by coughing and taking another sip of her drink. She loved him. The realization threatened to overtake her, and she had a difficult moment or two when the desire to fling her arms around him and declare herself was tough to subdue. She was in love with Sonny. The knowledge was the sweetest thing to have ever happened to her, and what a place to realize it. Frog Central, of all things.

"Miriam, you have a strange expression on your face. Are you sure you're okay?

"I couldn't be better, Sonny. Now, what were you saying about your professor and the fish pond?"

After supper Sonny and Miriam drove around for a while longer, neither of them ready to end their time together. Sonny had trouble keeping his mind on his driving and his eyes on the road. Her letter to him had shaken him like nothing else had done in his life. He'd been swamped with so many emotions at once – raw and all-consuming rage at the animal who had violated her in such a manner, hurt for what she must be feeling, uncertainty at just what his reaction to her should be, and, finally, an intense longing to grab her and hold on for the rest of their lives so that he might protect her from anything like that happening to her in the future. It was that final realization that helped him to know, once and for all, that he was in love with her. He'd been interested in her from the first, and over time he'd come to feel affection, camaraderie, warmth, gentleness, and more than a healthy dose of lust. Ultimately, though, he'd recognized the tenderness for what it was, and he couldn't imagine a life more empty than one without her in it. He'd gone out the next afternoon and bought a ring. The wedding band was one of simple gold, with tiny diamonds embedded around its circumference. The engagement ring mirrored that row of stones, with a solitaire diamond and two emeralds in a filigree design in the center. He thought it the most unusual ring he'd ever seen, and he knew it was perfect for Miriam. It was in his pocket now, and tomorrow he planned to ask her to wear it and promise to be his wife.

Tonight he was content just to be with her, to have her sit near him in the car and see her smiling and relaxed. It was more than he'd hoped. Sonny knew she could have been hysterical, withdrawn, angry, even bitter and hateful toward all men in general. Those feelings were understandable under the circumstances, yet, somehow, Miriam was dealing with the aftermath with a courage that baffled him. He only knew he'd never been more grateful to God for anything in his life, nor had he been prouder of anyone. Miriam was a remarkable woman. Tomorrow he hoped she would agree to be his.

The sun had begun to slide toward the slope of the horizon when Sonny pulled up in the driveway behind Isabel's house. Slipping his arm around her shoulders, he pulled her close and hugged her tightly, breathing in her customary fragrance. Her hair smelled like warm cream, and he felt himself respond to the nearness of her. He'd never felt this kind of awareness for any other woman, and the depth of the want inside him was staggering. Pulling back slightly, he reached up to cradle her cheek in his palm. She smiled at him again, and he knew he was lost.

"Miriam, I was going to wait to say anything to you until tomorrow, but I find that I can't. I hope I'm not rushing you, but . . . oh, Lord . . . I may as well get this over with." Sighing in frustration, he cleared his throat and blurted out, "Miriam, I love you."

Her eyes searched his face as they filled with tears, and he thought for a moment he'd made a mistake. Then Miriam reached up to press her cheek to his, and she whispered, "I love you, too."

"Really?" he asked, an incredulous note in his voice.

"Really," she said as she nodded.

He hugged her again and laughed. "Oh, Miriam, honey, I love you so much. I can't believe you feel the same way. It's too good to be true. I've waited forever to find you, to love a woman the way I know God intends for every man." He kissed her, and then kissed her again, his eyes glowing with a light that had Miriam blinking from its intensity. The brightest star in the night sky was insignificant next to the sparkling fire in Sonny's eyes. Settling back against the seat, he drew her close and urged her head onto his shoulder. Nestling beside him, she took his left hand in hers and stroked his fingers in a nervous up and down motion.

Speaking softly, she told him of how much she'd dreamed of hearing him declare his love for her and of how frightened she'd been of finding love because of how she'd seen her father pervert it.

"What if I'm as bad at loving someone as Daddy was? Sonny, what if I can't let myself trust you and this love that's between us? Daddy started out loving Mama, and look what it became. I'm terrified of hurting you because of my own fear and uncertainty."

"Honey, we're both going to hurt one another from time to time. We're imperfect human beings, flawed and sinful. We're bound to get impatient, frustrated, angry with one another from time to time. Our emotions will get between us, and sometimes we'll simply misunderstand one another because we're two unique individuals. What we need to remember is that God has given us this love. It's a gift from Him to us, and we need to commit to one another and to Him to guard it with all our being. We need to be honest with each other at all times, and agree to talk about everything instead of letting our hurts get out of control. If we nurture this gift, and allow Him to help us to keep it precious between us, I don't think we'll need to worry about anything spoiling it like your Mama's and Daddy's love was spoiled."

"I've been thinking about what you said, about letting God take the sting out of what Charlie did to me. I want to pray to let God do that. I don't want one night's betrayal to color the rest of my life, Sonny. I want to heal. Do you think I can? Do you think I can put this behind me and get on with the life I want to live?"

"Of course I do, and, honey, I want you to know I'm already so proud of you for the courage you've shown. You aren't angry and bitter, lashing out at people and punishing them for what Charlie did to you. Your heart is bruised, but you've not allowed it to become twisted and ugly, and I think that's remarkable. You're stronger than you know, and with God's help, and mine," he paused to kiss her again, "you can heal."

She reached up to hug him again, then drew away to kiss his cheek.

"Oh, I think we can do better than that." He smiled as he moved to touch her lips with his own. Miriam's body sizzled with the emotion racing through her. Sonny's lips were the softest she'd ever imagined, and when he kissed her the warmth flooded her whole being, making the soles of her feet burn with its intensity. She knew instinctively that he could seduce her with his mouth alone, and before they were swept away, she knew it was time to stop.

Sonny sensed her hesitation and drew back slightly. He rested his forehead to hers, then sat back once again.

"Oh, honey, I could stay like this forever, but I don't think it's wise. I'm going to walk you to Isabel's back door and tell that dear lady goodnight so that no one will draw any false conclusions about our behavior tonight. Your reputation is precious to me, as are you, so I think it's time we call it a night."

"Thank you, Sonny, for understanding. You take my breath away, and I find it difficult to think at all when we're together like this."

"Much more talk like that and I'll lose my resolve. Come on." Opening the door, he scooted out and then drew her out as well, holding her hand as they ambled to the kitchen doorway. Miriam stepped inside first, calling Isabel's name.

"I'm in here, children. Come in, Sonny, and I'll have Miriam play for you what she's learned."

"I'm not ready to play for anyone, Isabel. It's only been a few weeks. I'm still working on the exercises you gave me to learn the notes and a few basic chords. I can't believe Sonny wants to hear me do that."

"Oh, but I do," Sonny insisted. "I'd love to hear you play."

"But you're so accomplished, Sonny. I heard you

at Seth's wedding. Maybe later-" she started to say.

"Nonsense, child," Isabel interrupted. "You know 'Joyful, Joyful, We Adore Thee' well enough. Play that."

"Just remember, Sonny, you asked for it." Miriam sat at the piano. She found the hymn in the book and settled herself on the bench. She played in a stilted, uncomfortable manner at first, but then, as she became more absorbed by the music, she relaxed and played more easily. Clearly she was still learning, but Sonny marveled at how well she played the song. She was very talented, and he could see by the expression on her face how much she loved what she was doing. As she finished, the room was hushed. Rising from his place on the sofa, Sonny walked to her and sat beside her on the piano bench.

"Honey," he said as he took her hands in his, "that was beautiful. I know you're still a beginner, but you play very well. You love playing, don't you?"

"More than I thought I would, yes. It's as if the music has been a part of me all my life, and I just didn't know how to express it before now. I still love to sing, but playing the music adds a new dimension to it that I've never known before. I can almost forget that anyone else is listening. Do you like what I played?"

"Very much. If you keep working, you're going to eclipse my ability in a very short time. Thank you, Isabel, for bullying her into it," Sonny teased as he turned to the elderly lady seated beside the piano.

"Walk her home, son. It's late." Isabel smiled at Miriam's young man. "And you come see me again soon, yes?"

"Yes, ma'am. I'll look forward to it."

Sonny led Miriam out into the back yard and up the steps to the door of her apartment.

"I don't usually go up this way," Miriam explained, "but I didn't want you to walk into my apartment by way of my pantry."

"Your pantry? What are you talking about?"

"There are steps in the garage that lead up into my apartment by way of the pantry. They're wider and sturdier, and so I use those most of the time."

"I'd like to be given the 'insider's view' of your pantry some day, honey. In the meantime, it's late, and I want to pick you up about 8:30 tomorrow morning. Is that too early?"

"No. I'll be ready. Good night, Sonny," she responded softly.

Leaning down to press his lips to hers, he kissed her gently and whispered, "Good night, honey. Dream about me."

"I already do."

"See you tomorrow then."

"Good night."

He stared at her for another moment and then made himself turn away and walk down the steps. It was so difficult to leave her. If things went well tomorrow, he thought to himself, he wouldn't have to leave her too many more times. Whistling a cheery tune, he drove down the road to his motel.

Chapter 17

Miriam hummed to herself as she set about getting ready for bed. This day hadn't ended as she'd expected this morning; she couldn't quite believe it. Sonny loved her! She wanted to sing the news to everyone she saw, to everyone who could hear her. Never in her most secret imaginings could she have seen this day coming. She had known Sonny was fond of her, but she'd convinced herself long ago that she was past marrying age and too flawed to ever have anyone love her. She was still afraid that she was going to do something to ruin it.

Walking into the bathroom, she picked up her hairbrush and began her going-to-bed routine. As her mind cleared with the familiarity of her tasks, she thought of her mother.

"Mama, I have the most wonderful news. Sonny Williamson told me tonight that he loves me. I still can't believe it. He's such a good man, Mama, so smart and wise, caring and understanding. He makes me feel good about myself, like I can do more, be more, somehow, because he believes in me. He didn't turn his back on me when he found out about Charlie. I'm so relieved I'm almost too weak to stand. I was certain he would end our friendship for sure. But Mama, I'm so afraid. I don't know how a man and a woman are supposed to love each other. You and Daddy weren't exactly shining examples of a caring husband and wife. I don't blame you for that; you tried your best, and long after I would have given up and left him. Still, I don't know how to behave, what to say, about loving him. I don't want to hurt him or disappoint him. I want to give him all the love and support he's given me. I'm scared."

Miriam changed into pajamas and brushed her teeth, turned the bedside lamp out and she climbed into bed. Fluffing her pillow, she cradled her head in her arm and looked to the shadows playing on the ceiling from the wind blowing tree limbs across the street lamp. Before she could even understand what was happening, the fear rose up in her like some great choking cloud. Her mind raced as she struggled to breathe. Almost as if she could hear the words aloud, her worries danced in front of her eyes.

"Oh, God," she thought, "I can't do this. I spent my entire childhood trying to win Daddy's love, and I failed miserably at it. He cares nothing for me even today. I've been invisible to him all my life. Maybe whatever was in me that kept Daddy from loving me was the same thing that made Charlie believe he could use me like he did. How can I be what Sonny needs? How do I know if what I'm feeling is love? I've never known what that is. If I try to love him, I'll fail at that too. He'll end up hating me just like Daddy." She swiped at the tears and tried unsuccessfully to slow her breathing to something less than hysterical. "Even if we manage to be happy for a while, it can't last. Mama thought she'd found happiness with Daddy, and look how that turned out. What if I wind up turning on Sonny? He'd be better off walking away from me. I'd be a bad wife."

Miriam counted the tics of the clock as she waited for the panic to ebb, but even after her tears were stilled her mind wouldn't calm. She lay huddled in a tight ball, shivering, until the skies had begun to lighten with the coming day. Finally, exhausted and numbed from the spent emotion, she slept. Even in sleep, however, the fear followed her. She dreamed of being lost in a huge building with dozens of doors, and every time she looked into a room for a way out, she saw her father or Sonny walking away from her, heedless of her cries to wait, to help. The knocking on the front door startled her from her restless slumber and, disoriented, she peered at the clock to see that it was 8:30. Groaning, she knew Sonny was waiting for her on the landing. Heartsick and miserable, she dragged her robe on over her pajamas and stumbled into the front room.

"Sonny, I'm not ready. I overslept. Can you come back in an hour?" In spite of her best effort to keep the tears from her voice, Sonny heard them and called out to her.

"Honey, what's wrong?"

"I'm fine. I'm just not ready," she lied.

"I'll wait here on the steps until you can get ready, okay?"

"Oh, Sonny, don't do that," she begged. I don't know how long it will take me."

"I don't mind," he insisted. "It's a beautiful day."

"Please," she mumbled, "please, I can't do this."

Hearing her soft voice, Sonny was instantly concerned. "Miriam, I don't want to go and leave you like this. Can't you open the door?" The concern in his voice was evident as he pleaded with her. "I won't come in, I promise."

Shuddering, she cracked the door open and squinted into the bright sunlight of early morning. Sonny stiffened as he saw her haggard face and haunted, tear-swollen eyes.

"Miriam! What's happened?" At the shake of her head, he began again, "Come out here on the steps. No one will see you, and I need you to tell me what's wrong. Please," he begged, frightened by the tumultuous emotion on her face. She hesitated for so long he thought she would refuse, but she shrugged and stepped onto the porch. He urged her onto the top step and then sat beside her, putting his arm around her shoulders and squeezing gently. "What's wrong?" he asked again.

The tears flowed down her ravaged face as she explained to Sonny about the fear that had overwhelmed her last night. She told him how afraid she was of hurting him, of being miserable because she didn't know how to love someone, of believing deep down that she didn't deserve to have anyone love her, otherwise her father would have loved her as well. Her pain was so deep, her stuttered explanations so heart-wrenching, that Sonny felt the tears begin to gather in his own eyes as he listened. When her explanation ended on a sad little whisper, Sonny could think of nothing to do but gather her to himself and hug her as he stroked her hair and told her that all would be well. They cried together for a long time, her tears coming in soul-wracking sobs as she clung to him.

"Oh, God," he breathed the prayer, "help me. I don't know what to do. What do I say to her to take away a lifetime of rejection? Give me the words, Father, please. I love this woman, and I know you love her. She is your child. Show me what to do.

"Miriam," he murmured, "I love you. I believe with all my heart that you are the woman God created for me to be my wife. I don't believe for one minute that you're going to do anything to mess up our relationship. There's nothing you could ever do that would stop me from loving you. That's my promise to you. You can't get rid of me that easily." He smiled as he stroked her hand. She responded with a watery grin of her own.

"I know you have been rejected, first by your father and then by Charlie's cruelty, and I can't even begin to understand the depth of the agony you've experienced. No one should have to bear such a heavy burden. All I can do is reassure you that you are God's child, and He loves you. He'll never turn away from you either. He'll help you to heal if you'll let Him. He wants to do that for you, honey. As much as I'm in agony over your grief, the Father is even more so, and He can take your fear away if you allow Him to do so."

"Sonny, I'm so afraid."

"I know you are, baby, I know. If you like, we can take a drive this morning. If you think it will help, we'll find a back road and explore a while. We'll talk about silly things and you can get your mind off everything, just for today. Do you think that will help?"

"I don't know, but I do know I'll go crazy in this apartment letting this fear have free reign. Why don't you go knock on Isabel's back door," Miriam suggested. "She'll give you some banana bread while I get ready."

"Okay, that's an offer I can't refuse." Assisting her to her feet, he wrapped her up in his arms and soothed her again as the mockingbirds beckoned to one another and the wind soughed in the trees. Patting her back, he turned her to the door of her apartment. "Take all the time you need, honey. I'll wait for you at Isabel's." Kissing her briefly, he added, "I love you. Believe it."

"Okay, I won't be too long."

Thirty minutes later a calmer Miriam made her way to Isabel's back door. She had showered and dressed in a sleeveless cotton dress with blue periwinkles splashed across it in a cheerful pattern. White sandals and a flowing blue scarf knotted at her waist completed the look, and, at least on the outside, she appeared more composed and ready for the day. Inside her stomach was quivering and her legs were so shaky she could barely stand.

Hearing Sonny's chuckles as she opened the screen door, she found he and Isabel enjoying an ice cream float as well as the promised banana bread. Turning at the noise, Sonny jumped to his feet and drew Miriam into his arms as she approached the table.

"Hey, you look terrific. Are you feeling better?" he asked, still very concerned.

"Yes, I'm a little better. The shower helped to soothe the rough edges away." Miriam walked across the room and into Isabel's waiting arms, needing the comfort her elderly friend had given her time and time again.

"My child, my dear child," Isabel crooned as Sonny looked on. "You are so precious to me, to us. We'll do everything we can to help you through this dreadful time, but Sonny was right when he said that you must trust God to give you solace as well."

"Oh, Isabel, I'm trying to listen for God, but it's so hard. I've believed myself to be a misfit for so long."

"You're not a misfit, Miriam. Nothing of the sort. You will not take on your father's failings and call them your own, do you hear me?" Isabel spoke fiercely. "In the short time you've lived here I've come to love you as my own child. You are kind and compassionate, giving and mindful of others. Your students loved you, I know, and they are the best judges of character we sometimes have. If you had been insincere or disdainful of them, would they have responded as they did to you? I think not. A sweet soul shines from your face every time I look into your eyes. You must begin to believe that of yourself, child, as everyone else believes it."

"Isabel is right, Miriam," Sonny added as Miriam wept quietly. "I love you, and I know how much your family loves you. Don't sell yourself short. Don't sell our Heavenly Father short. Now, are you ready for our drive? Isabel has given me an idea of how we can spend the morning, and then we'll come back here and pick her up and all go to lunch at Lucille's. I've a hankering to see those frogs again."

Wiping the tears from her cheeks, Miriam sniffed a time or two and turned to the back door. Sonny smiled at Isabel and followed Miriam to his car parked in the driveway.

"I'm sorry about these tears. I don't think I've stopped crying in the year and a half since Mama died."

"There's nothing wrong with being emotional, honey."

"There is if you can't function because of them."

"I haven't seen them debilitate you yet. Give

yourself more credit than that."

Miriam remained silent as he crunched down the driveway.

"Where are we going?" she asked in a hushed little voice.

"Isabel told me about a summer carnival not too far out of town. It sounded like fun. We can ride the Ferris wheel and eat cotton candy, and maybe we'll wander the livestock barn and look at the animals. I'll even try and win you a prize on the midway. Would you like that?"

Smiling, Miriam found the idea had definite appeal. "I'd love to go to the carnival. I haven't been since I was a little girl."

"Well, then, let's go," Sonny urged as he grinned. Miriam sat beside Sonny and listened to the soft music playing on the car radio and thought about what happened in the past week. When had life gotten so complicated? Huh, she thought, mildly disgusted with herself, when hasn't it been complicated? Why had she thought her life could be simple? Before she could sink into the beginnings of despair, she upbraided herself and looked out the window at the world going by. The day around her glowed warm and sunny with a refreshing morning breeze blowing in through the windows. The wildflowers were everywhere, and the birds were crying out their joy at such a perfect summer day. She had the most remarkable man in the world sitting beside her, and Mary Elizabeth and Polly were about to have babies. She had an understanding boss and an uncomplicated job to return to on Monday, and Isabel Barnes had kept her from being so lonely for her mother. You see, Miriam, she thought to herself, there are blessings everywhere if you just take time to see them. With the day spreading before her with fresh promise, she found she could put last night's paralyzing panic attack away and concentrate on the reasons she had to feel good about her life. She resolved to think only about this day, this moment, and enjoy it as much as possible.

Sonny turned off the highway and into a pasture that had been converted into a parking lot. He drove past the balloons and flags flying gaily in the breeze and parked in the nearest empty space in line. Emerging from the car, Miriam could hear the sounds of the carnival up ahead – the calling of the barkers, the squeals and laughter of the children, and the music that floated on the warm rivers of air. The smells were delightful, as well; popcorn, cotton candy, hamburgers, and hot dogs wafted their aromas over the fairgrounds and made her stomach grumble. She'd not taken time to eat any breakfast.

"Oh, Sonny, what a grand idea! I can't wait to get in on the fun."

Relieved to see that the strain around her eyes had diminished somewhat, he took her hand and led her to the ticket booth. "Let's get a move on, then. I want to do everything!"

Sonny bought their tickets and led Miriam to the food tent straightaway. "I'm hungry again," he insisted, "and I know you didn't eat anything this morning. Let's see what they have for us to feast upon," he encouraged.

Askance at the prices, Miriam started to protest, but Sonny would have none of it. "You are to worry about nothing today, honey mine. Choose anything that suits your fancy."

Miriam took him at his word, and soon they were enjoying apple strudel and steaming hot coffee. Nothing had tasted this good in a long time. Wandering the carnival grounds half an hour later, they saw children enjoying the merry-go-round, couples scrambling onto the roller coaster, and elderly couples strolling along arm-in-arm. They looked at the winners of the jams and jellies competition, marveled at the intricately stitched quilts that had won the top four prizes, and laughed together as Sonny hit enough balloons at the dart throw to win Miriam a stuffed rabbit. She couldn't have been more charmed. Realizing that time was getting away from them, they hurried to the Ferris wheel and rode three times before returning to the car and the short trip into town to meet Isabel for lunch.

She was already seated at a table when they entered the diner, sipping iced tea and scanning the menu. Looking up, she smiled at the obvious joy on Sonny's and Miriam's faces.

"I see you two enjoyed yourselves," Isabel greeted them.

"It was such fun, Isabel," Miriam told her. "We rode the Ferris wheel, and look what Sonny won for me. I can't remember when I've spent a more perfect morning," she said.

"We took in the sights, that's for sure, and now I'm starved," Sonny added. "What's the special on Saturdays?"

"It's fried pork chops with apple rings, and it's worth some consideration," Isabel told him. "I think that's what I'll have. Their broccoli rice casserole is good with it, too," she added.

"I'm sold. Where's Linda when you need her?"

"Doesn't work on Saturdays," Isabel told him.

"What a shame, and just when I was getting to

know her, too," he teased.

They ordered lunch from a sweet young waitress with long brown hair and a shy smile, then had a lively time talking and laughing together for over an hour. Sonny had insisted that both women order dessert, so they had shared a huge piece of strawberry shortcake.

Once Isabel had driven off, Sonny turned to Miriam and asked her to walk up to the square with him. They found a bench under a magnificent oak tree and sat together for several minutes, idly chatting, but mostly just listening to the breeze ruffle the trees and the songbirds call to one another. Miriam felt more peaceful than she had in weeks, and sitting with Sonny, nestled in the crook of his arm, feeling his thumb idly grazing her upper arm, was more soothing than the best sedative medicine could boast.

Sonny wasn't in the most tranquil of moods, however. He had decided that this was the time and place to propose to Miriam, and as a result the dive bombers were doing loop-de-loops in his midsection. He chastened himself for being a coward, then finally took a deep breath and turned to the woman sitting beside him. It's now or never, son, he thought to himself.

"Miriam, I'd like to ask you something," he said.

"Sonny, you look so serious. Is anything wrong?"

"No." Steadying his nerves, he spoke what he'd been rehearsing all week. "Miriam, last summer when Solomon and I took a wrong turn and landed you in the dirt, I never could have imagined that those circumstances would bring us to this place and time, and yet God has a way of bringing His best out of even the most unusual turn of events. Through the letters we've written and the times we've spent together, I've gotten to know what a special woman you truly are, how giving and caring you are, how much you value your family, how sincerely you are seeking to follow after God, and I've come to love all those things about you. I love you, more than I ever dreamed I would love anyone. I'd like to spend the rest of our lives showing you how precious you are to me. I want to wake up beside you every morning, hold you when you cry, laugh with you when you ruin dinner, struggle and dream and work for a future hand in hand with you, and only you." Reaching into his pocket, he withdrew the box and held it out to her. "Miriam, will you marry me?"

He opened the box and showed her the ring he had purchased. With a tearful sheen in her eyes, Miriam stroked the ring and looked into the face of the man she had come to love more than her own life.

"It's the most wonderful ring I've ever seen. Sonny, every instinct in me is telling me to say 'yes' and never look back, but I don't think that's wise under the circumstances. Will suggested to me last weekend that I take a few days to get away from everything and do some thinking. I hadn't seen the need until now. Would it be asking too much of you to wait until I take that time before I give you an answer? I want to be sure I'm ready to make that kind of commitment to you. Anything less would be unfair. I'll go down to Corpus Christi this upcoming weekend; I'd like to see the beach. When I get back, I'll have an answer for you. Will you wait?"

She saw the disappointment in his face, but she saw the love shining in his eyes. "I'll wait as long as you need. I love you."

Miriam threw her arms around him and hugged him tight. "Oh, I love you too, so much. Thank you for being patient with me. I have the feeling it won't be the last time I'll need it." She smiled an uncertain smile.

Chapter 18

The world seemed to drop away as Miriam maneuvered the car closer and closer to the sand. Her stomach was dropping away as well; she could feel the loop-de-loops as she took each turn. What had made her take off on this little adventure anyway, she wondered for the hundredth time? Drat that Isabel for being so eager to loan her this car. She'd never driven this far from home in her life, but Will had encouraged her to get away, to go somewhere. She'd known that she'd needed this time away, but to be doing it had her jumping out of her skin. Chewing on her lower lip, a recent habit she detested but couldn't seem to break, she followed the signs to the parking area behind the dunes.

Emerging from the car, Miriam was struck by the force of the wind. It was almost a gale, it seemed to her. Walking past the cabanas, she felt her feet sink into pure, white, fine sand. She dug her toes into its depths and grinned. Just like a kid playing in a sandbox. Deciding she liked this sudden carefree mood, she watched the sand sift through her toes for several minutes. Giggling, she kicked as she walked up the dune.

The roar of the surf interrupted her light-hearted reverie, and Miriam looked up to stare in wonder at the ocean before her. Sure, she had taught her children about the oceans of the world, but staring into such restless, endless blue and feeling the wind strike her in the face was indescribable.

"Dear Lord," she prayed quietly, "it's incredible. Thank you for bringing me here" The whitecaps rushed toward shore in a rhythm as old as time, and the roar of the surf whispered through her spirit like the gentle cadence of a favorite lullaby. She walked toward the water with an eagerness she'd not felt in a long time. Will had been right; she'd needed to be here, to experience the timelessness and open beauty of the ocean. The water washed over her feet as she strolled along, and she listened with joy to the haunting cry of the gulls and the delighted squeals of the children as they jumped the waves offshore. Miriam watched the different families scattered up and down the sand as they flew kites or built sandcastles, tired moms keeping a watchful eye and sunburned dads trudging out for one last swim. The panorama before her soothed her battered soul.

With a smile on her face – a genuine smile and not those phony things she'd adopted to hide the misery that had become her life – she threw off her wrap and strode into the waves with ever-growing confidence. To her surprise she found herself laughing out loud as she jumped wave after wave, exulting in the cleansing sunshine and wind and water. Miriam had read about individuals who heard the roar of the ocean's surf and tasted the salty air and responded with restlessness and sorrow. There was nothing sad about this day for her, however. The wonder she felt was balm to her battered spirit, and in that moment Miriam felt the ugliness of her father's abuse and Charlie's brutality that had held her in their punishing grip loosen just a little. She recognized the hope that flooded her being and knew the tears on her cheeks were the beginning of healing.

Unaware of time or distance, Miriam walked for over an hour, allowing herself to cry everything out of her system – the anger, the guilt, the blame, the grief. She had been frozen inside herself, doing what was necessary to survive each day but never opening up any of her true personality to anyone. How many years had she lived inside the cocoon she had created for herself, unaware that she'd done so? How much of the true spirit that was Miriam had been dimmed from her fear of rejection? She wanted to feel again, even if that meant feeling hurt. God knew she'd endured everything her father had inflicted and survived. She refused to let Charlie's brutality ruin her life.

On a spurt of energy Miriam jogged back to her car. The sun had begun to descend behind the dunes and the wind was decidedly cooler. She'd drive back to the motel and eat the ham sandwich and apple left over from lunch. Rather than the emotional exhaustion that had dogged her steps for weeks, she felt again the physical fatigue that comes from healthy exercise. It was a change for which she was profoundly grateful. Rather than the escape it had become, sleep once again was a respite, a renewal of her spirit for the day to come. She had forgotten how good it could feel to be normal.

Setting off across the two-lane road that bisected the coastal waterway, she marveled at the hush that had fallen over everything as dusk encroached. The winds had softened to a whisper and the raucous birdsong had been stilled. A river of fire kissed the water as the sun disappeared below the low hanging cloudbank nestled against the western horizon. Fingers of orange and red reached out to the blue of a sky that faded from the powder blue of a baby's blanket to the midnight blue of a woman's velvet gown. She watched, awestruck. Enthralled by the sight, she almost missed the drive into the parking lot and found herself wrenching the car harshly to the right. "Whoops, better watch it, Miriam," she scolded. Coasting to a stop, she put the car in park and reached for the door handle. Unbidden, Sonny's face came to her mind.

"I knew I'd bring you with me, Sonny. You've become the best part of me this past year, and I love you madly. I hope I can find an answer for you while I'm on this little sabbatical. Are you praying for me, Sonny? Don't stop; oh, please, don't stop."

The motel room walls were painted a light blue, with a beige and brown sea shell design on the bedspread and curtains. The furniture was utterly forgettable, finished in a light shade and marred with hundreds of scrapes, dents, and cigarette burns. She was less than pleased, but at least the room was clean and serviceable. It would suit her purposes well enough.

She stripped off and got into the shower, washing away the fatigue of the drive and the sand from her excursion on the beach. She shampooed her hair and was pleased to note that it was growing once again. She wasn't sure she'd ever wear it as long as it had been before her impromptu cut, but she liked the feel of her fingers stroking through it. Maybe a little bit of length would be okay.

Snuggled into her old chenille robe, Miriam

polished off the meal that Isabel had packed for her earlier that morning, then drank the last of the milk from the mason jar in the cooler. Stretching out on the bed, she fluffed the pillows behind her back and reached for the book she'd tossed there when she'd unpacked. Fifteen minutes later she tossed it back onto the bed. Her mind just wouldn't focus on the words. She stared at the bland painting on the wall. Soon she was talking to her mother.

"Mama, what am I doing here? I'm so tired of thinking about everything all the time. I want my life to be easy for a change. One day would be a gift. I've got to put Charlie out of my mind and never think about him again. How do I do that, Mama? And how do I put to rest all the ugliness that has filled my mind since that night? Why can't I just accept myself for who I am and believe the good things Sonny and Isabel and the family say about me? I don't want to feel broken any longer. I want to be the whole person Sonny believes I can be. What do I tell him next week? He wants to marry me, Mama. I've never wanted anything more in my life. Can I risk it? What if I turn on him like Daddy did to you? I love Sonny too much to do that to him. It just feels hopeless, and I'm too much of a coward to take the risk."

Feeling miserable, Miriam lay back on the bed and brooded as she stared at the ceiling. Looking over at her novel, she couldn't bring herself to pick it up. The story held no interest for her. She thought about what Sonny had said to her, about asking God to take the sting out of her memories of Charlie's attack. The idea to read from the Gideon Bible she'd seen in the bedside table earlier came to her on a whisper. Turning over on the bed, she retrieved it from the nightstand and opened the pages to the Psalms. She read several and realized that she was no longer as restless. Idly turning pages, she read snippets of Scripture as she came across them, with no rhyme or reason. When she reached I John, she was drawn to the words of chapter four, where it discussed love. Maybe this would give her an answer about Sonny and his proposal. When she reached verses 17 – 19, everything in her stilled. She read it again:

'By this, love is perfected with us, that we may have confidence in the day of judgment; because as he is, so also are we in this world.
There is no fear in love, but perfect love casts out fear, because fear involves punishment, and the one who fears is not perfected in love.
We love, because he first loved us.'

Miriam read the words again, letting them sink deeply into her spirit. If there is no fear in love, she thought, then I have no reason to be afraid. I know that God loves me. I know my mother and Lizzie and my family love me. Isabel loves me; Sonny loves me. That's why Daddy can't love us. He's afraid. He was afraid of losing Mama's love, of being betrayed by Uncle Jim, so he pushed them away before they could hurt him. That wasn't my fault. Seeing a tear splash onto the page before her, she reached up to wipe it away and found herself weeping openly at the truth that had just struck her. It wasn't my fault, she repeated to herself. Marveling at the weight that seemed to lift from her shoulders, she said it aloud. "It wasn't my fault. Oh, Mama, I'm not the one who failed. I did love Daddy, and I loved you, and that love was pure. Daddy was the one who failed me, us. So if I didn't fail Daddy, if there wasn't something wrong with me, I don't have to be afraid of messing up the love I have for Sonny. I can love him openly because I know God loves me first. I can tell him yes."

The tears turned to laughter as she realized that her heart felt healed; for the first time in her life she felt whole. She didn't feel the wrenching emptiness that had been with her for most of her life. The cocoon she'd built around her heart split open; she could swear she heard the sound of the fibers ripping. She knelt by the bed and prayed that God would help her to never spin those shackles again. She thanked Him for His faithfulness to lead her to the words that helped her to see the truth, once and for all. She wept out her gratitude for her mother's love, the circumstances that had brought Sonny into her life, and the freedom she'd found to spread her wings and become the Miriam she was meant to be. In the deepest part of her heart, she felt a tiny spark ignite, and as it fanned into life, she found that the pain of being raped was gone. Yes, she still grieved for what Charlie had taken from her, but the agony had been lifted. Her anger was but a mere whisper of what it had been for all these weeks. She could even feel sorry for Charlie and Gladys for the emptiness in their lives.

Walking into the bathroom, she splashed cold water on her face and smiled at the new woman she saw in the mirror. The lines on her brow were gone, and the sadness in her eyes had been replaced with a sparkle she'd never seen there before. Changing into her pajamas and brushing her teeth, Miriam crawled between the sheets and almost drifted into the most restful sleep she'd ever known. This time no nightmares invaded her dreams throughout the long night. She didn't know what to call the feeling that had stolen over her spirit, but Sonny would tell her when she explained to him the miracle that had happened in her life. It was called peace.

The next morning Miriam was up early, eager to explore Corpus Christi and bask in the joy that had come over her the night before. She found herself smiling the most ridiculous grin she'd ever seen as she combed out her hair after her shower, and, to her even greater surprise, she didn't care if it looked ridiculous or not. She ate a huge breakfast at a local café and then left an extravagant tip for the young girl who had been her waitress. Life was good, and she wanted to spread the happiness around.

She bought a few silly trinkets in the gift shop she found as she wandered around town, enjoying the palm trees and the ocean breezes that seemed to follow her wherever she went. It felt incredible. Later in the morning she walked the beach on Mustang Island again, pausing to marvel at the breeze that ruffled her skirt, the heat from the summer sun that soaked into her shoulders and warmed the sand as she walked, and the insistent cry of the seagulls as they waddled along the shoreline, digging with their sharp beaks for whatever the water surrendered to their foraging. Finding an abandoned cabana, she pulled a notebook from her canvas tote and composed a letter to her father. She was certain he'd never see it, but something within her seemed to compel her to commit her thoughts to paper. If for no other reason, she was determined to share her experience from the night before with Sonny and her family, and writing it down might help with the telling of it down the road.

Dear Daddy,

I loved you for a long time, in spite of your earnest

efforts to kill any feeling that I had for you whatsoever. But my young and foolish heart insisted that there was hope if I just kept trying. I've come to realize now that you couldn't let yourself love me. I represented every fear, every nightmare you'd ever had, and loving me was just too risky. You couldn't open your heart up to that much hurt. I know now that the one who lost out, ultimately, was you. Oh, I've lived in fear most of my life, too, and it was a fear you helped to nurture by your coldness and abuses, but I'm not going to live in fear any longer. I know that I'm a person who is worthwhile. I know that I have people in my life who love me, who care deeply for me, and from now on I'm going to make sure I love myself as much as I love them. I'm not a failure. The one who has failed is you. You had the love of the most wonderful woman in the world in your hands, and you threw it away. You threw the rest of us away, too, but we've held on in spite of you. I'm sorry for all you've lost, but I don't intend to lose another moment of the life I've been living in self-doubt and regret. I hope someday you can find a way out of the hell you've created for yourself. I'm even going to pray that God will help lead you out of the miserable existence you've chosen. I'd like to get to know the man you were, the man Mama married. I think she would want that.

Miriam

Tucking the letter into her tote, she slipped her sunglasses on and walked to the water's edge once again. Shielding her eyes from the glare of the sun on the water, she stared across the waves for a long time. A hymn she used to hear her mother sing came to her mind, and she hummed it to herself.

"When peace like a river attendeth my way, when sorrows like sea billows roll, whatever my lot, thou hast taught me to say, it is well, it is well, with my soul."

An urgency she hadn't expected rose up within her, and she couldn't wait to get back home to see Lizzie and T.J. and be with Sonny. She sprinted back to the car and drove over to the motel, gathering up her belongings and checking out with the clerk at the front desk. In less than thirty minutes she had stopped to buy a hamburger and chocolate shake for lunch, gassed up the car, and was steaming up the highway toward Cedar Springs. She found a station on the radio playing current country hits and hummed along as she made her way back to a future she couldn't wait to begin.

The sun was just beginning to sink into the distant pastures as Miriam turned off the highway into Cedar Springs and drove past the post office and into Lizzie's driveway. The lights shining from the windows welcomed her as they had never done before, and she smiled as she realized that the lights were just the same. She was the one who was different.

Retrieving her suitcase from the back seat, she strode to the front door with a purpose in her step that was new. Tapping lightly on the door, Miriam entered the front room and looked up to see Lizzie standing in the hallway. Even bigger than she had been just two weeks ago, she made her lumbering way to Miriam and did her best to wrap her arms around her for a hug. Realizing that her arms just weren't long enough, she shifted her bulging midsection sideways and tried again. Miriam leaned over in order to accommodate Lizzie's girth.

"Oh, Mim, I'm so glad to see you. Come sit down, and help me put my feet up. I'm not sure I'm going to last another month. This baby gets bigger every day, and he kicks up a storm now! I feel like there's a boxing match going on in my innards. It's not too comfortable when he really gets going."

Shifting down onto the sofa, Lizzie sighed as Miriam pulled her legs around and propped them on a pillow. She sat at the foot of the couch and addressed her sister.

"Are you and the baby all right, though? You're not overdoing it, are you?"

"Oh, goodness no, we're fine. How could I overdo anything with that circling buzzard of a husband of mine? He hardly lets me lift a finger. It's getting more than a little irritating, too, Mim. I'm not an invalid; I'm just having a baby. He behaves like I'm the first woman to ever accomplish such a thing! He hovered so at church last week that I threatened not to go back until the baby is born if he didn't give me a little more elbow room. I don't remember that he behaved this way when I was expecting T.J."

"You never passed out when you were expecting T.J. He was so scared he was bloodless for days after that. You're just going to have to be patient with him. At least it won't be for too much longer."

"It may not be for even that long. I saw Dr. Meyer yesterday. He said the baby could come early because he's bigger than T.J. was. He said this one could weigh as much as nine pounds!"

"My goodness. What have you been feeding this

child?" Miriam teased.

"Nothing out of the ordinary, believe me. I don't think he can get much bigger without bursting right out of me! Are you hungry? I've got some fried chicken and potato salad left over from supper."

"I'm starving, and I'll get it," she hastened to add as Lizzie moved her legs in preparation to stand up. "You stay right where you are." Walking toward the kitchen, she turned around as the quiet in the house registered with her. "Lizzie, where's Toby and the kid?"

"They're at Grammy Ida's for a while. I guess he saw how tired I've been, so he offered to take T.J. to his folks' for a couple of hours. His mother would keep that boy indefinitely if I'd let her. She's so crazy about him, and she and Earl are good help. I count my blessings that we have them to count on when we need them. Toby should be back with him soon, though; it's almost T.J.'s bedtime."

As if on cue, the door opened and Toby walked in with a very tired little boy slumped on his shoulder. Turning, he jumped back a step when he saw that he'd almost squashed Miriam. "Oh, Mim, I didn't see you. We weren't expecting you back until tomorrow. How was your trip?"

"Eventful. I'll tell you both after I scrounge up some supper. Do you need some help with this little guy?" she asked, rubbing T.J.'s back as she spoke to his daddy.

"Oh, no, I'm fine. You go eat and I'll put him down. I'll be back in just a few minutes." Looking toward his wife, he remarked, "I'm happy to see you with your feet up. You've been working much too hard this week. I asked Mother to come over on Tuesday and help out around here."

"Toby," Lizzie chided, "I'm perfectly capable . . ."

"I know, I know, but I don't care. You need to learn to be gracious about accepting a little help once in a while, Lizzie. And just so you can be irritated at me all at once, Thelma Collins stopped me in town yesterday and asked if the ladies at church could do anything to help. I assured her we would welcome some help. They'll be here Thursday." Smiling cheekily because he knew his wife couldn't say anything to his mother or Mrs. Collins without appearing ungrateful, he breezed out of the room with his sleeping son snoring into his neck.

Chuckling, Miriam headed in the direction of the leftovers.

"He's got me cornered and I know it, but you don't have to be so happy about it, Mim," Lizzie called after her.

"Oh, yes, I do," she responded to her frowning sibling in a sassy little sing-song voice.

"Ganged up on, that's what I am," Lizzie muttered to an empty room. "Ganged up on and not one thing I can do about it." Resting her head against the sofa pillows plumped up behind her, she willed herself to relax. Without warning the weariness crept over her as she lay quietly. "Little one," she crooned as she rubbed her swollen belly, "I'm sure you're snug and happy tucked up in there, but you're doing terrible things to my ability to move around or sleep. Aren't you just about ready to come on out and meet your family?" Chuckling at her own nonsense, Lizzie idly soothed her stomach, almost drifting off when the first contraction nearly swept her off the couch.

"Oh," she gasped aloud as she clutched at her

midsection. "Where did that come from?" Gone almost as quickly as it came, Lizzie brushed it off and evened out her breathing. Pulling the afghan from the arm of the couch, she draped it over her legs and lay back against the cushions once again. She could hear Toby speaking softly to T.J. as he got him settled for the night, and the clatter in the kitchen as Miriam raided the refrigerator made her smile. How good it was to have Miriam under their roof again. She had worried herself almost sick ever since Mim had told her about the rape. Silently she urged Miriam to hurry up so she could tell them about her trip to the beach. Mary Elizabeth had seen the light in Miriam's eyes and knew it portended better news. Comfortable and warm once again, she found herself unaccountably sleepy in spite of her best efforts to remain awake. Feeling herself drift, she moved to sit up when a second contraction gripped her. Toby walked into the room at that moment and saw the twisted expression on his wife's face.

"Mary Elizabeth, what's wrong?"

"I don't think we're going to have to wait any longer to welcome this baby into the family. She's ready now."

"Are you sure?"

"Toby, I've been in labor before, and I remember what it felt like. Trust me."

"I'll call Dr. Meyer," he told her as he thundered into the kitchen.

"Whoa, there, mister, are you trying to wake the king with all the noise? When did you invite the elephants into the house?"

Taking the plate and glass from her hands, Toby directed Miriam to go into the living room and sit with

Mary Elizabeth. "She's in labor."

"Now? Are you sure?"

"She says she's sure, and I'm taking her at her word."

"Are you calling Dr. Meyer?"

"As fast as I can."

Miriam walked into the front room to find Mary Elizabeth sitting upright and rocking back and forth, breathing deeply as she stroked her stomach.

"Oh, Mim, it looks like that talk of ours is going to have to wait . . ."

Miriam had walked to the front door and stared out at the driveway at least a thousand times since sun up. She'd never spent a more restless night in her life. After Toby had driven Lizzie off to meet Dr. Meyer at his clinic, she'd checked on T.J., still sleeping soundly, thank goodness, and had then lain down on the couch to wait for some news. When she'd awakened around 6:30 she couldn't believe she'd slept for so long, and where in the world was Toby? Shouldn't this baby be here by now?

Hearing T.J. stir, Miriam reluctantly left her post and hurried to change and feed her nephew. He was clearly happy to see his Auntie Mim, but his face registered his dismay when she walked with him into a kitchen that was not occupied by his mother.

"Where's Mama?" he asked.

"Mama and Daddy are at the clinic, bringing home your new baby brother or sister," Miriam explained. "Won't it be fun to have a new baby in the house, sweetie?"

"I want Mama," he demanded.

'I know, sweetie, and so do I. I wish your daddy

would -" Hearing the front door, she snatched up T.J. and hurried into the front room. A very tired, but clearly delighted, Toby, reached for his son and grinned into Miriam's expectant face. "They're fine," he told her.

"Well, is it a boy or a girl?"

"It's a girl, but you aren't going to believe the second part of the story."

"What second part of the story? Is Lizzie . . .?"

"I told you they're fine, all three of them."

"Three of them?" She frowned. "You mean, she had twins? Lizzie had twins?"

"You couldn't be any more surprised than I was, or Dr. Meyer, for that matter. He said he never heard more than one heartbeat. They surprised all of us."

"Toby, if you don't tell me everything, and right this minute, you'll get no breakfast from me!" Miriam declared.

He smiled. "Can you cook while I tell you? I'm starved."

While Miriam fried bacon and cut dough for biscuits, Toby told her about the birth of their two daughters, Anna Elizabeth and Ava Christine. They weighed a little over five pounds each, which explained Mary Elizabeth's discomfort of late. Two babies! Born a little earlier than expected, but both perfect. Toby wanted to shout it to the entire town, but he figured he'd settle for letting Will know a little later on in the day, and then maybe dropping by the parsonage and letting the pastor know. That should spread the news.

"When can I see her? And the babies?" Miriam wanted to know.

"We'll go up in a little while. Mother will be here about 9:30 to take care of T.J. for me. I swung by the house and told her. Woke her up, and you should have heard her shout for joy. Dr. Meyer said Lizzie is fine and can come home in a couple of days. Do you have to go right back to Martinsville? I know Lizzie is going to need some help for the first few weeks."

Frowning, Miriam thought about her circumstances. "I know I can take some time off, but I'm not sure how much. Why don't I go back to Martinsville this week and close up everything there? I'll need to give a week's notice at work and pack up my apartment. Could you come get me next Saturday? Maybe your mother, or the church ladies, could give Lizzie a hand until I get back. I'll be able to stay the rest of the summer that way."

"Aren't you going back to Martinsville for the school term?"

"No, I'm not. I didn't get to tell you and Lizzie last night, what with the babies' impatient arrival, but I've decided to get married instead."

Spluttering over the sip of coffee he'd just taken, Toby looked up with eyes as huge as saucers and asked, "You're getting married? Since when? When did Sonny ask you? Have you set the date?"

Laughing, Miriam got up to refill his coffee cup. "Now you sound like Lizzie. Give me a chance to explain, Toby dear, and all will be made clear."

"I'm not sure I can stand another surprise today, Miriam. I'm a new father, y'know." Standing up, he threw his arms around her and hugged her clean off the floor.

"Married," he said, shaking his head. "I'm happy for you, Mim. Sonny is the best guy I know." He chuckled as he considered his wife's certain response.

"Mary Elizabeth is going to have a fit."

Over biscuits and homemade dewberry jelly, Miriam told Toby about her trip to Corpus Christi and the healing she had experienced. She shared with him about her fears of ruining a marriage because of failing to find any love in her father, and how God had shown her that the failing had not been hers. She was giddy at the prospect of becoming Sonny's wife and the helpmeet of a minister, and she couldn't wait to tell him her answer.

"When I felt that sense of urgency about coming home, I thought it had something to do with my new sense of freedom. I had no idea it was because the twins were going to make an early appearance. Oh, Toby, two babies! Let's hurry up and get out to the farm. I can't wait to see Will's face when you tell him!"

Later on that morning Will and Miriam stood by Mary Elizabeth's bedside and stared down into their sister's beaming face as they gazed upon two cottony-blonde, wide-eyed baby girls.

"I still can't believe it. Dr. Meyer had just told me it was a girl when the contractions started up again. I thought something was wrong, especially when he said, 'Oops.'" She laughed at the recollection, although she hadn't laughed at the time. "Then out popped Ava, squalling and red-faced. She's going to give us a run for our money, you mark my words."

"They're beautiful, Lizzie," Miriam declared, wiping tears from her cheeks. "I'm so happy for you. What a day this has been!"

"You said a mouthful, Mim," Will said. "I thought Toby was joking when he said I had a niece, and then he said there were two! I wonder how much a double wedding costs the father of the brides. Toby, what do you think?" he teased.

"I think you'd better talk about something else. Barely born, these two are, and you're already telling me I have to marry them off. Give me a chance to breathe, will you?"

"That's not all the news for the Cahill clan." Toby smiled at Miriam.

"What else?" Mary Elizabeth asked. "Mim, did something happen in Corpus Christi? Will, if you sent her down there and she got hurt -."

"Hold, on, Lizzie. I'm fine. Going to Corpus Christi was the best thing I could have done, and I'm grateful to Will for bullying me into it." Moving over, she slipped her arm around Will's waist and hugged him as she announced, "If Sonny will still have me, we're getting married."

The next five minutes were loud and rowdy. The nurse came in to scold them for making too much noise and wound up taking the babies back to the nursery, clucking in disapproval as she went.

An hour later Will and Mary Elizabeth were smiling through their tears as Miriam finished up her accounting to them of what she had experienced on her sojourn.

"It never occurred to me that Daddy has lived his life out of fear," Mary Elizabeth remarked.

"But it makes sense," Will added. "He was too afraid that Mama had been with Uncle Jim to want to know the truth, so he assumed the worst and punished all of us. Mama must have seen his fear and hoped that in time she could convince him of the truth."

"She tried for over 20 years. I've never seen anyone work so hard for something in my life. What courage it must have taken to put up with his tantrums and beatings day after day."

"You mean what love," Toby chimed in. "She loved him enough to work for that change in him when he never gave her one minute's hope that her efforts ever made any difference."

"We have endured so much as Tom Cahill's children," Miriam told them, "but Daddy is the real loser. He had it all – Mama's love and devotion, our love and trust, and a lifetime of happiness and good times – and he threw it away because he was too stubborn to listen to anyone. I'm not sure at this point there's any reason to hope he'll ever change, but what I learned in Corpus Christi is that I can change. I can lay aside my fear and get on with my life because I'm not to blame, for any of it. You have no idea of the freedom I felt when I realized that for myself. I felt like I could fly," she exulted.

"Then this is a time of new beginnings for all of us," Will announced. "Now that you're going to become an old married lady, Mim, what are your plans?"

"Well, I guess I should let the groom know first."

"Here, here!" Toby laughed. "I think the groom should definitely know that he's going to have to get his best suit pressed."

"I think I should pack and load up Isabel's car, then write Sonny a letter and ask him if he could come next weekend. I should be back on Saturday. Lizzie, can you manage without me for a week?'

"Of course. I've got the best crew of helpers in the world, and you just wait until everyone gets a look at my two girls. They'll be standing in line to hang out diapers and wash bottles. We'll be fine."

Miriam hugged her sister, then Will took his turn

before they left her to rest for the afternoon. Toby kissed her, twice, and promised he'd be back after supper. "Nice going, Mrs. Woods," he whispered to her as he bent over the bed.

"Thanks, honey." She smiled into his beloved face. "I love you, Toby."

"I love you back. Your mother would be as proud as she could be, Mary Elizabeth," he said.

"I think so, too. Bye, y'all."

Miriam's suitcase was sitting by the door – she'd barely had time to unpack it before needing to load it up again – and she had just sat down to compose a letter to Sonny when Toby walked into the front room. "Well, T.J. is down for a short nap. He was so excited to see his mother and his two new sisters. Can I help you with anything?"

"No, I was just going to write Sonny so I could mail it on the way out of town."

"Then I'll leave you alone; I think I might stretch out for a short nap. Don't leave without waking me," he asked of her.

"I promise," she assured him as she returned to the stationary paper on the desk.

Dear Sonny,

I'm home, and I have wonderful news! Mary Elizabeth had her babies. Yep, I said babies. Two perfect, beautiful little girls are now resting in their mother's arms at the clinic – Anna Elizabeth and Ava Christine. I had barely gotten back from my trip to Corpus Christi when she went into labor. Even the doctor wasn't prepared for twins! I can't wait for you to see them. Do you think you could come to Cedar Springs this weekend? I'm on my way back to Martinsville to resign my teaching position and pack up my apartment. Toby will pick me up Saturday morning and bring me back here. I've decided not to return to teaching in the fall. I'd like to make a fresh start away from everything that happened, so I'm moving back into Mary Elizabeth's house to help care for the girls.

I have so much to tell you about my trip to the beach, but I won't make you wait to tell you that I've decided I'd very much like to be your wife. If your offer is still open, my answer is yes. I love you.

Miriam

Chapter 19

Miriam sat in Isabel's garage apartment Saturday morning packed up and ready for Toby to swing into the driveway. She had just spent a physically and emotionally exhausting week, and getting back to Cedar Springs was the most important thing on her mind. She hoped Sonny was waiting for her; she couldn't wait to see him.

Saying goodbye to Mr. Robinson and Melissa had been difficult enough, but bidding Isabel farewell had been wrenching. She'd come to love Isabel Barnes as much as she'd ever loved her own grandmother, and leaving her was difficult to do, in spite of the reason why. She'd sat for hours with Isabel, sharing with her about the trip and her revelation about her father, about the twins and her joy at having these precious new babies in the family, and about her hopes for a future with Sonny. She had played the piano on several evenings, delighting in how it soothed her and filled her spirit with light. She hoped to continue lessons someday.

The most difficult moments had come when she went looking for Annie. She thought back to the past Tuesday afternoon as she waited for Toby's knock on the door.

Annie had been nothing short of astonished to see

Miriam standing on her front porch that afternoon. She'd ushered her inside and poured icy cold lemonade for both of them.

"Daniel is with Aunt Sarah, working in her garden this afternoon. I'm sure he's muddy from his toes up and having the time of his life, so I have all day. What are you doing in Martinsville, sweets? Last I knew you were headed for home. What's happened?"

"More than you know, and I'll tell you everything, but first I wanted to share some good news."

"I'm all ears, sweets. Give," Annie encouraged.

"I'm getting married." Miriam smiled as she announced her news.

"Hot dog! I knew it! Didn't I tell you last year? Annie Buchanan didn't just fall off the turnip truck, and I knew something was afoot. Oh, Miriam, I couldn't be happier for you." She ran around the table and grabbed Miriam in a hug that forced the air of her lungs in a huge whoosh and surely bruised half her ribs. "Have you set the date? I'll be on the front row; just tell me when to show up."

"I don't want you on the front row. I want you standing beside Mary Elizabeth at the front of the church. Will you stand up for me, Annie? Please?"

"Oh, sweets, nothing would make me happier! You know I will. So, spill. I want to know how this came about," Annie demanded with her irrepressible smile warming Miriam all over. Oh, how she had missed this dear woman.

"I'll have to start my story by telling you about a man named Charlie Carpenter -" Miriam began with a solemn tone to her voice. For thirty minutes Annie listened with Miriam's hand clasped tightly in hers, hugging her once when Miriam described the rape, and then wiping tears with a tissue as her friend told her about moving in with Isabel and working for the Robinson's, going home, and to Corpus Christi, and finally about writing Sonny with her answer.

"Oh, sweets, what you've been through. Did you cripple that no good, gutter-crawling, sniveling bully for life for what he did to you? No? Good, where is he and I'll do it for you. I'll throw in Gladys for nothing. Let's see; should I blind her or just cut off both her arms?"

"Why does everyone react with such anger? You, Sonny, Toby, Will, you all want to hurt Charlie and Gladys," Miriam remarked.

"Didn't you? Weren't you angry enough to inflict permanent harm, Miriam?" Annie asked incredulously.

"Yes, I confess I did. It's been some time now since I've dealt with my feelings, I guess, so I'm not as intently angry as you are. Only natural, I suppose."

"You bet it's only natural, sweets."

"I did leave Gladys with a not-so-fond remembrance of me," Miriam mused aloud.

"I think I'm going to love this. What did you do?"

Miriam told her about threatening Gladys with the scissors and then breaking the glass in the kitchen. Annie hooted with laughter at the idea.

This is my last week in Martinsville, Annie. I'm going home to help Lizzie with the babies and make wedding plans. I'll go by the school tomorrow and take care of my resignation. Will you help me pack up my room?"

"Of course I'll help. I'm going to miss you, though. I've grown used to having you around, lady. Aside from Buck, you're the best friend I've ever had."

"I don't know how I'd have gotten through one day of school if you hadn't been there for me. I love you so much, Annie, and I don't want to lose you. Your friendship is one of my greatest treasures. I want you to meet Sonny, and I want him to get to know you and Buck. Promise me we can stay friends, Annie."

"You don't need to worry your pretty self about that one, sweets. I'm not going anywhere." The tears trickled down her face as she reached to hug Miriam once again. Soon Miriam's tears joined those of her friend. They spent the next two hours planning the dress Annie would wear, exulting over Miriam's new life as a minister's wife, laughing about the twins and Seth's soon-to-be-born little one, and making plans for keeping in touch with one another. The time the two women spent together that afternoon would be a sweet memory in Miriam's heart for years to come. Smiling to herself as she recalled Annie's renewed offer to work Charlie over with Daniel's baseball bat, Miriam was startled to hear a car horn honk in the driveway.

"My goodness, have I been sitting here for that long?" She scolded herself as she dashed into the bathroom to comb her hair and apply fresh lipstick. The knock at the door had her rushing to let Toby into the apartment. Opening the door she found herself swept up into a fierce embrace that had her clutching the shoulders of the man who had grabbed her, concerned that they'd overbalance and both wind up on the floor.

"Sonny!" she cried in delight. "What are you doing here?"

"What am I doing here? Foolish woman, how could you even ask such a question? What you should have asked is how in the world I waited an entire three days to accost you after I got your letter. The choir at First Methodist will be talking about my reaction to your answer for years to come," he told her as he cradled her face in his hands and kissed her senseless.

"What does my letter have to do with the choir at First Methodist? Can we sit down? You've taken me by surprise once again. Do you plan on making a habit of doing this?"

"Every day of the next 50 or so years."

They sat together on the sofa, Sonny holding her hands in his as he gazed at her. He couldn't seem to take his eyes from her face.

Kissing her yet again, he told her, "I love you, Miriam. I'm going to tell you that every day of the next 50 or so years, too. I'm going to tell you that you're beautiful, and sweet, and the most amazing woman in the world. I couldn't keep it bottled inside for one more minute, so I called Toby and asked him if I could come get you. He seemed happy enough to say, 'yes.' I think T.J. and the girls are conspiring to keep him and Mary Elizabeth from ever sleeping through the night again."

"I'm so glad to see you." Miriam grinned at him as she stroked his cheek. "Now tell me about your reaction to my letter," she prompted.

"I was running late for practice, so when I dashed for my front door I saw the mail scattered around the drop box. I scooped it up and tucked it into my folder, intending to look at everything when I got back home. Well, just as choir was wrapping up, I took my folder to the storage room and the mail fell out. I saw your return address as I was gathering it back into a stack, and I couldn't wait until I got home. I ripped into it and skimmed it until I read your yes. I thundered down the corridor back into the sanctuary, yelling 'wahoo' at the top of my lungs and dancing down the aisle. When Mrs. Sanderson finally got my attention enough to ask me what was going on, I grabbed her and swung her around yelling, 'She said yes! She said yes! You're all invited to the wedding!' They were still chuckling as I ran out the back door to find a telephone and call Toby."

"Oh, Sonny, I'm so happy you feel that way. I felt the same way when I realized last weekend in Corpus Christi that I could tell you 'yes' and not be afraid any longer."

"So tell me about your trip to the coast. What happened?"

"I'll tell you about it in the car. We have a great deal to load and a pretty good drive ahead of us. Shouldn't we be going?"

"Yes, I suppose that does make good sense. Can we stop at Lucille's one last time for breakfast? I left so early this morning I didn't take time to eat, and besides, those frogs are calling to me."

"I don't think the frogs have anything to do with it. You just want to see Linda again," she shot back as she reached for a box.

"She has been on my mind lately, I will admit. Think she'd run off with me if I asked her?"

"Oh, no you don't, Reverend Williamson. You're mine, and Linda is going to hear about it the minute we walk in the door," Miriam declared as Sonny grabbed her for a hug. "You'll just have to settle for me and a waffle."

"It's a deal, Miss Cahill."

An hour later Sonny and Miriam were glorying in a gorgeous summer morning as they made their way back to Cedar Springs. The crepe myrtle trees were a vivid pink against the hazy blue of a summer sky, and fat cotton ball clouds danced across the landscape in a succession of fascinating shapes. The sun was warm, the breeze exhilarating, and no two people anywhere in the world could have been as happy and these two as they traveled over the winding black top. Sonny listened intently to Miriam's accounting of her experience in the Corpus motel room, stopping her only once or twice to ask her to clarify a point.

"I'm not excusing what Daddy did to us. He put Mama through Hell. I wonder sometimes if her illness didn't progress so quickly because she didn't have the will to continue living as she had for all those years. But I do think I understand why he behaved as he did. He was afraid, Sonny. He thought he'd lost a part of himself because he believed Mama had been with Uncle Jim, and that I wasn't his daughter. When the truth of that finally made sense to me, I realized that there wasn't anything wrong with me. I was a whole person, not flawed and unlovable, like Daddy made me believe. I realized, too, that I didn't do anything to lead Charlie on. He raped me because his life is twisted, and I was just his, and Gladys', hapless victim. I'm sure I was too trusting of her and her good intentions, but the alternative is to become cynical and suspicious of everyone and his motives, and I can't imagine living my life that way either. I'll just have to be more careful from now on."

"That's right. From here on out all your dates will have to be cleared with me," Sonny told her.

"David Walker Williamson, that's not what I meant, and you -"

Laughing helplessly, Sonny squeezed her hand

and told her, "I'm joking, honey. No man is going to get within fifty feet of you from now on, and you can be sure I'll see to that! Your epiphany is such good news, Miriam. To have you come back from Corpus Christi this full of life and ready to face any challenge is more than I could have hoped for." Chuckling, he remarked, "Why do we pray for God to work things out in our lives and then find that we're surprised when He does so, and most of the time to an even greater degree than we could have thought to ask? So much for my faith," he said ruefully.

"You're not lacking in faith, sweetie. I think we all have low expectations where God is concerned because we have such a poor understanding of who He is and how much He loves us. He desires to do so much in our lives, but our finite minds can't wrap themselves around the idea that He is God and His love and mercies are infinite. We just need to be expectant as we pray."

"My sweet Miriam, you do astound me with your insights." Sonny smiled into her face before turning his attention back to the road.

"Sonny?" Miriam asked.

"Hm?"

"When do you want to get married?" she questioned shyly.

"How about Tuesday?"

"You're joking," she burst out.

"Yes, actually, I am."

"Oh, you," she fussed with a smile on her face. "I'm serious. We need to make some plans, don't you think?"

"I do indeed," he agreed. "I graduate in December, but we won't be assigned a church until the spring, with the idea that I'll begin my ministry there in

June." At the questioning look on her face, he replied, "Just the way we Methodists do it. Ministers are moved around in June. I think I could find a job for a few months in Cedar Springs, just to have a full-time income. We could rent an apartment in town. What do you think?"

"Would you object to my going back to work at the library? I can get my part-time position back, Mary Elizabeth says. The extra money could go into our savings, and I could be close enough to help with the babies when she needs me."

"I think that's a great idea. What do you think about a December wedding? The church would be decorated for Christmas, and we could add our own touches for the ceremony. I'd rather like to see you in your wedding dress in a canopy of evergreens and red ribbons."

"When is your graduation?"

"December 11th," he told her.

"Is that a Friday?"

"It's a Sunday."

"How about the following Friday evening? We could fill the sanctuary with candlelight," she suggested.

"December 16th it is."

Pulling the car over to the grassy verge, Sonny pulled to a stop and turned to his fiance'.

"What are you doing?" she asked, laughing.

"I can't properly seal the bargain with a kiss and keep both hands on the wheel at the same time," he told her. Sobering, he stared into her face for several timeless moments before softly demanding, "Come here."

Pulling Miriam into his arms, he stroked her cheek with the tips of his fingers, just a feather-light tough that nevertheless sent huge bolts of lightning skittering down Miriam's spine, and then slowly lowering his lips to hers, he kissed her with that same feather-light touch, once, twice, and then pressed his mouth firmly to hers in a kiss that warmed them both from the inside out. His arms enveloped her in a tender hug, and her fingers slipped into the hair at the nape of his neck to stroke and soothe. The honking of a truck horn as it rumbled by startled them both into breaking apart, and waving at the elderly farmer, Sonny urged Miriam to sit beside him as he once again merged into the sparse traffic on the old farm to market road.

For the rest of the trip back to Cedar Springs, Miriam sat with her head on Sonny's shoulder and her arm wrapped around his waist. Sonny hugged his bride-to-be to his side and steered the car with his left hand, grateful for this quiet time together. There was little need for conversation at the moment; their hearts were too full of wonder that the miracle had happened and they were together, this time for good. Miriam thought of her mother, and soon her thoughts became a silent conversation with the woman who had loved her so completely.

"Mama, are you close by? Can you see how much I love Sonny, and how much he loves me? I hope so. I know you'd like him, Mama. He's so good, and so patient, and he makes me dream such dreams – of a home with polished hardwood floors and a huge four-poster bed, a kitchen painted blue and yellow, and a black and white spotted dog who sleeps in the window seat of our bedroom and goes with me to get the wash off the line. And he makes me dream of babies, too, and a nursery with Battenburg lace pillows and a wooden rocking chair.

He can cheer me up when I'm down and make me laugh until I'm breathless. Did you feel like this when you first married Daddy? Did you dream these kinds of dreams? Did you hang on because you still loved him? Could you see through his fear? I'm sorry you lost your hope for a happy future, Mama. I'm sorry you traded your dreams for a life of ugly words and sadness, angry rages and Daddy's fists. No one deserves what you suffered, Mama. I still miss you every day, and I still cry when I remember those last few days of your life and how sick you were. I had so much I still wanted to tell you, to ask you. I wish you could see Lizzie's sweet baby girls. I know you'd love Polly and be happy because she makes Seth so happy. You'd be proud of Will and the work he wants to do on the farm. We're doing well, Mama, and I'm just selfish enough that I still want you to be here to share it with us. But I can't wish you back to what your life had become with Daddy; I know you're in a place of joy and beauty and light that is infinitely better than anything you could have had here. I couldn't take you away from such perfect love and the sweet fellowship you know now no matter how much I miss you. I love you, Mama."

"Sonny." Miriam sat up and looked at the face that had become dearer to her than any other on earth. "When we get settled back home, will you go out to Mama's grave with me? I'd like to introduce you to her and tell her about you."

"Sure I'll go with you. Have you been out there other times to talk to your mom?"

"No, I couldn't bring myself to go to the cemetery after her funeral. It was just too painful. I talk to her quite a bit, though, and I think I'm ready now. Will you hold my hand?"

"I can't think of anything I'd rather do. Miriam," he added, "have you been back to your father's house since you moved out last year?"

"No, Sonny, I can't go back to that house. I hate it. I hate my memories of that run-down, useless farm. Unspeakable cruelty lives in those rooms, and I hear the echoes of the tears and cries of unhappiness every time I think about growing up in that miserable place. I don't want to see Daddy, and I'll not dwell on a past I couldn't make better then or change now."

The next 40 miles were traveled in silence until Sonny spoke quietly once again. "I haven't told you about my grandfather's farm, have I?"

"No, you've never mentioned it," Miriam told him as she sat up from her resting place against his shoulder.

"I spent most of my childhood at my grandfather's farm. It was over in Hartsville, and Dad and Mother took us to visit every chance they could find. My grandmother died when I was four; I don't remember her. Mother worried that Pops wasn't eating right or taking good enough care of himself, so at least every six weeks or so she'd spend an entire day baking up pies and cookies, meatloaf, scalloped potatoes, green beans and creamed corn, cornbread and rolls, and we'd head off to her Daddy's farm. He fussed that she fretted over him too much, but he never told her to stop bringing the food. I know he loved her for it, and we loved going to Pops' farm. He had an old mule named Queen Victoria who loved to see us. We fed her sugar cubes and carrot sticks, and once in a while I'd put Gideon or Esther on her back for a ride around the corral. We fed the pigs and named the barn kittens and climbed the huge live oak in the yard to watch the lightning bugs dance at dusk."

"It sounds like every child's idea of paradise," Miriam remarked.

"That's the perfect word for Pops' farm, honey. It was paradise."

"Do you still go out there to see him?" she asked.

"You have no idea how much I've wished lately that I could. I've wanted to tell him about you and get his advice about a hundred times. Pops died three years ago, Miriam. At 77 I guess he just wasn't strong enough to fight off the pneumonia that winter. Mother and Esther cleaned out the farmhouse and sold the place to a young couple who moved here that summer from Nebraska."

"I'm so sorry, Sonny. I know you miss him as much as I miss Mama."

"Yes, I miss him fiercely. But I missed that farmhouse, too. I can still smell the way the hay sweetened up the summer breeze, and I can hear the chickens cackling in the back yard. The screen door made a peculiar sound when we opened it; sometimes I think I can still hear someone walking through that door into the house. When Pops died, I felt like a part of my life had been taken, too. A big chunk of my childhood was gone forever, and I grieved for it as much as I grieved for Pops. I couldn't make myself go out there, even when Mother asked me to take the truck and move the last of the furniture back to our house. I couldn't do it, but I realized last summer that I had no choice. Making my peace with the past wasn't easy, but I knew I needed to let go of the house and move on."

"What happened?"

"I drove out to the farm and walked around for the better part of the morning. I watched the young woman who lives there now rock on the front porch and bring her clothes in off the line. I saw her husband out in the cotton, working tirelessly in spite of the heat that was already simmering. I heard the baby crying from the cradle just inside the front door, and I remembered. I let every sweet memory flood my being until I was so overwhelmed I wept. I hadn't cried like that since Pops' funeral. I embraced everything from that old farmstead that I could – every aroma, every sound, everything. And then I told Pops how much I missed him and the farm. I had myself a long talk with him as I leaned on the fence and let the sound of the breeze in the pecan trees comfort me. I was greedy with wanting to remember everything I could, to take all of my childhood memories with me when I left, to hold close to my heart for when I grow old. I thanked God for allowing me to grow up in that house, and for having a grandfather like my Pops, who loved me and taught me so much about being a good man. I was afraid my heartache would overwhelm me once or twice, but now I know I needed to face the emotions and not try to run from them. You know what I mean. You had to face the ugliness of what Charlie Carpenter had done to you; you couldn't hold in that anger. I knew that if I was going to have peace with losing Pops, I had to do it. He told me once that it's more important to be grateful for what I've had, even if it's been taken from me, than to spend my life afraid to risk the having for fear of losing it."

After several moments of silence, Miriam remarked, "Your grandfather sounds like a wise man."

"He was."

"I'll think about what you've said, too," she promised.

Hugging her close, he smiled. "That's my girl. I do love you."

'I love you, too, even if you are as obvious as an irate skunk."

"Saw through me, did you?"

"Be pretty hard not to," she told him as she laughed gently. "Look, we're almost to the turn off. I can't wait for you to see the girls, and you won't believe how T.J. has grown."

Exiting the highway for the two-lane road into town, Sonny navigated around a tractor pulling a load of hay and around the bend to the town square. Turning into the post office parking lot, he braked and turned to the puzzled young woman sitting beside him.

"Before we get to Mary Elizabeth's, I need to take care of some overdue business," he told her, pulling a box out of his pocket. Reaching for Miriam's hand, he told her, "I want everyone to know that we're to be married. Will you wear this?"

"Oh, Sonny, I'd forgotten how beautiful it is. Yes," she assured him, "I'd be honored to wear your ring."

Slipping it onto her finger, he hugged her one last time before pulling back onto the road for the last hop to Mary Elizabeth's home. The silence that greeted them as he turned off the motor was pierced by the wailing cry of a very unhappy baby.

"Oh, my," Miriam exclaimed with a grin. "Looks like we got here just in time! Come on."

"Are you sure? Maybe I should just go -" Sonny suggested hesitantly.

"Don't be silly. They're just babies, not delicate pieces of priceless glass. Besides, I need your help to get my things unloaded," Miriam scolded with a grin on her face.

Sighing deeply, Sonny popped the trunk and reached for one of the boxes he'd loaded earlier that morning. He followed Miriam up the front steps and walked gingerly into the living room. It was pandemonium. T.J.'s sizeable collection of blocks was scattered across the floor, and he was sitting in the midst of them crying as if his heart would break. Toby was trying to get his son to pick them up while unsuccessfully soothing one of the twins as she screamed and wailed in his ear. Mary Elizabeth wavered in the doorway with her other daughter in her arms, her hair in uncharacteristic disarray and the tracks of recent tears on her face. Miriam hurried to T.J., picking him up and attempting to calm his tantrum.

"Is this what happens when I'm gone for a week?" she asked Toby.

"It's been crazy," Toby told her. "Anna here was up most of the night with colic, so we were up most of the night as well. I haven't been able to put her down long enough to play with T.J., so he's angry. He's been throwing blocks for the past ten minutes. Mary Elizabeth is exhausted, and out of compassion for her sister's unhappiness, Ava feels compelled to join in with her own furious cries. We're at our wits' end."

Reaching for Anna, Sonny spoke up, "Toby, have you got a hot water bottle?"

"Sure, in the bathroom."

"Would you heat up some water no warmer than this little one's bath water? And Mary Elizabeth," he said as he cradled Anna, " do you have any peppermint?"

"Yes, I do. I keep it for tea," she answered him.

"Good. Go crush two leaves and make some very weak peppermint tea, please," he instructed her. "We're going to make this young lady feel much better," he crooned to the infant nestled in his arms. In just a few moments Mary Elizabeth was back with the tea in a bottle. Sonny fed Anna about an ounce, then he burped her and placed her face down across his lap with the hot water bottle cradling her tummy. He rubbed her diaper-clad bottom and spoke softly to her while she whimpered. In no more than ten minutes she was sleeping soundly, the distress of a few minutes ago gone. He looked up with a grin on his face to see everyone staring at him in wonder.

"My little brother used to suffer with colic. This helped him," he explained. "Why don't you take care of Ava, Mary Elizabeth, and Toby can play with T.J. now. I suspect he'll be needing a nap himself in just a little while. I'm going to sit here with Anna in my lap. No need to disturb her just yet. She's had a tough day. Miriam, want to sit with us a while?" He smiled as he looked up.

She joined him wordlessly, clearly in awe of the miracle he'd just wrought. "You're amazing!" Miriam exclaimed softly. "You've effortlessly restored order to chaos."

"Sometimes the situation calls for an objective view, that's all," he told her. Looking down at the sweet bundle in his lap, he stroked her back and whispered, "Isn't she something? I think I'd like five or six of these for ourselves. How do you feel about large families, Miriam?"

"I grew up in a family of four, and I wouldn't trade one moment of the life I've lived with Lizzie and the boys. I think at least that many is essential," she agreed.

"Fifteen minutes later the blocks were put away and T.J. was tucked in for a nap, as were Ava and Anna. The adults were gathered around the kitchen table with glasses of peppermint tea and slices of pound cake the minister's wife had dropped off yesterday afternoon.

"Whew! I don't ever want to spend another night like last night again," Mary Elizabeth remarked.

"Amen, honey. I've been as miserable as poor little Anna. I didn't know what to do to help her, so a couple of times I cried with her."

"So did I," his wife admitted. "T.J. has been so jealous and unhappy with the time we've needed to give to the twins, and I feel guilty for neglecting him. Mim, I don't think I've ever been as glad to see anyone if my life," she assured her sister.

"I'm happy to be back home, too." Reaching over to grasp Sonny's hand, she added, "We'd like to share some news. Think you're up to it?" she asked, her eyes alight.

"Never been better," Toby assured them.

Holding out her left hand, Miriam told them, "The wedding is December 16th."

Chapter 20

A new kind of bedlam reigned in the kitchen for several happy minutes as Sonny and Miriam were hugged and congratulated. Breathless, Miriam told them about her plans to stay with them until the wedding and then that she and Sonny would live in Cedar Springs and work until they could move into their new church home in June of the following year. Toby told Sonny of several places he thought might give him a temporary job, and soon the two young men had drifted out the back door to sit under the live oak and discuss ideas. Before long the conversation took on a much more serious note.

"Sonny, have you given any thought to what needs to be done to Charlie Carpenter?" Toby asked his future brother-in-law.

"I know what I'd like to do to him, but I'm not sure it's the right thing to do."

"Why not? He needs to be taught a lesson. Maybe I'm just explaining away the ice in my gut every time I think about what Miriam endured, but I can't believe God would judge us too harshly if we gave him back some of his own. We wouldn't do any permanent damage; we'd just rough up his face a little bit." He smiled grimly at the idea.

"If you would promise me that this would be more intimidation than anything else, I'd like to teach him that lesson myself. Think Will and Seth would go with us?"

"In a heartbeat. Will and I have had several long talks about how we might handle this dirtbag. We can go in a few weeks, after Polly has her baby and things settle down."

"Count me in, brother. I'm just dying to get my hands on that guy."

Miriam and Sonny had agreed to walk to the market for Mary Elizabeth later on that afternoon. The day was pleasant in spite of the lingering summer heat, but Toby was sure these two wouldn't have noticed anyway. They were so absorbed in one another as they set off hand in hand that donkeys with wings could have swooped in over town and neither would have noticed. Sonny told Miriam more about his family, and she cooed over the girls and whether or not Polly's baby would be a boy or girl. She talked about how grateful she was to be out of Martinsville and yet how she missed Annie, thinking to tell Sonny that she'd asked Annie to stand up for her in the wedding. She'd like to have Lizzie as well; could he find two groomsmen, did he think. He assured her he had been trying to decide between his two younger brothers, knowing he'd surely hurt the one left out, but now that wouldn't be necessary. Both Gideon and Caleb could be his best men. Sonny shared with Miriam that Esther had reluctantly completed her first year of secretarial school, but she had adamantly refused to return in September unless her parents agreed to she and Chad's engagement. More discussion than goes on in a presidential debate had ensued, along with the extraction of several fervent promises, before his mother and father had agreed to the engagement at last. There was to be a party in October or November; he hoped she'd go with him. The minutes they spent together were precious and reassured them over and over that they were God's best for one another. Miriam wasn't sure her feet ever touched the ground.

Sonny kissed her goodbye at the door an hour later, promising to be back in a couple of weeks. She waved him out of sight, happily unaware that he had decided to make one more stop on his way back to school.

The farmhouse looked even more forlorn as he navigated his way along the overgrown lane. Shaking his head with sadness, Sonny emerged from the car and gingerly stepped over the sagging boards of the front step to knock at the front door. He waited so long that he concluded that no one was at home and had turned to leave when he heard the door creak behind him.

"What do you want?" the figure behind the screen asked in a gravel-laced voice, a menacing scowl on his face. "I don't want no trespassers on my place."

"Mr. Cahill? My name is Sonny Williamson. May I speak to you for a moment?"

"What for? I don't know you. Go on and leave me be."

"Mr. Cahill, I'd like to talk to you about Miriam," Sonny politely insisted.

"Well I don't want to talk about Miriam. Now git!"

"Mr. Cahill, I'd like to marry your daughter, and I thought the proper thing to do would be to discuss that with you, but I can see I'm wasting my time. I'll go.'

"Come back here for just a minute. You want to marry my ungrateful girl, you say? Come in, come right in here. I've got something to show you, boy. Maybe after you read it for yourself you'll see just what kind of a girl you think you want to marry. Might just make you change your tune about my uppity oldest child." He sneered, shoving a soiled envelope into Sonny's hands.

"What is this, Mr. Cahill?"

What's it look like? Are you stupid or something? It's a letter, proving what I've known about that girl and her no-good mama all along. Just read it, and then get out."

Sonny looked around the room to find a seat, but seeing the condition of the furniture, he chose to stand where he was and read the letter.

"Mr. Cahill, this changes nothing about my desire to marry your daughter. If anything, it only makes me want her more. She's lived with a great deal of unhappiness in her life, and I think I'd like to spend the rest of my life trying to make up for it if I can. I know I love her enough to try." Handing the letter back, he moved to go. "Now if you'll excuse me, I need to be on my way."

"What do you mean? Did you read this? Do you know what it means about Miriam?"

"Sir," Sonny countered, "have you read the letter?"

"Didn't have to; I know what it says. I've known it for years."

"I know what you think that letter says, but maybe you should read it for yourself. Seems to me it's way past time. Good day, Mr. Cahill."

Tom Cahill stared at Sonny as he walked back to his car and backed around in preparation to drive away.

"What does he mean, I should read the letter?" the

stoop-shouldered farmer wondered aloud. "I know what it says," he insisted. Walking into the kitchen, he sank into a chair at the worn old table and reached into the envelope for the letter. He held it in his hands, staring, until the sun descended behind the trees and the shadows in the room lengthened. With fingers that trembled, he opened the yellowed pages and read.

Dear Christine,

My heart is heavy after reading your last letter, but I have decided to risk Tom's anger in order to send you this final word. I'm sorry he misunderstood our friendship. In all candor, I had hoped in the beginning that we might someday prosper our relationship with one another, but after seeing your face the day you met Tom all those years ago, and witnessing for myself how much you love him, I knew my cause was hopeless. I couldn't be angry for long, however, because I saw how happy you made my brother. I know that in the beginning he loved you, as well. How in God's name could he have mistaken our familial relation for anything more? It staggers the imagination. I ache for the pain you must endure, and I grieve for the ignorant, jealous, malevolent man Tom has become. I'll never understand how he could believe that we would betray him, the two people who love him most in the world, nor that he could look at that precious daughter and not know deep in his soul that she is his own. He is truly a fool. In light of Tom's repeated abuses I feel I must terminate our friendship. I couldn't live with myself if I were to cause any harm to come to you or that sweet baby girl. I will pray for Tom to come to his senses, and I will pray for your safety and that of little Miriam. If he can somehow get past this ludicrous notion that has possessed him, I will gladly welcome him back into the family fold. As it stands now, I can't bear the sight of him for what he has come to believe and for how it makes him behave. May God have mercy on him for his stupidity.

In brotherly affection,

Jim

"No, no, it can't be," Tom spoke aloud the denial that had been ricocheting through his thoughts as he read the letter. "No, I couldn't have been wrong. She did betray me . . . and Jim . . . he must have . . . NO!" he roared in anguish as the crumpled letter fell to the floor. Stumbling from the kitchen, Tom shoved the back door open and ran down the steps, reaching the hay pile in the barn before he collapsed.

Life in the little house behind Cedar Springs' post office settled into an unsettled routine of sorts. The twins needed to be fed or changed around the clock, it seemed to Mary Elizabeth's sleep-deprived mind, and T.J. was fractious more often than not since Anna and Ava had come home from Dr. Meyers' clinic. There was an endless pile of diapers and t-shirts that needed to be laundered, and the adults needed to eat once in a while just to keep up the pace. How they managed at all was a mystery to the tired young mother, but clearly she knew they couldn't have managed any of it without Miriam. She was a Godsend. Miriam admitted to being fatigued at the end of the day, but her energy was boundless as she washed clothes, made meals, rocked unhappy children, and kept the house tidy, all with a song on her lips. Mary Elizabeth concluded that it could only be love. A letter came for her about every third day, and she quietly disappeared for a few moments to read Sonny's latest missive to her, only to reemerge from her room with a sweet smile on her lips and a dreamy look on her face. Sonny shared his most secret dreams with her – dreams about ministering to a congregation of people and how he hoped they could become an extended family for one another. He longed to teach them and share his love of gospel music with them. He wrote at length about his dreams for their life as husband and wife. One paragraph had so filled Miriam with longing that she'd walked around in a daze for the rest of the afternoon.

"I want to sit with you on a big front porch, rocking in the swing as the rain falls in soft little plops. We'll talk quietly about how much fun we have together in bed, trying to make babies, and we'll remember each touch, each caress, each kiss, until we can't breathe for the wanting of one another. Oh, Miriam, how I long to see you stand before me in the soft light of a candle's glow and memorize every feature, every shadow and hollow, of your sweet form, and know that we've come to one another pure in body as well as in spirit. I want us to revel in one another, awaken one another, and know the joy of snuggling under the covers and giggling with one another, knowing the laughter will soon turn to sighs as we discover one another all over again. I love you, Miriam, with a palpable knowing that God meant us for one another."

Miriam was standing at the sink washing dishes

four weeks after she and Sonny had last seen one another, dreaming of her wedding dress and just how she wanted it to look when an unexpected sadness rose up in her and threatened to swamp her. She dried her hands and staggered to the kitchen table just as the tears fell, and soon her entire being was engulfed in great gulping sobs over which she had no control. This was how Toby found her several minutes later, and he hastened to try and comfort her as she wept.

"Miriam, what is it?" he asked. "Why are you crying?"

"Oh, Toby, I'm so lonely for Mama. I thought I'd cried every tear I had for her long ago, but I guess I haven't," she managed to explain. Toby reached for his handkerchief to dry her cheeks, encouraging her to continue. "I wish Mama could be here to watch me walk down the aisle. I want to pin a corsage on her, sitting there smiling at me in a new organdy dress and dabbing her eyes with an embroidered handkerchief. I want to share this with her, and knowing that I can't is killing me."

"I know you miss Christine. A girl should have her mother with her on her wedding day, but that's just not to be. You can picture her there, a smile spread over every inch of her face, and know she'd be happier for you than anyone else there. She prayed every day for you to find your life's mate from the day you turned fourteen years old."

"How do you know that, Toby?"

"She told me not long after Mary Elizabeth and I got married. She told me I was God's answer to her prayer for her Lizzie, and she was praying just the same for you. Somehow I just know that she knows those prayers have been answered. She would have loved Sonny almost as much as you do, I think. He's the finest man I know."

Sniffing once or twice, Miriam smiled as a new wave of weeping overtook her. Hugging Toby's shirtfront, she soaked it with tears until he was baffled at how to help her stop. Awkwardly patting her back and murmuring, "There, there," for no reason he could quite understand, he was about to give up when a sleepy Mary Elizabeth appeared in the doorway.

"Toby, what's wrong?" she asked.

"Come see to Miriam," he said as his eyes pleaded with her to take this emotional female off his hands. He looked so plaintive and so helpless that Mary Elizabeth had to hold back the chuckle she felt bubbling up as she moved to sit beside her distraught sister. Thankfully Toby slipped away as Miriam talked to Lizzie about her grief.

Sinking into the overstuffed armchair beside the fireplace, Toby raked his fingers through his hair and marveled at the emotional makeup of women. He'd seen his share of female tears, but no one cried as much as Miriam did. She cried when she was angry, or sad, or frustrated, or happy. He wondered if there was an emotion known to man that wouldn't bring on her tears. She was a puzzle for sure. Still, next to his wife Miriam was the most loving, giving woman he'd ever known, so maybe a waterfall of tears wasn't the worst fault a person could have. Sure kept a guy on edge, though. He hoped Sonny was up for the challenge.

His reverie was interrupted by the ring of the telephone. Man, he still wasn't used to that thing! He'd been delighted when his dad told him it was their gift to him and Mary Elizabeth when she'd announced her pregnancy last year, but often days went by without a single ring. He leaped to grab it now lest it wake the kids, who were all three sleeping at the same time, a feat he considered nothing less than a miracle, and found his brother-in-law on the other end.

"Toby, I thought I'd call with some news," Seth's voice rang out over the connection.

"Seth, old man, what's going on?" Toby asked him.

"You have a nephew."

"So soon? She's not due for several weeks."

"You're surprised? I nearly had heart failure when Polly told me she was having contractions. Men just aren't cut out for this kind of thing, Toby."

"Tell me! Is everything all right?"

"We had a scare, but Polly and Jonas Alexander Cahill are just fine."

"What kind of scare?"

"The baby was breech. Tried to come out backwards. The doctor thought he might have to do a Caesarian section, but he was able to turn him and deliver him without surgery. Her mama was pretty worried for a while. I didn't get too alarmed until the doctor told us after he'd been born what might have happened. I nearly fainted right there in front of Polly's father and Reverend Mitchell and half the congregation. What a story that would have been!"

"Hey, congratulations, Seth! Let me call Miriam and Mary Elizabeth to this telephone. They'll have my hide if I don't let both of them have a turn at you. Just hold on," he advised as he hustled to the kitchen to call the women to the phone.

Mary Elizabeth was so excited about the news that she might have squealed in delight had it not been for her sleeping offspring. Seth told her that Jonas had dark red hair and the softest skin he'd ever touched. He was a big boy, weighing in at just over eight pounds. His daddy could already see him pitching in the big game. Men!

Miriam told Seth the news about her upcoming wedding, and he assured her that they would be there, newest member of the family in his best blue suit. He promised to take a few pictures with the camera Polly's dad had given them and send them off as soon as he could. Polly and Jonas were home from the hospital and doing fine. Wasn't life glorious?

Mary Elizabeth and Miriam talked for days about the goodness that seemed to be flowing all around the Cahill clan. Seth and Polly's little one had arrived safely and all was well, and Seth was delighted with his son. Ava and Anna were doing well at five weeks old, and maybe T.J. would revert to his sweet self one day soon. His jealousy was understandable, but his mama was about at her wit's end to know how to handle him.

Miriam's wedding was well into the planning stages. She had been in touch with Sonny's mother about colors and Sonny's ring size, and Mrs. Williamson had astonished Miriam with the eagerness she had shown to welcome her into their family as a new daughter. She refused to use the term 'daughter-in-law.' She told Miriam it implied a distance and formality she despised; Sonny's new wife would be a member of the family in every way that Esther and Rebekah were. Molly Williamson had invited Miriam to call her "Mother," and before Miriam could blink twice plans had been made for a day of shopping in the coming weeks. Sonny's mother insisted that she take Miriam out to get to know her better and help her to pick out some of the essentials for a new bride. Miriam decided she loved this woman already, even if she couldn't keep up with her.

Lying in bed every night, Miriam found her thoughts turning more and more to her father. She was so angry with him for the bitterness that he'd allowed to warp his soul, for the backhanded slaps and ugly accusations, for his apathy when it came to his farm and providing for his family. She wanted to erase every memory of him from her mind forever, and yet, there were moments when she hungered for the kindness and understanding of a father's touch that she wept with the loss. Accepting that she still loved him had been a shock, but love him she did. She had moments when she couldn't for the life of her understand how there could be any love left for him after the way he'd abused them; it baffled her. Miriam knew, as well, that she grieved for what he had lost by the way he'd chosen to live his life. He had the love of the finest woman Miriam had ever known, and he chose to throw it away. He could have made a happy life with her and the four of his children. God knew they'd tried again and again to find a way into his affections, but he had withstood their attempts to reach him until they'd finally given up. He could be enjoying his grandchildren and spending his days reminiscing with his sons and being cosseted by two adoring daughters; instead, his life was as empty and desolate as the ramshackle old house he inhabited on the worst farm in the entire county. The thought of him living out there alone brought tears to Miriam's eyes, but she had accepted that there was nothing more that she could do.

Chapter 21

Mary Elizabeth hurried to answer the knock at the door with something less than anticipation. Nursing the twins had depleted her resources, and she was exhausted. In addition, every loud noise lately startled Anna, and once she had begun to cry, Ava felt it her clear obligation to join in with the general confusion. They both wanted to eat at the same time, be held constantly, and their collective wailing could stun small mammals with the onslaught of the sound waves.

T.J. had been unhappy with the addition of these two interlopers from the first day they arrived home, so he demanded that his mom hold him constantly now, and yesterday he'd pleaded with his mother to nurse again, too. Mary Elizabeth was certain she'd have run away from home by now if not for Miriam's capable help and Toby's remarkable patience with their son's ever widening ornery streak. And now someone was knocking at the door.

Standing outside the screen was an elegantly dressed gentleman of about fifty-five with silver streaks in his chestnut brown waves and watchful eyes the color of fog over the Little Cypress.

"Mary Elizabeth Woods?" he asked quietly.

"Yes, may I help you?"

"Honey, I'm your Uncle Jim," he explained.

"My uncle . . . ? Uncle Jim? Daddy's brother? Oh, please, forgive my rudeness," she apologized as she reached for the screen door. "Please come in," she invited.

Stepping out to provide him entrance, she spotted a thin man with iron gray hair standing to the right of the door. He was dressed in spotless dark khakis and a chambray work shirt, his hair was neatly trimmed and combed, and the deep tan on his face only partly explained the network of wrinkles crisscrossing his cheeks.

"Oh, I didn't know you had anyone with you -" she said, "Won't you . . . . Daddy?"

"Honey," her uncle interrupted, "I've brought Tom to see you."

"Daddy, you look so different," Mary Elizabeth remarked, still clearly recovering from the surprise of seeing her father and this uncle she'd never met standing on her front porch. They sat down on the sofa as she indicated and accepted her offer of iced tea.

Hurrying to the kitchen, she found Miriam folding the mountain of diapers she'd washed and dried yesterday afternoon.

"Mim, you won't believe what I'm about to tell you; I'm not sure I believe it myself. I don't know how to tell you," she gushed, "but Daddy and Uncle Jim are here."

"You can't be serious!"

"I'm perfectly serious. I've come to get them some tea and warn you to stay put," her incredulous sister whispered as she reached for glasses.

"I'm not going to hide in here like a criminal, Lizzie. Why can't I come into the living room with you?" Miriam argued.

"I'd like to find out why they're here first, Mim. Did you ever in your life expect to see Daddy at my front door? I'm still breathless, and I just think we should see what he and Uncle Jim want before we spring you on them."

"Well, I suppose you could be right," Miriam conceded. "I may listen at the door," she added.

"Eavesdrop all you want," she told her sister. "My goodness, I can't believe I just said that. Just stay out of sight." Picking up the tray filled with the drinks and a plate of cookies, she hurried back to the living room.

"Here we are," she announced as she offered them the refreshments. "I'm sorry for staring at the door, but you both took me by surprise." She smiled, albeit cautiously.

"I'm sure we did, and I'm sorry for just showing up on your doorstep like that," Jim Cahill explained, "but we were both so eager to see you that we sacrificed good manners for expediency. I apologize for catching you off guard."

"Oh, please, don't apologize. I'm very happy to see you both. Daddy," Mary Elizabeth turned and addressed her father, "you look so different."

Smiling sadly, Tom responded, "I'm just a foolish, tired old man in a new set of clothes, daughter, but thank you for saying so."

Had it not been for her innate good manners, Mary Elizabeth would have stared at them open mouthed until she drooled. To say that she was astonished to see her father and uncle was putting it mildly. She was so stunned it felt like her brain was stuttering while it caught up with the current circumstances.

"I'm afraid I don't understand."

"Honey," her Uncle Jim explained, "your daddy came to me two weeks ago with a letter in his pocket and a story to tell me. We've spent the time since trying to comprehend twenty-five years of anger and misunderstanding."

"You mean, you went to Uncle Jim?" the incredulous young woman asked of her father.

"Yes, I did. I found a letter your uncle wrote to your mama when I was digging around in the attic last year. If it hadn't been for Miriam's young man, I might never have read it for myself."

"But, why not?" Mary Elizabeth wanted to know.

"I was convinced I knew what it said. I believed Christine and Jim betrayed me years ago, and that Miriam was his child," Tom explained.

"Yes, I knew," his daughter told him.

"You knew?" he responded, astounded by her words.

"We talked about it last year. It was the only thing that made sense," she told him.

"Once I read Jim's letter to Christine I knew that I'd tortured myself and my family for years over a lie. I nearly lost my mind at the idea of what I'd done. Took me weeks to work up the courage to even approach Jim. Never believed for a second he'd welcome the sight of me, but he did. Seems Jim found God some years back and had already forgiven me," Tom softly concluded.

"I'd prayed for years that Tom and I could reconcile. I was just waiting for him to show up." Jim

Cahill smiled at his brother.

The shocked surprise registered clearly on Mary Elizabeth's face as she looked from one man to the other and back again.

"You mean, you've made peace with one another?"

"By God's grace, we have," Tom told her. "I'm one of God's own now, too, and I have His forgiveness. I've come to see you because I need to ask my children for forgiveness. There's no way to make up for everything I took from you children, but if you would allow me to be a part of your lives now, I'd like to be T.J.'s grandpa," her father beseeched her with tears in his eyes.

"Daddy, I can't speak for Miriam and the boys, but I would be delighted to have you be T.J.'s grandpa." She smiled. "I have a surprise for you, too."

"Daddy?" a soft voice spoke from the doorway.

Three heads swiveled to find a tearful Miriam hesitating at the edge of the living room.

"Miriam, child, I didn't know you were here," her father began as he stood. Slowly at first she made her way toward him, only to pick up speed as she threw herself into his arms and clung to the father she'd never known.

"Daughter, I'm sorry, for everything. I can never make up for . . . all . . . I've done . . . oh, I'm so sorry," he spoke as the tears tracked down his leathery face.

"It's all right," she sobbed. "We can begin from today. Oh, Daddy, I need you."

"Miriam, can you . . . could you . . . I need to ask for your forgiveness."

"You're forgiven," she said as she sobbed. "We

can talk . . . everything will be fine." She assured herself as well as him.

"God knows I don't deserve anyone's forgiveness for the way I've spent my life, but I'll try to make it up to all of you." His brokenness was almost more than Miriam could endure, and she hugged him even tighter as he wept.

"Uncle Jim," Miriam turned toward the smiling, benevolent stranger. "Thank you so much for bringing Daddy to see us."

"Too much time has been lost already," he told her. "I'm delighted to be reconciled with my baby brother. Now I can get to know my nieces and nephews." He grinned.

An unhappy wail interrupted everyone's joyous reunion.

"What's wrong with T.J.?" Tom asked, startled at the noise.

"That's not T.J.," Mary Elizabeth smiled. "That's the surprise I started to tell you about. You two sit down and Mim and I will be right back."

A few minutes later the young mother and her grinning sister walked back into the living room with a shy two-year old and two freshly diapered and sweet smelling baby girls.

"Daddy, I'd like you to meet your granddaughters."

A light shined in Tom Cahill's eyes that hadn't been there since the first year of his marriage to Christine. He'd let jealousy and hatred twist his soul for years, but the tiny spark that had been lit in his spirit a few weeks ago glowed with awe as he stared in wonder at the tiny babies.

"They're a miracle," said Uncle Jim.

"Such pretty little things," their grandfather agreed. "Your mama would have been as happy as a mule eatin' briars at the sight of these little ones."

Mary Elizabeth and Miriam responded by placing a baby in each older man's arms.

"Daddy," the proud mother said, "You have Anna Elizabeth, and Uncle Jim, you're holding Ava Christine."

"And who's this handsome fella?" Uncle Jim indicated T.J.

"This is my son, Uncle Jim. T.J., can you say hello to your uncle?"

"'lo," a very reticent toddler spoke quietly.

"T.J., come sit with me," his mother directed. "These gentlemen are a part of our family, sweetie. This is Uncle Jim, and this is your grandfather. He's my daddy, just like Toby is your daddy."

Struggling to comprehend, T.J. told them, "I have a Papa Earl."

"Yes, sweetie, you do, but you have a Grandpa Tom. How about that? You have two grandfathers who love you."

After a few minutes of intense scrutiny, T.J. hopped down from his mother's lap and approached his grandfather.

"You wanna play cars, Gra'pa?"

Smiling widely, Tom responded, "You bet, young 'un," and giving Anna to Miriam, he allowed T.J. to take his hand and lead him to his room. "We'll be back," he told them.

Miriam turned back to her uncle and asked, "What happened?"

"He showed up at my door two weeks ago and

asked if he could speak to me. I'd been praying for him to have a change of heart, but I was still unsure of what to expect when I invited him inside. He asked me to read the letter I'd written to your mother twenty-five years ago and then he broke down in my arms. He'd been consumed with rage for so long, and to at last be confronted with the truth of his mistakes was almost more than he could bear. I feared for his sanity for a time. Facing the man he had been was the hardest thing I've ever seen anyone do, and knowing he'd lost his chance to make amends with Christine was the most difficult truth of all. He's done some mighty powerful soul searching lately. I got him to agree to speak to my minister, and I believe Pastor Stuart was able to help him find some real peace. I don't know what went on in their sessions together, but I do believe that Tom is a changed man."

"I'm still not sure I believe it yet," Mary Elizabeth said in a shaken voice. "How has he come to terms with the abuses he's inflicted on us, especially Miriam and Mama?"

"I can't tell you that, Mary Elizabeth; I just know I'm grateful for the end result. I've missed Tommy for many years. I'll enjoy every minute I can spend with my little brother from now on and be grateful for each one."

"It's too much to take in, Lizzie," Miriam spoke with wonder in her voice. "After a lifetime of wishing, we finally have a daddy. We've got to tell Seth and Will!" she exclaimed.

"Miriam, honey, don't do that." Uncle Jim's words startled her.

"But, why not? This is good news!"

"Your father needs to face his sons in his own time. They'll sort out their feelings for one another when the time is right, but your daddy needs to have his say in order to quiet the demons that have been eating away at him. Do you understand?"

"Yes, I guess I do. It's going to be hard to keep quiet, though. I feel like I've just found out that there really is a Santa Claus!"

Toby was a bit more skeptical about his father-in-law's change of heart, but listening to him at supper that night and seeing the light in his eyes as he helped to feed T.J. and rock the girls impressed him that maybe Tom had come through a refiner's fire. He was happy for Miriam and Mary Elizabeth that the family breach had at long last begun to heal, and he told Tom that he was welcome anytime. Mary Elizabeth insisted that he come to dinner Sunday after church, and her father eagerly agreed.

Miriam found that she could rejoice in her miraculous news as she wrote to Sonny later on that evening. She told him what her father had said about perhaps never reading the letter at all if Sonny hadn't suggested he do so, and she thanked him for his diligent prayers on her father's behalf. The letter overflowed with Miriam's joy, and when Sonny read it a few days later he found the sheen of tears in his own eyes as he rejoiced with her that Tom Cahill was indeed a new man.

The first week of October arrived in a flurry of autumn leaves and the promise of a frosty winter. The skies were a pale blue with just the hint of wispy clouds high above the trees, and the breezes exhilarated as well as chilled. Miriam loved being outside and found every excuse she could to take walks. She crunched the leaves underfoot and breathed deeply of their rich smoky aroma, hugging her sweater close and imagining Sonny's arms around her shoulders. She found her footsteps taking her to the farm unbidden one Saturday afternoon, and soon she was striding up the lane she'd sworn not so very long ago she'd never visit again. How strange it felt to be walking up to the house to which she'd promised she'd never return and find that all she felt was an eagerness that in itself was a wonder.

Rounding the last bend, she was astonished to see the changes that had been wrought on the old farmstead. The sagging beams on the front porch had been replaced with new lumber, and a fresh coat of white paint adorned about half the timbers. The windows were sparkling clean, and the screen on the door had been replaced. Stepping into the living room, she looked around wide-eyed at the plain, but spotless, green cotton curtains at the windows and the checked slipcovers on the sofa and chairs.

"Daddy?" she called. "Are you about?"

"Miriam, child, I'm out back. Come on through the kitchen," came the muffled sound of her father's voice.

Miriam wandered through a house that had seen a great deal of scrubbing of late, and the kitchen gleamed beyond her wildest imaginings. Stepping onto the back porch, she looked up to see her father perched halfway up the ladder, nailing new lumber to the awning along the roof line.

"Look what you've done around here!" she exclaimed.

"Quite a change, isn't it?" he replied, resuming his hammering.

"I can't believe how nice everything looks, Daddy. You've been busy."

"Taking a new look at the house shamed me more

than I care to admit. I know I can't make up for the years I spent as a lazy old sod who didn't care if his family had a solid roof over their heads or not, but somehow I feel like I'm making some amends, even if they're only to Christine's memory. I miss your mama, Miriam," he finished softly as he climbed down the rungs of the ladder.

"I know; I miss her, too. I still talk to her, though."

"I've begun talking to her too, these past few weeks. Felt like I needed to apologize to her most of all, even if it's just to her memory. She put up with so much, and I let her slip away from me because I was too blind to see the truth."

"You have to put it behind you, Daddy. There's nothing we can do to bring Mama back or change the past. All we can do is look forward to tomorrow."

"How can you . . . I was hateful to you all your life, treated you like a servant girl instead of my own daughter. How can you even stand the sight of me?"

"I love you," she replied simply.

"God knows I don't deserve it," he whispered.

Reaching her arms around his waist, Miriam hugged her father gently as she nestled her head against his shoulder. Drawing her close, Tom Cahill softly added, "I love you, too, child."

Clinging to him, the tears flowed down her cheeks as she sobbed away a lifetime of childish hurts and heartaches. They stood like that for some time, Tom soothing her back as she cried, thanking God again and again for the miracle of restoration. When her tears had dried and the sobs had become mere sniffles, Tom looked down into her face and said, "Come inside with me and

I'll pour us some coffee. Want to risk it?"

"When did you learn to make coffee?"

Two days later Miriam fluttered in front of her mirror, tweaking her hair and worrying that her dress wasn't dressy enough or the shoes the wrong color or her earrings too bold. Despite Molly Williamson's words of welcome and acceptance, Miriam was scared to death about the impression she was about to make.

"Lizzie, will I do, do you think?"

"For goodness' sake, Mim, you look fine. I've never seen you quite this nervous."

"You've never had to meet a mother-in-law before," Miriam complained.

"I beg your pardon, my sister dear. Who do you think Ida Woods is?"

"That's different; we've known Toby's parents since we were kids."

"Once you marry her son, it's different," Lizzie insisted. "Stop picking at your hair. You're going to make a fine impression. Besides," she began as the knocker on the front door clacked, "it's too late. She's here."

Lizzie opened the front door to find a well-dressed woman standing before her with a dazzling smile on her face. She was tall and slim, with dark hair that waved around her ears and gave her delicately oval face definition and contrast. Her pale complexion was flawless, but there was a fine network of laugh lines around her eyes that changed her from intimidating to welcoming in an instant. Mary Elizabeth sized up Sonny's mother in that moment and found she liked her very much. In many ways she reminded her of Christine, and that should put Miriam at ease as well.

"Please come in, Mrs. Williamson," she invited.

"Oh, my, please call me Molly. I'm eager to know Miriam's family. If you don't mind, I'd like to get started right now. Where are those babies I've heard so much about?"

Indicating the padded quilt on the floor, Mary Elizabeth directed her guest's line of sight to the girls lying there with teething rings in their hands. Exclaiming delightedly, Molly Williamson swooped down onto her knees and began talking to the girls as if they could understand every word she spoke. Looking on, their mother just marveled.

"May I hold them?" she asked. "One at a time, of course," she added, laughing.

"Sure," Mary Elizabeth told her. "Why don't you start with Ava; she's the most outgoing one of the two." Seeing Molly's questioning glance, she told her, "In the green shirt."

Cuddling the baby, the older woman patted the floor beside her. "Care to join me? I'm much more comfortable on the floor most of the time," she told Mary Elizabeth.

When Miriam walked into the room she found her sister and future mother-in-law laughing together like old friends as they each held a baby girl in their laps and stretched their legs out on the quilt. She was taken aback.

"Mrs. Williamson?" she questioned hesitantly.

"Hello, my dear. I'm just getting to know Lizzie and these delightful young ladies. She tells me that Toby's mother has T.J. for the morning. I'll have to spend some time with him my next visit. Are you ready to go shopping?"

"Yes, ma'am, I guess so. I'll just get my purse."

Rising from the floor as gracefully as she had sat, Molly hugged Mary Elizabeth and kissed her briefly on the cheek.

"I can't wait until my Esther gets to know you. She's 19 and all aflutter over her young man, but I'm not sure she knows a thing about the practicalities of being a wife and mother. My advice continues to fall on deaf ears; perhaps you will be able to help her better understand what's waiting for her."

"I'll look forward to that. I can't wait to meet Sonny's family. If Mama were still alive, she'd be telling us that anyone with half his wits and one eye could see that Sonny and Miriam are made for each other. We feel like we've added another brother to the family already."

"I'm delighted to hear you say that. This is going to be such a happy wedding, don't you think? And I want you and Miriam to know that while I can't take the place of your own dear mama, not that I would ever presume to do so, I'd be happy to help with anything either of you need. Putting a wedding together is not the easiest of chores."

"I'll remember to squeak if I find myself overwhelmed. Thank you for offering, Molly. You two have a good time," she added as Miriam walked back into the room.

"Don't wait up!" Molly chuckled as she whirled Miriam out the door.

"My goodness," Mary Elizabeth remarked as the door breezed shut. "Girls," she addressed her daughters, "now I understand where Marcus Thompkins got his energy. She can suck the air out of a room before you realize what's happening." Chuckling, she sat back on the quilt to play with Ava and Anna until their nap time.

Out on the highway, Molly Williamson sped up to accommodate the Saturday morning traffic as she and Miriam made their way to Ascension.

"I know it's a bit of a drive," she was telling Miriam, "but we have all day, and there are several dress shops we simply must visit. I have some grand ideas about your trousseau; oh, I can't wait to get you into the stores and try out some of those dresses. We need to consider shoes, purses, hats, and nightwear, of course. What size do you wear, my dear?"

'I'm an 8," Miriam told her.

"Oh, to be a size 8! I'm a size 12 because I'm so tall and raw boned. I felt terribly gawky when I was a girl, but once I turned 15 the edges smoothed out a bit and my body seemed to belong to me once again. Then I met Mr. Williamson, who is 6 foot 2, and I've never felt ungainly again.

"I'm going to so enjoy outfitting you today, Miriam. I know just what you need in order to be properly attired as a minister's wife, and your coloring is just perfect for all the lovely blues and plums and dark greens that are in fashion now. We should look at something sedate in navy for church services, and a bolder blue print for the ladies' meetings."

Molly was lost in her own ideas for several minutes when Miriam spoke quietly. "Mrs. Williamson, I appreciate your wanting to do this for me, but I feel like this is a great imposition. I don't know when I could possibly repay you for the clothes and accessories you're talking about buying,"

"Miriam, my dear, I don't want you to pay back a cent of this. I want to do this for you because I love you already and am utterly delighted at the prospect of your being my son's wife. This is my gift to my new daughter. I'm going to have such fun; I'd hate for you not to be able to join in with me. Can you do that?"

"You overwhelm me, I must confess, but I'll try." Miriam smiled in return.

"Good." Her mother-in-law smiled and patted her hand. "Now relax and tell me a little about your brothers and that delightful sister of yours. I want to get to know your family."

Several hours later, Miriam sat with Molly in a brightly lit café, sipping iced lemonade and trying to catch her breath. The woman was a dervish! She'd hauled Miriam from one shop to another, pondering dozens of dresses and suits, blouses and skirts, belts and shoes, until even Miriam wasn't sure what had been loaded into the trunk of the car. A few purchases stood out, however, including an exquisite ivory colored linen suit. The lapels were embroidered with rose buds and vines in soft colors of sage green and mauve. Miriam thought it the loveliest thing she'd ever owned. One of the dresses Molly had insisted she buy was a sleeveless tunic in navy polka dotted Swiss with a wide white collar and white belt to match. The skirt rustled as it settled over the petticoat sewn into the garment, and Miriam felt as feminine as Molly insisted she looked when she tried it on. There were sweaters in bold autumn colors, loafers, pumps, a strappy pair of sandals, and four of the most frivolous hats a woman ever imagined wearing on her head. Miriam loved them all. Smiling as she eased out of her shoes and wiggled her aching toes, she thought yet again of the negligee set Molly had found for her wedding night. It was satin with a fitted lace bodice. The lace straps criss-crossed in the back where it attached to the floor length skirt. The robe was thin chiffon with pearl buttons and elastic at the wrists of the long, puffy sleeves. Miriam looked at herself in the mirror of the dressing room and couldn't believe the image before her was actually her. The idea of standing before Sonny on their wedding night in that gown took her breath away, both in fright and excitement. She knew so little, and her only experience hadn't exactly given her the sexual awakening she'd imagined for herself. What an understatement, she thought.

"Miriam, why do you have such a strange smile on your face?" Molly asked her softly.

"Hm? Oh, I was just thinking about how much I love the ivory suit. I'm going to wear it when we leave for our honeymoon."

"I think you'll be the loveliest bride anyone has ever seen, my dear." Taking a deep breath, Molly broached the subject she'd had on her mind all day. Small wonder. It had been on her heart ever since Sonny had confided in her several weeks ago about his bride-to-be.

"Miriam, I'm about to take a great leap into something that's none of my business, but I only bring it up because I love you and Sonny so much. So here goes," she declared. "Are you worried about the honeymoon?"

Her face the color of a ripe plum, Miriam stared at Molly for a long moment and then took a hasty sip of her drink.

"Never mind, my dear, I'm sorry I've embarrassed you this way. We'll talk of other things."

"If I can stop this ridiculous blushing, I would like to tell you something. I know that we hardly know one another, yet, but I've been thinking about this for days. I think I'd be more comfortable in the car, though. Can we start back?"

" I'll pay this check and we'll be on our way."

Ten minutes later Molly had aimed the car out of Ascension and was glorying in the countryside through which they were driving on the way back to Cedar Springs. With a quick prayer for the right words, Miriam confided in Molly about the rape. In tears by the end of the telling, Miriam scrambled in her purse for a tissue and looked up in surprise to see tears on Molly's cheeks, as well.

"Oh, Miriam, my dear girl, I'm so terribly sorry that you've been subjected to such a brutal awakening. What kind of man could do such a thing? But I'm even more in awe at how you have overcome. Your life is a triumph over what might have driven another woman mad. You're a marvel."

"Oh, no, Mrs. Williamson, I'm not a marvel. Any victory I've had over what Charlie Carpenter did to me has been God's doing, not mine.'

"Yes, of course, you're right, and I thank the good Lord that He has wrought such a miracle in your life. But, sweetie, there are many women, even Christian women, who would have been so bitter that they couldn't have let God heal them of such an ordeal. You've not hardened your heart; I find that incredible. My dear Sonny has been led to quite a young woman, I must say."

"I think he's quite a guy," Miriam said, blushing anew.

"I can see that you do, and that makes me very happy. Now, you're worrying about how to approach your wifely duties, we'll call them, aren't you?"

"Yes," Miriam admitted. "I hope and pray that

when the time comes my love for Sonny and the desire he's awakened in me will wipe out the memories of that night, but I'm still unsure of how I'll respond. The thought of hurting Sonny gnaws at me."

"Well, I think we can put your mind, and heart, at rest. Shall I try?"

"Fire away." Miriam grinned.

"I have seen for myself the love my son feels for you; it shines out of his eyes like a beacon. You clearly love him just as much, too. I have no doubt that you will both work very hard every day to keep that love alive and precious between you. You're going to be patient and giving with one another, tender with one another's feelings, and talk for more hours than Carter has liver pills, getting to know one another. Any of this sound possible so far?"

Responding with a smile, Miriam answered, "Barely possible."

"You're a sassy little thing, aren't you?" Molly Williamson laughed. "Now then, as long as you and Sonny remember to be honest with one another, and loving in your dealing with one another, I know God will bless every aspect of your marriage. Believe me when I tell you that Sonny is worried sick about hurting you, too. The good news is that he trusts God, and you, and he has faith that you two can work it out. Okay?"

"Okay," Miriam agreed.

"Whew! Thank goodness that's over," Molly exclaimed. "I've been wondering how I was going to get that out and not hurt or embarrass you. I have a tendency to be somewhat blunt from time to time. I'm sure you hadn't noticed."

"Well," Miriam drawled, "maybe a little."

"Good, and since I'm being so blunt, let me remind you that I'm not fond of your calling me 'Mrs. Williamson,' all the time. If you're uncomfortable with Mother, why don't you try calling me 'Molly.' Okay?"

"Okay, Molly, I'll give it a try."

"See that you do, or I'll have to lash you. I prefer wet spaghetti, don't you?"

"I can see where Sonny learned to tease so well."

"Oh, my, I hope it doesn't bother you too much."

"It's one of the things I love most about him."

"Tell me what you have planned for the wedding ceremony. Have you chosen the music?"

Entering into this more lighthearted mood, Miriam explained what she hoped to do for the wedding as the miles sped away. She'd had such a marvelous day, getting to know Molly Williamson and finding out how their relationship might develop. What a surprise Sonny's mother had been, open, fun-loving, generous and caring; it was so much more than she could have hoped for in a mother-in-law. She prayed the rest of the family liked her when she attended Esther's engagement party in a few weeks. Time was speeding by quite quickly, and she and Lizzie hadn't even started on her wedding gown.

Chapter 22

Sonny pulled up in front of the post office just as the sun was setting. The crickets greeted him with a cacophonous noise that shivered along his nerve endings. He flexed his shoulders in an attempt to relax the tension, but his efforts were useless. This trip and its purpose had not been his idea, but he had agreed wholeheartedly to the plan. It was the right thing to do. Emerging from the car he found the grim faces of Toby and Will staring back at him.

"Sonny," Toby acknowledged.

"Toby, Will, you boys still okay with this?"

"Yep," Will said as he nodded. "This needs doin', and I'm dead certain we're the ones to do it."

"Where's Seth?"

"On his way."

"Do we know how to find him?"

"I asked around some, and the waitress at the corner diner was happy to tell me what she knew. Seems she's got her cap set for him and is real unhappy that he won't give her the time of day," Will told Sonny. "He comes into town every Saturday night for supper, she says, so all we have to do is wait."

Two pickups rumbled up the street before they spotted Seth's vehicle in the distance.

"Here he comes." Toby indicated with a nod at a third truck turning the corner two blocks up.

Pausing at the curb, Seth rolled down his window and asked, "We got a plan?"

"Enough of one," Toby responded.

"Get in," Will suggested to the others.

The slamming of the car door echoed down the storefronts of Main Street, then Sonny circled the block and parked in front of an office storefront two doors down from The City Café. In relative shadow themselves, they had an open view of the lighted sidewalk in front of the eatery. Everyone coming and going was in clear view.

"Think we'll spot him?"

"Yep."

"You sure?"

"Tall, black hair, pretty boy smile, boots and jeans, Miriam said," Sonny answered.

"We'll know him," Seth insisted.

"Low life does that to Miriam, he's done it to someone else," Toby began.

" - and the swagger'll give him away," Will concluded for his brother-in-law.

For the next 35 minutes the four occupants of the blue sedan popped their knuckles, flexed their arms, and tried to remain calm as a steady group of customers came and went.

"Must be good food," Seth idly remarked.

"Don't remind me." Will groaned.

"You are always hungry, little brother." Toby chuckled.

"Not my fault." He grinned. "I'm just a growing boy."

"There he is," Sonny interrupted.

Four pair of hostile eyes watched Charlie Carpenter laugh as he escorted a young woman into the café.

"Looks just like Miriam said," Toby added.

"I'm going to enjoy breaking that perfect nose of his," Seth remarked.

"What about the girl?" Will asked.

"I think we should follow them when they leave," Toby suggested.

"I agree," Sonny said. "We never planned on his having a date."

"Should have."

"Too late now."

"Shouldn't take too much longer."

"Then we wait."

Before another hour had gone by the object of their interest emerged with his young lady on his arm. They watched as he helped her into his pickup and said something to make her laugh.

"Ever the gentleman," Seth derided.

Keeping at a safe distance, Sonny followed the black truck as it drove to the end of Main and turned north. About two miles out of town he turned onto a country road almost hidden by a canopy of sycamores.

"Where's he going?"

"Maybe she lives out there."

"Don't see any lights."

"Could be too far to see any. Kill our lights, Sonny, before you turn."

"Good idea."

Sonny lost sight of Charlie's truck a dozen times on the twisting, dusty road, but his tail lights reappeared a few hundred yards up ahead.

"He's not going to any house."

"I think you're right."

"Looks like he has other plans."

"She might like what he's got in mind."

"One way to find out."

"Slow down, Sonny," Toby warned. "He's hit his brakes."

"Roll the windows down," Will advised as Sonny drifted to a stop. They listened for fifteen minutes but couldn't hear anything beyond the faint strains of country music coming from Charlie's radio. A loud crack broke the silence, and the four men in the car jolted as if they'd been struck. The truck rocked back and forth for a moment, then Charlie's date screamed.

Miriam's self-appointed vigilante committee leaped from the car and ran to the truck, their feet pounding on the dirt track. Sonny and Toby reached the passenger door just as the pretty young redhead lunged for the handle. Gasping, she fell into their arms, and clearly terrified, struggled mightily to get away.

"Miss, it's alright. We aren't going to hurt you," Sonny said.

"We're not here to harm you." Toby spoke gently. "We're here to see your boyfriend."

"He's not my boyfriend." She trembled as she spoke. "He was about to . . . I just met him tonight . . . Where did you . . .? oh, my," she murmured as she slumped into Toby's arms.

"Just like a female," he remarked, grinning.

"I've got her," Sonny said. "I'll take her to my car and be right back. Don't start without me."

"Wouldn't dream of it."

Toby walked around the truck to find Will and

Seth holding Charlie firmly by the upper arms, and, to his way of thinking, thoroughly enjoying the cowboy's tirade.

"What do you think you're doing?" he demanded of them, hopelessly trying to wrest himself free. A bug on display might just as well have tried to undo the pins. "Who are you? Did you follow us out here? I'll have you arrested."

Seth and Will snickered. "I don't think you're going to want to call the sheriff about this," Seth declared.

"Bad idea," Will intoned.

"Then what . . ." looking around to see Sonny approaching, he decided to appeal to him. "I'd like to know what this is about," he demanded.

Sonny and Toby moved to flank Will and Seth, and after several long moments of silence in which they watched Charlie begin to sweat, Sonny finally spoke.

"We've come to see you about a young woman named Miriam Cahill,"

"I don't know who you're talking about -" Charlie protested, only to be cut off by Toby's heel connecting with his left knee cap. "Hey, what are you doing?"

"You're going to want to shut up and listen now," Toby snarled.

Sonny began again. "You and your friend, Gladys, arranged for Miriam to go on a date with you last May. Starting to remember now?" Sonny asked, seeing the sweat pop out on Charlie's forehead. "You took advantage of her, and you shouldn't have done that, Charlie." He spoke slowly and softly. "No one deserves to be treated the way you treated Miriam, and it looks like we stopped you from making a similar mistake tonight with the young lady now waiting in my car. So this is what we thought we'd do. You need to know how it feels to be helpless, Charlie, and since Miriam can't do it, we're going to take care of it for her. And just so you'll know later why we did this to you, these are her brothers, that's her sister's husband, and I'm the man she's going to marry."

Nodding to Seth and Will, Sonny stepped back and allowed Charlie to jerk free of their grasp. In a desperate attempt to get away, he lunged for the door of the pickup truck, but Sonny's stunning blow to his solar plexus doubled him over as the breath whooshed out of his lungs. After that Charlie didn't have much of a chance. Just as he'd promised, Seth delivered a fierce right to his nose and had the pleasure of hearing it snap. The blood gushed down his face as they each took their turn, Toby blacking his eyes and Will bruising his jaw. They left him in the dirt on his hands and knees, spitting blood and crying like a baby.

Walking back to the car, Will muttered, "That was too easy."

"Mama's boy, too; I knew it," Toby declared in a disgusted tone. Opening the rear door, Sonny bent down and addressed their passenger.

"Mickey, are you alright?"

The tearful young woman sat up and wiped her eyes, nodding slowly. "Why did you do that?"

"You're not the first girl he's driven off into the woods. We decided he needed to know how it feels to be on the receiving end of an assault." Sobering, he added, "He raped my fiance'. These are her brothers."

"I'm sorry," Mickey whispered.

"May we take you home?" Toby asked.

Smiling shyly, she said, "I guess I do need a ride."

"Good enough," Sonny grinned. Executing a wide

turn through the cow pasture, Sonny headed the car back to town.

"Think that diner might still be open?" Will piped up. "I'm starving."

Raucous laughter echoed on the night air as the sedan's lights faded into the distance.

Chapter 23

Shorter days, colder nights, and wedding plans heralded the blustery arrival of November. Miriam and Mary Elizabeth had bought the fabric for her wedding gown, and they spent many afternoons stitching and sewing in seed pearls. The cap for the veil would be covered in seed pearls as well, and the gown itself boasted a high neckline with lace insets in front and back and a short lace train. Miriam couldn't believe how magical the garment looked already, still in pieces spread out across Mary Elizabeth's sewing table. Sonny assured her in his many letters that his brothers were being fitted for new suits and his sisters had bought new dresses for their holiday nuptials. She had splurged with the last paycheck she received from the school district and bought Annie's and Lizzie's dresses. They were similar to Miriam's, with straight necklines and lace overlays, long sleeves and full, tea length skirts. She chose a soft green for Lizzie and powder blue for Annie. The organist promised to brush up on his Mozart; they wanted him to play one or two short pieces as well as several of their favorite hymns as guests entered the church. She still had yet to arrange the flowers and greenery; that would need to be coordinated with the pastor's wife since there would be traditional

Christmas decorations in the sanctuary. Martha Tate volunteered to make the wedding cake; she'd been so excited that Miriam had said 'yes' that she'd shed a few tears. They agreed on three tiers, decorated in holly leaves with red berries and trim. As the items on her 'wedding list' were slowly checked off, Miriam realized that she was getting married, in just six weeks! There had been so little time to think about what she'd committed herself to doing, but when she did contemplate her future she was giddy with the idea of being Sonny's wife.

Sonny's academic deadlines were piling thickly one on top of the other, so he had not been able to get back to Cedar Springs since he'd driven her home from Martinsville. The letters had been myriad, filled with plans and ideas and promises of the great joy they would know once they became man and wife. His uncle found Sonny a part-time job working at the local funeral home. This hadn't been his first choice, but counseling with families would certainly be good experience for him, and the pay was excellent. With that in mind, along with Martha Tate's promise to take Miriam back at the library at her old salary, he asked her to look for an apartment or small house they could rent. She had found a house just a few blocks over from Lizzie's. Old Mr. Miller had passed away at age 97 earlier in the summer, and his children had cleaned out the house of everything but a few pieces of furniture and some basic items in the kitchen. Unable to find a quick buyer, they asked the minister at their father's church to look for renters until they could decide what to do with the house and remaining furnishings. He smiled as he thought of Miriam and Sonny. The house was perfect for them, and the rent was more than affordable.

Miriam fell in love with the two-bedroom cottage. The wide front porch boasted a swing and two rocking chairs, plus a concrete ramp that had been added to the east side for Mr. Miller's wheelchair. The living room was equipped with a fireplace and Mrs. Miller's piano; Miriam was overjoyed at the prospect of playing again. There was a bed, dresser, and bedside tables in the master bedroom, plus a dining table and chairs in the kitchen. Molly had promised a few pieces from her father's home to fill in the empty spaces, and Miriam had quite a few things left over from her year in Martinsville. She was sure they'd get along just fine, and she couldn't wait to show the house to Sonny. Determined to keep it a surprise, she'd mentioned nothing of her find in the last few letters, but waiting for him to see it was causing her some sweet distress. Keeping secrets was so difficult, especially when they were such happy ones.

After giving the minister a deposit, he gave her the key, and she and Lizzie set to work. They washed the curtains and re-hung them, then added new ones they had stitched. There were lace curtains in Miriam's home once again. Toby and Miriam's dad painted the bedroom a sunny peach, and the kitchen gleamed in pale mint green. Miriam found cup towels with red cherries on them, and framed and hung up several exquisitely detailed sketches of red fruit she'd found in a yard sale a few weeks ago. They looked very smart above the window. She bought new sheets for the bed, and her mother's quilt brought the old iron bed to cheerful new life. She added throw rugs to the floors and found flowered pillows in the five and dime that were a lovely russet color. They worked well with the new paint. The house was slowly becoming a home, her home; her face shone with happiness and pride at what she had already accomplished.

Before she knew it, the day of Esther's engagement party was upon her. Sonny had driven into town last night and had stayed with Uncle Thad and Aunt Margaret. He told her to expect him about 8:30 the next morning. He couldn't wait another minute to see those babies, he'd teased.

Miriam awoke Saturday morning to a cold drizzle that fogged up the windows and a lazy wind that stirred up the autumn leaves still gathered in corners and huddled next to tree trunks. She barely noticed. She helped Mary Elizabeth prepare breakfast and change the girls' diapers on auto pilot; Sonny occupied her mind to the exclusion of almost everything else.

She was drying the last plate when she heard the doorbell chime. Toby had just opened the screen door for Sonny when Miriam flew through the hallway and launched herself into his arms.

"Oomph!" Sonny exclaimed as he staggered back two steps.

Laughing, Miriam declared, "Oh, Sonny, It's been so long!"

"I'm happy to see you, too, honey, but it's getting difficult to breathe here," he wheezed, chuckling.

'I'm sorry," she apologized, only fractionally loosening her grip.

"Mim?" Mary Elizabeth spoke from behind Toby. "Invite him in for Heaven's sake."

After the requisite hugs and handshakes, Sonny sat on the sofa snuggled up to Ava, or was it Anna, he wasn't quite sure, paying homage to T.J.'s castle he was building out of blocks, and trying to sip his hot chocolate. He looked across the room at Miriam, holding one of her nieces and smiling at him, her eyes alight with love, and thought to himself, "Yes, God, life is good."

"Sonny," Toby said, interrupting his reverie, "how are your classes coming along?"

"Not badly. I've finished all but one paper and one homiletics project."

"What kind of homiletics project? What is 'homiletics,' anyway?"

"It's the art of preaching," Sonny explained, chuckling. "I wonder sometimes why there has to be a complicated word for everything. Every graduating ministry candidate has to preach a sermon for a panel of professors and graduate students so he can be critiqued. It's nerve-wracking, standing up in front of a group of men who have been preaching for years, knowing there's no way possible for you to say anything interesting or original without drooling, throwing up, or passing out. I've been dreading it for weeks."

"Come on, it can't be that bad," Toby argued.

"Oh, no? Ask my buddy who had to do his a couple of weeks ago. Instead of properly quoting the scripture where it warned to beware of the 'fiery darts' of the devil, he said 'diery farts.' They're still hooting about that one."

"Did he say that?"

"Hard to imagine, isn't it? He was red-faced and miserable for two days."

"Poor guy. I guess I can understand why you'd be a little nervous about it, too."

"More than a little."

"I'm sure you'll do a very good job, Sonny," Miriam spoke up. "Just imagine that you're explaining something to me."

"Honey, if I imagine that you're there with me I'll be so star struck I won't get a coherent word spoken. You don't know what your smile does to me." He leered at her.

"You're terrible, Sonny Williamson. Here I am trying to help and you -"

"Easy, honey, I was only kidding. I appreciate your suggestion, but you are entirely too distracting and that's the truth. I'll figure something out. Maybe I can imagine Dr. Smitherman with a cream pie in his face. He's such an old sourpuss anyway; we talk about his sullen demeanor and pessimistic outlook. I know that God can use anyone with a willing heart, but I've often wondered just what, if anything, about that old relic has ever been willing. Well, willing to do anything but complain and criticize. He's a master at that!"

"On that note, I think we'd better get going," Miriam laughingly suggested. "This conversation has nowhere to go but down. Lizzie, will you take Anna for me? I'll take these cups to the kitchen and get my coat."

"Here, Sonny, I'll relieve you of Ava," Toby offered, leaning over his daughter.

'I almost hate to make her move, Toby," Sonny protested. "She and I were just getting to know one another."

"You've got plenty of time for that, Uncle Sonny. Haven't I told you that Mary Elizabeth and I are planning on the kids spending the weekend with you and Aunt Miriam once you get back from your honeymoon? We thought we'd get off by ourselves for a couple of days."

"Miriam!" Sonny yelped at his fiance'. "Do you know about these plans?"

"What plans?" she asked as she walked back into the room.

Toby and Mary Elizabeth burst out laughing as they saw the good manners warring with the terror on Sonny's face.

"Joking, old son, joking," Toby replied as he patted Sonny's shoulder.

"You should know him well enough by now, Sonny," Mary Elizabeth reminded him. "Now you two go on and have a good time. I'll take care of my hapless husband."

"Promise?" Toby waggled his eyebrows at his wife.

The easy bantering followed Miriam and Sonny as they made their way to the car parked out front. Miriam scooted next to her husband-to-be in order to get warm more quickly in the frigid automobile's interior.

"Where to?" he asked as he drove around the block toward Main.

"Somewhere we can neck?"

"Why, Miriam Cahill, how can you even suggest such a thing?" Sonny drawled.

"You thought of it first, and don't you deny it, Reverend Williamson. I could tell by the look on your face."

"Guilty. That's not where we're going, though, is it?" He sighed.

"Of course not; no necking until after we're married."

"Spoilsport," he moaned.

"We're going to 817 West Lancaster Avenue."

"We are? What's there?"

"You'll see. Turn left at the next corner."

When Sonny pulled up to the house he realized this was the home he and Miriam would share in the first few months of their marriage. He smiled as he looked at the trim little yard and the front porch.

"Mmmm, I've already got some plans for that swing," he told her.

"In front of the neighbors? What will everyone say?"

"They'll know just how much I love my new wife."

"Come on; I want you to see the inside," she told him as she stepped out of the car. Swinging the front door open, Sonny was astonished to see how much she'd already completed.

"Miriam, look at what you've done. I'm proud of you; this has taken some work."

"Every minute I was working I could imagine us in these rooms, eating together at the kitchen table, sitting on the sofa in the evenings talking, and other things, going upstairs to bed together," she concluded, turning to face him.

Growling softly, he drew her into his arms and lowered his mouth to hers. The kiss was filled with every promise he'd ever made to her, and to himself, about this relationship and how hard he was going to work to make her happy. Soon Miriam was clutching his arms and moaning as their embrace grew more intense.

Drawing back, Sonny expelled a long breath and whispered, "We'd better not stand here much longer. Show me the kitchen."

They wandered the house hand-in-hand for the next fifteen minutes. Sonny was clearly delighted with the homey touches and the obvious love that shone in

Miriam's labors. Walking back to the car, she asked him if he'd make one more stop with her before they went back to the house.

"Anywhere you say. What've you got in mind?

"I'd like to introduce you to my father."

"Sweetie, I've already met your father."

"That didn't count. He's nothing like the man he was when he threw you off the porch. I've asked him if I could bring you out today, and he told me he'd very much like to see you. Would you do that for me?"

"I'd be honored." He smiled.

They drove out to the farm, exultant to be with one another after such a long separation. Sonny noticed the changes in the old farmstead as soon as they rounded the corner of the driveway, and he expressed his surprise to Miriam.

"Isn't it amazing? Anyone who no longer has any faith in miracles should see my father now. He's a different man. In my wildest dreams I never imagined I could be reconciled to him, but here we are. Oh, Sonny, I've had such a joyous time getting to know him. I can see glimpses of the young man Mama must have known and loved, and I understand, at least a little, why she endured the abuse and unhappiness for so long. The regret still shadows his eyes, but only time and God's mercy can help him to overcome the grief of what he lost."

"Only his home-going will afford him the ultimate healing. He's paid a great price, but from what you've told me in your letters, God has done a powerful work in his life. I'm going to enjoy getting to know him and being his son-in-law."

With tears in her eyes, Miriam kissed Sonny's

cheek and dashed from the car. The front door opened to find Tom Cahill standing with his arms outstretched, waiting for Miriam's hug.

"Miriam, girl, I'm mighty glad to see you. Thank you for bringing your young man to see me today."

"I'm happy to see you, too, Daddy. How are you?"

"Why, I'm fine, child. I've been spending some time with your Mama's Bible. I've been comforted to see her handwriting in the pages, and her comments and thoughts helped me to realize again just what a fine woman my Christine was. How she ever kept faith with God with my bullying and blaming all those years is a mystery to me, but I'm grateful for you childrens' sake that she did. She raised you all right fine, and I'm proud of her and of all of you. Thank you for trusting me with it." He smiled into her face with the light of tenderness shining in his eyes.

"Oh, Daddy," Miriam whispered. She grabbed him in another fierce hug as the tears poured in earnest.

"Here now, what's this?" her father questioned. "Miriam, child, the time for regrets needs to be over. I could cry myself dry every day if I brooded over what I've done to my family, and I'd be feeling most sorry for myself. I know what I gave up with my mistrust and scorn. But what would be the use? God tells us to look ahead and trust Him for the past, and with His help that's what I'm trying to do. You need to do the same, daughter. We can't wish for what we can't change."

"I'll try," she promised, sniffing and swiping at the tears on her cheeks. Sonny's footfall on the steps drew her attention, and she turned to extend her hand to his and draw him into the circle she shared with her father.

"Mr. Cahill, it's good to see you again. I'm glad to see you doing better," Sonny greeted the elder man.

Clasping Sonny's hand in a firm grip, Tom responded, "I'm grateful to you, son, for having the courage to dare me to see the truth. A few months ago I wouldn't have believed I could ever find joy in my life again, but the good Lord is a man of His word, isn't he?"

"Yes, sir, He is."

"You young folks come into this house and warm up. I've got some coffee on, and I bought cinnamon rolls this morning. We'll warm some up to go with our drinks."

Escorting Sonny and Miriam into the house, Tom breathed deeply and felt the joy every parent knows at seeing one of his children truly happy. It was a new experience for him, but, oh, how grateful he was to see it for himself and know that he was being restored to his children. God did indeed still work miracles. Miriam insisted on serving the rolls and coffee, so Tom and Sonny sat at the table with smiles for her ministrations, and Sonny asked Tom about his plans for the farm.

"I've found that I want to make the farm a success, Sonny," Tom explained. "I know what the community thinks of me, and they'd be right to think so about the old man I was. But now I've found a little spark of pride within myself, and I'd like to make some changes on this place. Make it arable again, leave it better than it ever was for Will and the rest of the kids. He's got some ideas about doing some things different; reckon it's time I hear him out since he's done some good things this past couple of summers. He sure seems to love puttering around this little farm. Guess any love of farming he's got came from somewhere else. Sure couldn't have come from me," he concluded as he smiled sadly.

"Daddy," Miriam scolded as she placed the tray on the table, "take your own advice, please. We're not going to look behind any longer, isn't that what you said?"

"Yes, daughter, I said that, and I'm trying to live by what God says. I aim every day to 'forget what is past and press on toward the mark of the high calling,' as the Scriptures say, but coming to terms with the evidence of your sin isn't easy, especially when I know how much I hurt you by how I lived."

That's true, Mr. Cahill," Sonny spoke up, "but we have a Heavenly Father who doesn't keep score, or condemn, and His forgiveness is complete in Christ Jesus. Your children have forgiven you just as well."

"I know," Tom spoke earnestly. "I can't begin to understand how they could, but I'm mighty grateful to the Lord that it's so. I surely don't deserve it."

"None of us deserve the blessings we receive; thank Heaven we don't receive what we do deserve as sinners before the Lord. What a misery that would be." Sonny grinned.

"Miriam, child, I like your young man." Tom turned to his eldest daughter with a grin of his own. "Tell me about your plans for the weddin'."

Recognizing her father's attempt to lighten the mood, Miriam told him about the decorations for the sanctuary and the wedding cake and food for the reception. He listened avidly as he sipped his coffee, thinking back to his own wedding day and realizing anew just how much his life had changed in such a short period of time.

"Daddy -" Miriam paused as she spoke. "Sonny and I would like to ask you something."

"Well, what is it, child? You look so serious."

"Oh, no, it's not anything bad," she reassured him. "We'd like to ask you to walk me down the aisle."

Tom stared at Miriam for several moments while the clock's tick boomed into the shimmering silence and he swallowed repeatedly over the huge lump that had formed in his throat. With tears shimmering in his eyes, he smiled and told them, "I'd be honored, daughter. When and where do I show up?"

Wiping tears of their own, Miriam first, and then Sonny, hugged her father and laughed together as they once again made plans for their special day. Driving away an hour later, Miriam waved one last time and watched Tom walk back into the house.

"Promise me Esther's engagement party will be at least a little light-hearted, Sonny," she begged, sniffing with the return of her tears. "Whew, I'm not sure how much more of this emotional intensity I can stand."

"Raucous would be a better word to describe this party. Marcus is my cousin, remember, and he wasn't raised in a vacuum. Several others in my family are just as exuberant as he is, and when we get together, it's a wild ride. You're going to love every minute of it, and I'm going to love showing you off. This may be Esther's party, but I'll be doing some celebrating of my own, my dear."

"Stay close by me, please?" she begged. "Marcus by himself can be a little intimidating."

"I'll stay close, and that's a promise, but not because you're going to need me. Mother is almost as excited about seeing you again as she is having Esther get married."

"I'm happy to see her again, too. She's delightful, Sonny. She's so comfortable with herself that she puts everyone around her at ease, too. I've never known another woman as confident and outgoing as she is. I'm hoping some of it rubs off on me."

"She is very self-assured, and I love that about her. She can be accepting of others because she is so confident herself. I've often thought that her people skills were never properly utilized as a farmer's wife. She could have been just as at home as the wife of a diplomat or politician. No one's going to get the best of Molly Williamson!"

"That's true, but it's more than just her extroverted nature. She doesn't intimidate anyone else with the force of her personality. She can be comfortable in any situation, whether it's dressed up for church or in dusty jeans digging in the kitchen garden, and she is gracious in every circumstance. Everyone is welcome to make themselves at home with her; that's quite a gift she possesses."

"Rebekah has that gift, too. You'll see it today at the party."

"I can't wait to meet your brothers and sisters. You've shared so much about them I feel like I know them already."

Reaching down to squeeze her hand, he reassured her, "They can't wait to meet you, too. Rebekah has big plans for her new sister-in-law, so don't say I didn't warn you."

"I can't wait."

Alighting from the car at Toby's and Mary Elizabeth's once again, Sonny sniffed the air and his eyes grew wide. "Is that lunch I smell?"

"Yes, it is. Lizzie's pulled out all the stops to impress you. She's baked a ham, so what you're smelling is probably cloves and pineapple."

"I smell that, but I smell sweet potatoes, too," he told her.

"She's serving sweet potato casserole with cranberries and pecans, butter beans, lettuce and tomato salad, homemade pickles, devilled eggs, and pumpkin pie."

"I may be marrying the wrong sister," he teased as they walked up the driveway.

"You're going to regret that, mister," she threatened as she tickled his ribs. "I'm going to serve you cold canned soup every night for the first month!"

"Promises, promises," he taunted.

The two were still laughing helplessly as they entered the house and pitched in to put the meal on the table. Ava and Anna had begun to sit at the table and eat mashed bits of food, so every meal was an adventure. Sonny marveled at how well Mary Elizabeth managed and how much help Miriam was to the scheme of things. He couldn't wait to see her in action with a child of their own.

"Mary Elizabeth," he groaned an hour later, "that was the best meal I've ever had. Please don't tell my mother I said so, though, or she'll disown me."

"Your secret is safe with me, Sonny. Thank you for the compliment, but it doesn't seem like so much. Every woman cooks for her family."

"Yes, every woman cooks, but few women have the gift for making a home like you do. Your meals are incredible, not just because they taste so good, but for the love that radiates from this table as you gather your family together. You are a marvel."

"Do you hear that, Toby? A marvel, the man says." Mary Elizabeth prodded Toby as she stacked plates.

"I agree with him, honey. I'm sure I've said so at least once," Toby told her.

"Maybe once," she agreed, 'but it's clear he knows how a woman likes to be appreciated. Sonny, have a talk with him," she demanded with a smile.

"There's no way for the two of us to emerge from this confrontation unscathed, Toby," Sonny told him. "We are outgunned and outmatched. What do you say we grab these children and make a run for it while we still can? I'll help you get them down for their naps. I can use the practice."

"Sonny, old man, you've got a deal," Toby quickly agreed.

When Miriam emerged from the bedroom that afternoon, dressed for Esther's party, Sonny could only stare. She was exquisite. Her hair had grown into a lovely short bob with curls framing her face, and her cheeks were aglow. The dress was a delicate cream color, with a lace bodice and full skirt. The neckline plunged in a modest vee, and the long sleeves and drop waist added to the ethereal quality of the garment. A pearl necklace accentuated the luminescence of her skin. Walking toward her, Sonny took her hands and spoke quietly,

"You're so beautiful, Miriam. I can't believe the love I see shining in your face is for me, but I'm grateful. I hope I remember to tell you every day how much I love you." He kissed her cheek, then turned to accept her coat as Toby held it out to him.

"Remember that she's staying with my parents tonight," he told Mary Elizabeth. "I'll bring her home tomorrow afternoon."

Tucking her hand into the crook of his arm, Miriam kissed Mary Elizabeth on the cheek and smiled at Toby as she turned to the door.

"Have a good time, Mim," her sister called.

Miriam remembered later that if felt like she was floating as she made her way to Sonny's sedan. Was this how Cinderella felt as she traveled to the ball? It was certain no girl ever had a sweeter or more handsome prince.

Chapter 24

"There must be forty cars in front of your parents' house, Sonny!" Miriam exclaimed as they pulled up. "You didn't tell me this was going to be a coronation," she scolded. "How am I going to bear up under the scrutiny of so many faces? I'll never remember their names!"

"No one expects you to. As a matter of fact, no one expects you to be anything but yourself, so relax. This is nothing more than dinner with the folks."

"You don't expect me to believe that, do you?" she huffed.

"Well, no, I guess not, but I thought it might help you to think so." He grinned. "Honey, you already know Marcus, Uncle Thad, Aunt Margaret, and Mother. They can't wait to see you again, and once everyone else gets a look at you in that dress, they won't care if you remember their names or not. I'll stay close by, like I promised, so stop worrying. Esther will have to watch out or we'll forget the reason we've gotten together to celebrate in the first place."

"Oh, I doubt that, but I appreciate your reassurances. Soothing her skirt with nervous fingers, she replied, "Might as well take the plunge."

"That's my girl," he said, patting her hand. He walked around the car and opened the door for Miriam just as a whirlwind in a lavender dress came flying down the steps and launched herself into Sonny's arms.

"Oh, I thought you'd never get here! I've been watching the door for ages. Look at what Mother made me wear, Sonny! I asked her if she'd hem up a pair of Caleb's slacks for me, but she wouldn't even talk about it. Now I'm stuck in this thing!" his youngest sister declared with disgust from her perch in his arms.

"You look lovely, Rebekah," Sonny assured her, smiling down into her frowning face. "Besides, you may as well get used to it. You're going to have to wear a dress for Esther's wedding, and mine, you know."

"Don't remind me. Hey, maybe you could elope instead."

"No chance, Huck. Mother would skin us alive and hang our hides above the fireplace. You'll just have to pretend to be a girl a little longer." Turning to Miriam, Sonny stood Rebekah back onto the ground and introduced his baby sister and his bride-to-be.

"Oh, Miriam, you're even prettier than Sonny said!" Rebekah exclaimed as she wrapped her arms around Miriam's waist. "I've been waiting to meet you forever. Esther and I are so happy to have another sister in the family; now we won't be outnumbered anymore. Come on, you two, you have to see everybody. We've been waiting so long for you to get here!"

Rebekah grabbed Sonny's and Miriam's hands and dragged them up the driveway to the front porch.

"Easy, there, pal; you don't want to pull us over on our faces. I don't know about Miriam, but I'm just entirely too handsome in this suit to get mussed. Why don't you run on and tell Mother that we're here. We'll follow right behind you, I promise."

"Okay!" she called, already in a lope across the porch. She flew into the house, her youthful impatience causing the screen door to slap back into place and the front door to bounce on its hinges as she flung it open.

"Whew! You weren't kidding about her, were you?" Miriam exclaimed.

"She's a perpetual motion machine. I'm crazy about her."

"I can see that. I like her already, Sonny. She's delightful. Why did you call her 'Huck'?"

"Huck Finn," he told her. "She's reminds me of him. Her free spirit and untamed exuberance would have been right at home with Huck and Tom Sawyer out on the river, thinking up mischief and winding up in trouble."

'I think you're right. Huck suits her."

Sonny and Miriam reached the front door just as it was flung open once again, this time by Esther and Molly. Miriam glimpsed the crowd waiting to welcome them and took another fortifying breath.

"Sonny," his mother spoke, "come into this house and bring my new daughter with you." Smiling, she kissed his cheek and turned to wrap Miriam in a hug. Miriam found herself overwhelmed by a cloud of green chiffon and lavender toilet water.

"Let her breathe, Molly," a distinguished gentleman in a dark suit lightly scolded from behind them. "Son," he addressed Sonny, "it's grand to have you home. Introduce me to your young lady."

Herb Williamson clasped Miriam's hands in his own and kissed both her cheeks with loud smacks. She smiled as she looked up into Sonny's father's face and loved him. His cheeks were weathered from a lifetime of sun and wind damage, but his blue eyes danced in just the way Sonny's did, and his smile held the warmth of a summer day. His silver hair, still thick and full, refused to be tamed in spite of the intense combing he had given it earlier that evening. Miriam realized that this is what Sonny would look like in thirty years, and the idea pleased her. Turning her gently toward the crowd, he introduced her to Esther and her fiance', Caleb and Gideon, and the rowdy collection of relatives. "They'll sort themselves out later. Now, you must come with me into the dining room. We have some spiced apple cider and snacks to hold us over until dinner, and it would be my pleasure to make you a plate."

"Thank you very much, Mr. Williamson," Miriam said as she smiled. "I'm so happy to have been invited tonight. It's such a pleasure to meet you."

"Miriam, my dear, we are grateful to God for bringing you into our son's life. We've seen already what goodness you've brought to Sonny, and we're honored to count you as our daughter. With that in mind, do you think you might call me Tuck?"

"I'd be honored to . . . Tuck?" she asked, puzzled.

Chuckling, her explained. "My full name is Herbert Tucker Williamson, but Molly calls me 'Tuck.' It's her nickname for me. I thought that might me easier for you at first than 'Dad.'"

"Yes, it will be. Tuck it is," Miriam said, grinning.

The rest of the evening was a blur of bright lights and laughing, happy faces as Miriam was plied with questions about wedding plans, her family, her year of teaching, and at least a hundred other things Sonny's family thought to ask. She met Chad and was able to see for herself why Esther loved him so much. Sonny's eldest sister was petite, with dancing eyes and hair that fell in thick waves the color of ripe wheat. She was soft-spoken and genteel, but Miriam caught glimpses of the core of steel her dainty frame concealed. Caleb and Gideon were typical teenage boys, running wild, eating constantly, and full of vinegar. They reminded Miriam of Will and Seth at that age. Uncle Thad kept the entire company in giggles with his family stories, and Molly's sister-in-law, Charlotte, played the piano while everyone sang. Miriam ate until she thought the zipper on her dress was about to pop open, but everything was so delicious. There was roast beef, turkey and dressing, scalloped potatoes, green beans, beets, cabbage, okra, fruit salad, yeast rolls, pecan and cherry pies, peach cobbler, and an enormous cake decorated with violets and offering congratulations to Esther and Chad. Before she knew it, 10 o'clock had come and gone and the guests gathered up their things to head for home. Soon the house was quiet. With the leftovers put away and the house tidied, the family gathered into the kitchen for hot chocolate before they retired for the night. Everyone had exchanged their party finery for pajamas and robes, and Miriam relaxed as she sat between Sonny and Rebekah and sipped her hot chocolate, content to listen to Tuck and Molly as they discussed the day with their children.

"Well, Esther, was the party to your liking?" her father asked her.

"It was even lovelier than I could have hoped. Thank you, Mother, for everything you did to make it so special. Daddy, I know you spent more money than you should have to make everything so beautiful. I'll remember this night for the rest of my life."

"You only get engaged once, daughter," Tuck told her. "It should be memorable."

"I wish we could eat like that every night," Gideon said. "Mother, do we have any pie left over? I could use a snack."

"Why does that not surprise me?" Molly said. "It's a little late for pie, dear. How about a turkey sandwich instead?"

"May I have one of those, too?" Tuck asked his wife.

"You're hungry, too?" she asked, incredulous.

"I talked more than I ate at dinner, wife," he declared.

"If you're making sandwiches for them," Sonny spoke up, "I'll take one, too, please."

"Molly," Miriam said, "why don't I help you make some sandwiches?"

Working beside her future mother-in-law to prepare this late night snack pleased Miriam inordinately. She wanted so much to be a part of this remarkable family, to be accepted and valued for who and what she was. She saw the obvious love Sonny's parents shared, but somehow she sensed more than that between them. They had been so in tune to one another this evening, for one thing. From across the room Tuck sought out his wife's face, only to find her already looking at him, the love shining from her eyes. Miriam had seen them exchange those looks several times this evening. They had finished one another's sentences several times over dinner, as well. She marveled at what they seemed to share. Slicing bread, Miriam decided to ask Molly about her relationship with Sonny's dad.

"May I ask you a question?

"Of course you may."

"Sonny has told me quite a bit about you in his letters to me, and I've seen for myself tonight what a close family you are. He's told me about you and Tuck and how much you love one another. I've seen that too."

"I do love Tuck very much," Molly told her as she worked.

"How do you two do it?"

"Do what?"

"How do you keep that love so strong between the two of you? You seem to be in such harmony with one another. I have the feeling that what you and Tuck share is rare, even among happily married couples. I want my marriage to be just as special. How do you do it?"

"My, you do ask tough questions, don't you?

"If you'd rather not talk about it –"

"Oh, my dear, that's not what I meant. I'm happy to talk about my marriage to Tuck, especially with you as you're about to become a married woman yourself. I just meant that there's more than one simple answer to it. I think it's because we're best friends first. We talk about everything, and we share what we think and feel with one another. We put the other first, looking for ways to serve each other as husband and wife. We support one another, and we're honest with one another. Most of all, though, I know that I married a very special man. He's been blessed with a wisdom beyond what most men have, and he uses this wisdom to seek God's best for himself and his family. He loves us unconditionally, and because he does, he is our encourager, our nurturer, our provider, our guide. He's taught his children well, Miriam, because I see so many of those qualities in them as well. What Tuck and I have is rare, but I believe with all my heart that you and Sonny will share that same kind of relationship. The secret is to never take it for granted."

With tears in her eyes, Miriam reached out to hug this remarkable woman. "Oh, Molly, I know already how blessed I am to have Sonny, and now I've seen tonight that my blessings have been multiplied because of his family and the way you've welcomed me. I love you already."

"Oh, sweetie, we love you already as well. You're a light in our lives as well as Sonny's, and don't you ever forget that," she said, her eyes bright with the sheen of tears, too. "Now, let's feed our crew." Picking up the tray of sandwiches, they turned to the table where the rest of the clan was engaged in a lively game of I, Spy. As she listened to the teasing and laughter, Miriam knew in her innermost being that this must be what God intended families to be, and that this kind of family life was the one she wanted to build with Sonny.

Walking with Sonny into church the next morning, Miriam was astonished at the number of people who congratulated her with hugs and handshakes, calling her by name and wishing she and Sonny well for the upcoming wedding. How did everyone know her? When she posed the question to Sonny, he laughed and told her, "Mother and Rebekah, that's how. Mother has been so excited about this, she's told the postmistress, the butcher, and everyone here at church. It helps that she's lived here for 30 years and knows everyone in town. I hope you don't mind. This has been my church home ever since my diapers were changed in the nursery, so they feel like a member of their own family is getting married."

"I guess I don't mind. I'm just a little taken aback. I've never had such a welcome from anybody else." Smiling, she told him, "It makes me so proud of you, to see how they love you and wish you well."

"I'm the one who is proud, walking with the prettiest girl in the entire congregation this morning."

"I'm sure I'm not the prettiest girl, but I'm happy you think so. Thank you."

This was a larger congregation than the ones Miriam had attended at home and in Martinsville, but she found she liked the more formal architecture and style of worship. So many voices blending together to sing the hymns made chills race along her arms; the harmonies were lovely. Surely this must be a glimpse of the angel choirs in Heaven.

Miriam found it difficult to concentrate on the words of the message with Sonny's arm around her shoulder and his familiar after shave tickling her nose. He was so solid, so steady, and she couldn't seem to stop thinking about actually being married to him, living in the same house with him, sharing a bathroom sink and a closet, eating meals together, sleeping in the same bed. She felt herself blushing and deliberately homed in on the words of the minister. Lusting after your husband-to-be was one thing, but to do it in church! She smiled to herself as she worked to keep her mind from wandering any farther down that particular road.

After the services had ended, she and Sonny were swamped once again by well-wishers. The trip into the fellowship hall took an extra fifteen minutes just because so many people wanted to hug Sonny and shake her hand and ask about some detail of the wedding. She was smiling into Sonny's face as they turned the corner into the large room only to be jolted from her thoughts by a boisterous "Surprise!" The whole church had crowded into the room, which was decorated with fresh flower arrangements and balloons and a huge banner that said, 'Congratulations, Sonny and Miriam.' She stared at what she was slowly realizing was a wedding shower for the two of them.

"Did you know about this?"

"I had no idea. How did Mother keep Rebekah from telling us ahead of time?"

"Maybe that's because your family knew nothing about it," Mrs. Rogers told him as she escorted them to the long table at the front of the room. "It's the best kept secret in the history of the ladies' missionary group." She was beaming at them. "You two have a seat at this table. Pastor Hiram would like to say something."

"Sonny, you know we love you and consider you a part of our family. We have prayed for you, as we pray for all our children, that God will accomplish his purpose in your life, and we have seen that come to pass as you are soon to graduate from seminary and marry this lovely young woman. Therefore, we would have been remiss not to add our good wishes as the two of you embark on this life God has chosen for you. Please enjoy the refreshments, and then you've got some gifts to open."

With a sweep of his hand he directed their gaze to a large round table so laden with gifts it seemed to groan from the effort of holding them up. Sonny gaped, and Miriam found her eyes swimming with tears.

"Oh, Sonny, look what they've done. Have you ever seen anything like it?"

"Never," he told her, his own eyes misty. "They're unbelievable."

Chapter 25

After the last hug, the last kiss, the last cry of 'Good luck' and 'We love you,' Sonny and Miriam pulled away from the church with his car, and his dad's, laden with wedding gifts. They'd received dishes, glasses, pots and pans, towels, sheets, wash cloths, pillows, cookbooks, hand towels for the kitchen, baking dishes, a hand crocheted sofa throw, picture frames, and enough groceries to fill a good-sized pantry. Miriam was still stunned by the generosity that had been extended to them by this loving church family.

"Oh, Sonny, can you believe this? We won't need to buy anything for years. Did your mother make a complete list of these gifts? I want to get started on my thank-you cards right away."

"I'm sure she did. Why don't we pack up as soon as we get to the house and head for our place. Hm, our place. That's the first time I've called it that, and I like the way it sounds."

"So do I. Can we fit everything in your car?"

"I doubt it. We'll take as much as we can, then I'll ask Mother to drive over with the rest next week.

She'll jump at the chance to see you again. She may even help you get things settled at the house."

"I wish you could stay. I'm going to miss you."

"I'll miss you, too, but these last few weeks leading up to graduation are going to be hectic. You have so much to do to get ready for the wedding, you'll be too busy to miss me."

"Don't believe that for a minute. It's easy enough to keep my mind occupied during the day with chores and caring for the kids, but at night I get so lonely for you I ache all over."

"I feel the same. We'll just have to be comforted by the fact that it won't be much longer now."

"Four weeks, I know, but it feels like a lifetime."

Pulling into his parents' driveway, Sonny reached his arm around Miriam's shoulders and drew her close. "I'll just have to leave you with plenty to remember me by," he said as he lowered his mouth to hers. The kiss swamped her with its fire, and she responded in kind, pressing herself close to him and threading her fingers into his hair. Soon they were drawing apart and gasping for air.

"Oh, my, Reverend, what you do to me."

"Miss Cahill, you have no idea."

They walked arm in arm up to the house, hoping to delay Sonny's departure for school as long as possible. She hummed as she packed her things, thinking back over the past two days. The Williamsons were gracious, and she'd been overcome with emotion at the way they had opened their arms and hearts to her. Thinking about Esther's party, and the family gathering in the kitchen afterward, Miriam reminded herself to send a note of thanks to Tuck and Molly for making her feel so much at home.   She decided as well to send notes to each of Sonny's siblings; she wanted to work on being their sister as soon as possible.

Sooner than Miriam had planned, she and Sonny were hugging everyone goodbye and heading down the road toward Cedar Springs. Sonny drove as slowly as he dared, enjoying the intimacy he and Miriam shared as she sat with her head on his shoulder, talking quietly with him as the miles sped by.

Unloading the car at the house took less time than either one of the young people had hoped, and with more kisses along the way, he drove her to Toby's and offered his final goodbye before driving off toward school. Miriam closed the door behind him, resting her head on its smooth surface and feeling the tears as they trickled onto her cheeks.

"What is it, Mim?" Lizzie asked from the sofa behind her.

'I miss him already," she told her sister.

"I'm sorry, but maybe what I have to show you will cheer you up." She smiled as she beckoned Miriam to follow her. Walking into the bedroom Miriam had occupied since the summer, she stared in awe at the completed wedding dress hanging from the closet door. Never had she seen anything more exquisite in her life. Walking toward it in a daze, she stroked the lace and seed pearls with trembling fingers, enjoying the sound of the rustling the petticoat made.

"Try it on, Mim. I've been dying to see you in it."

With Mary Elizabeth's help, Miriam soon found herself staring at the image of a lovely young woman with chestnut curls in the dress that would herald the beginning of her new life.

"Oh, Lizzie," she whispered, unwilling to break the mood that had settled over them. "Thank you, oh, thank you." She hugged Mary Elizabeth, then turned to the mirror once again, not altogether convinced that she wasn't dreaming this entire thing.

"You're so lovely, Mim."

'I wish Mama could see me."

"Maybe she does, somehow."

"Do you think so?"

"I like to think that she can see T.J. and the girls. Foolish notion, I guess, because I don't think God allows glimpses of the family anyone has left behind. That would be too painful, don't you think? The Bible says there are no tears in Heaven, after all."

"Sonny told me that he believes that the saints in Heaven who have gone before us can see the entire scope of our lives, all at once."

"What do you mean?"

"Well, since Heaven is timeless, infinite, he thinks that everyone already in Heaven has seen the end of the story. Mama has already met our children and knows how everything has turned out in their lives."

"What a lovely idea. My, does it ever surprise you at the intensity of his thoughts?"

"Constantly. He's so smart, and his faith is such a vital part of his life. I think his thoughts are often on a different plane from my own, but that just gives me one more reason to love and admire him. Oh, Lizzie," she burst out, turning to face her beloved sister, "I want so much for my marriage to Sonny. I see how in tune you are with Toby, and the harmony that exists between his parents, and I want the same thing for us. It's so scary, thinking about this huge feeling that exists between you and not wanting to do anything to damage it or hurt him."

"Toby and I grew up together before we eloped four years ago; we've known each other since childhood. Being married to him changed that, though. It's like our lives didn't begin until we became husband and wife."

"What do you mean?"

"He's a part of me now, and I'm a part of him. We are no longer just Mary Elizabeth and Toby. There's a oneness that ties us together, and that bond is what we try to nurture and help to grow strong. Even when I'm working in the house, or caring for the kids, he's a part of my thought processes, my actions. What I do I do in part for him, because he loves me, and because I love him. I want to please him, to take care of him and protect him, to see him happy and enjoying his life. I want to be some of the reason he has joy in his life."

"How does it happen? How did you and Toby come to feel that way?"

"You and Sonny will find as the years go by that you will share not only the same experiences, but you'll tell one another things that no one else knows. Your private world together will be yours alone, where no one else can intrude, not even your children. I love knowing that Toby knows me that well, and that I know him, too. That intimacy will be what helps you find your own harmony together."

"I hope so. I love him so much."

"I've come to realize that Mama stayed with Daddy in part because she had that harmony with him in the beginning, and she desperately wanted to find it again during those years that he was so hateful and angry. I think she loved him so much that she couldn't give up on the man he had been, so she waited, and prayed that who he had been with her in their private world would come back to her, somehow."

"I think you're right. I'll never agree with her decision to stay with him, especially when he was so physically hurtful, but I can understand loving someone so much that you never lose hope that he'll change. I'm just sorry that she didn't live long enough to see what Daddy has become."

"I'm not sure he would have changed if he hadn't lost her. It took something that drastic to cause him to even consider that he might have been wrong about her those many years."

"Oh, Lizzie, and look at what he's lost."

"Yes, but look at what he's gained. He's a new man, and the perfect love and perfect forgiveness that Mama has found will be his someday. I think she'll be waiting for him when it's his time to go, and together they'll know perfect oneness in Heaven for eternity."

"You're going to make me cry. Help me out of my dress, and I'll help you make supper. Toby should be back from his mother's house soon, and I know three children who are going to be hungry, sleepy, and grumpy."

"I think you're right."

Chapter 26

An uncharacteristic snowfall dressed the landscape in feathery white as Miriam stood at the mirror in the church parlor. She surveyed her reflection one last time before she walked down the aisle and became Mrs. David Walker Williamson. Mary Elizabeth had worked tirelessly the entire week, making sure that everyone and everything were ready. Annie and Buck had arrived two days ago, and she and Lizzie stood behind her now, their dresses floating around them in filmy loveliness, their faces wreathed in smiles at what was about to take place. Miriam had seen Molly and her new sisters this morning at the breakfast brunch the ladies of the church had hosted for her. She had been able to relax and spend a happy two hours with the women who meant most to her in the world, and she still luxuriated in the memory of their hugs and good wishes. She was coming to realize what a powerful thing it was to be a part of the company of women, to share a history with Mary Elizabeth and her girl cousins, to have the wisdom and insights of the ladies at church who had been her mother's friends and her first female role models. Women like Martha Tate, Emily Perkins, Ruby Sarver, and Evelyn Brown had given her an understanding of what it meant to love and care for others. Now she had added women like Polly, Annie Buchanan, Isabel Barnes, and Molly Williamson to that foundation, and she realized her life was richer because of her ties to these exceptional women. Today, she smiled to herself as she realized she had taken her place among them. Miriam had grown up.

Sonny's graduation had been thrilling, watching him walk across that platform and officially become Reverend Williamson. Her heart had swelled with the emotions bombarding her – love and affection, admiration and pride, and endless joy – and her heart beat like a trip hammer as she clapped and rejoiced in everything Sonny had accomplished. The drive back to Cedar Springs had been quiet; on the eve of their wedding words were unnecessary. Sonny's kisses as he bid her good night told her everything she needed to know.

Now, as she stood ready to accept her bouquet and walk down the aisle, she thanked God for bringing her to this place in her life, and she whispered to her mother once again of the love and gratitude she would forever feel for the woman who had raised her with unconditional love and steadfast goodness. The music from the organ swelled, and she looked to Annie and Lizzie as they realized it was time to go.

Sonny stood at the front of the church, looking out across the sanctuary at the people who loved him and were his friends, and at those who had joined his life since he'd met Miriam, and he whispered his own prayer of thanks to the loving Heavenly Father who had led him to this moment in his life. His attention was directed to the back of the sanctuary as the doors opened and Annie and Mary Elizabeth walked in on their husband's arms. Then he saw the smiling face of Tom Cahill as he stood beaming in his new suit, proud to be escorting his eldest child. As Sonny directed his gaze to Miriam, his breath caught and his eyes grew wide. He'd only thought she was beautiful before, but this woman who stood waiting her turn to advance down the aisle rocked him to his toes. Statuesque and slim in her dress, she looked to him with the love she felt for him shining in her eyes, and he knew he'd never forget this moment or the feeling surging through him. He watched through a blur of tears as she and Tom approached, and he knew that taking her hand to begin this journey with her was the culmination of everything that had gone before in his life. Everything he'd done, everything he'd learned, had been preparing him for this moment, and that realization caused his spirit to soar with the joy he knew he'd never be able to put into words.

A hush fell over the congregation as the minister asked everyone to bow in prayer, and then, as the pastor uttered the 'Amen,' they heard the opening strains of "Be Thou My Vision." Confused, Miriam and Sonny turned to find the source of the music; they had not planned to have this song in the ceremony. With a gasp, Miriam looked to see Will standing at the piano, tears on his cheeks as he sang with such love in his voice that she felt her own tears begin to fall. She looked at Mary Elizabeth, who was weeping openly, and nodded. Looking around, she saw her father staring at Will, as well, the tears pouring down his face. The warmth that began in her heart spread to her limbs and made her entire body tingle as she realized that Will, too, had been reconciled to their father, and in making his peace with Tom had been healed from the hurts his father had once inflicted. Joy such as she had never known pulsed through her, and she silently sang her praises to God for the wonders He had wrought in their lives.

With the tears still damp on her cheeks, as well as Sonny's, they exchanged their vows and were triumphantly heralded as Reverend and Mrs. David Walker Williamson among thunderous applaud and happy laughter.

Walking into the fellowship hall to prepare for the receiving line, Miriam and Sonny were caught up in the hugs and kisses from both their families. Delighted to see Tom getting along so well with Tuck, Miriam let the love she felt wash over her in a great flood. It carried her along as they cut the cake and visited with everyone who crowded into the splendidly festooned room, smiling and laughing and vowing to commit every moment of this remarkable day to her memory, to bring it forward and let it warm her for all the years to come.

She laughed as Rebekah caught the bouquet, then she and Sonny were in the car and driving away from the church to begin their lives as husband and wife.

Miriam stood at the window of her hotel room and looked out across the water to the storm building in the distance. Some may have scoffed at her desire to honeymoon at the beach in December, but because of what had happened here, Miriam thought it the perfect place to celebrate her marriage to Sonny. They had spent three blissful days walking along the sand, finding a different kind of pleasure in the churning water, the sharp winds, and the stormy, low flying clouds. The fierce energy in the wintry landscape made Miriam feel more alive, more vibrant, than she had felt before in her life. Sonny had taken her to several lovely restaurants, and they had browsed the downtown shops, buying one or two souvenirs of these first few days together. They took photographs of one another, and asked an elderly gentleman enjoying coffee in a brightly lit café to take a snapshot of them together to have as a special momento of their honeymoon in Corpus Christi.

She looked over her shoulder to watch Sonny sleeping peacefully under the coverlet. It was still early, not yet seven, but Miriam had awakened before dawn, her mind so filled with the past three days that she couldn't go back to sleep. Their wedding night had found them in a homey motel just outside of Houston, exhausted from the events of the week. Miriam had taken a hot bath in an attempt to soothe her nerves, but she was still trembling as she walked into the room where Sonny waited for her, doing some pacing of his own. Everything in her stilled, however, as he looked at her, and she felt the freedom of that moment begin to thrum low in her body. She had been so afraid of disappointing him, so agitated because she was so innocent, so naïve about the things that transpired between married people. But then he walked across the room to enfold her in his arms, frame her face in his hands to kiss her, and her agitation fled. She breathed deeply of the scent that was his alone, and felt the gentleness in him as he soothed her with his touch, and the need to know him as her husband filled her. His murmurs of reassurance, of comfort, of love, had seduced her, and she had soared in the knowledge that no one had ever touched her in this way, no one had ever made her feel what Sonny made her feel, and no one but she had ever been with Sonny as she was now. Their love had reduced the entire universe to this one moment, this one place in time, between them alone, and Miriam understood what Mary Elizabeth had been trying to tell her about that private place she and Sonny would build for themselves. They had faced one another in bed much later that night, laughing together that they were married, and nothing had ever felt as good as being together.

With the images from the past three days stirring her, Miriam crossed quietly to the bed and lay down beside Sonny, stroking his cheek, soothing her hand down his back, waiting for his eyes to open so that she could tell him once again how much she loved him and how happy she was to be his wife.

Chapter 27

Spring had come. March had given way to April, and everything was a riot of color as new life was born in all living things. Miriam exulted in the sight of the daffodils in her front yard, grateful to the former owners for providing such a sweet bit of sunshine in a yard still brown and dull from the sheen of winter. Several Sunday afternoons had found her driving with Sonny into the country to walk among the fields of bluebonnets, marveling at the rich, blue oceans of blooms filling the pastures. Her marriage had bloomed as well, filling her heart with a joy she'd never thought she could know. Sonny was everything his mother had told her and more – loving, thoughtful, patient, and fun. He'd held her as she cried when she'd forgotten about the cake in the oven and nearly set the house on fire, then he'd grabbed a cloth and helped clean up the sooty mess. He'd brought her daisies after being apart from her one particularly long day. He'd walked with her on the square late at night, listening to the sounds of the crickets and watching the community around them settle down to sleep. They'd spent hours at the kitchen table or snuggled on the sofa, talking about everything Miriam could imagine – their families, their faith, Sonny's hopes for a first church, and they had pledged their love to one another endlessly, with words, and caresses, and sighs deep in the nighttime.

They rubbed up against one another's rough edges once in a while, too. Sonny never put a shoe in the closet. Miriam found them in the kitchen, the hallway, on the dining room table, and in the bathroom. He never seemed to notice that she had tripped countless times already. She cleaned and dusted so much that Sonny found himself dumped from his comfortable spot on the sofa more than once so she could fluff the pillows beneath him. Balances had been sought, and found, and later they had laughed together at one another's quirks and bad habits.

On this particular morning Miriam had arisen early to see Sonny off for work, a duty she found delightful, and then set off on a secret errand of her own. Now she stood alone in a small cemetery as the sun beat down on her head to warm her and remind her of the rebirth going on around her. There was still a bite to the wind, but it was the lazy bite of a contented cat, curled up in his master's lap, chewing gently on his toy. Standing before her mother's grave hadn't taken as much courage as she'd once feared; it seemed almost natural to continue the talks she'd had with Christine all her life, even these past two years that her mother had been gone.

"I love you, Mama. Losing you hasn't diminished my love for you. If anything, I love you even more now than I did before." Living on her own these past two years had given Miriam the opportunity to see for herself that the values she learned at her mother's knee were true, and right for her own life. Miriam had needed her mother's courage countless times, and it had not failed her. She had needed her mother's patience, and kindness, and steadfastness, and they had not let her down. She had come to understand the love that had held her mother fast when Daddy had been so cruel, for she had found that love for herself when she met Sonny.

"Mama, so much has changed since your homegoing. Do you know what has happened? Did you know somehow that Lizzie had her baby girls, and that Seth is a new father? Did your spirit quicken when Daddy's heart was changed? Can you see how happy I am with Sonny? Do you know already that I'm carrying his child? You're going to be a grandmother again, and even though this baby won't know the joy of having his Grammy holding him in this life, I'll tell him about you and the things you taught me. He'll know you, and love you, and someday when he meets you in Heaven he'll know your voice and the love in your hands; I'll have told him what to expect.

"I'll bring Sonny to meet you soon. He promised me he'd come. I think he'll be surprised to learn that I've come today on my own. Somehow knowing I'm a mother now made it easier to take this step; I'm not sure I understand why. I'm so excited to tell him our news about the baby. He's going to be the best daddy ever. He had a good teacher in his own father, and his love for our Heavenly Father will stand him in good stead as well. I miss you, Mama, but I know now that in losing you I've somehow found myself. Thank you, Mama; I'll be back soon."

With purposeful strides Miriam turned and made her way back down the pathway and onto the sidewalk. It would soon be lunchtime, and Sonny would be home from work to share a sandwich with her. Maybe she'd make something special today. She had something very special to tell him.

An hour later, as Miriam stood at the stove stirring the gravy, she heard the screen door creak and the sound of her husband's voice. "Miriam, honey, I'm home . . ."